STRANGE IN SKIN

Sara V. Zook

PLANETTOPIA PUBLISHING LLC

I dedicate this book to my children, Coen, Avery and Lucas.
They inspire me daily to keep reaching and keep growing as a person.

Prologue

Wes. Where was Wes?

Emry's eyes struggled to focus as he came to. His muscles ached from leaning against the cold steel of the tower with his feet propped up. He got to his feet. The sudden noise of his boot knocking over an empty beer can startled him. He ran his fingers through his hair and took a deep breath. He realized it had happened again.

He licked his dry lips and stared up at the darkening sky. Why did it keep happening? Why couldn't he control it? He let the questions linger in his thoughts momentarily and then pushed them aside. He wouldn't allow himself to dwell on it anymore. He had to face it, the answers would never come.

He was on the top of the tower, the sound of crickets humming from below. He had come here to relax and talk with his friend, Wes. But Wes was gone.

He hurried around the winding stairwell running down the side of the tower, his hand tight on the railing for support. Had Wes gone home and left him here? Surely not.

He slowed halfway down the ladder and looked to the ground below. Nothing but empty cans. He smashed one of the cans near his boot in frustration, then kicked it over the side. He peered over the railing to watch it fall, but his eyes strayed to a different spot on the ground. A sudden burning crawled up from his stomach and into his throat. There was something near the ladder. His mind struggled to catch up to the racing thoughts. It couldn't possibly be, could it?

Emry gripped the ladder tighter. His boots clanked with every hurried motion against the metal as he made his way to the bottom.

He realized he had been holding his breath and took a moment to gasp in air. He looked toward the ground again. He was three quarters of the way down. His stomach tightened at what he saw.

He knew what it was. Wes, his best friend, lying in a twisted position on the ground, his lifeless eyes staring up at Emry. Shards of bones poked through his broken body as dirt and blood speckled his white t-shirt.

Emry couldn't take his eyes off his friend. He bent down to touch his arm, then decided against it as he slowly backed away. Wes had fallen from the tower somehow.

What had happened? Why couldn't he remember?

Panic settled in. He felt as if his lungs were collapsing. His stomach churned and he covered his eyes with his arm, unable to bear looking at his friend any longer. This was real. This was really happening.

Unable to contain them, tears streamed down his cheeks as he turned around, his eyes searching for the path that led out of the woods. Finding it, he ran as fast as he could as the adrenaline pulsated through his body; the darkness of the night right on his heels.

Chapter 1

I shuddered as I gripped onto the diminishing mound of pamphlets in my hand. My footsteps echoed off the hard prison floor. I looked at Buck Brady beside me.

"Creeped out yet?" Buck asked.

"Yeah, actually." I had felt like a prostitute the entire time I had been here. The prisoners hadn't taken me seriously. They didn't care about their souls, they just wanted to make nasty comments to me inviting me into their cells.

"Looks like you've caused quite the commotion. These guys are going to be fired up all day now. Look what you've done," he teased.

"I guess they don't act like this to my father."

A shallow chuckle croaked from Buck's throat. "Not exactly. Wonder why Pastor James sent you down here today? Not really a place I would want to send my daughter to."

I hadn't a clue. "Mrs. Anderson needed him this morning."

"Mrs. Anderson." He repeated the name as if he was going to back it up with more words, but instead, hesitated. "Strange," he blurted out.

I narrowed my eyes at him as we came to an abrupt stop at a bunch of unoccupied cells. "So, these ones are empty? Is that it?" I pulled back the sleeve of my sweater to get a look at my watch. It dangled loosely on my scrawny wrist. "It's almost noon already."

"There's one more inmate in the very last one. I think it would be okay to skip him, honestly."

"Why should I skip him?" I eyed Buck warily.

"It's just Emry Logan down there, but you've wasted half your day on this crap."

"Crap? You think my father's ministry is crap?"

He instantly looked remorseful. "That's not what I meant."

I didn't know exactly why I was becoming so defensive of my father's ministry to the inmates. I felt that this was a total and complete waste of time. These men had no interest in repentance, or knowing Jesus or the Bible. These men seemed hopeless, and I wanted to run out of here and never make the mistake of stepping foot in this hellhole again. I had thrown each and every paper at the feet of the prisoners so they wouldn't touch me. I was afraid of getting too close to them, afraid they'd grab hold of me and never let go. Or even worse, that some of their corruptness would rub off on me and seep into my skin, ruining me. I felt way too pure to be in their midst, maybe even too good. I was about to change my mind and turn around and leave when Buck began moving down the corridor again.

"Alright. Follow me."

A feeling of emptiness washed over me as we came to the end of the hallway. Buck stepped in front of the cell first, lifting his arm to show me the last inmate. I hesitated and then bit my lip and took a step forward, waiting to hear the man say something rude and totally inappropriate, but to my surprise, the man didn't even look up.

My eyes strained as it seemed the light was very poor at this end, and I realized that part of the fluorescent light bulb was out, making the yellow glow even more intolerable here. The prisoner had his back turned to us, as he was seated in a small wooden chair. His head was down, and his shoulders slumped over. I looked to Buck to question what he was doing. He just seemed to be sitting there, thinking.

Buck shrugged, giving me no answer.

What was I supposed to do here? Should I just toss the brochure on the floor like I did with the others?

"Um, sir?" I whispered, sounding out of breath, my heart thumping wildly in my chest. There was no response. He sat completely motionless.

"Logan, turn around here!" Buck snapped.

Slowly, the man composed himself and turned around. I gasped at his face. He was so young, barely in his twenties. His face was clean shaven and his rusty brown hair combed back by his fingers. He stood, but his eyes were still looking down at the floor. He was tall, lean, and built, his muscles exposed underneath the too-small orange jumpsuit he wore.

"Um, hello," I said. "This is just a pamphlet for you to look over if you want."

He finally looked up at me, his blue eyes piercing and beautiful as if they sparkled in the gloomy, dark corridor, unaffected by the yellow fluorescent. I found myself staring at his eyes, unable to look away. They were gleaming because they were wet, wet with tiny pools of tears, yet not enough to make them spill from beneath his eyelids.

"It just basically tells you what we're about, and how we can

12

minister to your spiritual needs." I realized this was the most I had spoken to an inmate the entire time I was here, and he wasn't speaking back. He looked utterly sad, and I knew then that he had been crying while sitting there slumped over. My mind raced with why this man was here. What could he have possibly done to deserve to be locked up in this dungeon? It was as if they had secluded him to this section of the prison, away from everyone else. Without hesitation, I put my hand in through the bars, holding out the brochure toward him.

He stepped closer to me.

Buck changed his stance, as if on guard, ready to intervene if necessary.

I gave Buck an uneasy look, and then my head turned slowly back toward the inmate he had called Logan. He stared back at me with those sad, beautiful eyes, as I realized there were tiny freckles darting over the bridge of his tanned nose and his cheeks. A strand of hair fell in his eye as he looked down at the floor and then back up to meet my gaze. He gently took the piece of paper out of my hand. I pulled my arm away.

"Thank you," he whispered. His eyes were glued to mine. He didn't seem to realize that Buck was there beside me.

I nodded and crossed my arms together in front of my chest, feeling a chill in the air around me. I looked down at the ground and then toward Buck, my stomach in knots.

"Ready?" Buck asked.

"Yeah," I mumbled and turned to leave.

"Excuse me, Miss?"

I felt the muscles in my stomach tighten at the sound of the inmate's voice. I spun back around.

"She's all done here, Logan. Go back to what you were doing." Buck's voice had an edge of real anger to it this time.

I ignored Buck and took a few steps backward to where I had just stood and peered in at him.

"Are you related to Pastor John James?"

"Anna," Buck huffed impatiently, and I realized his concern at once about giving this prisoner too much information about myself.

"Anna, is it?" The prisoner raised his eyebrows slightly.

I heard Buck make another huffing noise, annoyed that he had let my name slip out so easily. "That's none of your business, now is it, scumbag?" Buck pressed his chest against the bars, trying to be as intimidating as possible. His eyes looked fierce. The young man stood a few feet away from the door of the cell, his face completely expressionless.

I found myself standing directly beside Buck, dangerously close to the bars, and staring into those glorious blue eyes. "I'm his daughter," I suddenly blurted out.

"What are you doing?" Buck grabbed my arm and whipped me around as I found myself being dragged down the corridor.

Why did you just say that? My heart began to pound as I realized that this man had been in here for a reason. He had done something terrible to be locked behind bars in a prison. He was dangerous. Here I was blurting out silly things. Buck must think I'm a complete idiot.

14

We got out to the front lobby and Buck grabbed my coat and turned to look at me, still furious.

"He's locked up, Buck. It's not like he can hunt me down or anything." I tried to make it seem ridiculous, the way he was acting just now, although I knew he was right.

He held up the coat for me. I put my arms in the sleeves that had been dampened by the rain. "You have no idea what he's capable of," Buck said.

I pulled the coat around me as my fingers clumsily attempted to clasp all the buttons together. "I'm really sorry."

"Anna, look, it's no big deal, okay? You aren't in any danger. You don't have to worry about it."

Buck bit his bottom lip as if he was pausing to think, and then his eyes softened again as he saw how upset I was getting.

"Please don't tell my father," I begged, thinking of how upset this would make him if he knew.

He sighed. "It's not really a big deal, like I said," he repeated. "You were just being nice. You're always nice." He forced a smile. "I won't tell your dad," he added, putting his arm around my shoulders and guiding me toward the door. "Look, the rain stopped."

I turned toward my pale yellow car parked right outside.

"It was nice seeing you today."

I nodded and took off out the door. I practically dove into the driver's side of my car.

***

I carefully put the white porcelain plates down on the huge oak table that fit perfectly into our little dining room. My mother bounced around like a ballerina, carrying in a pitcher full of iced tea and bowl after bowl of food for supper. The table was soon filled with piping hot mashed potatoes and vegetables, the steam rising and disappearing beneath the beautiful antique chandelier that brightly lit the square room.

"Seems like an awful lot of food for just us," I mumbled.

My father came in and gave me a quick peck on the cheek and then held out my chair. "Please, sit." Matthew, my disabled brother, came around the corner as my mother wheeled him toward the table to his usual spot. His eyes became enlarged as he saw all the food. He clapped his hands together excitedly and we all laughed. Seeing Matthew so happy made me feel better. I didn't know why I was in such a sour mood, but the events of the morning had haunted me throughout the day.

We all piled mounds of food on the beautifully decorated plates and were silent for a minute. "Prayer, shall we?" my father said.

Bowing my head, I found it difficult to concentrate on praying. I heard my father's words, thanking God for the day, the food, those who prepared it, but my mind kept wandering back to the jail and Emry Logan. He knew my name. Anna James, Pastor John James' daughter.

"So how was your day today, Anna?"

My head snapped up, and I realized that I was the only one not

16

eating. Matthew was digging into his mashed potatoes.

"Well," I began, realizing my mother was staring at me intently,

"I made it down to the jail."

"What?" My father practically jumped out of his seat. His eyes shifted to my mother, who set her fork down and began chewing on one of her fingernails. "You went down there?"

"Uh, yeah." I narrowed my eyes at her. She hadn't told him? I thought this had been his idea.

"Why on earth would you do something like that?" he demanded.

I could see him begin to lose his temper, something that rarely ever happened. He was always in such control of his emotions.

I sighed and then scooped my spoon into the middle of my own potatoes and let them slide back off again. "I thought you two had this all planned out. You know, the pamphlets and all."

"I had no idea. I would have never sent you down there. Were you alone?"

"Well, if you don't count Buck." I peered into my father's eyes, which now seemed wild and alarmed.

"Helene?" He demanded an answer, knowing where to place the blame right away.

My mother shrugged and tried to smile. "Honey, somebody needed to do it. You were busy with Mrs. Anderson and all. How's her son?"

I was amused at the way she attempted to change the subject. There was no getting around it, though.

"I would've done it tomorrow."

"Honey," my mother said calmly, her voice never rising, "you can't do it tomorrow."

This seemed to silence my father momentarily. "Do you have any idea what those men are like, Helene? Anna should never have gone down there to listen to those filthy mouths."

My father knew exactly what kind of things had been said to me. It made me slightly embarrassed that he knew. I gnawed on a dry piece of chicken and swallowed hard. It seemed to stick in my throat, and only the cool gush of iced tea allowed it to go down.

"Anna, it wasn't so bad, was it?" My mother nodded toward me.

I looked away from her. "It was fine, really. Buck kept things under control."

The meal went on and nobody mentioned my little visit to the prison again.

"I'm going to bed," I told them as I dried the last plate and put it away in the cupboard just above my head.

"Okay, Hun." My mother came over and kissed my forehead.

"Night." My father was sitting at the table reading his paper. He looked up at me momentarily and then continued reading, his glasses falling down to the bottom of his nose.

"Night, Matthew." I gave him a quick kiss and hurried up the stairs.

The privacy of my own room felt so peaceful and relaxing. I quickly took off all of my jewelry and placed them each carefully into

18

their specific spot in the cherry jewelry box perched upon my dresser.

I changed into my flannel pajamas and looked in the mirror to pull back my hair. I pressed my lips together tightly and then released them. I turned my head from side to side, inspecting every angle of my face. *This is stupid,* I thought after a few minutes. Why should I care what I look like? I have never cared much before.

I sat down on my bed. A feeling of guilt rushed over me. Why was I feeling like I was hiding something from my parents? Nothing really happened today.

I closed my eyes in the darkness quickly, and then reopened them. A sliver of moonlight came in from my window, making shadows appear on the adjacent wall. I closed my eyes again and tried to relax. I did feel tired. This day was exhausting in so many ways. It was nothing at all like I had expected it to be.

I knew that the world was generally bad. I knew that bad people existed out there and that terrible things happened to many different people on many different levels. However, I had never really come into contact with any of it. Nothing ever bad had happened in my family. My parents didn't really fight. Sometimes someone from the church would leave and go to another church or move away, but that wasn't so horrible. At that jail today, those men stunk of impurity, of sin. They weren't the type of people I was used to being around, which were proper, well-behaved Christians. Seneca's crime rate was pretty low. Every once in a while you'd hear of a kid getting into trouble with drugs at the local high school or someone had too much to drink and drove home a little tipsy, getting a DUI, but that was about it. No one was ever murdered. Were those men murderers? What had they done to get such a punishment as being locked up behind bars? There were bad people right here in Seneca, I realized.

They weren't acting out, obviously, because of where they were, but they were still here right in the middle of our little nested, secure town.

The realization made me shiver. I pulled a side of the comforter up and swaddled myself in it.

Shutting my eyes again, I took a deep breath and listened to myself exhale. The wind was beginning to pick up outside. Rain again, maybe?

My mind began to drift again. I was beginning to fall asleep, and then I saw his face. Emry Logan. I repeated the name multiple times in my mind. I pictured his beautiful face as if he was standing in front of me again. His head was bent downward toward the floor, his rusty brown hair falling into his face. I pictured his arms, his biceps protruding even underneath the bright orange jumpsuit and how slowly he stood up, so tall and lean, almost graceful.

I realized how much I had been thinking about this particular inmate all day. Of course I was upset by Buck's reaction, and now my father's. They made me feel as if I had done something wrong, something very wrong. I kept going back, trying to uncover exactly what it was I said or may have done that would necessitate such strong reactions. So I had told him I was the pastor's daughter. So what? Buck had been the one to actually say my name, not me. And my father, well, I thought I was just doing what he had wanted me to do. I had no idea he hadn't known I was going down there, but I still felt bad about it nevertheless. Amongst all these thoughts that drifted through my head all day, Emry Logan was still right there in the midst of them all, the most centered thought.

I wondered why he was in jail. He was so young, younger than me for sure. The other prisoners actually looked like bad people to me. They had a rough look about them that screamed 'I'm dangerous' out to everyone who looked in their direction, but Emry Logan, he looked … perfect. He looked as if he could walk into the church with that orange jumpsuit on and nobody would even consider him dangerous at all. And he seemed so very sad. Was it a mistake that he was in there? It had to be, I decided. He looked like he couldn't hurt a fly. I remembered seeing his slumped-over shoulders and how motionless he had sat in the chair. No wonder he was so distressed. He must have been framed. I started to become outraged at who exactly had done this terrible thing to him, who had made him so sad that he would have to sit there and feel such pain.

Wow. I sat straight up in bed. When was the last time I had ever thought about someone so intently?

I couldn't remember. I had never been fixated on someone like this before. I felt the lump return in my throat. I searched for an answer. It had to be because I was so stricken by his pain. I felt genuinely awful for him having to be locked behind those bars. And then in my mind, Emry Logan suddenly looked up at me and his blue eyes fixated on my own tiny brown eyes and remained there. I tried to remember the striking color as they lured me in.

Emry Logan. "Emry Logan," I whispered, allowing myself to

speak his name in the darkness. It sounded like music rolling off of my tongue.

"Goodnight, Dear." I realized at once my mother had my door cracked open and was peering in at me.

"Night!" I blurted out, immediately embarrassed and falling back down in the bed, my head indenting into the pillow.

Had she heard me say his name? I held my breath for a moment, listening to my heart. No, I decided. She hadn't. It had barely been a whisper.

My head was spinning from the emotions. I felt remorseful. I was being secretive. I usually told my family everything, but I couldn't tell them I was thinking about one of the inmates that I had met today. Well, sort of met. My mind jumped ahead to tomorrow morning, getting up and going to work in my mother's antique store, and suddenly, I felt as if I didn't really care. Work sounded boring. When had I ever really been bored with my life before? *Never bored, always content*, I thought. But there were other people out in the world; exciting people that fascinated me, like Emry Logan. I was absolutely intrigued, but couldn't quite put my finger on why. I wondered what he would be doing down in his jail cell at this exact moment. Would he be sleeping? Perhaps he was reading a book. Maybe he was sitting on that chair again, his mind drifting, his mood depressed and sad.

No, that's no good. I immediately shook the thought from my head. He didn't wear sad well. His kind of sad made me feel sad. He deserved to be happy. My eyes snapped back open and moved to the white ceiling above my head. My eyes traced around the outline of the stationary ceiling fan. What was the matter with me? I felt so alive. A funny feeling filled the pit of my stomach. I felt like such a child. This was absolutely silly. I'm a grown woman thinking of ways to help a criminal escape from a prison I didn't believe he deserved to be in, but I didn't know that for sure. It was exhilarating, this feeling. I smiled at the way I felt, then I shut my eyes tight, pulled the covers up over my head, and forced my mind to be empty to try to get some sleep. Every time I tried, there stood Emry Logan again.

Chapter 2

The next few weeks seemed to drag on, especially since it rained almost every single day. I glared at the gray clouds hovering above my head and cursed them as I wished they would go away. The air was getting colder as winter approached and soon snow would cover all of Seneca. I wanted to enjoy the remains of autumn. It was my favorite season, after all, with the red and gold leaves. However, this nasty weather had made the leaves turn straight to brown and fall off the trees in a hurry. The wind continuously whipped them in spiral swirls on the ground.

It had been almost a month since my notorious jail visit. My parents hadn't brought it up again. My memory of the morning had gone from front burner in my mind to the back as I busied myself with Christmas choir practice, and business at the antique store had suddenly picked up. It had seemed so long ago, just a dull ache now.

On a Friday after a busy day at the store, Sammie decided to walk with me back to my house. She was a part-time hire who sometimes came in to do inventory when things got too hectic. She had bright green eyes and red, frizzy hair that was usually pulled back into a messy ponytail. It seemed as though she never stopped talking. She was a few years younger than me and only lived a couple houses down the street.

On days like these I forced myself to walk, even if it was getting chilly. Walking let me clear my head from the day, unwind, and I knew there were only a few precious days left for walking before winter really set in full swing. However, with Sammie by my side, it was difficult for my head to clear properly with her jabbing away in my ear.

"And then I didn't know what to say, you know?" Sammie paused to look at me, to make sure I was listening, which I only partially was.

"So what are you going to do?" I asked, trying to pretend as if I cared. I truly just wanted to be by myself right now and not try to keep up with Sammie's drama.

She sighed as if this were so terrible. Two men. She had two men chasing after her. Dreadful. "I just don't know. I've been with Tim for three years. Three years is a long time. But then, on the other hand, Dave is so cute. And he's different from Tim, too, you know?"

No, I didn't know. I didn't even know what it was like to have one guy chasing after me. Guys weren't exactly drawn to someone like me. My background was intimating, first of all, and then there was my appearance. I rarely stopped to look in the mirror before I left in the morning.

"I sure hope I can figure this out soon before I lose them both. That's what they say, you know. You have two men, and then suddenly both of them go and you're left all alone. I couldn't imagine what that would be like."

I gave her a hard stare. She was talking to *me* about being alone. I had never really felt alone while living with my family, but recently something had changed in that regard. There was this strange sense of loneliness wearing on my every move. That's probably the reason for my being in such a sour mood lately, I supposed. And then there was this weather, this dark gloom creeping in all around me, suffocating me, and then the clouds lurked overhead, adding to my misery. I threw my hood up, put my head down, and picked up my steps so that I was almost jogging down the street and away from her.

"See you later, Anna!" I heard Sammie call out from behind me. I was sure by the tone of her voice that she was frantically waving her arm up and down at me.

Once I saw my brightly lit house directly in front of me, I slowed my pace. Sammie was long gone.

The curtains were tied back in the living room, and I could see Matthew propped up in front of the TV and my mother walking around the room, her lips moving slowly. More than likely she was singing.

I stepped in a puddle of mud as I reached the door of the mailbox. I moaned, my frustration growing. I felt the cold, murky water seeping in through my shoe and drenching my sock. *Just great*, I thought. I grabbed the mail and rushed up the sidewalk to the front door.

"Anna!" Matthew greeted me.

"Hey," I said, bending over to take off the wet shoe.

"What now?" my mother asked, stopping her pacing to watch what I was doing.

I grunted in annoyance. "Oh, I stepped in a mud puddle getting the mail."

She continued to watch me struggle to get my foot out of it. "Here, I'll take the mail," she offered, stretching out her hand.

I quickly hopped into the kitchen on one foot and tossed the mail onto the counter. I went to turn and go toward the stairs to go to my room and change out of my clothes, when my eyes caught sight of my name on a small off-white envelope.

Ms. Anna James, 305 Walker Lane. Then I glanced at the return address. Seneca County Prison. I felt my heart skip a beat as I quickly snatched up the letter and put it under my arm before darting up the stairs.

I turned the small gold lamp that sat on my nightstand beside my bed on and sat down. I stared at the envelope in my hand for a moment. What on earth could this be? I tried to get my breathing under control as I quickly tore at the top of the envelope to get it open. A small piece of notebook paper was inside. I unfolded it and my eyes scanned the words.

Dear Anna,

My name is Emry Logan. I don't know if you'll remember me or not, but I was one of the men you gave your father's pamphlets to at the jail a little while ago. I hope I'm not being inappropriate by writing to you this way. I have read over the pamphlet and have a few questions. I was hoping you could come see me to discuss these things. I completely understand if you cannot and want to stay away from me, but I believe that you may be the only one who can help save me.

Hope to see you soon. E.L.

I sat there on the edge of my bed, feeling suddenly short of breath. My head was spinning. Emry Logan had written to me. He wanted to see me. A sudden gush of panic grabbed hold as the realization set in. Buck had been right. I had said too much. From just a little information, he had enough to track me down. How in the world did he get hold of my home address? He was trying to find out more about me. He was trying to lure me in. Why? For what reason? He was a hunter, and I, his prey. He was dangerous. He sat in that prison for a reason.

Ugh! I wanted to scream. My life had been so uncomplicated, and now it seemed as if everything was going to change, and I was the one to blame. I should have acted the same with him as I had with every other inmate. Why did he have to look so sad? Why did my emotions have to take control of my head? I felt so naive.

I stood up. That's it. I knew what I had to do.

I had to take this letter downstairs and tell my mother what had actually happened at the jail. I had to show her that Emry Logan, I mean an *inmate,* had written me a letter. He was thinking about me, stalking me. She would call my father and he would come home right away, rush to be by my side, and between the both of them, they would know what to do. Maybe Buck could help them find a way to stop this man before things got even more out of control.

I was halfway down the stairs, the letter in hand, before I began to scold myself. Turning around, I ran back up to my room and read the letter again. I thought I heard my mother's footsteps on the staircase shortly thereafter and quickly folded the letter in half and tucked it safely away in the first book that I picked up off my bookshelf.

You are so ridiculous, I thought to myself.

Emry Logan wasn't dangerous. Didn't I remember his eyes? *Remember his eyes*, I commanded myself. The face. His composure. Just a few weeks ago I had sat here and talked myself into what the real reason was that he was in prison. Of course. He was an innocent man who had been unjustly wronged. He didn't do anything—could not have done anything. Innocence was written all over his face. His sadness had pierced my heart, had filled me as if I felt it, too. I wanted to free him of his pain. He didn't look like he deserved to be in there. The other men, yes, they *looked* like they should be there. But not Emry. I refused to believe it.

I sighed and buried my face in my hands. What was I going to do now?

He wanted to see me. He wanted my help. He thought I was the only one who could save him. Save him from what? Himself? Hell? And why would he want me over my father, the pastor? He would know exactly what to do and say. If he wanted help with knowing God, that is. But if he meant from himself, maybe he thought of me instead. But why? How could I help him sort through his past? I had no experience with anything remotely bad. I was not one who could properly counsel someone.

Maybe he thought he would be more comfortable with me than my father. My father could be intimating at times, I supposed. He could get a very serious look on his face that could be misunderstood as intimidating from outsiders who didn't know him.

My parents definitely weren't going to approve of this. Shame washed over me. I had never been sneaky or secretive in my life. This I could not tell them. They wouldn't let me go, and I felt now like I needed to go. I needed to see what he had to say and more even, what I had to say back. Maybe I wouldn't have anything to say, but I had to go and see. I felt the impulse from the bottom of my stomach, a spark that jumpstarted me to life and could cast all of these gloomy storm clouds away. I felt that alive feeling again, and I didn't want it to go away. I suddenly felt very selfish.

If Emry Logan was dangerous, I would march right up to him and see exactly what the danger was. I couldn't stand the thought of not knowing why he was in there or what he wanted from me. He couldn't hurt me. Look where he was and look where I sat. I was free, and he certainly was not. That should be enough reassurance to know that I was not putting myself in harm's way by simply talking to a man behind bars.

And then I began to plot in my mind how I was going to betray my family's trust. I already knew for certain what my parents would think about all of this if they had actually known about it. They would be 100% against it. I could already tell that after my mother sent me down there, I was pretty much banned from stepping foot inside that building again. It was clear by how abrupt the conversation had ended, and how angry my father had been at my visiting to the jail. I could not let anything slip or anyone know what I was doing, or else it would all be ruined. My little feeling of being driven to want to do something for the first time in my entire life would be ripped away if I couldn't hold it together in front of them. I had to dig up all the deceitfulness from within myself and put on a good face for my parents. They couldn't know any different. It would hurt them too much, and it would steal away what little bliss I was feeling at this very moment of desiring the unknown. I wasn't asking for too much. I just wanted to know someone outside of my sheltered box, someone different, and someone interesting.

Confusion of what was going to happen filled the pit of my stomach, and I liked it. It was decided. I was going to go see Emry Logan the first chance I got.

I stood up and looked at my face in the mirror and grinned. Then I wiped the smile away as quickly as it had come and took off down the stairs to help my mother prepare dinner.

***

My scheming had to wait for a few days. I carefully planned it out at the store when my mother would leave to make her rounds to all of the widows of the church with lunch, which she did once a month. I peeked outside the antique store window as she and a few other women loaded up the back of a suburban with boxes of Styrofoam bowls full of piping hot vegetable soup and others with salad.

These days the store was left in my hands. I knew that Sammie would also be working on this particular day. She was checking inventory in the back and would appear periodically at the front of the store with items that needed to be replaced. She would say something to me every now and then, but I just kind of mumbled a response. My mind was far away, just a few miles, actually, down at the jail where I soon knew I would be.

"Sammie?"

"Huh?" She looked up, her red pouffy hair bouncing as she did so.

"I have an errand to run. I shouldn't be too long." I knew exactly when visiting hours were at Seneca County Prison. I had checked into it and double checked before I left the house this morning.

"You can manage for a little while, right?"

Sammie's smile beamed as if I had just entrusted her with my life or something. It made me want to laugh out loud, but I contained myself.

"Of course I can," she squealed.

I doubted there would be many customers, if any, this afternoon, anyway. A few snowflakes flittered down from the dark sky, and the wind started to pick up. It was the beginning of winter, and most people would be staying inside their warm houses all nice and cozy, not wanting to venture out to go antique shopping.

I gave her a quick smile and reached for my coat. I felt the weight of it in my hand as I had just pulled it from the closet this morning. It was my heavier coat, thickly insulated to protect me from the winds that so notoriously whipped around Seneca during the winter months. I could feel the chill settling in this morning and was glad that I had decided to bring it along. I glanced at my watch.

There were still fifteen minutes until visiting hours began, which gave me plenty of time to make it down to the other side of town.

When I reached my car, I realized that a customer had just gotten out of their car and was headed up the steps of the store. *Great*, I thought. I should go back in there and deal with it, but instead, I didn't. I couldn't waste a minute. Sammie could handle it.

The drive down to the jail seemed to take forever. The anticipation of getting there was awful. My mind swirled with all sorts of things. How exactly was this going to work? Buck wouldn't be there, I knew that at least. This was his day off. But who would be working the front desk? What if they recognized who I was? They would send me away immediately and probably tell my parents that I had been there. What excuse would I give my mom and dad? But a more important question was pressing upon me. How could I bear being forced out of the jail without first speaking to Emry Logan? An uncomfortable fluttering filled my stomach as I started to feel physically sick.

I parked in the large parking lot behind the jail, instead of in front of it like I had last time. The outside overhead lights were on because the clouds were making it dark outside. I pulled my coat around me and stuffed my hands in the pockets to keep them warm as I walked as quickly as my legs would allow up to the front door. There was the same black button. There was the camera. And there was that buzzing sound again. Click. The door was open, and I was in.

My eyes scanned the open room before me. There were a few police officers sitting at the desks that had been vacant before. They didn't seem to notice me. They were busy shuffling papers and staring at their computer screens. I looked toward the plastic screen where a stout woman sat. I let a large amount of air exhale from my lungs.

"Can I help you?" she asked.

I took a few steps closer and smiled. "Yes. Hi. Are visiting hours now?" Of course I knew they were.

She looked at a large metal clock hanging on the wall behind her.

"Yes," she said. "Sign in here."

I bent over the clipboard that she had handed me. There was a single piece of paper with a few names scribbled on it already. It was asking me for my name, who I was intending to visit, the time I arrived, and my relation to the particular inmate of interest. I swallowed hard. There was that lump in my throat again. This would be proof that I was here. Buck would know. If he didn't discover it, someone else surely would.

Think fast, I ordered myself. *Think, think, think.*

I wrote down a fake name. Amy Wright. It was the first name that popped into my head at the time. I wrote down Emry Logan, 10:58 a.m., and relation: Sister. I set down the clipboard and flashed another smile at the woman working behind the desk. Would she become aware of my being overly nervous?

She smiled back, though, making me feel slightly better. "Follow me," she said and popped out from behind the plastic screen, shutting half of a door behind her as she did so.

She led me to a separate waiting room where there were a few chairs. Some of the chairs were already occupied with people waiting to visit other inmates. A few glanced in my direction, others continued to sift through magazine pages. I sat and tried to keep my head and eyes down. My attention drifted to the pale red carpet on the floor, and I felt nervous once again. What if they asked for ID?

They would want to see Amy Wright's driver's license, and then what would I do? The fluttering returned and I closed my eyes, trying to make the nausea disappear. I realized I was more nervous about seeing Emry than about getting caught. What was I going to say to him when we were finally face to face?

"Follow me," a harsh voice said. I was suddenly startled from my daze and looked up at another unknown police officer, who seemed to be aggravated.

I followed the other people to another room that had a row of chairs and desks with a wide plastic screen in front of each one that went all the way up to the ceiling. A large black phone sat on the desk, connected by a short cord.

"Caldwell, Strong, Hepburn, Lance," the officer shouted out. I quickly caught on that he was saying the last names of the visitors and the order in which they were to sit. He pointed to the last few chairs.

"Davids, Olgson, Wright."

I sat down in the very last chair and looked up at the scratched plastic screen in front of me. There he sat, directly across from me. Emry Logan. My heart began to thump at the exact same time the lump returned in my throat. I remained like that for a few seconds, my body paralyzed by the apprehension that overwhelmed me. Emry stared at me for a moment. Then I saw his hand reach for the phone on his side of the screen, and I automatically removed my sweaty hand from my warm pocket and felt my fingers slide over the greasy phone with a firm grasp.

"Hello," he whispered, his brown hair resting in the corners of his eyes as he positioned his head slightly downward.

"Hello," I whispered back.

"My sister?" He raised his eyebrows, as I realized they must have told him what I had written down on the paper.

I felt a tense chuckle escape my throat. "Well, I had to put something down."

He didn't say anything for another moment, just stared at me with those insanely glorious blue eyes.

"Well, I don't have a sister, but I have to admit, I am surprised."

"You are?"

"Well," he began slowly. "Yes. I mean, I didn't think you would come." Of course he didn't. He thought I would be smart enough to stay away like everyone else thought of me, too. "I honestly didn't think the letter would get to you. I figured someone in your family would see it first and destroy it before you ever got the chance to read it."

I swallowed, the lump somewhat dissolving now. That probably would've happened if I hadn't been the first to retrieve the mail that day. "Well, that didn't happen."

"And what did you think? Of my letter, I mean."

I studied him for a minute. He was sitting there so perfectly still, not fidgeting at all like I felt I was. His face seemed hard, yet gentle, and I felt myself memorizing the position of the dark freckles on his cheeks before I looked away, embarrassed by my actions. "I don't know what to think." I hesitated for a moment longer, still so unsure of what I was saying. "You wrote that you thought I was the only one who could help you?"

This time, Emry turned away. He looked down at his fingernails, and it seemed I had triggered something that troubled him from within.

"Have I upset you by coming?" I asked, suddenly wishing that his sadness would go away as I felt an ache deep from within from seeing his sudden pain.

"No, of course not." He looked up, and a smile played on his lips but not enough to come blatantly forward. "I'm so glad you came. No one visits me here." He took a deep breath and pushed the hair out of his eyes with the back of his hand. "No one talks to me. You were the first one that had said anything to me in months that day when you brought in your dad's papers; besides the guards, that is. I thought, this girl is kind. She must be to talk to someone like me. Maybe I'll write to her, and here you are, but I didn't think you'd come."

"My father doesn't know I'm here," I quickly blurted out.

Emry nodded his head slowly, and then I realized he had already understood that before I even had to come out and say it. He knew that when I wrote down Amy Wright on the piece of paper. "I'm sorry you had to lie."

I shrugged as if I was an old pro at the deceit game. I didn't think he bought it. "Okay," I began, feeling slightly calmer at the moment. I could hear the whispers of everyone else on their phones, but couldn't hear specific words being said. "So, what exactly do you need saved from?"

He snorted out a short laugh. My eyes immediately darted to a small dimple in the side of his cheek as he did so. His beauty was astounding. How could such a creature be locked up behind bars, behind this disgusting plastic screen right now?

"Everybody needs saved from something. Even you." He eyed me curiously.

What was he talking about? I wasn't the one in prison. I was completely free. What gave him the right to suppose such a thing on my life? He didn't even know me. I moved the phone over to my other hand.

"So why are you in here, anyway?" I asked as casually as I could, but really, I had been dying to ask that question since the first time I saw him.

He looked down again, his face so serious. When I found myself unable to stare into his glistening eyes, I would pay extra attention to all his other facial features, his strong jawline, the way his small ears protruded ever so slightly from the sides of his head.

"I don't really like to talk about myself," he said. He looked up and stared deep into my eyes as if trying to read my response. "I've been poked and prodded continuously in here about … everything. I'd much rather talk about something else."

I felt a little twinge in my stomach, not nervousness, but more like disappointment. I wanted so badly to know why this beautiful, young man had been arrested in the first place, but I could see very clearly that he would give me no such satisfaction on the subject right now. I decided not to pursue it any further. "So what do you want to talk about, then? Why did you want me to come?"

"I know I made it sound like I wanted to talk about God, but I don't. Not now at least." He hesitated for a moment, gathering his thoughts. "I didn't think you'd come," he repeated.

"You keep saying that, but I did come. I'm here. So now what?"

"Let's talk about you."

Confusion took hold of me again. I wanted to be here, but at the same time, things were getting too dangerous again. This was supposed to be about him, not me. "What do you want to know?" I felt the words slipping off my tongue before I had time to stop them. I wasn't able to take action of my thoughts around him. My lips just opened and the opposite of what I knew I should be saying came out.

He smiled a little, his teeth perfectly white against his tanned skin. I felt my heart flutter momentarily in my chest as I saw how the smile illuminated his features even more. I realized I was holding my breath and tried to look at anything but his face, hoping to make the stupor go away.

"I want to know all about who Anna James is."

The way he said my name was enough for me to go right back into a trance. It was seductive, yet hung on the edge of taunting as if he knew this would create some sort of reaction within me. Whether I showed it or not, I wasn't entirely sure. I seemed to be so out of my element here in so many ways.

"There's really not a whole lot to say. My life isn't very interesting," I told him, unsure of what to say exactly. Talking about me would bore him to death. He would probably rather sit in his cell than listen to my life story.

"Believe me, you have me interested."

He continued to stare, his eyes so piercing I felt that fluttering sensation return. My emotions were on a roller coaster ride, and it felt like

I was on the verge of physical sickness at any moment, but somehow I was still holding it together.

"Do you live in a pretty country house with a white picket fence with a perfectly green lawn or something?" he asked, amusing himself.

I shrugged. "Pretty much." My mind was racing, my lips slipping again, as I began jabbering away about my family, what I did every day, and church life. He listened intently, or perhaps politely—I wasn't sure which. He would ask questions and I would answer. It seemed to go on for quite a while like this. He was poking and prodding me about my life. I finally sighed and leaned my head up against the wall beside me, feeling exhausted from having to remember all the dull aspects of myself.

"So," I said, "that basically sums up me."

He nodded, and I wondered how bored he truly was. "Which is who, exactly?"

I thought for a moment and then smiled. "I guess the girl sitting across from you right now."

"See?" he said. "That realization right there, that's interesting."

I saw his eyes move down to my lips and then slowly back up to my eyes. I immediately looked down at my hand. "I don't know."

"You do know who you are. There's not a classification system to it. You can't just say one word and be like, yeah, that's who I am. You stick to what you know, what you believe in, and that's who you are. And let me tell you, Anna, that's rare."

"Rare? Me?" I chuckled. I had always felt so completely ordinary. Sheltered, yes, definitely, but still very ordinary.

"Someday you'll realize that I'm right." Emry blinked his eyes warmly at me.

"I want to know *something* about you. I know nothing. It's not really fair." Now I was the one waiting for a reaction, but I found none. He didn't say anything, so I decided it was safe to go on.

"How old are you?"

"I'm twenty-two." Finally, an answer.

"I'm six foot three, blue eyes, brown hair," he added, grinning.

I couldn't help but smile in return. Perhaps my being here did make him somewhat happy then, at least enough to forget his sadness for a brief period of time.

"Where did you grow up?" I thought I may as well continue while I was on somewhat of a roll now that the focus was no longer aimed toward myself.

"Right here in Seneca."

"You did?"

"Why does that surprise you?"

I pinched my lips together with my teeth and then released them as I felt the sudden self-inflicted pain. "Because I know a lot of people in Seneca, or have at least heard of them between my father's church and the store."

He ran his fingers through his hair once more. It was such a simple action, yet he was so wonderful and graceful as he did so. My eyes watched the strands of hair fall toward the back of his head. "Ever heard of

Lainey Tritt?"

I began to search my memory. Lainey Tritt. The name sounded vaguely familiar, but I kept drawing a blank when trying to pinpoint where I had heard of her before. "Sounds familiar."

He paused and then continued. "Lainey Tritt adopted me when I was a baby." He waited to see if that triggered anything in my memory. It hadn't. "She lives over near Canyon Park in a slummy part of Seneca, I guess you could say."

Emry Logan was adopted. I didn't know what this meant to me, but it seemed that it proved my theory that he was out of place here. By the looks of him he didn't belong to somewhere like Seneca. I, of course, did belong in Seneca. I was average-looking. I could blend in easily. Even on my best day I doubted someone would give me a double take as I walked by.

"Was she a good mother?" I asked when I realized he was not giving me any more information willingly.

His head went to the side and back up again. "Lainey did the best she could with what she had."

"Does she visit you here?"

"I told you, no one visits me here. She's got dementia really bad. She's not doing too well. It wouldn't surprise me if she didn't remember me at all anymore," Emry said.

I was horrified by his words. Not remember him? How could someone forget Emry Logan? He hadn't said one impolite word to me the entire time I'd been sitting here. He was trapped and all alone, and I just couldn't wrap my mind around someone forgetting all about him.

A big heavy door slammed shut on the other side of the room. A police officer came stomping in.

"One minute!" he shouted out to all of us.

I glanced back at Emry, panic settling in my eyes. He realized that I didn't want to go and smiled. "This won't be the last time we talk, will it?" I quickly blurted out. I must be losing my mind.

I heard him chuckle into the phone. He seemed genuinely delighted by my comment. "That all depends on you, my dear."

"I hate this plastic screen thing. It makes me feel like a prisoner, too," I said, wrinkling up my nose to show him my disgust.

Emry's smile faded and he looked down, his sadness returning.

"I'm sorry you're here," he whispered. "This is a terrible place for you to be."

"I'm here because I want to be."

"Can I write to you?" he asked.

I saw most of the people around me already standing up and heading toward the door, their conversations already ended.

"It's probably not the best idea," I warned him. "I'll come back, though, if you want me to." Our eyes met.

"Yes, of course I do."

"Time's up." The officer took a step my way.

"Goodbye, Emry Logan." I forced myself to smile as I hung up the phone, but my heart felt heavy and I didn't want to go. I had barely found anything out.

Chapter 3

The next week went by painfully slow. Every waking thought I had belonged to Emry Logan. It became apparent to me that I was becoming obsessed; obsessed with finding out about him, why he was in jail, the next time I would see him, and all about his life. It was exhilarating, yet exhausting at the same time. And then I started to feel depressed again. Winter was still trying to move in. The air remained brisk and cold, but snow had yet to remain on the ground. I didn't know when I would be able to see him again. My mood was altered by the moment. I was hoping my family wouldn't be able to notice the changes in me, though I had my doubts. It felt as if I jumped at any little question they asked me, fearing that they thought something was off. I was fearful that they'd start asking me questions about my emotions, and I wasn't sure if I was going to be able to handle those questions, or more specifically, handle the lies that I knew I would tell them.

I walked through the motions of every day like I was supposed to, like what was expected of me, but my mind was never where I was. I was constantly picking at my brain and plotting my next move, but I had to be so careful. I couldn't keep going down to the jail every day to talk to Emry. I couldn't be Amy Wright. No one ever visited Emry, and for his sister to suddenly show up and be there all the time would be a dead giveaway. I was going to get caught if I wasn't cautious, and I wasn't sure how to do that quite yet.

Buck was on my mind as well. He was the one that would recognize me immediately if he saw me at the prison. I was trying to think of a way to get around Buck. I had to memorize his schedule, and the only way I knew how I could do that was to actually get to know Buck better as a friend. I wasn't very good at female friendships, let alone having one with a male. I didn't really know how to go about it exactly. Everything seemed so risky. I felt caged in, a prisoner in my own house, just like Emry. I felt so helpless. Why did things have to be so difficult? Furthermore, I kept questioning over and over again why I was so focused on the very thought of Emry Logan. After hours and days of tearing myself up about it, I finally gave in. He wasn't disappearing from my mind, so I decided to stop focusing on the reasons why this was happening to me. I had to focus on other things, like trying to get closer to Buck in order to get closer to Emry.

"Anna!" my mom hollered at me. I was lounging on the couch in the living room, flipping through stations on the TV with Matthew. I couldn't find a thing I wanted to watch, and it was starting to irritate me.

"Anna!" she called out again.

I grumbled a little as I made it seem like such a big struggle to get off the couch, and I handed the remote to my little brother. I rounded the corner to the kitchen where my mom stood, her hand stretched out toward me, holding the cordless phone. Her facial expression was peculiar, one I was not familiar with, but it looked suspicious. She eyed me for a moment and then her lips curled into a smirk.

"There you are," she said in a lower tone of voice. "Here." She took a step closer, pushing the phone toward me.

"Who is it?" My eyes narrowed at her and my heart began thumping. There was that anxiety again, something that was beginning to feel all too familiar. I rarely received phone calls. And why was my mother acting so strange?

She practically grabbed my hand, ripped open my fingers, and forced the phone into my palm. "It's for you."

I tried to slow my heart down by taking a deep breath. It didn't help much. Had Emry Logan called me at my house? What was I going to say to him in front of *her*? I turned and walked into the dining room, an attempt to get what little privacy I could. "Hello?" I whispered into the receiver.

"Hey, Anna."

I knew that voice. It was a male, but it wasn't Emry.

"Do you know who this is?"

And then I heard him chuckle, and it confirmed my assumption. "Hi, Buck."

He laughed again, a little louder this time. "Yeah, it's me."

And then a flutter began in the pit of my stomach, not out of nervousness but out of excitement. Buck had called me. I hadn't had to track him down. He had come to me. This was all too perfect. "What can I do for you?" I turned around slowly, leaned against the back of one of the

46

dining room chairs, and caught sight of the bottom of my mother's dress scurrying around the corner. *No privacy*, I thought.

"Well, you know Seneca's Frost Fest started, and every year I try to go. I thought to myself, you know what, I'm tired of going alone. It's just no fun. I should think of someone to go with me this year, and then I thought of you."

"Me?" I probably sounded as surprised as I was. This was completely unexpected. Since when did anyone, let alone a guy, think of me?

"Yeah, you. I mean, we're friends, right? We practically grew up together and all."

I listened to the silence for a moment, not sure what to say back. I was just so excited that Buck had called, that now there was an even greater chance I could get the information I needed from him.

"So," Buck said, "were you planning on going? I mean, did you maybe want to come along with me?"

I smiled. I saw my mom peek her head around the corner this time. She caught me looking happy, and I saw her eyes burst to life with delight. "Sure," I said. "Sounds like fun."

"Alright then. How about I pick you up tomorrow around noon?"

Tomorrow was Saturday. "See you then." I turned the phone off and made my way back to the kitchen to face my mother.

"What did he want?" she asked, bouncing up on her toes and then back down again.

"He wants to take me to Frost Fest tomorrow."

My mother clapped her hands together in excitement. "Is it a date?"

I watched her eyes grow wider as she waited impatiently for my answer. Her reaction almost made me burst out laughing. "I think so." I raised my eyebrows.

She hugged me tight and then stood back to take a look at me. "I'm not a child, Mother. No big deal." But it was a big deal. This was my big break. Finally, something was going my way for once.

"I know, I know. It's just … Buck is such a nice young man. Your father just thinks the world of him, you know."

I nodded and then headed toward the stairs to go to my room. Did Buck have a crush on me? Impossible. I stepped onto my soft purple carpet and shut the door quietly. It *had* sounded like he was asking me out, though. That's not exactly what I wanted. I didn't want to have to pretend to like him more than a friend just to get information out of him, but I would if that's what it took. Maybe I wouldn't have to cross that line. A little flirting wouldn't hurt anyone. I wasn't the least bit interested in Buck in that way. He was too short, he had these big glasses, and he seemed so awkward pretending to be a big, bad police officer when he was truly so meek and scrawny. I could have come up with a long list of reasons why I could never like Buck in that way. He was just a friend; a friend that I needed to help me get back into Seneca County Prison.

How was I going to act toward him? Did I even know how to flirt? I laughed and went over to my mirror. I was grinning at myself, a devious sort of grin, because I knew the games were about to begin.

***

"What are you going to wear?"

I turned around to see my mother hovering over me as I picked through sweaters in my closet.

"Probably a sweater and jeans. It's Frost Fest, remember? It's outside."

She ran her hand over the top row of shirts. She was on a mission. I had so many clothes, but I hardly wore any of them. Some were still left over from high school, some as far back as ninth grade.

I just hadn't taken the time to get rid of this stuff. I probably should, I decided. I was never going to wear half of these clothes again.

"Here." My mother took down a hanger from the top and held out a black turtleneck. "This always looked nice on you, Honey."

I stared at it for a moment. "Alright." I grabbed the shirt and pulled the hanger out. Black turtleneck and jeans it was.

"And wear those cute boots, too," my mother added as she left the room so I could change. "Those ones I bought you for Christmas a couple years back. You know the ones I mean."

I watched her disappear and quickly changed. I ran a comb through my hair and then smoothed it down with my hands so some of the static would go away. I sighed. I just prayed that I wasn't going to slip and say something stupid. All I had to do was be friendly. I needed Buck to trust me.

The clock on the wall said 11:45. He would be here any minute. I glanced out the window. Buck's shiny silver sports car pulled up beside the house. I grabbed my purse, tucked it under my arm, and headed downstairs.

"Morning, Mrs. James."

"Why hello, Buck." My mother opened the door wider so he could come in.

"How are you doing, Buck?" My father took a step toward him to shake his hand.

"Just fine, sir." He shook my father's hand and looked my way.

I walked in and shuffled past my parents. They were making this a big ordeal. Of course, I had never gone out on a date before, so I guess this was all new and exciting to them; especially since they liked the guy so much.

"Ready?" I asked, anxious to get away from my parents.

He smiled at me. "You look nice."

I blushed and quickly put my head down so no one would see. "Thanks," I mumbled.

"Have a good time!" I heard my mother shout behind us as we walked down the steps of the porch toward the car.

Buck opened the car door for me, and I quickly got inside. The smell of a very strong strawberry air freshener filled my nostrils. I tried to hold my breath for a moment, the smell hitting my sinuses full force as I could feel the sudden twinge of a headache developing.

"So did you go to Frost Fest last year?" Buck asked as we drove down the wet back roads toward the highway.

I tried to breathe normally as I slowly eased myself into getting used to the smell. "It's been a while."

"I try to come once a year. They have some great ice sculptures. This year's theme is fairy tales."

"Oh."

I tried to sound excited, but walking around in the blistering cold was not really my idea of fun. I would rather stay in the warm car and ask a million questions about Emry Logan. It was on the tip of my tongue, but I clenched my jaw together tight. *Get control of yourself*, I thought over and over again. Gain his trust, be nice, that's all.

***

I was surprised at how many people were actually out walking about on this chilly day. The streets of downtown Seneca were covered in beatifically carved ice sculptures, from Cinderella's carriage to Tarzan swinging from a tree made of ice. There were food stands all around, too, the smell of piping hot apple cider filling the air.

"Let's go get some of that cider to warm us up a bit," Buck suggested. "It smells wonderful." *Better than your car*, I thought.

I sipped on the delicious warm apple cider as we walked around. We saw a few people from our church, each one giving us a surprised, but approving smile as they saw us there together. We walked around for a while, and then my fingers started to go numb from the cold. I scolded myself silently for forgetting my gloves at home.

Buck and I made small talk as we walked, enjoying the day and the sights around us. He seemed genuinely happy that I was there by his side, and I was happy to be out of the house and building a friendly relationship with a cop.

We headed back toward Buck's car, and he shut the door behind me as I got in. I figured he was about to take me home. Where do I go from here? I had to ask to see him again, but I didn't want to sound too interested in him either. I rubbed my hands together as he turned on the heater and tried to sift through the thoughts going on in my head, trying to make sense of what exactly to say.

Buck turned toward me. "Hey, are you hungry?"

I paused, thinking about it for a moment. I actually was kind of hungry. All that walking had made me build up an appetite. "I am, actually."

He grinned. "Me, too. We could go grab a quick bite to eat; that is, if you didn't need to get back home or anything."

"No, I don't need to get back. Let's go." I smiled back at him, even though his sickening air freshener was rushing to my brain. This was absolutely perfect. Dinner would give me an opportunity for some serious talk with Buck.

**

The restaurant he took me to was a family favorite. It was called Mae Mae's, and it was kind of rundown looking in the inside, but the food was all homemade and fantastic. We sat and ordered and waited for our drinks. I folded my hands together in front of me and looked up at Buck, who sat directly across from me, his lips pressed together as he studied my face.

"You know, I'm still trying to figure you out," he said.

I raised my eyebrows. I had no idea what that was supposed to mean. "How so?"

He played with a small pink packet of sugar that had been sitting on the table and flipped it between his fingers. "Why is it that a girl like you doesn't have a boyfriend?"

A girl like me? I pretended to be thinking about what he had said for a moment before giving any sort of answer. "I'm a pastor's daughter."

"That just means you were raised right, Anna, not that you have a warning label on your forehead." The waitress set Buck's iced tea down on my side and my water in front of him.

"Thank you," I mumbled to her, and then politely waited until she was out of sight before switching glasses. "Well, sometimes it feels that way. Certain things are expected of me, and I think it intimidates guys."

Buck took a noisy slurp of his iced tea. "Are you trying to say that men aren't attracted to you, Anna?" His eyes narrowed as if he were offended. "Or is it that you aren't attracted to men around here?"

Great. A trick question. "Well," I began, trying to be cautious not to upset him, "from my point of view, it's like you grow up with everyone here. From the time you're five you know everyone and you know everyone they've dated in the past, and it's just like you almost wish a new group of people would come in, people you know absolutely nothing about."

"Oh, I see. We're boring to you."

I laughed at the way he said 'we'. I could sense his irritation and we hadn't even been served our food yet. I was ruining my chances. "That doesn't go for everyone, Buck; especially not you." I thought I'd sounded convincing enough. I waited for his reaction, and I saw his eyes soften a bit and realized I was making progress. "How could someone like you be boring? You're a policeman. You have a dangerous job."

Buck sat up a little straighter in the booth. That had done the trick. I had gone straight for the ego boost, and he had taken the bait. He was too easy to figure out. Being a policeman to him meant obtaining the title of, *watch out, I'm a big, bad cop now, so stay out of my way*, even though that title didn't apply to him. "It is dangerous."

I had to refrain from rolling my eyes. That was exactly Buck's problem. Buck actually thought he played that part. At least I didn't deny the dullness that made up my life. "So tell me a little bit about your job, Buck."

He grinned with pride. "Well, you know, its bad guys versus good, protecting the innocent and locking up scumbags."

"Do you ever think that some of those scumbags could be innocent?" I asked, twirling the straw around in my water.

He looked up, a confused expression on his face. "No."

54

"No? Never?" His response had been so cold-hearted.

He paused to think for a moment. I guessed he was going over the inmates in his mind.

"Here you go," the waitress said, putting down our plates of food in front of us. "Anything else I can get you right now?"

"No, thank you," Buck replied.

I shook my head, and with a turn of her heels, she walked away.

Buck stuffed a fork full of pulled beef into his mouth and started talking with his mouth full. "You know, there are a few men in there—they did minor things, robbery, assault, things like that—and they're pretty tolerable as people. I can actually have a conversation with them and call them by their first name, that sort of thing."

"So," I said, picking through my salad and digging out a few brown pieces of lettuce and putting them off to the side. "Not everyone in there has done something terrible?"

"No, not everyone, but we do get a lot of inmates who have done the unthinkable. Ever since they made the jail so much bigger, it seems like that's a lot of who goes through there, but sometimes they don't stay long."

His words alarmed me. "What do you mean?"

Buck took another noisy slurp of his drink and set it down on the table just as obnoxiously. "Well, some of them get transferred to other prisons." He paused and took a good look at what I was doing. "You're that interested in my job?"

I wasn't sure if this turn of subject was the beginning of an interrogation, so I decided I should stop asking so many questions. "Of course." I gave him a huge grin. "I don't know much about the police life."

Buck grinned back. "You just know the church life."

I sighed, realizing he wasn't catching onto anything. "How's your dinner?"

"Great," he said, patting his belly. I laughed. "Yours?"

"Delicious. We always come here when we go out to eat."

"Best place in town." Buck waved down the waitress to get another drink.

We sat there in silence, finishing our meals. My salad actually wasn't that great this time, but I kept managing to pick through it and act like I was truly enjoying it.

Buck finished his food first, and then wiped his mouth with a napkin. "So, I hope I didn't scare you when you were down at the jail with the way I was acting."

"Not at all." I was glad he was talking about this again.

"Good. I mean, those guys can be real jerks, and I can't just let them walk all over me. I didn't like to show you that side of me."

"Really, I understand, Buck." I bit my lip, hesitating for a moment, but my impatience was getting the best of me. "There was that one prisoner, the very last one." He looked over my shoulder off into space, trying to recall exactly who I was talking about. "You didn't seem to like that one very much. He must be one of those ones who did something unthinkable," I said, anxious for some sort of answer.

"Oh, yeah, I know who you mean. Logan." The way he called him by his last name with such emphasis of emotion showed how much he really loathed him. "He's definitely a scumbag. That's the one that I slipped your name to. Sorry for that. I overreacted on that one."

That one. He couldn't even bring himself to say his name again. "That's okay," I quickly said.

"No, I feel bad. I was a jerk. He just really gets to me."

"Don't feel bad, Buck. You're a good police officer." I wanted to ask more. Should I? Buck could be such an emotional mess. One minute he was extremely happy and the next he seemed so down. It was hard to juggle the situation without knowing which way it would turn out. "What did he do? Logan, I mean."

Buck waved down the waitress again. "Do you want another drink?" he asked me.

"No."

"Can we get the check, please?" He turned his head toward me again. "I'm not really supposed to talk about those kinds of things."

"Oh." Disappointment filled me again. Was I ever going to be able to find out why he was in there?

Buck must have been able to read the disappointment written all over my face. "Hey," he whispered, putting his finger under my chin and lifting my head up. "I know I can trust you, Anna. This stuff I talk about, cop stuff, it's between you and I, right?"

I felt a little glimmer of hope as I was breaking down the wall. "Of course. You have my word." I regretted saying that as soon as it had slipped out of my mouth. I never liked to promise things. I grew up getting scolded whenever I said that. It wasn't supposed to be used lightly. I guess Buck probably knew that, and that's why he found me so trustworthy.

He leaned across the table to get closer to me. I felt myself leaning in as well, the suspense taking hold of me. What was he going to say? Emry's a thief, a drunk, or a drug dealer?

"He killed his best friend. And not by accident either. He threw him off a really high tower," Buck whispered.

I had been way off. Buck was saying that Emry was a murderer.

I suddenly felt like I couldn't breathe. I backed away from Buck, probably too quickly, and struggled to regain control of myself. Could this possibly be true? Could beautiful, wonderful, sweet Emry have done such a dreadful thing, and furthermore, to his own best friend?

Buck immediately saw my shock. He rushed to the other side of the booth to sit next to me and put his arm around my neck, trying to comfort me, but my mind was still spinning from the picture forming in my head of Emry looking down from a tall tower to the ground where his friend's body lay motionless.

"Hey now," Buck hissed. "It's okay. Please don't be upset. I know it's scary to think about, but I'm sure he's forgotten about you. I'm positive he has. He's not going to come after you or anything. I wouldn't let that happen, anyway."

Pull it together! I commanded myself. *You're acting ridiculously.* But then I felt a little relieved as well. At least he thought I was scared, as if there was a reason to my sudden hyperventilation.

"Come on, let's get you going home."

I allowed Buck to pull me to a standing position out of the booth. He tossed some cash onto the table, and we walked together out of the diner. He stayed very close behind me, I guessed he thought maybe I would faint from fear or something.

The car ride home was mostly silent. Buck didn't know what else to say to comfort me, and my mind was still trying to wrap itself around the situation at hand. I had gotten what I wanted, an answer to my question, and I knew I should truly feel fear. I had gotten absurdly close to an alleged killer, but for some reason, the shock of hearing the reason of why Emry was in jail was not because I was afraid of him. I felt sorry for him. This all had to be a mistake, but murder wouldn't be treated lightly.

This wasn't just something he could walk away from and be released from jail, not any day soon, at least. This was a real mess, and I felt a hollow feeling forming in the pit of my stomach. Why was I being so harsh toward Buck for being an emotional mess? I was the one who was acting like a drama queen with my ups and downs. This was not something I felt I was capable of helping Emry with. This was beyond me. I was too insignificant to help Emry. *I was helpless*, I thought.

Surely there was more to the story. I had to start digging up Emry's past. How would I ever start to do such a thing? I felt determination again, a purpose to all of this madness within myself. It was the only thing that helped make the void slightly disappear and somewhat bearable. I had to redirect my thoughts once again. I was going to have to become more focused, or else Emry would be lost to me forever in the lifetime of a prison sentence.

"Just great!" Buck shouted out.

My eyes flittered upward to look through the windshield toward the foggy road in front of us. I couldn't tell where we were as I hadn't been paying attention. Buck pulled over to the side of the road.

"Do you feel that?" he asked me.

I looked toward him and then back to the road as the car came to a complete stop. "Feel what?"

Buck took a deep breath. "Flat tire." As he jumped out of the car, I felt the sudden rush of cold air hit my face from the open door.

I pulled the handle of the car door on my side and slipped out into the afternoon air as well. The fog was thick, settling a few inches off the ground. I had trouble seeing my own feet as I looked down at the road. Buck was already bent over the culprit tire, trying to see how much damage had been done.

"How bad is it?" I walked over and stood behind him. I could see the tire sagging. "Do you have a spare?"

He huffed as if suddenly irritated with himself. "You'd think I would, but you know, I don't. I don't even have a donut." He kicked at the tire with his boot. "I can call someone. It shouldn't take too long for us to be picked up." He crossed his arms in front of his chest. "Sure is getting colder, huh? We'd better get back in the car and try to keep warm."

I saw him eye me slightly, and I realized he was thinking he could keep me warm until someone showed up. Would he offer me his coat or put his arms around me in the car? I wasn't sure what he had planned, but I nervously started straining my eyes to try to look through the fog.

"Hey, we're on Livingston Street, aren't we?" I asked, taking a few steps away from Buck and a few closer toward the open field across the road.

"Yeah, I think. Why?"

"Mrs. Anderson lives on this road, and if this is the field," I said, crossing the ditch and hopping into the field, "her house should just be right up there." I pointed for him. "We could stay there until someone picked us up. It'd be warm there." It would get me away from having to be that close to Buck. I didn't want to give him too much of the wrong impression. Friendly, yes, but not *that* friendly.

Before Buck could object to my little scheme, I started walking through the field toward where I was almost certain the house would be.

"Anna, wait up!" Buck yelled out from behind me. "I have to get my phone!"

I slowed my pace a little but continued to walk. He could catch up. And he did. My boots trampled the frozen ground beneath my feet. It must have rained while we were in the diner. Ice seemed to be covering everything. Every few steps I would feel my boots slip, but then I would steady myself before falling down. We walked like this side by side for a while, our breaths exploding into miniature clouds in front of our faces as we went along.

"You know Mrs. Anderson, don't you?" I asked him.

"Oh, yes. Mrs. Anderson is a … nice lady."

61

He said it strangely. I wasn't sure what he meant about it. Buck seemed to say everyone's name in a weird way, though. It's like he held grudges or something, knew something about everyone.

"She's always calling my father for one thing or the other. Usually it's her son that calls, though."

"It's not like she's that old," Buck commented as if I had meant she were elderly or incapable of taking care of herself.

"No, she's not." I hadn't really thought much about it before. Mrs. Anderson had always seemed older to me because her kids were at least a good ten to fifteen years older than myself, but really, she was around the same age as my parents. She had just had her kids at a young age. I wondered why I had never really thought about that before. "She's been through a lot, though."

"You mean with her husband's death and then Ernie's?" Buck asked. "It's actually been a long time since both of them passed." He said it without a hint of sympathy.

I slipped on the ice again, but this time I felt Buck grab hold of the back of my arm, steadying me.

"Thanks." He didn't release his grasp, but continued to keep a firm hold on me to make sure that I wouldn't be able to slip again.

Mrs. Anderson had had some troublesome hardships to deal with in the last decade or so. Her husband had suddenly killed himself. Mrs. Anderson was the one who found him hanging by a rope in their bedroom. No one knew why he had done it, and nobody liked to mention that it had happened either. Suicide was a very difficult thing to deal with. Not only had that loved one died, but we believed that his soul would be damned as well. That's what we were taught in the church. I couldn't really ever remember seeing Mrs. Anderson's husband. I couldn't picture his face in my head.

And then around five or six years later, Mrs. Anderson's middle child, Ernie, died in a fishing accident. He had been at the lake by himself and campers found him face down in the water, drowned.

I didn't know her well, but she was probably an emotional wreck, devastated by the loss of those around her, and rightfully so. She never came to church, but she seemed to need extra guidance from my father, and if she was really depressed, her son, Lauren, would call my father to try to help her.

Lately, it seemed like a regular occurrence. Mrs. Anderson, the unstable widow of Seneca. She had turned into 'the creepy lady' to the little kids who wanted nothing to do with her and would double dare each other, especially around Halloween, to walk down her long driveway and catch a glimpse of her in her house, as if she were a witch or something, like her house was now haunted by the ghost of her dead husband.

"She just needs a little more spiritual help than others," I finally said, trying to defend the poor lady. "It may have been a while, but who knows how long it takes to get over some of the things she's been through."

"You're right." Buck sounded sympathetic now, more toward me catching him being heartless rather than judging Mrs. Anderson.

The field was coming to an end as I could see trees directly ahead and then the opening that was the entrance of her long, narrow driveway. The fog seemed to have lifted a little in this area, and I looked around me and saw that everything was truly covered in ice.

"Must've rained." Buck was having the exact same thoughts. "Hey, hold on for a sec." He abruptly stopped and pulled his cell phone out of his pocket as it was humming on vibrate. "Hello? Hey, Frank." He turned around and started having a conversation with one of his buddies. I guessed he had given someone a call while we were still at the car. "Yeah, if you wouldn't mind. Um, it's Livingston Street. Well, that depends. Do you want to change a tire in the cold, or would you rather hook up the car to a tow truck in the cold?" He chuckled. "Okay. Sure. Thanks. See ya." He snapped the phone shut and smiled as he headed back to where I stood. "Help's on the way."

He said it as if we were in danger.

We began walking down the driveway again and rounded the corner. Mrs. Anderson's house would be within sight soon. My eyes skimmed past the fading fog toward where I knew the porch would be. Suddenly, my crunching steps came to a halt. "Anna, what the…?"

"Shh!" I hissed at him, squatting down behind a bush to hide myself so I could observe more closely. Buck automatically hunched over next to me.

I could see Mrs. Anderson's house clearly now in the distance. She was outside standing in her yard with a pretty white lace shawl wrapped around her head. Pieces of her brunette hair were sticking out of the sides. She laughed suddenly, the sound echoing over to where we were, and then she lightly touched the side of a man's face who was standing in front of her. I squinted a few more times to confirm who exactly it was.

"Pastor James?" Buck mumbled, just as surprised as I was.

Pastor James, my father, was standing there in the yard not seeming like a pastor but simply an ordinary man now, a man that was uncomfortably close to another woman; a woman that was not my mother.

I watched the two of them obviously conversing, but I couldn't hear what they were saying to each other. Then suddenly Mrs. Anderson took a step up on the wooden porch stairs and turned with an outstretched hand toward my father. He stood there for a moment before stretching out and taking her hand in his own, and together the two of them walked up the stairs to the front of the porch.

My heart felt like it was going to leap right out of my chest. I gasped and then covered my mouth as a shrill, piercing sound had started to escape.

My eyes were glued to the front of the house. I couldn't move, feeling as if my feet were cemented to the ground. They conversed for a few more minutes in front of her door, and then suddenly my father bent downward and kissed her hand. He held it for a moment longer before she gave him a kiss on the cheek. He then turned away to head toward his car. Mrs. Anderson watched him leave before removing her white shawl and going into her house.

What in the world was going on? Had I really just seen what I thought I had? My father, the loving, respected, honorable Pastor John James, was having an affair? I felt that familiar lump return to my throat.

My entire body felt heavy and weighed down. Clenching my hands together, I could feel the nails digging into the palms of my hands. Fury overtook every emotion, reigning champion now. I wanted to stand up and scream at the top of my lungs.

"Anna," Buck whispered, "that wasn't what it seemed. It couldn't have been. Anna? Anna?"

I wasn't listening to what he was saying. I could only feel the rage overwhelm me as the tears began to sting my eyes and rush furiously down my cheeks. I found the strength to stand up, turn, and start running as fast as I could down the driveway again.

"Anna!" Buck called after me. "Please wait!"

I couldn't turn around and face him. I couldn't look at him and have him see the shame in my eyes, shame for my hypocritical father's actions. All this time, all these calls to our house and him running over here, all for this. I wanted to throw up. This couldn't be happening. Not to me. Not to my family. Somebody else's, but not mine. This wasn't how things were supposed to be.

I ran even faster, my boots skidding lightly over the hardened ground beneath each step. Before I knew it, I was in the field again. My lungs were burning from the sprint, but I barely noticed it. The ache in my heart was so great. And then suddenly my legs gave out on me, and I crumbled to the cold ground in the field, the tall, thick weeds sticking out around me, and I began to sob violently and threw my face into my hands on the ground and just surrendered to the sadness that filled every aspect of me. I had never felt so betrayed in my entire life. My own father, the one who had raised me to be different, to follow the Bible, was committing such a sin as adultery.

What was to become of my family now? How could I go back there and face them all? Was I going to tell my mother and brother, or would I just go on about my life as if I had never been there, never seen that? My mother wouldn't be able to go on. My father and the church were her life. Our reputation would be ruined. It *was* ruined. Buck now knew, too. I couldn't face any of it, didn't have the strength to. This was too much for even me to bear.

I heard Buck rush to my side, felt his hand on my back as I still had my face buried in my hands as the tears freely flowed. "Anna, please," he begged.

He wanted me to get up, to look at him, to talk to him. There was no way that I could. I couldn't get up and go home. I wanted to stay here on the ground and freeze to death in this field.

"Leave me alone," I cried. "Please, just go."

"Don't be silly." He wrapped his arms around my back and gave me a gentle hug. "Just look at me for a moment, will you?"

What other choice did I have? I was so completely humiliated. I tried to calm down, but the pain so agonizingly deep. I couldn't inhale properly, and my breaths were coming as short gasps. I turned to face him, standing up with his help, but I couldn't bear to look him directly in the eyes.

"Anna, I know what you're thinking, and you're wrong."

"She kissed him. They held hands!" I yelled out in disgust, another sob escaping along with the words.

He hugged me tight then, my face pressed against the shoulder of his coat. "Listen to me; you have to calm down."

"And then what? You'll just take me home."

"Yes," he said. "You have to go home. I don't want to tell you what to do, but I don't believe what I saw. I don't believe it for one moment, and I don't think you should be so quick to doubt your dad, either."

He was lecturing me now? I pushed him away and began stomping back toward the car "Where are you going now?" he asked, not in such a hurry to catch up as he was before.

"To the car. Take me home!" I shouted, wiping my wet face and runny nose with the back of my hand. A peculiar, numbing sensation took the place of the rage, and suddenly I was a little calmer and no longer crying. I just felt empty all over. My heart throbbed with an ache I had never felt before.

I saw Buck's car up ahead. I didn't bother to turn around to see where Buck was in relation to me. I opened the door on the side of the car and slammed it shut. I closed my eyes and leaned my head against the headrest, trying to picture Emry in front of me. There was no plastic screen between us.

There was no one else around us. There was just me and him together, and alone at last. He was staring at me with those big blue eyes and smiling with a dimple suddenly appearing in his cheek. I let the memory of him overcome everything else flittering recklessly around in my head, and for that exact moment, I felt some peace in my soul.

Chapter 4

My father wasn't home when I got there. I was thankful for that. I hadn't said another word to Buck and didn't even say goodbye when I got out of his car. He sat in front of my house, though, waiting to make sure I got inside okay. I had hoped that most of my tears had dried by the time my mother would see me, but I was sure my face was slightly puffy from my recent breakdown.

I attempted to open and close the front door as quietly as I possibly could so she wouldn't come running over to me right away. I even made it up to my bedroom and changed into my pajamas and collapsed on my bed in the darkness before anyone noticed I was home.

"Anna?" My mother pushed open my door a little, the light from the hallway making the room glow, but not enough to get a good look at my face. "I didn't hear you come in. How was it?" she asked. "Did you have fun?"

"I had a lot of fun," I answered in a flat tone.

"Buck's such a gentleman, isn't he?" She stepped into the room a little closer to me.

I didn't answer. My mind was still going a million miles an hour. I found it difficult to concentrate on giving my mother the kind of responses she wanted.

"Are you hungry?" she asked, realizing I wasn't interested in talking.

"No, we ate. I'm actually feeling really tired. I think I'm just going to go to bed."

My mother sat very still on the edge of the bed for a moment, hoping I'd change my mind and want to give her more details about my date with Buck, but I didn't. She got up and headed toward the door.

"Okay, Honey. Goodnight."

"Night. Oh, mom?" She turned around. "Where's dad?"

"He's at a meeting at the church right now. He'll be home soon. Why? Did you need to speak with him?" she asked in a more quiet tone.

"No, just wondering," I quickly said, watching her shut my bedroom door.

I laid there in the dark for a while, trying to sort through all the different emotions I was feeling at the same time. I turned onto my side and curled my knees up to my chest and hugged myself into a tight ball on the bed. The tears came on again as I pictured my father hand-in-hand with Mrs. Anderson. I tried to squeeze my eyes as tightly shut as they would go to make the images disappear, but they wouldn't. I tried to make the sudden sobbing stop, but then I realized that I could let it all out here. I didn't have to pretend to pull it together for Buck or hide the barely dried tears on my face from my mother. No one could hear me as I buried my face in my pillow. No one could see me. I could let it all out. I needed to release all the tension somehow, or I was going to explode.

The hours on the clock continued to turn, and I realized that it was very late into the night. My father had probably come home and was asleep now. Everyone was asleep. Everyone but me. I felt physically exhausted all of a sudden and flipped my wet pillow over to the dry side. I laid very still in the darkness for a few minutes longer just inhaling and exhaling routinely. That numbness had returned, and I was grateful to have gotten rid of some of that stress. I closed my eyes, and this time I did fall fast asleep and didn't wake up until the sun had come up again.

***

The proceeding days were almost intolerable. I tried to keep busy, which was the hardest part. I had nothing to do, but I wanted to steer clear of my father. When he would come in the house, I would go out and try to get some things down around the store or go shopping alone. Most evenings I would find myself at the library, looking through law books trying to figure out how much trouble Emry was in and if I could find any information as far as court hearings or the average prison sentence of convicted murderers, but every state was different and the terminology wasn't exactly the easiest for me to understand. I often found myself giving up and slamming the books shut. Then I would just sit there and mull over how irritable of a person I was becoming, how nothing seemed to be working out in my life all of a sudden. I would just sit there, arms crossed, sulking. I felt as if I had nowhere to go.

I would go from feeling sorry for myself, too sorry for my mother. It wasn't fair that she didn't know.

But then I would get to thinking that it was possible that she did know. Could she be so blind as to not see what he was doing? Was she actually just letting him get away with it? But then I would feel instantly guilty every time the thought crossed my mind. The matter of the fact was that in reality *I* had been that blind. I would have never in a million years thought my father capable of such a transgression.

Snowflakes floated down from the sky overhead as the sun had already set, and I inhaled the brisk air deeply and tried to hold it in my lungs as I walked to my car. I watched the lights flicker out in the library and someone appeared at the front door to lock up. They had kicked me out again. I had stayed until closing.

I drove home in another one of my moods. It was dinnertime, and I knew I would have to sit at the dining room table with my father directly across from me. I didn't know if I could do it without exploding at him. I was so tired of trying to hide the way I felt from everyone around me. I knew this wasn't healthy.

I parked my car in its usual spot in the driveway and checked the mailbox before going up the walk.

It was empty. The smell of sauerkraut and dumplings filled my nostrils as I entered the warm house and hung up my coat and scarf on the rack beside the front door.

"Just in time," Matthew said to me, wheeling himself away from the dining room table a little bit so he could get a better look at me. "Come eat."

I smiled at him. I was grateful that he had no clue as to what was going on around him. I had to deal with the situation, and even though I was completely miserable, it was a relief to know that Matthew would always remain happy.

"Working late again?" my father asked, raising his eyebrows up at me as I passed through the dining room toward the kitchen.

"Uh-huh," I mumbled, refusing to make eye contact with him.

I found my mother with her back turned toward me as she twirled a spoon in a pot on the stove. I tried to see what else needed done in here to continue to make myself useful and busy.

"Hi, Hun," she said pleasantly. "You're a popular woman today." I eyed her suspiciously.

She smiled as she stuck her finger in the pot and then in her mouth. "You got a letter today. It's on the table. And Buck called, too. He wants you to call him back."

I stood there frozen for a moment. Where did she say the letter was? My eyes quickly darted all around the counter until I spotted a small pile of envelopes. I automatically wanted to run over there, grab it and sprint up to my bedroom, but I knew that that would only make me look like a crazy person. I recomposed myself, took a deep breath, and tried to walk as calmly and normally as I possibly could over to the counter. Reading my name, I immediately knew it was Emry's handwriting in the same off-white envelope he had sent the last one in, but instead of a return address stating it was from the jail, it was blank. I felt my pulse rate speed up.

"Who's it from?" she asked curiously as she continued to stir.

I shrugged. "Probably from Mandi Liswich. I talked to her not long ago. Do you remember her?"

Mandi Liswich was a girl I had gone to high school with that I used to be fairly close to, until she went away to college and then eventually moved out of town altogether. From time to time we would write to each other, so it was the fastest lie that entered my head.

"Of course I do. She was such a lovely girl."

"I think she's coming back to town to visit her parents sometime soon. I'll read it later. It's probably a long one." I shoved the letter into the pocket of my jeans.

Sitting through dinner was even more intolerable than I had anticipated. Everyone was chatty, and I found myself chatting along about nothing important, even speaking to my father from time to time, wanting nothing more than to shove every bite in my mouth, swallow it whole, and be done with dinner so I could excuse myself to my bedroom for the rest of the night to read my letter, but again, that would mean me not acting like my normal self. Not that avoiding the family the last few days was normal, but it was something that likely would go without question. I had to be extra cautious, I reminded myself. They would catch on if I made too many mistakes.

I was so relieved when I was finally able to reach the sanctuary of my bedroom. I almost hesitated for a moment, thinking that my mother would burst in at any second and want to see the letter for herself, but I knew she was still washing dishes downstairs and cleaning up from dinner. I sat down in a small wooden chair that was near the window and unfolded the envelope that was now crinkled from being inside my pocket.

Dear Anna,

I know you didn't want me to write, but it's been so long. I need to know what you think of me, if you think about me at all. You're all that I think about. Please come see me again. It feels like it's getting hard to breathe in here not knowing when and if you'll return to me.

E.L.

My heart ached with a longing to jump in my car and rush straight toward the jail to see him. He was thinking about me just as much as I was him. His letter was so short and simple, yet felt so powerful. Emry Logan was missing me. What could this all mean, and where did I stand now? The confusion came on again as my emotions overwhelmed my mind, and I struggled to think straight. I didn't know what I meant to him, but I knew what I had to do. I had to go see him right away.

Tomorrow, yes. I would go tomorrow. Amy Wright or Anna James, one of them would find their way into that jail.

"Anna!"

I jumped at the sound of my name being hollered up the stairs. "Yeah?"

"Phone!"

I grabbed the cordless from its charger on my dresser and hit the on button. As soon as I pressed my ear up to it, I heard the downstairs phone click off.

"Hello?"

"Hey, Anna."

It was Buck. Hadn't my mother said something earlier about how I was supposed to call him back?

I had forgotten all about it.

"Hey, Buck. Sorry I didn't get a chance to call you back yet." Emry's letter was still gripped in my hand as my eyes scanned over his words once more.

His breathing was kind of heavy in the phone as if he were out of breath. "Oh, no problem. Is now a good time?"

"Sure. What's up?" I folded the letter and pressed it in between the pages of the same book that held Emry's first letter to me. I put the book back in its place on the shelf.

"How are things going?"

It took me a moment to understand what he was asking. He wanted to know if I still had a relationship with my father, if my mother still held a relationship with him. I had forgotten he'd witnessed all of that. "Oh, same old, same old," I told him, hoping he wouldn't pry too much more.

"How are you holding up?" he asked, sounding truly concerned.

My irritable mood instantly returned. *Thanks, Buck*, I thought. I was beginning to think I could possibly be bipolar. "I'm fine, I guess."

He hesitated, sensing my unwillingness to talk to him about the matter. "Well, I thought maybe you might need to get out of the house, go out and do something fun."

"I do. What did you have in mind?"

"I don't know. Anything. How about ... I could make you dinner," he suggested.

I let out a small chuckle. "Buck, do you cook?"

"Hey now," he said, pretending I had hurt his feelings. "I can buy food and put it in the bowl to make it look like I cook."

It was a little funny to think of him capable of making a meal.

"Tomorrow night after work, come over to my place. I'll make you dinner, and maybe we could rent a movie or something, too."

I hesitated for a moment. This was definitely a date date. I did need out of the house though, and I did need to get closer to Buck to see if he could tell me any other information about Emry.

"Alright. See you tomorrow."

Buck's mood was lightened by my acceptance of his invitation. His voice instantaneously became louder and more cheerful. "See you then. Oh, and come hungry."

"Do you have to work at all, or do you get to have the day off?" I was pleased with how I snuck the question in at the last second.

"Actually, I haven't worked all week. Taking a few days off."

"Oh." Now I was the one whose voice sounded more cheery. "Well, I do have to work, so I'll be there sometime around six."

"Have a good night, Anna."

"You too."

***

I started off the next day in a pleasant mood. I got up bright and early, and planned out what I was going to wear. I decided that I was going to pull my hair back and put some makeup on. I was sure I still had lip gloss somewhere in the bathroom drawer. Of course, I wouldn't be able to actually apply the makeup until I was in my car later that day after telling my mother that I was going to go have lunch with Mandi Liswich somewhere out of town so I could have a little extra time. She told me to say hello to Mandi for her, and I easily got out to my car and parked a few blocks away from the antique store so I could put on the mascara and blush that I had stored away in my purse that morning.

I peered back at my reflection in the rearview mirror. I thought I actually looked pretty good, considering it had been years since I had worn makeup and also because of the fact that I was applying it in the poor quality of light from within my car. I put the car into Drive and sped off toward the prison, a fluttering sensation of butterflies in my stomach mixed with a combination of my heart beating unusually fast took over and only increased after I had parked the car.

The same pattern happened as before. I had to go up to the window and sign in. Who would I be today? Amy or Anna? I shuffled the thought around momentarily before writing down my own name on the piece of paper. It probably wasn't the best idea I'd ever had, but I was feeling a bit risky. Then I sat with a slightly larger group of visitors today than before in the same small waiting room area.

"Okay," a police woman said, coming into the room at last, "let's go." She looked down over her list. "Which one of you is Anna James?"

My heart felt like it stopped. Why had she pinpointed *me* out? Was something going wrong? I felt slightly dizzy as if with any quick movement I would black out.

I raised my hand unsteadily to reveal myself, but the officer barely looked at me.

"You'll have to stay here and wait. We have two people wanting to visit the same person, so what we will do is, we will split the time in half. I will come back and get you when it's your turn," she said.

I slumped back into my chair. My eyes darted toward the faces of the people now going into the room to see the prisoners. Which one was here to see Emry? He said he never had any visitors. I don't know why I was looking so intently, as if I could read their minds or faces and be able to tell exactly which one was going in to talk to him. My heart sank. I would only get to spend half of the time allotted with him today. I would have to share him. It made me agitated and furious. I clenched my hands into tight balls and felt them beginning to sweat from doing so. Patience wasn't my finest quality, and it sure wasn't coming into play now when I needed it the most.

I began to picture Emry. He was so close, yet I couldn't see him. He was talking to someone else now. Someone from his family? Had Lainey Tritt possibly come to see him? I had no idea because I knew nothing of him, really. Maybe a friend had come?

I started to become worried as the realization hit me that they'd soon pull that person out and I would have to pass by them. They would look at me, I would look at them, and we would recognize each other as a visitor of Emry. I didn't want anyone to look at me and wonder why their time had been split in half as well. I was trying to stay low key.

"Ms. James?"

I stood up, startled. The same police woman entered in from the other room and motioned for me to come forward. It was now my turn. I felt almost clumsy as my feet didn't seem to want to work. I passed through the narrow entrance and saw a row of people talking on the phones to each other.

Headed straight toward me was a short, thin woman with bright blonde hair and red lipstick. A young girl was by her side walking parallel to her. Their eyes were glued on me. The older woman seemed to be giving me a death look like she was furious and wanted to lash out at me, and before I knew it, they had walked by and were headed out the door, and the officer was directing me to go sit down where they had just gotten up from.

"And she's returned," Emry said into the phone when I first picked it up and held it to my ear. "You look beautiful, by the way. There's something different about you. Your hair. Your hair is pulled back," he complimented me, smiling, more talkative than usual.

I stared at his face. He looked happy today. I retraced the features that I had merely grasped in memory over the last month. Had his hair grown longer? He still had wisps of it in his eyes, some of it brushed back as he sometimes ran his fingers through it. And there were those eyes again. I felt as if I could get lost in them if I stared too long.

"What's wrong?" he quickly asked, seeing through me more quickly than most people.

"Who were those two girls that were just here?"

"I think you made her pretty mad," he told me, amused at the idea and laughing quietly to himself.

"I think I caught that by the way she was looking at me on her way out." I waited for a moment. He offered no further explanation. "Who was she?"

Emry's smile quickly disappeared. He looked away from me to his hand and tapped his fingers on the desk in front of him anxiously.

"You don't want to tell me?"

"No, I do. Well, I don't, no, but I will." He still had his head shifted downward as we sat there saying nothing for a moment. I hated wasting valuable time like this.

"Why is it so hard to tell me? Please," I pleaded, my eyes burning into his as he looked up just then.

He sighed. "Her name's Candace Ramey, and the girl was her daughter, Traci." I waited for him to go on.

He looked at my face again, and then up to my hair and down to my lips before returning to my eyes.

"Candy's my ex."

"Ex-girlfriend?" The words stuck as if they didn't want to come out. My mouth felt suddenly dry.

He slowly shook his head. "No. My ex-wife."

For some profound reason that I couldn't explain, I suddenly felt a very similar feeling to the one I had experienced when I saw my father with Mrs. Anderson that foggy evening. My chest felt like it was being weighed down, suffocating me as I found it very difficult to breathe, and a strange sensation zipped across my stomach and then shot outward to the rest of my body. Why did every emotion I seemed to get these days have to be so powerful and take control of every inch of me? I suddenly felt too warm and quickly took off my coat to try to cool down before I really did faint.

"You were *married*?" That word definitely stuck harder than the last ones.

"I know, I know," he said as if feeling remorseful. "It was a long time ago. It didn't last long, only about eight months." He rewet his lips with the edge of his tongue before continuing on. "I thought that we had had something once, but I was wrong. She had been in trouble, I had helped her out, and then one thing had led to another, and before I knew it, we were married. But the whole thing was a mess, a huge mistake that I wish I could take back. I regret every moment of it." He looked up and straight into my own brown eyes. "You have to believe me."

And then suddenly I did believe him, because it was hard to even begin to picture the striking Emry Logan actually married to someone who looked like her. She looked … I had to search for the words as I remembered her face … tacky and fake, in my opinion.

"I have no feelings whatsoever for her now," he added quickly.

"Was that your daughter, too?" Another heavy emotion overwhelmed me as I asked him that. My fingertips that were holding the phone were feeling numb, so I switched it over into the other hand, which felt just as numb as the other.

"No. Traci is … *was* my step-daughter. She's a good kid. I kind of feel bad leaving her with Candy."

I don't know why I felt so traumatized. I knew nothing about Emry at all. So what if he had been married and had this little family before in his past, and was now divorced and she was visiting him in jail? Why did it all matter to me so much?

"I'm so glad you came," he repeated. "You got my letter?"

All of the bad feelings washed away from me then and I smiled. "I did. That was very sneaky of you."

"I couldn't resist. I meant every word, Anna. You're all I think about. I can't explain it."

"Try," I said, quite boldly. "What is it you're feeling?" I really did want to know why he bothered with me, why he wrote to me with such a passion; saying he needed me and thought about me. I needed an explanation for all of it, for this craziness I had suddenly become caught up in.

He paused then and looked down, regrouping his thoughts. "I think you're the most beautiful woman I've ever seen."

Had he just really said that to me? A sudden joy filled my heart as I let the words sink in. I was beautiful? He should be looking in the mirror to see what I was seeing when I looked back at him. No, he was absolutely perfect. I, on the other hand, was just alright.

"Is that okay to say to you?" He thought he had possibly upset me.

"It's just strange to hear someone say that about me."

"Anna, you're truly breathtaking. The first time I saw you, I

83

couldn't look away. Every time I see you, I find another interesting facial expression of yours. I wish I didn't have to be blocked by this stupid screen." His eyes became angry and sad as he and I both realized that we were still sitting in this prison being completely blocked from having true contact with one another.

"I find you so fascinating. I want to get to know you better, know everything about you and everything you're thinking. I think it's intriguing that you're sitting here across from me yet again. You're either out of your mind, or you have the same strange kind of attraction for me, too."

The realization of it all hit me hard just then. The feelings had been there all along, but I had never been able to put a label on it before. I was attracted to this estranged criminal sitting before me. I *liked* him more than any other guy I had come into contact with in my entire life. He was gorgeous and muscular on the exterior and yet seemed to be so kind and thoughtful, too. But he was also an inmate, and the pieces didn't seem to fit together like they should. He didn't belong here, yet here he was, and here I was with him, too. This was all so wrong, yet all so very right at the same time.

"I know I have absolutely no right saying these things to you, especially like this, in here." He looked around at the walls that caged him in. "I've tried not to think of you, tried letting you go, but you keep racing through my thoughts. I'm being selfish, I know, by pleading with you to keep coming down here, and I'd understand if you felt the need to run far, far away from me right now."

I felt so mesmerized by what was happening. This was not what I had expected to go on today. He was pouring out his heart to me in this exact moment, and I didn't know what to say back, because the truth was that I felt the exact same way, but I had never actually told myself these things, I just tried to get around them, but the obsession was still there, the need and want to see him, the longing of the days that passed when I couldn't see him and the ache that filled me, even now, knowing that I had actually felt jealous when I had heard that he had once been married before.

"This is so totally wrong," I whispered, tears filling my eyes.

"I know. I'm sorry," he whispered back in a sad, serious tone.

"No," I stopped him. "I just didn't expect this, that's all." I looked up at him then and knew he could see my tears, but I didn't care. "I do feel the exact same way, Emry. I do want to be near you, get to know you. It just seems so unbearable to do it like this."

"I know. I'm so sorry. I shouldn't keep contacting you."

"Please stop apologizing. I'm not sorry for any of it. It's the only good thing I have going for me right now," I blurted out. I saw him stare at me, puzzled, but he didn't question me any further about what I meant by it. "It's just so unfair to have met you under these circumstances."

"I agree." He sighed again, and I thought he was about to look away, but he was still looking straight into my eyes, concentrating very hard on all of my reactions through my facial expressions, reading me like an open book. I suddenly felt very vulnerable. Emry was breaking down my walls one by one.

"One minute!" the officer shouted out to everyone.

"Ugh!" I exclaimed. "So frustrating."

"I know. It is."

I looked from his freckles, back to the blueness of his eyes. "I'll come back as soon as I can."

He didn't say anything, only nodded.

I stared at him for a few seconds more and then put my palm up to the plastic screen. I watched him put his hand directly across from mine on the other side, his so much larger. It seemed like such a cheesy gesture, but I didn't care. It was the closest I had to physical contact with him. I pretended there wasn't a screen, that for just a moment our skin would be allowed to touch, and I'd be able to feel the warmth of his hand against my own.

"Let's wrap it up, people!"

The moment was instantly over as I gathered up my coat and stood. Emry just sat there watching me.

"Goodbye." I mouthed the word, knowing he wouldn't be able to hear me anyway.

He didn't say or do anything back. He just sat there, watching me walk away.

Chapter 5

I was actually looking forward to Friday. I had it all planned out in my head. I would go to Buck's house, eat his food, make chit-chat, ask more questions about jail procedures and so forth, not get too close, and then go home. It would be simple and it would get me out of the house.

"You're going to lock up then?" I asked my mother as I glanced around the store one more time to see if anything else needed to be done.

My mother nodded her head slowly as she chewed on a large bite of donut that she had just stuffed in her mouth. She put the decadent pastry down and dabbed her lips with a small white handkerchief.

"Okay. Well, I guess I'm going to head out. I'll be home sometime later." I put on my coat and gloves, and wrapped a purple knitted scarf around my neck and pulled it up over my chin.

She took a sip of water and set the Styrofoam cup down in front of her on the countertop. "Have fun, Hun. Say hi to Buck for me." She smiled. I was becoming accustomed to that look she gave me, so full of hope that something was sparking between Buck and I. She so desperately wanted me to be happy, and what better way than to fall in love with a policeman that just so happened to be a member at the same church where my father was the pastor; and who also had grown up in Seneca, had graduated from the same high school, and lived just a short distance away?

I just didn't see it the same way. To me, growing up with Buck wasn't a good thing from my point of view. He had no mystery. You couldn't really hold a conversation about your past, because you already knew the past. I guess I had always assumed I was meant to always live with my parents and share a home with them. The friends I had had in high school were already married and some had little kids. Those that still remained single I held no interest for.

Why Buck had decided suddenly he wanted to show an interest in me, I wasn't sure. What I supposed, though, was that he was simply trying to settle. He viewed me as a prospect to be with, because we had similar backgrounds and maybe he thought that would be enough, but to me, I hadn't known any sort of passion or needing to be with anyone before, but what I felt when I thought of Emry or actually saw his face in person, this powerful kind of longing and happiness all at the same time, made me realize that I could be passionate about someone in this lifetime, and that someone was definitely not Buck Brady. I would not settle for anything less than the feeling I got from my beautiful inmate.

I saw Buck peek out of his front window when I pulled up in front of his house. It was just a small place on the corner of the street that had once belonged to his grandmother before she passed away. He had moved in here only a few months after graduating high school. I had never been in the house before, but it was a common place to drive by. I put my gloves back on and hoped he had not gone to too much trouble with dinner. *There had better not be any candles lit on the table*, I thought to myself.

A warm gush of air greeted me as Buck opened the screen door to let me inside. I instantly smelled the aroma of chicken cooking and something else I couldn't quite put my finger on, some sort of sauce.

"Smells good." I flashed him a quick smile as he took my coat from me and put it on the back of a nearby chair.

"I'm actually *trying* to cook. I'm using one of my mom's recipes." He looked at me for a moment and then raised his arm, gesturing to the living room. "Make yourself at home."

I watched Buck dart back into the kitchen, which was around the corner and out of sight. I began looking around at the tiny living room with its wooden rocking chair and pale gray loveseat with faded yellow flowers dotting it, the very worn orange colored carpet, and light green drapes hanging loosely on the only single window in the room. It was tidy, though, and much better than I had anticipated with a bachelor living here.

I walked over to a large bookshelf that consumed the entire side wall of the room, and my eyes swept over a row of encyclopedias that had probably been there since his grandmother had lived here and a few pictures that were beginning to collect a fair amount of dust. They were mostly photos of Buck holding up fish, a deer that he held up by the antlers that he had just shot, and another one of him and his brother, Jackie. I had forgotten about Jackie. It had been years since I had seen him. He had been in the military and had married a girl from Venezuela. The last I had heard, they were living somewhere down south, possibly Florida. I couldn't recall the exact details. And the last picture was a close-up of his grandmother's smiling face.

"Are you doing alright in there?" Buck hollered out to me.

"I'm fine, Buck. Do you need help with anything?" I strolled into the kitchen to see what he was up to. The kitchen was very much similar to the living room: Outdated cabinets, multicolored checkered linoleum floor, and golden countertops from the 1950s.

Buck stood over a pot on top of the stove, furiously stirring as it bubbled away. I immediately found the correct knob on the stove and turned down that particular burner.

"Thanks," he mumbled.

"What is it?"

"It's Fettuccine Alfredo, and there's chicken in the oven."

The Alfredo sauce is what I had initially smelled coming in, but I hadn't been sure what it was.

"Looks almost done. Can I help set the table or anything?" I quickly looked around to find the table, and was relieved that there were no candles. There weren't even any dishes on it yet.

"In that right-hand top shelf there," he told me, pointing. "Yeah, right there. You can use those plates."

I set the table quickly and poured us each a glass of ice water as he brought over the food. It did actually look appetizing, and I hadn't realized how hungry I actually was until I saw it. I had skipped lunch today, and had only had a small bowl of cereal for breakfast before going to the store this morning.

Buck sat down across from me and grinned, proud of himself for actually putting together this meal. "You don't get a homemade meal often, do you?" I asked him, taking a sip of my water.

"Does this dinner count?"

"No."

He shrugged his shoulders. "Then no, I don't, and when I do, I'm not the one to have made it."

"Can't wait to taste it, Buck."

He said grace quickly and then we filled our plates with pasta and chicken. The meat was a little dry, but the Fettuccine Alfredo was surprisingly good, so I just smothered my chicken in the sauce so I would be able to swallow it more easily.

We didn't talk about much of anything during dinner. We ate until there was not much left, and I helped him rinse off the dishes and put them in a small dishwasher he had hooked up beside the sink.

"It was really good. I have to admit, I'm pretty impressed," I said, seeing him instantly glow with pride.

He dried the water from his hands and tossed the towel onto the counter. "Why, thank you. That was a definite first for me."

"You should try cooking for yourself more often. It beats fast food every night."

I followed Buck into the living room. He sat down on the gray loveseat. I glanced around. I didn't have many choices to sit. It was either the uncomfortable-looking, hard, wooden rocking chair or the other side of the loveseat, so I sat down next to him, but tried to position my body in a manner that was away from him at the same time.

He smiled and his hand moved toward the remote, and then the TV flickered on. "So, I forgot to go to the movie store after going to get groceries today," he started to explain. "I don't have very many DVDs. Maybe something good will be on a movie station."

I watched him go through stations one by one and read the titles at the top of the screen as he searched for something to watch. I knew he had been secretly kicking himself for not grabbing a movie on his way home today. The TV offered very little choices as well.

"So, are you enjoying your week off?" I asked, anxious to get the conversation revolving around the jail.

A news channel popped up, and Buck rested the remote on the arm of the loveseat as he thought about the question momentarily.

"Yes and no."

"No? You'd rather be working?" I asked, surprised. But then again, I liked to keep busy, too. He was probably the same way.

He repositioned himself on the couch so that he could be slightly closer to me. "Well, I just get bored sitting around here all day. There's only so much sleeping I can do before I'm just not tired anymore." He chuckled at his own little joke.

"I know what you mean." I thought about all the questions I wanted to ask, and then tried to focus on the ones that I *could* ask. "So, how exactly does your schedule work? Do you switch shifts?"

"It really depends on the week. Mostly I am always daylight, but sometimes I get a few third shifts in there where I'm working until 7:00a.m. If I work so many days in a row, I get a few off as comp time."

This was going to be more difficult to follow than I had thought. He didn't seem to really know all the times he was working, so how on earth was I going to know when he was there or not there?

Maybe I could just start looking for his car, but the jail was so large and there was a parking garage.

Were there special places allotted just for police staff to park?

"So, what do you do?"

"What do you mean?" he asked, putting his arm up on the back of the loveseat, the smell of his spicy deodorant filling my nostrils as he did so.

"Well," I began slowly, "are you always at the jail when you work?"

"Sometimes there. Sometimes in the car driving around with my partner, Rod. Have you ever met Rod?" He paused to think for a moment. "No, I guess you wouldn't know him. He's something else. He's a riot." He thought about something in his head, Rod I supposed, and then laughed about whatever it was he was thinking about. "Your dad was actually down the other day passing around those pamphlets of his again." He stared at me, waiting for a reaction.

Great, I thought. He had just completely turned around the conversation and aimed it directly toward me. "Did he?" I didn't particularly care.

He nodded. "How are things going at home with all of that?"

I took a deep breath and found myself playing with the silver bracelet dangling from my wrist. I had suddenly realized that my father had given that bracelet to me a couple of birthdays ago and fought the urge to rip it off my wrist right then and there. "They're fine."

"Why won't you talk about it?"

"Because I don't want to." I found myself losing control, as if talking about this with Buck, who had seen it with his own eyes, would push me over the edge. I wished he had never been there.

"Calm down, Anna. I just think you need to talk about it, get it off your chest."

What did he know about anything? It infuriated me that he thought he knew what was best for me. "I don't need to get it off my chest. I need to forget it ever happened."

"Can you do that, though?"

"Do what?" I found myself still on the verge of almost screaming at him. I hated how he was making this his business.

"Forget about it?"

He didn't seem the least bit concerned that I was on the edge of making a scene and didn't seem to want to end the conversation. He just wanted to pry and dig his fingers deeper into the wound. "Of course not!" I yelled out, jumping to my feet. "I hate that I know this. I hate that he's done this to us, to my mother!"

Buck quickly stood from the love seat and took a few steps toward me.

"He acts like nothing's wrong! He puts on this big show, as if he's some perfect pastor who can do no wrong and everyone just goes along with it. *I* didn't even know anything was wrong, so how can I blame anyone else for not seeing through his little act? He's out visiting Mrs. Anderson, helping Mrs. Anderson, sleeping with Mrs. Anderson!" The tears came on strong, stinging in my raging eyes and streaming heavily down my cheeks.

"Hey, now," Buck whispered, pulling me in closer to him. He hugged me tight and I let him, not knowing what else to do. All I could think about now was my father, and I was so angry that I had allowed these feelings to overwhelm me, yet again. "Listen, you don't know what you think you saw is what is actually going on."

I pushed Buck away from me. "How can you defend him like that? It makes me honestly sick. How can you even go to church on Sunday and listen to him preach about God and about being a good person and doing all these good things when you saw it the same as I did? I *have* to be there, but *you*, you continue to go; why?" I screamed out, continuing to cry.

He took a step closer to me again, and I reacted by going backward. He threw his hands up in the air as if surrendering and didn't attempt to move closer. "I honestly don't think your dad is capable of something like *that*." He paused for a moment to assess my reaction. All I could do was just stand there and clench my hands up into fists, the nails digging in my palms. "I've thought about it. Believe me, Anna, I have. Pastor John James is a good man; one of the best."

I let a noise of disgust escape from my throat. He was fooled, too. "I can't believe this. You're taking his side. You saw what I saw, and you're *still* taking his side."

"Anna, I'm not taking his side. I just don't want you to be upset over this, because I really don't think it's happening the way you're thinking it is."

Buck was such an irritating person. He threw his opinions around and wanted me to just go along with whatever he said. "I know what I saw. How else would you, or could you, explain it?"

"I don't know exactly." He looked at me, not sure what to do or say next. "Have you tried talking to him about it at all?"

"Of course not!" I cried out. "I can't have that conversation with him. I would probably want to kill him if I heard him actually admit to it."

"Anna, you're overreacting."

"Whatever, Buck. Thanks for the lovely night." I took a few steps toward him to try to get to my coat.

Buck grabbed hold of me by the waist and swung me in closer to him just then. He had a silly smirk on his face, which only agitated me even more.

"Let go of me!" I cried out.

"Anna," he whispered, and then suddenly Buck's head bent down and his lips pressed tightly to mine. It only lasted a few seconds before he backed up to see my reaction. He was still smirking.

I immediately swung back my hand that was still clenched into a fist behind me and then released all of my fury and irritation as my fist collided with Buck's hard skull, directly on his eye.

He instantaneously cried out and stumbled backward, probably more from pure shock than from the actual blow.

"Not the reaction you were hoping for?" I asked, suddenly feeling calmer and better having released some of the built-up tension from within me.

He was holding onto his eye with his hand, suddenly furious with me now. "You're crazy! Why would you do something like that?"

"Why would you kiss me, especially in a moment like that?"

He squinted at me with his other eye, his hand still pressed against the one I had punched. "I was trying to get you to calm down."

"By kissing me?" I screamed.

He winced a little. "Do you have a ring on?"

I suddenly looked down at my still clenched fist. It was throbbing from hitting his hard face, and there on my middle finger was a ring with a sapphire stone on it in the shape of a heart. I looked back at Buck and felt a little twinge of guilt for hitting him now. "I'll go get you some ice."

I walked into the kitchen and began shuffling around his freezer, searching for an ice pack. The phone rang, echoing throughout the house. I turned around and stared at a large black phone hanging on the wall behind me and guessed it to be more memorabilia from his grandmother.

"Can you get that?" Buck shouted at me.

I slammed the freezer door shut and reached for the phone with my bad hand. It hurt as I did so. I started to wonder if maybe I had broken something. "Hello?"

"Anna, is that you?" It was my father.

"Yeah," I whispered, lowering my eyebrows. Why would he have called here? "Put Buck on the phone," he commanded me.

I thought about hanging up on him, but instead, I gently laid the phone down on the table and went to get him. "Buck, it's for you. It's the honorable Pastor John James."

He gave me a look of surprise, but didn't dare say anything to me about it as he tromped into the next room. His hand came down from his eye, revealing the damage I had done. It had already turned a deep shade of purple and blue as it began to swell. I didn't listen to their conversation. I just sat down on the loveseat and found myself staring blankly at the floor.

"Get your coat on," Buck instructed me as he came back in. He walked to a small closet near the front door and retrieved a coat for himself.

I stood up and looked at him cautiously. "That was fast. What did he want?"

He bit his lip slightly, still angry, but I could tell he was hiding something from me. "He didn't want me to tell you right away, afraid that you'd be upset, but I don't really see how you could get much more upset than you already are."

I continued to stand there, waiting for him to tell me what he was talking about. I put my hands on my hips impatiently. "Did he confess his undying love for Mrs. Anderson or something?"

"No, he wants me to drive you to the hospital."

"What for?"

He turned around and picked up my coat for me. "It's your mom. They think she's had a heart attack."

***

The ride to Seneca Memorial was a long, silent one. The roads were slick and wet. Buck drove cautiously, and too slowly for me not to keep losing my patience. I kept wondering if my mother was okay, what had happened, where was Matthew? Everything kept swirling around in my head. I glanced at Buck and saw the bruised, bulging eye. Probably another reason he was driving so carefully, I presumed.

Perhaps my mother had finally realized what exactly my father was up to with Mrs. Anderson. That had to be it. She now knew he was having the affair, and it probably broke her heart in half and gave her a heart attack from finding out. How horrible for her if she now knew. She was too fragile to handle something like this. Her heart was too delicate. She had always had irregular heartbeats since she was a child, and I knew she wouldn't be able to take something as devastating as this. My father was going to be the reason for my mother's death.

Once we were parked and inside, we headed directly for the cardiac floor of the hospital.

"Helene James' room," I said, trying to catch my breath from walking so quickly. I had decided that taking the stairs would ultimately be faster than the elevator. Buck and I stood in front of a large desk with four nurses sitting behind it. They didn't look particularly busy, but then again, it was almost ten at night. The hallways of the hospital were quiet, and everyone was whispering so as not to disturb those that were asleep.

"Are you a relative?" the nurse questioned me. She was chewing vigorously on a piece of gum.

"Yes. I'm her daughter."

"She's in room 1048. Go down the hall and it'll be on your left," she instructed me.

Buck followed me but remained a few steps back. I walked quickly to the end of the hall and hurried toward the door labeled 1048 in large gold metal numbers. I burst in and saw my mother lying in bed with all sorts of monitors and cords running to and from her.

"Anna," she whispered, reaching out her hand to grab hold of mine.

I rushed to her side, relieved that she was alright. I immediately felt the chill of her cold fingers as she touched me. My father was sitting on the other side of the bed directly across from me. I barely gave him notice, focusing all my attention to my mother, who looked pale and exhausted.

"What happened?" I asked, my eyes now moving accusingly toward my father and then back to her. She attempted a half smile. She always did this when she was trying to cover something up, trying to make things appear better than they really were. She had done this since I was a small child so I would feel better about the situation; only now, I could see right through it.

"I'm okay. Really."

I wasn't convinced. "What happened?" I repeated, adding a little more emphasis this time.

"She was having her palpitations again," my father explained. "She started getting sharp pains with them this time, though."

"You usually don't get them unless you're upset. What were you doing? Were you two fighting?"

My mother gave my father an uneasy look. A small wrinkle appeared between her eyebrows as she had a concerned expression on her face.

"Why would you think we were fighting?" she asked.

My eyes went to the floor. "I just assumed…" but I stopped. I couldn't talk about it like this, especially here.

A tall doctor came through the door. His hair was dark and he wore tiny, wire-rimmed glasses. He glanced over a page on a clipboard and then tucked it under his arm. "I'm Dr. Weston. I've come to reassess you, Helene." He flashed a smile full of bright white teeth. "Are you able to sit up a little for me?"

I moved out of his way so he could get closer to my mother. I watched curiously as he checked some of the monitors and then wrote down the information on the clipboard. He checked her pulse and her blood pressure and then walked in front of the bed to look at her.

"Looks like you've got some company," he said cheerfully. She nodded.

"How are you feeling?"

"Better, thank you."

"You're responding well to the medication. Very good. Any more pains?" he asked.

"No. Just tired."

"Yes, well, that's expected." He turned and gave my father and me a look over. "I'm going to keep Helene overnight for observation. We haven't totally ruled out a myocardial infarction just yet. I'm still awaiting the results of her cardiac enzymes and expect a call from the lab shortly on those." He turned his head toward my mother again. "Try to get some rest, Mrs. James. I will be in to check on you in the morning before I leave."

"Thank you, doctor," my father said as we watched him leave the room.

"You should go home and get some sleep," my mother told me.

"I just got here. I'm not going anywhere." I was irritated that she had suggested such a thing. I wasn't a child.

"Did you have a good night with Buck? Where is he?" she asked, still practically whispering.

"He's here." I glanced toward the doorway. Buck was obviously within listening distance as he peeked his head in the room for a moment so she could see that he was there.

"Oh my goodness!" my mother gasped. "Your eye."

Buck disappeared around the corner again, embarrassed.

My father gave me a hard, stern look. Had he already figured out I had done that?

"Um, I think he ran into the corner of a cupboard or something," I quickly spit out. "Where's Matthew?"

"Lydia has him," she answered. It was one of her friends from the church. "He was excited to stay the night."

We sat there in silence for a few moments, just listening to the hum of the monitors. There was a huge elephant in the room, and I grew more furious by the second that no one was acknowledging it.

"What were you doing exactly when you got these palpitations?" I asked, suddenly feeling brave, wanting to get this all off my chest. I wanted this weight lifted from my shoulders, because it wasn't fair to have to hide this any longer. It was too much of a burden for me to bear, too much for my mother. If my father wanted to be with another woman, we would turn our backs on him and never look back. I had little respect left for him now, anyway. It was time to tell the truth. If she didn't know already, which I assumed she did, it was time to expose this failure of a Christian man who stood at a pulpit every Sunday and made everyone else in the room feel guilty for their sins when a big, fat finger should have really been pointed right back at the pulpit to Pastor John James. The thought of him standing up there, believing he had any right to speak about Jesus repulsed me.

My stomach churned and my heart ached as I saw my mother in the hospital bed. And then I sighed, knowing that I was about to be a coward again. All of my strength dissipated when I realized that such a truth could possibly cause her frail heart to fail once and for all and then what good would the truth be if it had all been revealed and then the one honest, loving, respectful parent I had left, the one person who encouraged me and uplifted me, was gone? If she didn't know, I would not, could not be the one to sit here right now and tell her of my accusations toward the man she thought she knew and loved. It would still have to keep my burden bundled up inside of me, tearing at me, but safer there than to cause physical harm to my loving mother.

The silence was broken by the big heavy door to the room cracking open. I looked up, expecting to see Buck there. Instead, I gasped as Mrs. Anderson stepped into my mother's hospital room. I wasn't the only one completely shocked. My mother look horrified as well. And just with that one look on her face, I knew for absolute certain that my mother did indeed know something was up.

"Helene, how are you doing?" Mrs. Anderson asked, removing the hood she had over top of her head and exposing her brown hair streaked in gray, sticking out under a white lace shawl that she wore often.

I had never realized before how raspy and coarse Mrs. Anderson's voice was. It sounded as if she had been a chain smoker for years. Her face seemed hardened and stern, so much the opposite of my mother, but of course, she could never compare to her in my eyes.

"What is she doing here?" my mother asked, the question almost a hiss coming from her mouth. She suddenly looked even more upset than she had before as she looked toward my father.

"You really shouldn't be here," he said, standing.

She raised her arms up as if she meant no harm. "I know, I know. Please, I need to speak with you," she said to my father.

"Are you kidding me?" My voice sounded louder than anyone else's in the room. "How did she get in? Didn't they ask her if she was family at the front desk?" I found myself standing now, rage rushing through my veins. I wanted so badly to physically remove her from the room. She had caused this family so much pain, and now she had the gall to come to my mother's bedside while she was in the hospital? Who did she think she was? I felt the sting of tears filling my eyes without my consent. This seemed to be happening a lot lately. I was so out of control. I had too much built up. Mrs. Anderson had triggered an intense emotion from within me, and I was afraid that I wouldn't be able to refrain myself from truly losing my temper now.

Buck ducked into the room just then, a look of concern on his face for what was going on. Surely he didn't doubt my opinion now, seeing that she had come here in person only to interfere further with the relationship of my parents.

"This is not a good idea," my mother said, trying to sit up more now. Her voice still remained so calm. Why had I not genetically gotten that gene passed down to me?

My father walked toward Mrs. Anderson and looked over his shoulder to his wife laying in the hospital bed, her condition fragile. "This will only take a moment," he told her. "I'll be right back." He gave Buck a hard look on his way out.

As if Buck could read his mind, he suddenly came over to me and grabbed the back of my arm.

"Come on. Let's take a walk, Anna."

I was so stunned by what was happening that I didn't even put up a struggle. I looked back at my mother, into her suddenly very sad eyes, and my heart broke seeing her like this. I almost couldn't stand to be in this room for another moment, and allowed Buck to direct me out into the desolate hallway.

My eyes scanned the dimly lit corridor. Where had my father and Mrs. Anderson gone? They were nowhere to be seen.

Buck continued to walk further away from the room as my legs shuffled forward right along with him. He led me to a small waiting room, and I collapsed into a scratchy, stuffed arm-chair that smelled of some sort of lemony cleaner. A TV hummed quietly above our heads. Buck sat across from me and gave me a look. His eye seemed to be even worse looking than before, but I noticed he could open it wider than he had been able to earlier.

I knew I should be back there in that room with my mother. She was all alone and God knew what was going through her head right now. I didn't want to think about it. I didn't want to go back there, and I didn't want to see my father anywhere near Mrs. Anderson, the two of them standing even remotely close to one another. The thought made me want to puke. I slumped over and rested my head in my hands as the clock on the wall ticked, the noise starting to get on my nerves.

Why wasn't Buck saying anything? He was usually good for some sort of remark, always putting his two cents in. He just sat there, not even looking my way, staring off in a daze.

I suddenly felt the need to break the silence. "Buck?"

"Huh?" He looked up now, raising his eyebrows so high that it made thick creases in his forehead.

He looked tired.

I sat back in my chair and crossed my arms in front of me. "What do you think she wants?"

He sighed, probably hoping the conversation would be about anything but my father and Mrs. Anderson and the situation at hand.

Maybe he was afraid to talk about it, in case I would sock him in the face again.

"I honestly have no idea, Anna." He suddenly reached over and held his hands out. I automatically repositioned myself so that my hands were resting in his. I felt the warmth of his skin soothing. "Listen to me," he began, now looking directly into my eyes. "Everything is going to be fine."

I searched his one good eye for any sort of doubt. He seemed to be sincere. I had to admit, it did make me feel a little better for a moment, but life had been too perfect before. Something bad was bound to be thrown our way. This was definitely an obstacle that could potentially break up our entire family and the tightly-knit bond of trust that had seemed to always have been there as far back as I could remember. Something was happening to the James family, and anyone who tried to be insightful and look into the future would only surely be able to see disaster ahead. It was crouching all around me like shadows that never went away, always hovering, ready to pounce at any moment and come crushing down around all of us.

We sat there for what seemed like hours, my hands being held inside of Buck's. I could feel the sweat from our hands pressed together, but neither one of us seemed to mind. There was nothing left to do, nothing left to say. When we released our grips, we would have to go back and face reality.

The cruelty of it all truly sickened me. It was so much worse for me than Buck, but he too would have to be witness to my family's shame.

He already had.

My mind wandered to the only thing that could make me happy, the only person in the entire world I really longed to be with at this moment. Emry's face flashed before me in my head. He smiled and for a second, all of my worries were swept away.

"Anna."

I looked up at Buck, his eyes sympathetic toward me.

"We have to go back now." His eyes glanced up toward the clock, and then his hands fell, releasing mine.

I held them there in the air for a moment before pulling them in tight to my side. I stood up and nodded.

We walked more slowly back to my mother's room, everything around me a foggy haze. We passed by room after room, all the doors closed as I imagined each patient in bed sleeping. We passed by the front desk and the nurses sitting behind it, who eyed us silently as we walked on. There was a bench up ahead and a young woman sat there, her long brown hair covering her face as she slouched over ever so slightly. I looked at her as we went by, and she turned her head up and met my eyes. She was pretty, but her face was hardened. She was obviously upset by something. Was she going through something similar to what I was? Her lips were slightly pouty and her green eyes narrowed for a split second as I stared at her. Then she looked away, and I did the same as Buck touched my arm. I turned toward him and forced a quick smile.

"Ready?" he asked.

I nodded. He started to open the door. "Buck," I said quickly. He turned to give me one last moment of attention. "Stay close by me."

He opened the door wider, letting me enter first.

Chapter 6

The days following my mother's admission to the hospital whizzed by in a blur. I became full of responsibility for once with running the store, taking care of Matthew, and all of the housework. The holidays were in full swing. Everyone thought I should just close the store temporarily, but I welcomed any sort of activity that would keep my mind off everything going on around me.

My mother came home after staying in the hospital for a few days. They had put her on some sort of new medication to help regulate her heart rhythm, but she was very tired when she finally got home and seemed to constantly sleep. My father would pop in every now and again to see how she was doing, but he was spending a lot of late nights out. I never asked where he was going. No one said anything further about Mrs. Anderson, and my mother gave me no more indication that she had any knowledge that something was going on other than how she had reacted by seeing Mrs. Anderson that night at the hospital. I tried not to dwell on it anymore. I could feel the tension all around me, but with Mom being sick, I knew the problem wouldn't be addressed. For all I knew, perhaps they thought their reputation was far more important than getting at the bigger issue at hand, and even when she got better, nothing more would be said. I knew that nothing would be the same between any one of us, and I was sure that they knew that as well even if they tried as hard as they could to put up a good front to everyone else.

I spent my days tending to the antique store and thinking about Emry Logan, and then I would come home and make dinner and then lay in bed and think about Emry Logan. I became restless, anticipating the next time I would be able to see him, get to talk to him, or even touch his beautifully tanned skin. I would get out the book that contained the brief notes he had written to me and read them over and over, memorizing every word and the way he wrote the words as well. I found myself dreaming about him almost every night. Sometimes the dreams would be cruel as he would come close to me and hold out both of his arms toward me, yet I could never reach him no matter how hard I tried. And other times, I would find myself running down a dark corridor, much like the ones they had at the jail, and I would scream his name out. I would wake up in a panic, praying that I hadn't actually said his name out loud in my sleep.

I knew I was becoming someone completely different than I had been just a few months ago. I had once felt content with my life. And now, there stood a woman in the mirror who looked like Anna James, but she was worn down and beaten. I felt like digging my fingers in the ground and pleading for some sort of justice for all the good I had done. Didn't that count for something? Shouldn't something good come my way in return?

Emotions flowed through me that I had never experienced before. I had once boxed myself in, thinking everything around me was already perfect, that nowhere else in the entire world could I find such peace than with my family, the church, the store. Now I dreamed of helping Emry Logan escape from prison and running away with him to some tropical island where I imagined him holding me in his strong arms, and just being there with him would make all of my troubles here in Seneca go away forever. I'd be able to breathe again. These mood swings were agonizing to try to take control of. I felt like those teenage hormones that I thought had skipped over me were finally catching up. I hated my life. I wanted out, but I wanted to take Emry with me. My profound obsession with him only added to the craziness of my moods.

I heard the roar of an engine outside and hurried over to the window to see who it was. A black Mustang sat parked in front of the house. I didn't know anyone who drove a Mustang. Out of the driver's side, a short, middle-aged woman with dark brown roots protruding from her dyed blondish-colored hair, got out. She turned and stood to stare at the house. I noticed she wore overly large black sunglasses as she turned to slam her door shut. She moved to the back of the car and opened the trunk to retrieve a pink suitcase with red stripes.

I was still racking my brain with who it could be when I opened up the front door as she walked up the porch steps. She brushed right by me and threw the suitcase down on the hardwood floor with a loud thud.

"Annie, are you really that surprised to see me?"

Then I instantly knew who she was. "What are you doing here?" I asked. It was Carlin, my aunt.

She was my mother's baby sister. I hadn't seen her in probably over ten years. I never cared for her much. She thought she was better than everyone else. She was a free spirit, drifting from here to there, never living in one place for very long, and always wanting to experience new things to help restore what little youth she had left. She and my mother never saw eye-to-eye. My mother wanted a family, and Carlin didn't believe in the concept. They rarely spoke. I curiously examined her. She still looked the same, only aged with small wrinkles stemming outward slightly from the edges of her mouth and eyes. She had permanent indents molded into her forehead, and she had gained a little weight. She always referred to me as Annie, saying it in a spiteful manner. I could remember that even as a little girl, I detested the nickname. When I was little, I had always been relieved when her visits ended. Our personalities had always clashed.

She glanced around the room and huffed as if agitated by the way the house looked. "So I heard my sister is sick."

"Who told you that?"

She took her long black dress coat off and put one hand on her hip impatiently. "John called me."

"He did?" My voice cracked with surprise.

She nodded and tapped her stilettos on the wooden floor. "Where's Helene? Is she upstairs in bed?"

Before I could respond, she was already moving up the staircase toward my parents' bedroom. I didn't bother to follow. I sat down on the couch and tried to focus on the TV show that Matthew had on. I could hear the low hum of voices upstairs but couldn't make anything specific out. A few minutes later, my father came into the room and took a seat in the tan recliner.

"Your Aunt Carlin is here," he said.

"I've already seen," I mumbled, my eyes never leaving the screen of the television.

"She's going to be staying for a while."

I was about to protest, but then I quickly shut my mouth and decided not to waste my breath.

"I'm not saying you're not doing a good job," he continued, either reading my mind or sensing my growing irritation that her very presence caused. "I just think you could use a helping hand is all. Plus, I think it would be good to get Carlin back into the family. It would be good for her and Helene to patch things up and enjoy being sisters again."

Based upon my recent opinion of my father's intentions, I guessed this was merely another one of his schemes to take the attention away from him and give my mother, along with me, someone else to focus on so he could go off and parade over to his lover's house once again.

I didn't say anything back to him. Carlin would just cause problems. She always had. Even though my mother had never dared to say anything remotely bad about her whenever her name turned up in conversation, I had always sensed that something had happened between them to tear them apart.

"Why don't you go put fresh sheets on the spare bed?"

Why don't you do it yourself? I wanted to scream at him, but again, my inner hostility would do me no good at a time like this. I left the room to do as I was asked to do.

***

Another week passed. I was good at avoiding Carlin. I backed off and let her do most of the things that needed done around the house. It gave me a chance to avoid everyone else in the process. Some days I'd feel guilty as if I was abandoning my mother and Matthew when they needed me most, but then I would try to drive the feeling down and out of my mind and not think about it. My mother was gaining her strength back little by little every day.

"Anna?" my mother called. "Can you come here for a second, please?"

I paused just outside of my parents' bedroom and peered in. My mother was lying on the king-sized bed with her legs propped up. The curtains were drawn shut so that the sun couldn't shine in, and the only light in the room glowed from a small, crystal lamp on her nightstand.

"Are you feeling okay?" I asked, almost whispering because of the darkness.

"I just have a little headache. Come in and chat with me for a while." She patted a spot on the bed beside her.

I walked in cautiously at first and then settled down Indian style on the puffy checkered comforter. I looked up, and our eyes met.

"I feel like we're becoming strangers," she confessed, and I instantly felt guilty knowing that I had avoided being in this house as much as I possibly could.

I lowered my head. "I know. I'm sorry. It's my fault."

She put her hand under my chin and carefully made me look up at her again. She smiled, and it made me feel a little better. "So tell me how things have been. How is Buck?" Her eyes always did this little sparkle when she said his name. Maybe she was assuming that all of my time spent away had been with him, that we had bonded and found a connection and were forming this beautiful, passionate relationship together.

"I don't know," I replied.

"You don't know?"

"I haven't talked to him in a while. Since the night he drove me to the hospital to see you."

"Oh." The sparkle instantly disappeared and she was the one to look down now. I had disappointed her. "Then what have you been up to? Carlin says you're always running off somewhere."

I hated being cornered like this. Carlin was nosey and needed to stay out of my business. "Well, just keeping up with the store and going to the library. Nothing much."

"Anna, please don't worry about that store. It isn't going anywhere. Closing it for a while isn't going to hurt business. It's not the most popular place, anyway." She chuckled a little.

"How can you say that?" I asked. "You love that store. I want to keep up with it. You get tons of customers."

"Only the older ladies from the church." She smiled, amused I had guessed by picturing them in there shopping, chatting away as they always did amongst each other. "Carlin seems to think there's something not quite right going on with you, Dear. Is there anything going on you need to tell me about?"

Carlin had really put a bug in her ear this time. This conversation probably wouldn't even be happening right now if it hadn't been for her and her stupid opinions. I felt angry all of a sudden. "Carlin needs to…" I stopped. I couldn't explode on my mother like this. It wasn't her fault.

She raised her eyebrows. "Carlin needs to what?"

She needs to shut her mouth.

All she does is push her way into family matters that don't concern her. She just shows up after ten years and decides that she can be boss and do whatever she wants and say whatever she pleases. She's conniving, and she gets under my skin by simply looking my way, and I have no idea how the two of you even share the same blood, is what I wanted to tell her, but I couldn't.

She took a deep breath and leaned back in the bed. I guessed her headache was bothering her again. "Do you need me to get you some pills?" I offered, hoping to end the subject abruptly.

But she ignored me. "Carlin is who she is. I don't think there's a person in the world who can change that. But there's something you should maybe know."

I leaned in closer to make sure that I could hear her clearly. My mother never really talked about her side of the family. Her parents had died when she was young, her and Carlin had lived with one of their

117

cousin's for most of their adolescence. That was basically all I knew. I was intrigued that she was offering more information to me now.

"I know she can be irritating sometimes, well, most of the time. It probably seems to you that she and I don't have the best relationship, especially since she has barely been a part of yours and Matthew's lives, but there was a time when she and I were actually very close. We were best friends and sisters at the same time."

"What happened?" I asked impatient to know.

"Well," she began slow and cautious. She looked up at me again, perhaps uncertain if she should continue, "we were in love with the same man."

I was completely stunned. Was she saying what I thought she was? "What? Carlin was in love with father?" My eyes widened in disbelief.

"No, no," she quickly said. "Not him."

"Then who?"

"Another man. Someone before your father."

My mother was in love with someone other than my father? I guess I had never thought that possible before. Until recently, I had always thought of the two of them as having their marriage completely together, that they had never been with anyone else besides each other.

"His name was Russell, and he was gorgeous." I watched her eyes gleam in excitement as she said his name and remembered him in her head. "We were in the same grade. We were seniors, and Carlin, she was just a freshman. But he always hung around our house, and he seemed to show interest in both of us. He kind of dated both of us at the same time."

"Wow," I mumbled. "That's a little creepy."

"I know." She laughed. "We didn't care. He was so wonderful, and we could both be around him and share his attention and still be the best of friends at the same time. Then Russell did something unexpected. He did something that Carlin could just not forgive."

I found myself hanging on every word. I was discovering a different side to my mother, one never revealed to me before.

"He proposed to me."

"Did you accept?" I blurted out. Then I hesitantly looked behind me at the open door. What if Carlin was eavesdropping and heard us talking about this?

"Don't worry," she quickly told me. "I've sent her out on errands. She'll be gone for a while." I nodded, anxious to get back to her story.

"Yes, I did accept. He gave me a ring and everything. It devastated Carlin. She moped around for weeks and became so bitter toward me and everyone else around her, very much like how she is today. I never saw my happy, perky, baby sister again after that. She had really been in love with Russell, or so I assumed, that it had changed her so drastically."

"So then what happened with you and Russell? Did you marry him?"

She smiled again. "No. I gave the ring back. I couldn't stand to see Carlin like that. I thought by breaking things off with Russell that maybe she'd come back around, but she never did. It took a very long time for her to even talk to me again, and then once that happened, it was just civil, not sister-like anymore. Everything had changed."

119

"Wow," I repeated. "Why didn't you ever tell me this before?"

She chuckled at my reaction. "I don't know, Honey. I didn't want to bother you with it, to have you know that there was someone else before your father. Life is funny sometimes."

"Why are you telling me now, then?"

She thought for a moment and then sighed, bringing her forearm up to cover her eyes as if she had just remembered the pain of the headache again. "I just didn't want you to think Carlin had always been so … cranky."

"I can't believe she would hold a grudge for so long."

"I found your dad shortly after that and we got married, and Carlin, well, she's never found anyone who could compare to Russell. I suppose in her own mind, he had been the only one for her, and I had stolen that right from her, the right of true happiness. I guess I'm just as surprised as you by her staying here with us, and even though I don't feel like we're back to where we had been before Russell had come into our lives, I'm happy she's here. She's trying at least, trying as much as Carlin can try."

***

The time spent with Carlin was still torturous to me, even after my mother's little chat explaining why she thought she was like that. I, on the other hand, was quite amused that this Russell guy had been smart enough to choose my mother over her. Carlin was so self-centered it made me sick. Her presence put a downer on everyone's mood. She had this negative energy about her. Every small issue she made into a large one, and she also made it out to be about her because of her conceited, twisted ways. She was so melodramatic, she belonged in a theater. I couldn't seem to think of her as my aunt.

Aunts were supposed to be caring and yet sometimes better than parents because they always took your side and let you get away with murder. Carlin, on the other hand, was like some pathetic high school wannabe cheerleader who never made the squad and based the rest of her entire life off of that one negative instance. She spent all of her energy trying to make herself look like some sort of rich model/movie star, yet she honestly looked horrible. She looked worn down and was trying too hard to be young for her age. It was like she was never going to be able to accept that she was no longer a teenager.

"I'm going to go get some air," I announced one night after dinner was over and the dishes had been put away. Everyone had settled into the living room together, and I couldn't take another moment breathing the same air as Carlin.

My mother frowned. "Where are you going?"

"Probably the library again," Carlin assumed, rolling her eyes.

I stood up and walked toward the front door. "Actually, the library is closed," I informed her with just as much attitude as she had given me. "I guess I'll go to the store."

Carlin laughed out loud. I glared at her.

"For what?" my father asked, putting the newspaper below his chin to peer over at me.

I sighed, kind of huffing as I did so. "I don't know. Didn't you say we needed coffee?" I asked my mother quickly.

"What?" she said, confused as I had just made that up.

"Bye." I didn't stick around to look at all of their reactions. I just turned as fast as I could and headed straight for my car.

I actually did go to the store. I didn't specifically look for coffee, though I knew that I would have to go home with some just to *prove* that I had been there. I walked up and down the aisles. It was late enough in the evening that not a lot of people were there. I glanced at faces as I walked by, and I wondered if they thought I was strange because I wasn't searching the shelves like everyone else.

Maybe they thought I was intoxicated as I made it to the end of the store and decided to walk up and down each aisle again just one more time.

I was thinking about Emry, how it had been weeks since I had seen him. It felt like years. I was thinking about what he was doing. Was he sad and depressed again? Was he sitting there in his jail cell thinking of me, too? The idea that he was in jail thinking of me and I was in a grocery store thinking of him seemed lame yet romantic all at the same time. I was going to have to take a chance that Buck wouldn't be working and make it down there to see him sometime soon. Then my thoughts drifted to Buck. He hadn't called me, and I couldn't blame him. My family was seriously messed up, and in the process of it all, I was getting messed up, too. I would make distance between us if I were in his shoes. Plus, I had punched him in the eye. I wondered what he had told all of his cop friends when they asked him what happened. Had he told them the truth? They would surely have harassed him if he had.

Then I thought about Emry's sorrowful blue eyes again, like tiny puddles of the sea when they welled up, yet I had never seen him shed a true tear yet. He was good at controlling his emotions. He probably had had lots of practice. I didn't even know how long he had been in jail.

I looked up. What aisle was I in now? PAPER PLATES, GARBAGE BAGS, TIN FOIL hovered in bright white letters above my head. Up ahead I saw a woman round the corner in front of me. Wait a minute. I knew that person.

I hurried up and rounded the corner myself, but only peered around it hoping she would still have her back turned toward me so I could figure out exactly where I had seen her before. I pressed my back against the end of the aisle against some boxes of crackers. An older lady passed by me and gave me a disapproving look. I stared at her back briefly and then stretched my neck out so I could peek down the next aisle.

There stood a short, thin woman, wearing tight skinny jeans and a loose red short-sleeved sweater that exposed one of her shoulders. I watched carefully as she positioned herself with her back still toward me and stood up on her tiptoes to inspect a can of soup at the very top of the shelf. Her bright blonde hair bounced as she settled back on flat feet once again. For a moment, I was able to see her side profile. I gasped. It was Candace, Emry's ex-wife. He had referred to her as *Candy*. A pang of jealousy ripped through me just then, and I jumped back and pressed my body against the end of the aisle.

What a coincidence, I thought. Candace and I in the same exact store at the same exact time. Then I felt another emotion that I was not used to feeling. I suddenly wanted to watch her every move. I wanted to see exactly how she moved and memorize her facial features, because I knew that she had been with Emry. *My* Emry. He was more hers than he was mine. She had been married to him. Again, that sick feeling came over me. Jealousy and disgust all at the same time. She looked all wrong for him. How could he have ever been attracted to her? Then again, look at me. I was nothing to gloat over either.

I found myself stretching my neck to get another look at Candace. I realized she was gone, and then I found myself panic stricken. I raced down the aisle and glanced around to the next one. She wasn't there. My heart rate picked up as I practically ran to the next one, and finally, there she was. This time I didn't hide. I decided to pretend like I was browsing that aisle as well and I even walked by her.

What on earth was I doing? What if she had turned around to look at me? What if she recognized me and questioned me about my little visit with Emry? I wouldn't even know what to say to her.

I walked quickly down the rest of the aisle and straight out the doors. The wind whipped all around me as I felt the bands of cold snow-sleet mix fall violently into my face. It burned, but I barely felt it. I rushed to my car and tried to focus on slowing my breathing as I slammed my door shut. I leaned my head back against the headrest and closed my eyes. What was I now, a stalker? Why did I care so much about her anyway? He

124

told me he was completely over her and had no feelings for her whatsoever. But it irritated me that she had been there to visit him. What if she still loved him and wanted to be with him? She looked like the kind of girl that once she had something in her head, she wouldn't stop until she had exactly what she wanted, even if that meant destroying a girl like me. Then again, I felt the exact same way about her. She had her chance with Emry and had blown it. He didn't want her anymore. It was time for someone else to have a turn, and that someone was me.

I opened my eyes and tried to focus on the large automatic sliding door at the front of the store. It opened and I held my breath, but only a couple with a small child walked out. I watched one of them press the child against their chest as they ran toward their vehicle and tried to shield him from the sky belting ice their way.

I relaxed again. What was I going to do here exactly? I didn't want to go back home. I had barely been at the store for maybe a half hour or more. Carlin would surely still be awake when I got back. I had no interest in holding a conversation with her or having to listen to her try to hold one with me. We didn't like each other. That much was clear. She didn't seem to like my mother much either, so I wondered why she was even there to begin with. Maybe she was trying to steal my father away to get even. If so, she was in for a big surprise when she found out that my father was already taken by Mrs. Anderson.

The doors of the store opened a few more times, and a little while later I sat straight up in my seat as I squinted to make out who I thought was Candace. Whoever it was, they weren't too good at running in high heels as the accumulation from the sky had increased. Just a few parking spots down from me she stopped and threw open the trunk of her car. It was enough for me to recognize those skinny jeans. It was Candace. She was driving an old red clunker with quite a bit of rust around the edges. I watched as she jumped into the driver's side and started up the car, the engine coming to life as she turned the key and put the car in reverse. I found myself putting my own key in the ignition and starting mine as well. My hand moved to the gearshift. Now what? She started to pull out of the parking lot, and I frantically pulled my car out after her. I was going to follow her.

She drove quickly for the roads being so slick, and I felt nervous keeping up with her, afraid that the tread could make it through this winter without getting new tires might make my car suddenly slip. Scenes of me wrecking flashed in my mind as I imagined my car going off the side of the road and slamming into the guardrail. Maybe I would spin completely around and hit another car head-on or go into the wide, deep ditches that were on both sides of the road. My right hand moved to double check that my seatbelt was securely in place. Then it moved to meet my left hand that was gripped tightly on the steering wheel. There weren't many other cars on the roads. I figured everyone else was being smart tonight by staying inside and avoiding driving altogether, like I should be. I didn't even know why I was acting so psychotic now. What exactly was I expecting from this situation? I couldn't just follow her into her house.

Candace went to the edge of Seneca almost toward where the prison was, but then she turned down a narrow road that winded into a more country section of town. The snowy mixture falling from the sky started to come down harder in heavy sheets. I cranked my windshield wipers on high and strained my eyes to see. Her rear taillights had disappeared suddenly from my vision. Where had she gone? My heart began to thump in my chest. I slowed and thought I saw a lane up ahead on the right. I moved closer toward it and saw brake lights. Was that her? It had to be. A heavy mist lifted from the ground, making it even more impossible to see. I waited a few minutes, my car stationary in front of the lane, and once I couldn't see the brake lights anymore, I counted to 60 in my head, giving her a minute to get out of her car and into her house, then I pulled into the lane a little bit. It wasn't a very long driveway. I shut off my own headlights and the ignition next.

Now what? Was I going to go up and knock on her door, give her a friendly smile, and say, *oh, hi, I'm Anna James. I believe you may remember me from the prison. We were both visiting Emry Logan on the same day, and because of you, my time was cut in half with him. If you wouldn't mind, I would love for you to tell me everything you know about him. Oh, and by the way, I hate you too for having been married to him before.*

I almost laughed out loud. I *was* a stalker! This was just plain crazy.

I reached in the backseat and grabbed an extra scarf, a wool hat, and an extra heavy pair of gloves I kept as spare back there and put them all on, wrapping the scarf a couple times around my head so that really the only thing that remained uncovered were my eyes. I got out of the car and shut the door quietly. I felt the wind and wet moisture instantly hit my face. The bitter cold air sent a burning sensation down my throat as I breathed it in. Sleet hit my eyelashes, and I put my head down as I tried to stay along the edge of the driveway. After a few steps, I attempted to lift my head and saw the red car parked in front of a small brown house. A gust of wind blew again. It knocked me back a little. I struggled to regain my balance.

A yellow light flickered on in one of the front windows. I watched a figure move across the room inside and assumed that it had to be Candace. I moved closer to the window. I could see wallpaper with roses dotting it and a chandelier dangling from the ceiling. Candace came into view. She had already changed out of the clothes she had been wearing at the store and was now sporting an old faded black sweatshirt and gray sweatpants. Her damaged bleached blonde hair hung midway down her back. She was pacing back and forth in the room. I squinted my eyes to see what she was doing and realized she was on the telephone as she had a cordless tucked under her chin as she walked in circles, her lips moving frantically as she spoke.

I looked up to the sky. I pulled my scarf down so that the sleet and snow could freely hit my face. I could feel it pelt my cheeks and then melt, sliding down my skin in thick droplets. I knew I really shouldn't be here right now. This felt too dangerous for me. What would Emry think if he knew I had followed his ex-wife, had practically walked up to her front window and had been watching her? He would surely think I was completely insane, some sort of freak. I definitely felt like a freak now, and a foolish one at that by letting these crazy impulses take over me. I threw my arms up in the air in defeat. This was ridiculous.

I looked back toward the window. Candace was nowhere to be seen. I turned around and started back down the driveway to where my car was parked. I had almost reached it when I suddenly saw headlights flash my way and turn into the lane. I dived to the ground behind my car and ducked down out of sight, my body crouched low. An old Toyota truck rolled slowly by me and stopped right beside Candace's car. I peeked around the edge of my bumper. The truck's engine roared, and I could see its windshield wipers going back and forth as the passenger-side door opened and a girl jumped out, waved once to the driver, and ran to the front door to get out of the weather. I didn't get a very good look, but I knew at once that it had been Traci, Candace's daughter. Emry seemed to have spoken fondly of her. I was a little envious of that fact as well. I had no idea why. She was just a little girl, after all.

The truck backed out of the driveway and I waited until it was completely gone before getting back in my car. I turned the key in the ignition and backed slowly out of the driveway, even though I fought every impulse inside of me to floor it in reverse just to get out of there. I drove a little ways down the road before stopping the car and leaning my forehead against the steering wheel. I was on the verge of hyperventilating.

I had just drove to some stranger's house and watched her through the window in the middle of a snowstorm. Something was seriously wrong with me.

Heat from the car vents blasted my face. I just sat there for a few minutes with my body slouched over, my eyes closed tight. Emry's face popped back into my head as I tried to picture him as perfectly as he was. I tried to remember all the details of his face. His soft brown hair and how the edges just touched the outer edges of his eyes, his perfectly small, rounded nose and smooth cheeks dotted with freckles. I imagined his lips, the bottom one a little fuller than the top, and how they parted just a little as he breathed. His hands resting before him, the nails looking chewed, and his tan arms with biceps clearly visible underneath the orange jumpsuit. A prison jumpsuit.

A horn blasted loudly from behind me as I jumped so high my head actually hit the roof of the car. I looked in my rearview mirror and winced from the brightness of the high beams obviously meant to give me the hint to get out of the way. That's when I realized that I still had my car parked in the middle of the right lane. I put the car in Drive and pressed my foot on the gas pedal. It lurched forward, and with the adrenaline still zipping through my veins from the night's events, I recklessly sped down the slippery roads of Seneca.

I still didn't feel like going to my house. I felt like an emotional wreck, and I didn't want to have to walk in there and face all of them right away as I figured they'd all still be up watching TV.

The snowfall was lighter now. I turned down the speed of my windshield wipers. I eased up on the gas pedal and slowed the car down as well, trying to think of where I could go. I knew where I wanted to go. I wanted to go to Seneca County Prison, but I knew that was impossible and tried to erase the thought out of my mind as quickly as it appeared. I wish I had had more friends to turn to for a place to hang out. Most of the girls I had been close to in high school were now married and actually had lives. Most of them didn't even live in Seneca anymore. I felt cornered, as if there was nowhere else to go but home. I considered pulling off in some abandoned lot and sleeping in my car.

But that wouldn't be fair to my mother. She would be worried sick about me and probably already was with how I had left, not to mention the amount of snow that had just fallen down in the past few hours.

I began driving down a familiar part of Seneca, and then I breathed a sigh of relief as I neared the antique store and pulled into one of the front parking spaces. I shuffled through my pant pocket to see if the key to get in was still there. Sure enough, my fingers gripped tight around it. I removed the heavy scarf from around my face along with the long coat, both dripping wet from my recent stalking expedition at Candace's, and tossed them in the backseat.

Once inside the store, I flicked on the lights and took off my other coat to hang it up. I looked around and soaked up the silence for a moment before plopping down in an overstuffed antique leather chair in the corner of the front room and tried to relax. I tried closing my eyes, and a million different thoughts automatically ran through my mind. Maybe I should try this again. I reopened my eyes, and then after a moment, shut them tightly; only this time I pictured myself in a white box with nothing around me but pure white walls. I tried to focus on how there was nothing but white around me, nothing to look at but the whiteness, the blankness, as I tried to clear my head and not be so bombarded by the thoughts and emotions that now haunted me every second of every day from the moment I woke up, and sometimes even in my sleep. I deserved a few minutes of peace to reclaim my sanity that I had felt almost certainly slipping away from me tonight.

This was exactly what I had needed; a moment to myself, which is something that was rare and far between these days. It seemed like even in my bedroom in the very house I had grown up in that was supposed to be my place of comfort, I would attempt to do something such as this, but then I would hear a noise or someone's voice and the realization that Carlin and all of her shadiness was being allowed to lurk about the house provoked my emotions just enough to make me never feel comfortable there. A safe haven, that's what this store was. I needed to spend more time in silence like this. I was finally starting to feel better.

That serene moment ended abruptly as I heard a loud noise coming from the back of the store. I could feel the hair on the back of my neck rise as I sat up and listened, my fingertips indenting into the arms of the old chair. I heard someone's voice, almost like a hiss, and I swallowed the newly formed lump in my throat as I stood and slowly crept toward the back of the store.

Had I caught a burglar breaking into my mother's store? No one else had a key but me and my mother, and I knew she certainly hadn't stepped foot in here since her heart had started acting up again.

I gasped for air as I realized I had been holding my breath and my lungs felt like they were on fire from doing so. I walked on the balls of my feet and cringed as I heard one of the floorboards screech underneath me. I paused. I heard nothing. Then somebody rushed around the corner and slammed into me, the blow knocking me backward as I stumbled to regain my balance. I heard a loud thump as whoever had run into me had fallen onto the floor. Once I was able to stand upright again, my eyes scanned the floor in front to see what had happened.

"What are you *doing*?" a familiar voice snapped at me.

Carlin was lying at my feet, her hands behind her as she groaned in pain and gave me a disgusted look, as if this whole situation was entirely my fault.

"What am *I* doing?" I yelled back at her. "What are *you* doing?"

I watched Carlin get back on her feet. I offered her no help. She put her hand on her back as if she had pulled something, her eyes fierce with anger and aimed accusingly at me. "Helene asked me to get a receipt, and I dropped a metal box on my foot. I was coming in here to get some ice out of the fridge and …"She glared at me and pointed a finger in my face. "Look what you've done now!" Her face twisted in a pained expression.

I shook all over from how angry I was becoming, the intensity of the powerful emotion increasing by the second. "You came here for a receipt this time of night in the middle of a snowstorm?" I screamed, utterly outraged.

"I needed some peace and quiet," she began to explain, but then decided to direct the focus of conversation to me once again. "What about you?"

"Me?" I asked, suddenly feeling like shoving her with all my might and watch her fall back onto the floor.

"Yes, you. How was the store? Nice night for a little rendezvous, eh?" She sneered.

I had to hold both my arms straight by my side just to try to contain myself from hitting her. I couldn't stand this woman in front of me, and she was supposed to be my relative. There was no way that we had the same blood flowing through our veins. "What did you just say?"

"You heard me, *Annie*."

Keep pushing your luck, Carlin, I thought.

"Where exactly did you go, huh? I doubt you went to the store. Were you out meeting someone in particular?" she asked, still practically yelling as she did so.

The anger created tears in my eyes. I blinked them back. There was no way I was going to let someone like Carlin see me break down and cry. "My life is none of *your* business. I'm a grown woman."

"Ha!" She rolled her eyes. "You're hardly a woman, Annie. You're practically going on thirty and still living at home with mommy and daddy. Even the town cop has turned on you. You might as well admit it; your life is sad and pathetic."

"I wish you would just leave and never come back," I growled, clenching my teeth together. "Why are you here, anyway?"

"To take care of my sister."

Now it was my turn to sneer. "What a joke."

"Why don't you go hang out with your friend Mandi again? Mandi

134

Liswich was it your mother told me you went to see?"

My nails dug into my palms as I clenched my fists tighter and tighter.

"Funny story," Carlin went on. "I ran into Mandi's mom the other day, and she said her daughter wouldn't be home until sometime around Christmas."

She waited to see if that had done the trick, if I had snapped, but I just kept standing there as still as a statue with my arms down, hands clenched, and eyes glaring holes into her head as she did the same back to me.

Amused with herself, Carlin leaned back against the wall and crossed her arms in front of her. "So I thought to myself, I wonder why Annie would lie to Helene like that. I wonder who she is really seeing? Tell me, Annie, who does a girl with no friends see?"

I narrowed my eyes at her. "What exactly are you accusing me of, Carlin?"

She shrugged. "I don't know, but I do know that you're up to something, and that something is probably no good. I'm going to be watching you, little Annie girl, like a hawk until I figure out exactly what it is you're up to."

The tears came on and a drop escaped from my eye and raced down my cheek. I wiped it away quickly with the back of my hand. Carlin grinned deviously and made one sudden turn on her heels and disappeared out of sight into the back room.

"I hate you," I said, but it came out as merely a whisper.

I stood there in the silence; only this time it haunted me instead of giving me the freedom it had just moments before. I was so full of fury that all I could focus on was my need to release it. What was the one thing that could take all of my anguish away and replace it with a feeling of self-worth and hope? Emry Logan. The name echoed in my mind. I had to go see him. I needed to be with him once again, but even more than that, I needed to be beside him, be able to touch his face and his skin and breathe in the same air as he was breathing. I had to try to do something. It had been too long. But what was I going to do to be able to be near him? There had to be a way. Surely it wasn't an impossible feat.

My eyes frantically scanned the antique store. Surely my life was meant for more than this. I was meant to be with someone who would make my life one of excitement and spontaneity. I knew I was meant to be with Emry Logan. I had to get to him, to hear his soft voice once again, and to know that all of my recent craziness had meaning to it.

My heart fluttered as my eyes settled on something on the other side of the room. I hurried to the object that was spread out over the head of a faceless mannequin in the corner. It was an antique wig from the 1920s. It was a blonde bob cut, and it had been sitting here for years collecting dust. I suddenly smiled just then. Yes, I would be getting lost in the glorious blue eyes that belonged to Emry Logan very soon. I would be going to see him tomorrow.

Chapter 7

Darkness. It was the first thing my eyes opened to in the morning. I jumped out of bed and pulled back the thick curtains. More darkness. What time was it? Glancing back at the glowing red numbers coming from my alarm clock on the nightstand, I read clearly that it was 5:30a.m. Why was I awake so early? And then I suddenly remembered. Oh, yes. Today was the day.

I lay back in bed for a few minutes, staring up at the ceiling and trying to imagine how everything was going to happen. But then I realized that I actually had no real idea if any of this was going to work. All I knew was that I had to try and risk getting caught. It was a chance I was willing to take to get to Emry. I couldn't wait any longer. It felt like an eternity since I had last had the chance to see him. Maybe even longer.

I sat back up. There was no way I could just lay here in bed with this much excitement roaring within me. I felt so alert and jittery at the same time. I hurried over to my closet to try to find something to wear. I turned the light on and peeked inside. I frowned. I really wish I had had more of a sense of style than this. None of these clothes were going to work for what I had in mind. I was going to have to go shopping this morning, but how on earth would I be able to fit that in? I had to go tend to the store for a couple hours until venturing down to the jail. There was no way that a trip to the mall in downtown Seneca was going to happen for me today. I turned off the light and sat back down on the bed, crossing my arms and pouting as I did so. What was I going to do now?

Then a huge smile crossed my lips as an idea suddenly came to me. I stood and walked as quietly as I could down the hall to the very last door and stood in front of the spare bedroom. The door was cracked open a hair, and I prayed that it wouldn't screech loudly as I eased into the room, pushing it open wide enough for my body to fit through. My eyes began to adjust to the dimly lit room as I could see Carlin curled up on her side with a navy blue comforter wrapped securely around her, her body facing away from me.

I waited for a few moments, listening to the rhythm of her breathing. Then I looked toward the small closet in the room and Carlin's suitcase on the floor just in front of it. I was hoping that she had unpacked and put all of her things in the closet. Surely she had and wasn't living out of her suitcase any longer. I took gentle, light steps over to the suitcase. It was unzipped and hanging slightly open. I pulled it back to see it was empty. I moved to the closet next. The door made a shrill sound as I opened it. My heart pounded as I looked over my shoulder and saw Carlin's face. Her eyes were still shut. The noise hadn't fazed her.

I pulled the string dangling from a light bulb on the ceiling of the closet and gave it a quick tug. It cast a glow onto a row of designer dresses and blouses and also out into the room a little bit. I looked back at Carlin again. The light's edges ended just inches from her face. She was still sound asleep. I had to hurry. I tried to focus on the row of clothes in front of me. Carlin had so much to choose from. I just hoped that they would fit me. We were probably about the same size, height-wise. She was a little thicker than me around the middle, but if I had to guess, she would have bought most of these things a size or two smaller than she actually was just for pride's sake. My hands raked over many different styles and colors. She had a lot of black, though, which was probably the perfect color of choice for this particular day. Then my eyes met with a dress I instantly loved. The top part of the dress was gray. The sleeves looked like they would come about halfway down my arms. There was a silky black band that wrapped around the stomach area, followed by a smooth black skirt on the bottom that probably would extend a little past my knees. It wasn't too fancy and it wasn't too plain. I held it up to take a better look and then hastily pulled the dress and hanger from the metal rod it had been hanging from, yanked on the string to turn off the light, and darted out of the room.

***

The next few hours at the store went on endlessly. I was too excited to pay much attention to the customers or hold a very long conversation. They would ask how my mother was doing, when she was going to be back. I would say something short and simple in return, ring their order up, and give them each a quick smile before they left. The smiles came easier to me today. They were more genuine. I was extremely nervous, but I kept a close eye on the clock, counting down the minutes until I would be able to get out of here. When I could hardly contain myself any longer, I walked to the front of the store and flipped over the sign that said OPEN, to CLOSED. It felt nice not to have to answer to anyone about where I was going. I was now the only one in control of the store. I was just about to turn out the lights in the front room and lock up when the door swung open, a gust of cold air ruffling my hair up off my shoulders. I spun around.

"Sammie?"

"You going somewhere?" she asked, walking past me and then turning around to face me.

"Yeah. I was just locking up. I have errands to run," I mumbled, annoyed that I now had to explain myself. "I didn't think you were scheduled for today."

She shrugged, a red curl bouncing from her head as she did so. "I wasn't." She blew a bubble from her chewing gum and popped it loudly with her tongue. "I figured you might need some help."

"Oh, well, I don't." I just stood there and stared at her for a moment, and she did the same. I wanted her to turn around and leave immediately, but she wasn't budging just yet. Was she about to ask me a hundred questions? The anxiety of the situation was starting to build up. I still had to get ready, and she was wasting my time.

"It's no big deal if you have some things to do," she told me, taking a casual glance around the store. "I can watch over the place until you get back."

"No. I don't think I'm coming back today," I replied. "But thanks, though," I added. "I appreciate it."

She stared at me for a moment more as if she were trying to read my thoughts. Perhaps I looked as anxious as I felt and everyone could see through me today. I was probably more lively than usual with all this energy.

"Okay." Sammie took a few steps over to the door and opened it. "See ya later."

"Yeah. Later," I mumbled, closing the door myself behind her and locking it quickly. I watched her out the window until her car rumbled away down the road before turning on my heels and making my way to the back room to get dressed.

I unzipped the duffle bag I had carried in this morning and carefully unfolded Carlin's dress. I ran my hand over the smooth cotton and made sure that I hadn't wrinkled it by putting it in the bag. It looked perfect still. I wiggled off the clothes I had worn to the store and put the dress on over my head. I pulled it down over my hips and turned around to look at myself in the bathroom mirror. It was tighter than I usually wore my clothes, but it wrapped around my body as if I were made for it. I bunched up my hair onto the top of my head and wrapped a hair tie around it. Then I put what seemed like a zillion pins in it to keep it secured in place. I then proceeded to put on a thick coat of foundation on my face, followed by powder. I added some gray eye shadow to match the top of the dress and black eyeliner outlining the edges of my eyes. A shimmery cherry-red lip gloss polished my lips.

Lastly, I reached for the blonde wig and placed it on my gathered up ball of hair. I stood back from the mirror and gave myself a look over. I started laughing out loud. Who was that staring back at me? I definitely felt as if I had accomplished what I had set out to do, looks-wise. I was completely unrecognizable. I looked business-like, professional enough to be able to pass as Emry Logan's attorney. I put large silver hoops in my ears and added a layer of pale pink blush to my cheeks. I stared back at myself for a moment longer. I looked beautiful.

"Thanks so much, Carlin," I mumbled to myself, chuckling as I picked up my black dress coat that my parents had bought me for church years ago that I think I had only worn a couple times. I tossed it over my shoulder and flicked the light off as I turned to go out of the store.

During the drive down to the prison, I tossed names for myself back and forth in my head. What sounded lawyerly? I ran through the entire alphabet, sifting through names that popped into my head.

Before I knew it, I was pulling into the parking lot. I parked the car and turned off the engine. I crossed my hands in front of my lap and took a deep breath and exhaled loudly. My heart was thumping away uncontrollably. I closed my eyes for a moment and concentrated at the task at hand. Emry. Then I opened them, pressed my lips together in the rearview mirror, checked my teeth, and exited the vehicle.

Here we go, I thought to myself. *Amelia Roberts it is.* I repeated the name a couple of times to myself as I walked so I wouldn't stumble and mess it up, my black high heels clicking loud on the cement. I walked cautiously as I wasn't used to this kind of shoe, but I knew I had to play the part and walk in quick, long strides as I imagined a high-class attorney would.

Once inside the main entrance of the prison, my eyes immediately met with the woman positioned behind the plastic screen at the front desk. I recognized her as the same one that had been there when I had first stepped into this place to pass out my father's brochures. What was her name again? I searched my memory for the answer. I believe Buck had called her Tiff. I walked toward her and tried to keep my head held high, my shoulders back. Professional, I reminded myself.

"Can I help you?" she asked, sounding more annoyed than desiring to be helpful.

"I'm here to see a client of mine." I tried to steady my voice as the nerves were getting the best of me. My stomach felt instantly sick as anxiety took control over every inch of my body.

She raised her eyebrows impatiently. "I'll need your name, and the name of your client."

Remain calm, Anna, and maybe she won't ask to see ID that you don't actually have. "Of course. Amelia Roberts, here to see Mr. Emry Logan, please." I rested my hand on the little ledge in front of the plastic screen and tapped my fingers as if impatient that she was keeping me waiting. In reality, this short, stout woman intimidated me. My eyes drifted over to the rows of desks on the other side of the large room. To my surprise, just about every policeman sitting there had their eyes locked on me. I felt my heart rate increase again as the realization and dizziness hit me. My eyes moved from face to face to see if Buck was among them, but he wasn't there. Why were they looking at me? Did I really look *that* stunning, or was it because they could see through the act and I looked like a clown to them?

"Here," Tiff said in her flat tone.

I turned my attention back to her. She was holding up a plastic card that I assumed was some sort of pass to get back to where I needed to be. I hoped she wouldn't assume I knew where I was going, because I had no idea how to get back to where Emry was. I took the card from her hand. I almost thanked her, but decided against it. The attorney I was going for certainly wasn't the polite type.

"Paul will take you back to where you need to be," she told me. "Paul!" she called out, flailing her arms above her head, motioning toward someone.

I watched as a tall, gangly man with blonde hair so light it could almost be mistaken as white, stood. I heard a few of the policemen sneer and make comments to him as he awkwardly seemed to trip over his own feet at first before falling into a stride and walking hesitantly toward me.

"Paul, take Ms. Roberts back to cell number three-three-seven," Tiff instructed him.

He said nothing, but merely nodded his head and took off toward the doors just by the policemen's' desks. I stayed a few paces back and tried to swallow my fear as I knew that every eye would be on me as I walked by them. It felt awful to be the center of attention, a position I was certainly not used to. I prayed that I wouldn't trip over my own feet and

144

tried to make my legs take the same long, quick steps that I had practiced when coming in from the outside.

The heavy doors closed behind us, shutting out the group of policemen that had just been staring at me. I felt so relieved to have gotten away from them, to have fooled Tiff, and that my plan was working. I felt a boastful smirk cross my lips as I followed Paul down a corridor. He said nothing to me, and I wondered if he was shy or just the type of person who didn't like to make small talk with others. Nevertheless, I was grateful that he was the one leading me back into the depths of the prison.

We walked down more hallways. We were now in the midst of prison cells as inmates whistled and called out to me as I walked by. This time, it didn't bother me. I didn't even care. I worried more about the other officers looking my way than these men locked up in their cells. I didn't look their way or flinch as they made their remarks. I walked behind Paul with my head facing forward and my shoulders back. I was Amelia Roberts for the day. I was a big shot attorney. I was a professional.

Paul stopped in front of me and turned. "I'll go get him."

What did that mean exactly? Did he want me to stay here and wait, or was I supposed to know where to go? I watched him walk down the corridor alone, the whole way to the end where I knew Emry was. I felt a throb in my head with a sudden ache in both my temples. Adrenaline surged through my veins. Paul was far away now, but I could still see his arms lifted up in the air as he unlocked the entrance to Emry's cell. A loud click and a buzzing sound as the door came open, echoed down the hall, and I squinted to see clearly as a thin, tall figure emerged into the corridor, his hands being handcuffed in front of him, his head lowered. Emry.

And then suddenly they were both walking toward me. My heart pumped faster, if that was even at all possible. The palms of my hands began to sweat as I folded them in front of me and intertwined them together. Another policeman came up from behind me.

"You're Emry Logan's attorney?" he asked.

I turned to face him, hating the fact that I had to turn away from Emry as he was only yards away from me now. I nodded.

"You can come with me." He seemed friendlier than Paul.

I followed him to another room just around the corner. It had a more casual feel to it than the shadowy corridors that contained the jail cells and inmates within them. There were a few pictures of art on the wall, a large desk and chairs positioned around it. There was a glass door at the back of the small room that seemed to lead outside as the sunlight drifted in, giving it an even more pleasing feel.

The officer left, and I looked around apprehensively before tossing my coat onto the table and settling down into one of the chairs so that I was facing the door where Emry would soon be walking in through. And within minutes, he did.

Paul removed Emry's handcuffs as soon as he entered the room. My heart fluttered at how close Emry Logan was as he now stood before me. His head was still lowered. I stood and ran a hand down over the front of my dress to smooth it out and make sure it wasn't sticking to the pantyhose covering my legs. Paul lingered for a moment.

"I'll be right outside the door if you need me," he said in a hushed voice.

I nodded, wanting to say thank you, but again, refraining. The door shut behind Paul and Emry looked up then, our eyes meeting. I felt my breath come in gasps as he stared at me with those eyes so blue and beautiful that it was difficult to imagine that I could ever have the willpower to look away.

I suddenly didn't know what to say. He stood there on the other side of the desk, his face expressionless, with his hair in his eyes. I wanted so badly to reach over and wisp the strands back for him, but I settled for extending my hand out for a handshake.

He kept staring at me, ignoring the gesture. "I already have a lawyer," he said in a tone that seemed borderline angry.

"I figured you did." I drew my arm back, embarrassed. He didn't recognize me either. I had done a great job on the costume and makeup.

"So, who are you?" He eyed me suspiciously.

I smiled brightly, not able to contain it any longer. I was just so grateful to be able to see him after all this time and to be able to see him face-to-face for the first time. He was just so breathtaking standing before me. "Obviously not your lawyer," I replied almost smugly. My smile widened.

He glared at me for a second more, and then he practically climbed over the top of the table to stand directly beside me and studied my face intently. "Is it really you? Anna?"

I nodded, the blonde wig moving slightly with so much enthusiasm. "Recognize me now?"

"Barely." His eyes were illuminated as he looked me up and down, admiring what I had created of myself. "Wow," he finally said. "I wish you were my lawyer." He winked at me then, and we both burst into laughter. Then his face got serious and his eyes less stern and gentler as he looked down at the floor. "You did all this just to see me?"

I nodded, feeling slightly embarrassed again. Had I gone overboard? Was it too much? "I missed you." The words came out as a whisper.

I felt as if his eyes were penetrating mine. I could see my own reflection in those tiny pools of blue, but the woman standing with her short blonde hair and made-up face was unrecognizable.

"Can I take your hand?" he asked me.

I felt his warm fingers slide into mine before I could respond to the question. I had dreamt of his touch a hundred times in my mind, and now we finally had our chance at last. His hand seemed large as it completely consumed mine, and my heart heaved within my chest. And then he led me out of the glass doors and into the brisk winter air outside. The sun floated down on us as I focused on the warmth of his smooth skin and just being next to him. There was a small courtyard out here with a patio, a few trees that were barren, and a cement bench.

I leaned up against one of the walls, my back feeling the chill of the bricks through the dress. Emry stood in front of me, inches from my face. He towered over me even though I wore heels, and he put one arm above my head and leaned his palm against the brick. I could see his breath coming from his slightly parted lips as he bent over me. I felt the butterflies swirl in my stomach and the lump forming in my throat. I couldn't believe I was here at last with him, face to face. It had seemed an unattainable feat, yet I had somehow overcome the impossible. I felt paralyzed, our mouths so close, breathing the same air, our fingers still intertwined.

"Are you frightened by me?" he asked. I must have looked like a terrified mouse trying to crouch lower and lower as this young, beautiful, yet tall and muscular creature hovered above me.

I opened my mouth to say something but felt the words stick in my throat, my nerves getting the best of me now. I hesitated. I didn't want to say the wrong thing as it was hard to concentrate on thinking. My mind was so hazy at the moment.

"Are you frightened by me, Anna?" he repeated, lowering his arm and backing away slightly.

I frowned as we were no longer holding hands. "No," I whispered, wishing I wasn't such a tangled mess around him.

He turned, and I could hear him sighing, his warm breath fleeing upward in the chill of the air. He glanced back around to face me, running his hand through his brown hair. "Do you know why I'm in here?"

I pulled my back away from the brick as I could feel the cold creeping into my bones. At least the wind wasn't able to whip around so easily within these thick, brick walls. I looked down at my feet, the shiny black shoes that covered them. I nodded.

He seemed confused that I would know such a thing. "Why then?" he said sternly, demanding I tell him. "What did you hear?"

I didn't really want to repeat the horrid story, or the way it had come from Buck's mouth as if he were making a mockery out of Emry.

"Please, Anna, tell me what you know."

Now it was my turn to sigh. I looked up at him and saw a twinge of sorrow coming from his eyes. I hated that look. It was the one expression of his I was becoming most accustomed to. "That you supposedly threw a man off some tower," I told him. "Your best friend."

His face twisted in rage and he clenched his fists. "Who told you that?"

The lump in my throat was starting to burn. "Buck Brady."

"Buck Brady?" He sneered at the very name, just as Buck did with his. Well, that made the dislike between the two of them equal now. "That figures. He likes you, you know. It was so obvious by the way he acted around you that first day."

I instantly sensed the hint of jealousy in his tone. I felt a sudden joy at the realization. I watched him study me for a moment. I stared back but didn't say a word.

"Of course you know that," he continued. "You're a smart girl."

Then he froze in place for a moment, and I thought I had seen a sudden calmness come over him just then. He had made a realization of his own.

"Wait. You said supposedly."

I nodded, rethinking my words very carefully.

"What do you mean by that?"

"Well," I began slowly, "you didn't actually do it. Did you?" He walked closer to me, his face near mine.

"I don't know."

"You don't know?" I moved away from him in one sudden movement, trying to get to the opposite wall, away from him, anger filling me. So he was a murderer? So all of this nonsense going on inside my head, thinking about him every second of every day, was all for nothing? But as I swung my arm backward, I felt him grip onto it tightly, yet gently at the same time, and turn me back around to face him. He wrapped his fingers in mine once more and held me in place.

"You don't understand, Anna. It's complicated," he whispered, his eyes searching my face.

"Help me to understand then, Emry," I pleaded with him. I could feel the tears swelling in my eyes, and I didn't want them to fall for fear that they would carry black mascara the entire way down my cheek.

Emry began pacing between the narrow walls. He ran his fingers through his hair. I was beginning to realize this was an unconscious habit of his. "I've retraced my steps from that night over and over again. I don't think I did, Anna, I swear, but at the same time, I really don't know."

I lowered my eyebrows. "That's not helping me to understand when you say it that way."

He growled in frustration, and then took my hand once again and walked me over to the bench where we sat down simultaneously. He took a deep breath and exhaled loudly, trying to rid himself of the irritation with the heavy sigh. It must not have made him feel any better as he buried his face in his hands for a moment, and I focused my attention to the top of his head. I wanted so badly to run my own fingers through his hair and comfort him. I raised my hand, but then quickly placed it back in front of me on my lap. I waited, trying to be patient, letting him gather his thoughts. I was praying that he would be able to give me some sort of explanation. I couldn't bear the thought of labeling him a killer.

Emry Logan *could not* be a killer. It seemed truly impossible now while sitting next to him. Although, in the back of my mind my nerves stood on end from both desiring to be here and the desire to run out of here, knowing this wasn't safe but yet feeling safe by his side all at the same time. My mind spun out of control with contradictory emotions that it was beginning to drive me slightly mad with the agony of it all.

Emry looked up then, his blue eyes glistening slightly. "I'm sorry," he whispered. "I'm just so frustrated. I must be acting like a total lunatic."

I smiled. With our eyes locked on each other, my heart began to flutter, and I took a deep breath myself, feeling as if my lungs weren't getting the proper amount of air. "Don't apologize," I told him, my voice softer as well. I smiled again, hoping I didn't look frightened or angry with him, but wanting to enjoy this valuable time together. I wanted to help him to feel happy, if only for a brief period of time in this prison courtyard. He deserved that much at the very least. "You don't have to tell me anything if you don't want to," I added quickly, but not really meaning it. In truth, I wanted to know every detail. His life was such a mystery to me.

"No. I want you to know everything." He hesitated for a second. "It's just … I don't know how to tell you without scaring you. I don't want to scare you, although I understand if I do, but I mean, then again, you are

152

sitting here next to me face to face, so surely you're not afraid." He studied my face, trying to assess my reaction.

I looked away. Was I afraid? Not of him; I didn't think so, at least. I was afraid of this whole situation, of where exactly this was headed, because I felt like every day led me deeper and deeper into this emotional swirl that seemed inevitable to only spiral downward, me getting devastated in the end. But then, I felt there was no escaping it either. Emry had my heart cornered. There was nowhere else to go but toward him. He had finally given my life meaning, and the emotions I felt, no matter how insane they were making me act, were ones I'd never experienced before, and they were amazing. I was addicted to this craziness. No, there was no turning back now that I had decided.

"I'm a strong person," I said. Then I took his other hand in mine, the first action I had taken toward him, and I stroked his knuckles with my thumbs. His tan hands were smooth and warm. The very sensation of his touch overwhelmed me as I longed to be in his arms just then. "I feel safe with you, Emry."

He looked down at our hands and then pressed his lips together firmly. "I guess I'll just tell you the whole story. I'll begin with the part of the story of how they told me it happened."

"They?"

"The cops that arrested me."

"Oh." I decided I should probably shut my mouth and not interrupt him, or else he would never get to tell me what was going on.

"I'll just tell it my own way. Wes is my best friend.... *was* my best friend," he began. His eyes glistened with tears, and he quickly lowered his head so I wouldn't see. "He called me that evening. It was just about dark. He had had a fight with some girl he was seeing. I can't even remember her name. He bounced from girl to girl every other week. Anyway, he wanted to go throw back a couple of beers at this tower we always hung out at. It was way up in the woods, but there was an old path back there so we could just drive up to it. So I met him there, and he had had a couple of six packs with him. He just wanted to vent and tell me about this girl. He didn't seem *that* upset. Then after a while, the sun had set, and I was leaning back against the tower, staring up at the stars." Emry paused for a moment, remaining still, and then I felt his fingers stroke the inside of my palms, the sensation rippling up my arms. "Then I kind of blanked out. And when I sat up again, Wes was gone. I called out his name and there was no answer. I got up and looked down over the side, and that's when I saw what I assumed was him down on the ground in front of the tower. He looked like a speck, though; I was so high up. And then I began to panic. I climbed down to him and tried to wake him up, but he was dead. His eyes were staring up at me, his body was kind of twisted from the broken bones, and there was blood everywhere." He released his grasp from my hand to put it up to his face as I imagined his remembrance of Wes' body was too much for him to hold in.

I wrapped my arm across his chest just then and pressed my face against his shoulder. The scent of his neck filled my nostrils, and I breathed in deeply, trying to almost get a taste of it. He put his hand up on my arm and his head on top of my head, and we sat perfectly still like that for a few minutes.

"I didn't get any bars on my cell phone up there, and I didn't want to leave Wes like that, but I had to. I jumped in my truck and raced down the road until I did get reception, and then I called 911. And the police came up, along with EMS. They got his body, asked me what I knew. I assumed he had fallen, because I don't remember hearing anything strange. He didn't scream or call out to me or anything." I felt him sigh, his warm breath colliding with the skin on my ear. "The thing is: the police didn't seem to question what I had told them at all. Wes was gone and buried, and then one day the cops paid me a visit. It was Buck Brady and some of his men. They began questioning me about what had happened, and it felt as if they were accusing me or trying to get me to confess to something. I got very angry, and then suddenly something happened."

"What?"

"The next thing I knew Buck Brady's body was slammed into a tree."

"You hit him?"

"No." He let it go at that. "They left, but then the next day, well, that's when things got even weirder."

I pulled myself away from him so that I could look into his eyes once more. His side of the story seemed totally legit to me. How could anyone think of him as a liar? "What do you mean by weirder?" I raised my eyebrows in question.

He leaned forward and rested his forehead against mine. Our mouths were so close. I focused all of my attention to his lips and

155

memorized every aspect of them, unable to look away.

"Then they came to get me."

"The police?"

"Well, yeah. There was Buck Brady again, two other guys with him that I assume were cops but weren't in uniform, and your dad."

I jerked my head up so fast I almost fell backward off the bench. "What? Why was he there?"

Emry shrugged. "No idea, but he wasn't happy with me. He and Buck Brady were actually pretty mean. They gave me no chance to explain myself. They jerked me right out of the house and practically threw me in the back of the car."

"This doesn't make any sense." My thoughts were spinning. What business would my father have had with police matters? And him acting aggressively toward another human being, well, that was just something he never did. My father wasn't hostile. "But how could they arrest you? They didn't have any proof."

"They had a witness."

"But you said…"

He nodded. "Exactly. It was only me and Wes. They told me that this girl was there and had seen the whole thing."

"Who?"

"Her name's Stacy Helig. She's a waitress down at the diner. Sometimes she'd hang out with us, too, but not that night."

I repeated the name in my thoughts. I came up blank. Surely I would have seen her down there at the diner, though. We used to go there once a week to eat, if not more sometimes before my mother had been hospitalized. "I don't know that name."

He stared at me and then lifted his palm up in the air. I placed my hand in his. It still felt slightly uncomfortable. I felt strong emotions wash over me as his skin brushed against mine.

"Well, she said she saw me fighting with Wes, and then push him over the side."

"But you were the one who called the police," I said in a defensive tone.

"Exactly." He shrugged again. "They wouldn't give me any more information about her. I suppose I'll get to hear more of her side in court when she testifies against me. But I think they pulled her out of thin air."

I lowered my eyebrows in question, not fully understanding what he meant.

He recognized my clueless expression. "They paid her or whatever to get her to say what she said."

"But why?"

"To get to me. To have a reason to lock me up."

I sighed. Now I knew why he was so frustrated. This whole situation felt so wrong. He didn't belong here, yet here he was, trapped and all the while, I was trapped as well, being forced to be away from him every day. And the question of my father being involved irritated me further. He wasn't exactly at the top of my list as good doers anymore, but I didn't think him capable of harming another's reputation. Then again, I had never assumed him capable of cheating on my mother either. I tried to

157

shake the memory of him and Mrs. Anderson from my thoughts and return to the situation before me now.

"Okay. So, here's what I still don't understand." I stared straight into those beautiful blue eyes again and bit my lip as I tried to concentrate on all the details of his explanation.

"You doing alright?" a voice called out just then.

I quickly jerked my hands away from Emry, abruptly ending all physical contact as I looked up toward Paul, who was peeking his head out the door. Emry had had his back toward him, so I didn't think he had seen anything out of the ordinary except two people talking on the bench.

"We're fine, thanks!" I called back to him. Then I cursed myself silently for having being polite right then. I forgot that I was still Amelia Roberts. I watched him go back inside. Emry never even flinched or turned to look his way.

"You were saying?" he whispered, a smirk on his face from how jumpy I was.

His expression made me smile in response. I offered him my hand and he took it without hesitation.

"Well, you said you weren't sure if you did it. I think you used the term that you 'blanked out' or something along those lines. So what does that mean? How could you not remember arguing with him? Were you so drunk you passed out, or did you fall asleep?"

He stood up and lifted me to my feet as well. He walked to the far wall and put his back against the brick this time. "Anna," he whispered.

"Yes?"

"Have you ever felt like you didn't belong?"

I thought about the question. I felt like there was some hidden meaning behind what he was actually saying. "Well, I've kind of blended in my whole life, but not really fit in anywhere either. Does that count?"

He gave me a half smile, but it vanished just as quickly as it had come. "Anna," he whispered again.

The way he said my name ever so softly put me into an instant trance, making me feel slightly dizzy every time I heard it escape his lips. He took my other hand in his and brought my body closer to his chest. I thought I could hear his heart beating. It sounded like it was thumping just as hard as mine was. "I can do this *thing;* something happens to me sometimes when I concentrate real hard."

I let the words sink in. What on earth was he talking about?

"I know you're confused, but I told you I would tell you everything, and please believe me when I tell you that I have never even attempted to tell anyone this before."

I waited, while being still and silent. I felt as if I didn't know anything anymore, the confusion setting in as even those I thought I knew, specifically my parents, were complete strangers to me.

Emry was finally opening up, but I was almost afraid of what he was going to tell me. Would he say he could twitch his nose and turn into a ferocious beast?

"Tell me," I pleaded, because I did want to know when it came down to it. I didn't want to be left in the dark any longer. "You can trust me with anything, Emry, anything at all."

He looked at me, his eyes soft as he peered down at me. "I know. I do trust you, Anna. You coming here like this today, putting yourself out there, and pretending to be my attorney…"He stopped to laugh. I had almost forgotten that every time he looked at me now I still had this painted face, this tight dress on and this blonde wig on the top of my head. "This is something I will never forget." The way he said it sounded as if he now owed me. "I need you to understand. It's just so difficult to put into words."

"Please try."

He sighed. "Well, it's like I have this force inside of me. One of the things I can do is something like where I almost lose consciousness in a way. If I really focus hard enough, it comes to me, but not all the time. And lately, since I've been in prison, it hasn't happened at all."

I felt my head tilt slightly to the left, struggling to grasp this concept.

"It's like I go to another place, a different world." He stopped to perceive my reaction from his big secret that he had just exposed to me. "It's like I literally leave here and am there."

"In your imagination?"

He shook his head. "I think I need to be medicated," he joked. "I think at one time I tried to convince myself of that, but no. It's real. It's the most beautiful place you've ever seen, Anna." His eyes lit up as he relived the memory in his head.

"So you go to this place…?" It did sound insane. He was even crazier than I was.

"It's like I'm able to physically warp there. I can't really control when it happens, though. I don't know how to force it to happen when I want it to."

I was trying to be open-minded, really, but if he could only hear what he was trying to convince me of. "So you did this while on the tower; is that what you're saying?"

"Yes, exactly. I was laying back, looking up at the stars, totally relaxed and then bam, not here any longer, but there."

"Gone from this planet, you think?"

"This place is not Earth." He smiled. This little fantasy he had created within his mind really excited him.

"So, what happens to you here when you're not … here?" I asked, sounding just as foolish as he did trying to describe it.

He ran his fingers through his hair again, little pieces automatically falling back into his eyes. "I don't know what happens physically. I don't know if I'm really here anymore when I'm there. So that's what I mean when I say I don't know what happened here while I was gone. Had I fought with Wes and not known it, or was I not there altogether? I just don't know." He seemed sad again, yet still staring at me, waiting for a response to his madness. "But then there's something else, too; something new that I've just recently become aware of."

I waited for him to go on, unsure of how to respond right now, anyway.

"When I said Buck Brady slammed into a tree, but I didn't hit him?"

I nodded, remembering how odd it had sounded when he first mentioned it.

"That's because I willed him into the tree."

"Willed him?" I repeated.

"Yeah. I got really angry with their accusations and how he was treating me like some heartless criminal. I wanted to hit him, really, I did. I pictured him in my head flying through the air and his back cracking up against the tree that was a few yards away, and then suddenly, he did. He was really freaked out. Everyone was, including me." His eyes locked on mine. He let out a nervous chuckle. "I guess I'm giving away all my secrets to you."

His words pierced through me. He was confiding in me in a way he hadn't with anyone else, ever.

"Emry, I don't know what to say." I looked away from him, not wanting him to be able to see the doubt I was sure was clearly written across my face.

He released my hands and turned his back to me. "I know. This is why I've never told anyone. It sounds ridiculous, and it came out all wrong, just like I figured it would. You probably either think I'm making it up or that I need to be thrown in an institution." He whipped back around to face me. He put his hand under my chin to pull my face upward. "Tell me what you're thinking, Anna, please."

His eyes looked so sad. I thought my heart was going to burst from the pain I saw coming from within him. I had to at least try to believe him. I couldn't turn my back on him, not now.

"I've never felt like I belong," he continued. "I've always tried to blend in, and it seemed easy enough. I tried to make a life for myself here with Lainey and Wes, and even by marrying Candace, and look how that ended up, because I'm different. And only with you, Anna; only now have I ever felt like I've connected with someone on a different level. You and I. I felt it that first day I saw you. You drew me in with this instant attraction."

"You're not going to lose me, Emry," I reassured him. I grabbed his arm, and he pulled me in tighter; my head against his chest as he wrapped his muscular arms around me tightly and we stood there in the courtyard bound together. "I want to help you sort all of this out." And if that meant that he was manic and needed my help in that way, I would be there for him.

"That means so very much to me," he whispered, his arms wrapping around me tighter still. "You have no idea how much I've longed to have someone like you in my life."

"Emry," I whispered, knowing this would ruin the moment but needing to know despite the fact. I pulled my head back to look up at his face. "You said you didn't think it was your imagination; why? Can you physically touch things in this place?"

"Yes," he replied quickly. "I can feel the sunlight on my face, the water bubbling underneath my toes, everything."

I attempted to process what he was telling me. He thought he was able to just warp to another time, another place? A time traveler? What exactly? It seemed so profoundly preposterous. It was impossible for me to understand or believe. I decided I probably wasn't going to be able to, but nevertheless, I wanted and needed Emry Logan's arms around me in this very moment. He was still so beautiful and so innocent, almost child-like with this wild fantasy he had created around him, and I had to get to the bottom of it, no matter what. I wouldn't stop until I had and helped him gain his freedom as I did so. Together I was sure that we would be able to uncover everything. And what about this other *strength* he was telling me about; how he got upset and willed Buck to do something he had first imagined in his mind?

"So Candace knew nothing about this?" I suddenly asked.

"No." He frowned. "I'm sorry about her, you know."

"Don't be. It's in the past."

"Exactly, but still, I am sorry. She was just another cover for me to fit in. I got along with her and thought she was fun, but she really wasn't that way at all when I got to know her. She's conniving. She makes poor choices. She was dragging me down along with her. I felt bad for her, I suppose. I felt bad for leaving her, but I had to. It didn't feel right anymore. I just wish I had never married her, but if it makes you feel better…"

"No, really, Emry." I didn't want to hear any more about his having been married, and now I was the one sorry for having had brought the subject up. "I'm fine about it," I lied.

He remained silent then and took my hands. His head was lowered, his eyes shut, and I automatically shut mine, too. I just stood there, feeling the warmth of his skin on mine, the feel of his fingers completely intertwined in mine. I listened to our breathing and tried to place all of my concentration on just being in this exact moment with this wildly beautiful man standing before me.

It didn't feel so chilly out anymore. Actually, the sun was starting to burn through the back of my dress, and I could hear the lovely song of birds in the distance, the sound of a roaring ocean nearby. I opened my eyes and looked all around. I raised my hand to my gaping mouth and gasped in total horror at what I saw.

Chapter 8

I was no longer dressed like Amelia Roberts. I was Anna James again, dressed in cut-off jean shorts and a white tank-top. My long brown hair swirled around my shoulders as the warm breeze tossed it up and down. My feet were bare, and I looked down at the golden sand beneath my toes. I wiggled them a little. The sand was soft and sparkled gloriously as the sunlight danced off the tiny crystals.

Before me was an ocean containing silky water that looked so clear, as if it was made out of liquid glass. I could see a brown canyon below the water's surface plummeting downward. There were edges of rocky cliffs that were jagged and high above my head. There were holes in the tops of these rocks and just beyond them a red hazy sky with bright white dots sparkling in between darker red clouds. Stars perhaps? And just beyond the ocean, you could see where the water met land again, extending out into a velvety canvas of high golden grass.

My eyes were large in surprise as my mind made multiple attempts to process what my eyes were truly seeing. This was it. Emry had brought me to this very special place, this *world* that was so breathtakingly beautiful that Earth could not hold claim to it. And it was real. My toes were feeling the sand beneath them, I could feel the breeze on my skin and my lungs filled with the sweet aroma of the air. This place wasn't a figment of his imagination at all. And as quickly as that, all of my doubts about what he was trying to tell me were washed away. The thrill of this place made my head spin even faster than it had before, but in a good way. I felt so drawn to my surroundings. I wanted to belong to this world and be a part of its magnificence.

I turned around slowly, almost afraid that any sudden movements would make me disappear from this place and end up back at the prison. Just the thought of being in the prison again made me cringe.

I turned, and saw Emry in front of me, his bare back toward me as he was only wearing a pair of khaki shorts, his arms wide, every muscle bulging in a flexed position, and his head upward as he was basking in the light of the sun.

"Emry," I called out, my voice cracking slightly. I was hesitant to take him away from the peaceful moment he seemed to be having.

He turned then, his eyes widened in surprise at the sight of me standing there. "Anna? I don't believe it!" He hurried over to stand next to me. "You're here … with me … wow."

"This must be heaven." My eyes continued to span and take in every detail of wonder around me.

He chuckled and smiled again. His happiness had me smiling back as my eyes couldn't help but take in his wonderfully toned chest and abs. He looked like he was the one who belonged here, living as one with the beauty all around.

He had his arms around my waist in a moment, spinning me around and hugging me tight. "I'm so happy this happened, I just don't know how. How did this happen?"

I raised my eyebrows. I had no clue where we were, let alone how I had got here.

"I mean, we were just in that courtyard holding hands..." Another grin spread across his face.

"Amazing. I didn't know I could do that."

"Something tells me you're still pretty new at this," I said. He laughed back, agreeing.

A chillingly high-pitched whistle echoed through the rooftops of the caves that engulfed us. Had it belonged to a bird of some sort?

"I feel like I'm dreaming."

He grabbed my hand and pressed his fingers between mine so that they were intertwined. He peered down at me, his blue eyes gleaming softly in the glow of the light shining around us. "Anna," he said in almost a whisper. "Welcome to Evadere."

"Evadere?" I repeated, trying to make sure I pronounced it correctly.

He nodded. "That's what I call this place. When I was little, I found this old book titled Evadere. It talked about another world that was very beautiful and had wondrous things in it. It reminds me of this place."

"What's it mean?"

"Escape."

"Oh," I said in awe. "It suits." All around me my eyes found more and more to focus on.

"Everything is just so ... vivid here." This place was beginning to overwhelm me. "I feel like I don't even have the vocabulary to describe it, as if there aren't the right words to bring justice to it."

He dipped the edge of his toe into the glassy waters and then brought it back into the sand. "I know *exactly* what you mean."

I began to feel guilty about having not believed Emry when he was trying to tell me all of this. This was his big secret, and I was getting to actually be a witness to it all. And then a profound sorrow weaseled its way into my heart and mind as I realized that everything I had been taught as a child seemed somehow lost to me now. It was as if I had been lied to. The supernatural had been frowned upon, did not exist, and wasn't tolerated. And yet, here I stood, in another world, brought here by supernatural powers. It was as if I were just now waking up, finally seeing reality for what it was. Those that believed in these kinds of things were labeled as insane, locked up and abandoned from society.

Other things do exist beyond the boundaries of our minds. Perhaps no one knew, but surely someone did. There had to be others out there like Emry Logan. He couldn't be the *only* one. So who else walked among the human race with extraordinary abilities? It just didn't seem right. These types of people, or whatever they were, existed, and yet, we just locked them up? We ignored the fact because we didn't really believe it or we were afraid of something different? It was infuriating.

"Are you okay?"

I looked into Emry's beautiful blue eyes and felt the anguish start to melt away. He wrapped his arms around me, studying my face.

"It's a bit too much all at once, isn't it?" he asked. "I just tell you about this and then poof, you're here."

"It is a lot to take in," I agreed, my eyes scanning the motionless water.

"Let's take a walk," he suggested. "Clear your head a little?"

I felt the warmth of his fingers still intertwined in my own and followed along. "If that's even possible."

We walked along hand-in-hand on the beach for a while. I couldn't understand that if there was such a strong breeze, then why was the water so still and undisturbed by it? I had to try to expand my thinking as if I were dreaming, or in some sort of fantasy land where the normal rules I was used to didn't apply. Anything was possible in a place like this. And if anything did happen, I shouldn't be surprised by it.

"I feel like I have a million questions."

"I may not have many answers, but I'll do my best," he promised me.

"When did you first realize you were able to do this, to come here?"

He grinned as if he were remembering it all too clearly. "I was in high school, a junior. A bunch of us were out in the woods, bored and having a few drinks. I was on the tailgate of a truck staring into a bonfire, and then it happened. When I came back, I looked around me and saw everyone passed out and sleeping. I didn't know how long I had been gone, and I thought at first that someone had maybe slipped something in my drink, like I had hallucinated the whole thing, until it happened again."

"And you have no idea how it happens?"

"I'm sure there's an art to it; I just haven't been able to figure it out.

Like I said, I haven't been able to do this since I was in jail. This has been the first time in a long time."

"So what do you do when you're here?"

He shrugged. "I just explore, I guess. Sometimes I'll think about stuff or not think about stuff, depending. I can never get enough of this place. It amazes me every time. You can't even know how happy I am that you're here with me, too, experiencing it all." He grinned.

I was happy, too. This was amazing. How could I have ever doubted him? How cruel had I been just a few moments ago, acting like one of *them*, the people who doubted that there was anything more out there, that there was no way that anyone could just bounce from world to world? I was so happy that no one else knew Emry's secret. No one else could *ever* know.

"What else do you want to know? I love getting this off my chest."

"Not even Lainey knows?"

"No. I guess I should tell you more about all of that. Lainey adopted me when I was three. My parents supposedly couldn't take care of me, that sort of thing, when I was born. Then I was in the foster system until Lainey came along, and I think she was lonely. Her husband had died, and they never had any kids or anything. I was replacing him sort of. She was just so much older than a mother with a little kid should be, though. She didn't ever really treat me like a kid. I came and went as I pleased, and she would be there to give me a meal and a roof over my head. It was a strange relationship, but it worked somehow."

"And your real parents? Have you ever tried looking for them?"

"Well, yeah, actually, right after I turned eighteen. Henry and Trisha Logan were the names on the birth certificate, but I think they're fake."

"Fake?"

Emry stopped walking, bent, and picked up a white rock. He tossed it across the water and it skipped playfully a couple times across the surface before sinking. "The only reason I say that is because those names can't be linked to anyone. I've hired different guys to try to locate them, and they always say the same thing. There's no information on any Henry or Trisha Logan who were married and gave up a child. So I've pretty much given up on the idea."

I let that all sink in. Emry Logan abandoned, and his parents put down fake names on his birth certificate? Did they know he was *special*? Were they like that and trying to hide the fact? I was sure he had thought about all these things, so I didn't bother bringing them up. I didn't want to risk upsetting him either or talk about him being abandoned. I could only imagine what a beautiful baby he had been. How could anyone have ever given him up or not wanted him? It was truly heartbreaking for me to think about.

"Have you ever seen anyone else here?"

"Not a soul."

"That's interesting."

"It is, isn't it?"

We walked away from the beach and into a patch of golden grass. It was like silk beneath my feet and felt wonderful and soothing to the touch. Red clouds rolled overhead. They were just a shade darker than the sky itself.

"And you haven't been able to *warp* anywhere else? Is that the right word for it?"

He laughed. "I don't know what to call it either. Call it anything you want. And no, just here. Always here."

I inhaled a big gulp of fresh air. The sweetness of it enlightened my taste buds with the new sensation and taste. "Okay. So, you said you tossed Buck Brady into a tree by willing him to do that with your mind?"

He nodded, listening intently to the question at hand.

"So, why are you still in jail? I mean, can't you just will yourself out or whatever?"

"Funny you should bring that up," he said. "I've thought about that many times. Here's the thing. First of all, I've never been able to do anything like that before until Buck had upset me with the accusations about Wes, so I have no idea how I did it to begin with. I've thought about conjuring up those emotions that set me off in an attempt to break out of there, but really, what good would it do me? I mean, they'd just hunt me down again and throw me right back in jail."

"So why do you ever go back?"

"To Earth, you mean?"

"Yes."

He pressed his lips together. "I haven't explored but only a portion of this land. I don't have the first clue how to live here or what to eat. What if the water's not safe? I just feel too insecure. I would love to be able to stay here, but it doesn't seem feasible." Emry turned toward me, his hands sliding over my shoulders and holding me in place. "Is this all making sense to you, the answers to your questions?"

"Actually, yes. Basically you're just as clueless as I am at this point?"

He grinned. "Exactly." His eye turned toward one of the edges of the cliffs. "Do you think you can climb? I want to show you a favorite spot of mine."

"I can try."

The cliff was steep and jagged. The soles of my feet felt like they were getting stabbed with each step upward. Emry would pull himself up first and then reach down and help me by practically pulling me up to the next landing. I had never tried mountain climbing before. The movements were a struggle for me, and my body ached and ultimately refused with each attempt.

As we reached the final hike to the top, Emry reached his hand down to me one last time. Beads of sweat glistened on his forehead, and his hair came down to stick in his eyes as he lowered his head to look at me.

"Ready?"

I reached up and felt his hand lock around mine and then my body being lifted upward to the very top. The rock itself seemed brittle and unsteady as our feet cautiously stepped on it. Emry led me to the edge of it. It came to an abrupt sharp point that extended over the water.

"Now look down."

I glanced at him hesitantly.

He gave me a reassuring smile. "Don't worry. I have hold of you."

I carefully walked to the outer part of the roof of this cave, making sure to shift the majority of my weight to the balls of my feet. I heard a few pieces of rock crack underneath my feet. Emry's strong hands were gripped tightly around my waist. I stretched out my neck so I could peer downward.

The water was below us at a great distance, but it was as if I was staring into a sheet of perfect glass. Seeing through the clear water was an underwater cave that seemed to plummet endlessly in a spiral under the water. It was like a gigantic hole that stopped where the water's surface began. I gasped for air as I realized I had been holding my breath.

"Oh, Emry," I whispered. "That's incredible. I don't even know what to say. I feel like I could stare at that for hours."

He pulled me back. "Could you imagine falling into something like that?"

I thought about it for a moment. "Can you imagine what kind of creatures are lurking in that dark hole?"

He raised his eyebrows at the thought. "I don't think I want to find out."

"Me either."

We went back over to a flatter area of the cliff and sat down. Emry wrapped an arm around me, and I leaned over to rest my head against his neck. You could see even more of Evadere from up here at this height. The golden grasses extended upward and looked as if they touched the red

175

sky. It seemed like miles and miles of gold everywhere as the sun danced off every aspect of this place and illuminated the whole thing. The white dots of stars were like diamonds that stuck out against the rose-colored sky even in the sun. I looked away and closed my eyes for a moment, just trying to concentrate on being here alone with Emry and feeling his arm pulling me in tightly, safely.

"You have to tell me what you're thinking," Emry pleaded. "You know everything, and I feel like I know nothing."

"What do you want to know?"

"You're here with me now in my beautiful Evadere." He grinned smugly at the name he had created for this place. "You know more about me than anyone else, and the only response I've gotten from you are facial expressions. I need to know your thought process to it all."

What was I going to say? I had doubted him, and I didn't want for him to ever know that, because it had been such a disgraceful thing to do to this beautiful creature sitting before me who had never felt like he belonged to *my* world because he probably didn't. He belonged to some place like this, and how did someone like me become so fortunate as to experience something like this? I didn't feel like I even deserved to be with him, let alone for my eyes to be able to see this place. "I'm just trying to wrap my mind around it all." I looked up into his eyes and then looked away again, hoping he wouldn't be able to see how sad I was suddenly becoming. I didn't belong here. I belonged to Seneca, to live my same, expected, dull lifestyle there until I was old and gray and then I would die there.

176

"I think it's the most beautiful thing I've ever seen," I told him. "More beautiful than anything I could have ever pictured in my mind on my own. And, I think you're beautiful, every part of you." I felt bold, as if I could tell him anything in the way of how I felt toward him. It was almost as if this were my last chance, the last time I would get to be with him all alone in this way. I tried to shake the sudden burden of loneliness so I could enjoy this moment and what I had left of it now. "I've always been drawn to you. There's something about you, and now I know what it is. You are different, but not in a bad way. You're kind and gentle. You're a good person, Emry. You have these remarkable gifts and strengths, and the fact that you've told me your secret, well, that's just crazy to me."

"Why?"

"Because who am I to know these things? I'm just an ordinary girl without anything special. I feel like you've wasted your secret on me," I blurted out.

I could tell instantly that my words had pained him as his eyes gave it all away. He pulled his arm away from my shoulder and positioned himself so that he was still very close but directly in front of me, face-to-face. "Don't say that about yourself, Anna. You are special. You're a good person, too. I don't know much about you, but from what I can tell, you're caged in just as much as I am. It's like you have no sense of freedom, or any way to express who you really are."

"Too much is expected of me."

"By others. But what do you want for yourself? Have you ever asked yourself that question?"

177

I buried my head into my knees, attempting to hide the tears that had come on so quickly and that were now racing down my cheeks. "I hadn't until I met you."

"What do you want, Anna?" he asked more sternly.

I cried into my knees for a few minutes before being able to talk again. He didn't try to interfere with my moment of emotional release. "I want a life of my own. I want to be my own person. I feel like everything around me, everything I have ever known is a lie."

"It's not a lie, Anna; it's just that there is so much more to be realized."

I looked up at Emry, feeling the burden of everything that had been heaved upon my shoulders lately and wanting to let it all go, wanting to cave in and tell Emry everything. It wasn't fair that he told me all about his life and I told him nothing. Why was I trying to be so brave? I didn't need to hold all of these things in anymore. I had someone I trusted and could talk to, someone that would listen. I needed to finally get it all out in the open. He wouldn't judge me if I told him about my father, about Carlin, my mother being in the hospital.

"Emry, there are these things that have been going on lately," I began.

"What kind of things?" He lowered his eyebrows as if concerned.

I felt a lump in my throat and swallowed hard. It didn't budge. "It's my family," I told him.

"They're not what they seem."

I went on to tell Emry everything. It all came gushing out. Once I started, I couldn't stop talking. I told him about Buck Brady and his interest in me, how I decided to play along just to know more about Emry, how Buck's car had gotten the flat tire and we saw my father with Mrs. Anderson at her house, how upset I had been and my mother's heart condition. I told him about my mother's reaction to Mrs. Anderson showing up at the hospital and then about Carlin and the dark cloud she had brought into our already demented household. I even told him about Russell, the man my mother had been engaged to and who Carlin had also loved. It seemed like Emry had sat there forever, listening to me go on and go about all of my so-called problems.

When I was done, I felt so much better, so relieved to have gotten it all out. I leaned between Emry's legs and bent over to rest my forehead against his hard chest. I felt his hand touch my head and then begin to repeatedly run through my hair.

"Those other times you came to see me, you never mentioned any of this. I had no idea," he whispered, his other arm wrapping around my back to comfort me.

"I didn't want to bother you with it," I replied.

"Why?"

"Because," I said, irritated with myself that I now had burdened him with all of my insignificant dramas. "You're in jail, Emry. You have much bigger problems to deal with."

Emry chuckled, the noise vibrating in his chest and radiating to my head. He placed his fingers under my chin and gently pushed my head up so that he could look into my soggy brown eyes. "You've done so much for me. The least I can do for you is listen. I want to know what's going on in your life, Anna; you have to believe that and know that."

"I'm sorry."

"Listen to me. You have a lot going on. Don't think of your problems as less to deal with than what I have to deal with."

"They're not even close to being the same."

"I wish you didn't have any problems," he admitted, his eyes penetrating into my own. "I've only created more burden for you."

"I don't regret meeting you, Emry. The burden that I carry is that I feel as if my whole life has been a lie." I stood up and walked to the edge of the cliff, peering down at the wonder below me, the red skies overhead. I let the intense sorrow that I should be accustomed to fill me to the point of more tears. Emry immediately came over to me. He stroked the back of my head, his fingers running down the nape of my neck. "I don't understand."

I turned around and looked at his beautiful face and all of its features that I had instantly loved. I didn't want him to see my pain, but I was tired of trying to be brave, tired of hiding what I was truly feeling. "All of the things that were imprinted on me as a child, from being raised in the church, in a religious family."

"You're doubting God?"

"If there is one."

Emry looked horrified that those words had come from my mouth. "Anna, do you even realize what you're saying?"

I suddenly felt ashamed by his reaction, a sudden heat bursting forth in my cheeks. "You do believe in God?"

"How could you not?" He put his hands in the air and turned around slowly looking at his beloved Evadere, this world that had found him and attached itself to him. "Anna, just look around you. This didn't all just happen. Someone created it."

The stars twinkled overhead at me, and I did feel foolish. Emry was right. How could I just turn my back so easily on my faith?

"It'll be hard to look at Earth in the same way after being here, but there's beauty on Earth, too, Anna, and again, someone put it there." He hugged me against his chest. I pressed my face into his bare skin, inhaling the scent of him. "Nobody took me to church when I was a kid. You're lucky in the way that you have that background. Me, I don't really know what I'm talking about when it comes to that stuff, but you do. But I think I've really always believed. Sometimes even a guy like me prays. Does that seem stupid?"

I smiled. "No, not at all."

"Really, it's not so hard to believe there's a bigger power out there than yourself." He smirked.

No, not after today especially, I thought. My outlook on life had changed. There was this whole other realm out there. There was more beyond just ourselves.

"I don't know why I just said that. I think I was headed more in a direction of blaming God for everything going on in my family right now. It's like nothing ever happened to us. We were bound together by an unbreakable bond, the kind of love that doesn't falter. And now, one thing

181

after another keeps happening. We're a mess." I sighed, shutting my eyes as the pain returned.

"Listen, nothing can always be perfect. Maybe these things were always there, you were just blocking them out. I could see you doing that. Now you see there's more out there, and along with it came the realization that everyone around you who you thought were perfect aren't, and it seems like a lot to handle all at once because you've let your walls down and along with it, reality has set in."

I thought about what he was saying for a moment. Could that be true? Had my family always been this way and I just sort of ignored it?

"So really, I'm a mess, too."

"Well," he said grinning. "Look what you've accomplished today. Pretending to be an attorney to get to be close to an accused murderer, traveling to another world ... seems normal enough to me."

I laughed at his sarcasm. "You're right."

"I know I'm selfish dragging you into my world ... bad choice of words."

I laughed again. He always had this way of making me feel better even when I felt at my worst.

"I know you should run away from me, and if you want to go, I won't stand in your way."

"Emry," I tried to stop him.

"Just please listen. I don't want you to go, Anna, but I don't know how this whole thing is going to turn out. I mean, have you thought about it?"

"You didn't do it, Emry. You'll get out of there." But the truth was I had thought about it. That's why I was so afraid this was the last time I'd be near him. That thought terrified me, but I wanted to be strong for him and not give him any doubt that he might be in prison the rest of his life. I couldn't bear that sort of truth if it was what was headed in our direction next.

He took my hands in his and ran his thumbs over my skin. Then he released one hand to run his fingers through his hair. "There's more to the story than just accusing me of killing Wes."

"What do you mean?"

"I don't think it's a coincidence that right after Buck gets magically thrown through the air and into a tree, I get arrested. Something else is happening. They're afraid of me. Your dad's involved, too."

"Father..." The word stuck in my throat.

"I don't know what exactly his involvement is. I don't really know what's going on, or if they blame me for what happened to Buck, but my suspicions are pointing in that direction. Something more is going on, and Wes has just been a cover-up to get me locked up."

He was probably right. What did they know, and why would they be afraid of Emry to have to falsely accuse him of murder and even get a witness to say that she saw it, to make sure he wouldn't be able to get out of jail? And what exactly was my father's involvement in this whole situation? It sent a chill up my spine. "I'll get to the bottom of it," I promised quickly as my mind was suddenly buzzing with how exactly I was going to be able to do this.

"No." Emry pulled away from me so he could look straight into my eyes to get his point across. "I don't want you involved in this mess."

"I'm already involved," I argued. "You can't expect me to just sit back and do nothing."

He nodded. "That's exactly what I expect you to do. This is a dangerous situation, I can feel it." His eyes were narrowed at me and he had a stern look on his face, making him look even more beautiful. I didn't want to make a promise to him that I knew was impossible for me to keep.

"You're not going to listen to me, are you?" He had seen straight through it as if he had read my thoughts that exact moment.

"I don't know if I can stand back and do nothing. The feeling useless part will kill me."

"Well, it will kill me to know you're digging around in this mess and my not being able to do anything to keep you safe."

I could see his point. Maybe I could try to promise or cross my fingers behind my back or something. "How much danger do you think I could get into?"

"I have a *really* bad feeling about it."

"But, Emry, those involved are Buck and my father. They wouldn't do anything to me," I said, thinking to myself that there was little if any danger involved.

He shook his head. My attitude toward the situation irritated him. "Buck Brady is a bad man. He's the type that wouldn't hesitate to turn on a person, even a friend. And Pastor John James, I'm sorry to say it about your dad, but there's something off about him, too."

"The affair?"

"No. Something else. Like I said, I don't know what, but my gut tells me it's bad." He wrapped both arms around me and squeezed tight. "I know you want to help. I know your intentions are good. I'm going to miss you so much when we get back."

"Let's not go back," I pleaded with him, tears streaming down my face. I felt like such a huge bawl baby with him. "Please, Emry."

"Shh," he comforted me, stroking my hair, my cheek pressed firmly against his chest. "It'll be alright. It'll all work out. You'll see."

I pulled back slightly to look up into his eyes. "Then why does it feel like this is it? This is our one moment, and then we'll be torn apart?"

He wiped a tear away from my eye and tried to flash a smile, but he was just as sad as I was. Maybe he felt the same way: that this was it, but now he was the one being strong, putting on an act.

"Nothing this strong can stay apart. Do you feel it?" He put the palm of my hand on his heart. The thump of his heart beating on my hand sent a sensation throughout my entire body, making my own heart throb. "We are meant to be together, Anna James. And so we will."

"Emry, I can't bear the thought of being away from you again."

He put his finger up to my lips, hushing me. "You have to believe that we'll be together again, and we will. Just try to stay out of trouble, please," he begged.

"I promise I'll try." That was all I could give him.

He smiled, knowing that I wouldn't be able to not get involved because he was involved, which tied me in as well, but being careful about what I was doing, and I would, was better than nothing.

"No matter what happens, we belong together. Never doubt that," he whispered.

"I won't. And I'll never forget Evadere." I was sad to leave. This place truly was an escape from today's pain.

"I doubt it will be soon to leave your imagination and you can revisit anytime you like." He smirked again and drew me closer, his finger tracing the outline of my lips.

"Just a figment of my imagination. How sad." I smirked back.

"How crazy."

"We are crazy."

"That we are."

He leaned in toward my face. I felt the warmth of his soft, gentle lips pressing against mine. I could feel the intensity of his emotions being poured out in that glorious kiss, and I felt all of my own anguish turn to mush in that instance as I moved my own lips hungrily against his and kissed him back.

It was almost too much passion to bear. My heart throbbed in one big ache. I could feel his heated breath against my own mouth as he kissed me again and again, his fingers digging into the hair on the back of my head as my own hands slid up and down the smooth, tan skin of his back.

"What's going on here?" I heard an angry, unfamiliar voice shout out.

I pulled my head away from Emry's and looked around. We were back in the courtyard at the prison, our arms around one another as a small group of policemen stood at the door of the courtyard, watching us intently. At the head of the group of men stood a very outraged Buck Brady. He came storming over to us, and I could only gasp in horror as he tore the blonde bob wig from my head, my long brown hair falling down all around my face and shoulders, and the equally horrified look on Buck's face.

"Anna?" Buck asked, his tone one of uncertainty. He searched my face for a moment, realizing the lengths I had gone to dress up as Emry Logan's attorney. Then he glared at Emry and pulled violently at my arms, tearing me away from him.

"No!" I screamed, panic stricken as I held one arm outreached toward Emry as the other was being dragged away by Buck.

Chapter 9

I cringed in pain as Buck threw me carelessly like a rag doll down into a hard chair in one of their interrogation rooms.

"Do you want her handcuffed?" I heard one of the officers ask.

"No," Buck huffed. He crossed his arms in front of him and glared in my direction. "Give me a moment, will you?"

"Sure thing."

I was so angry that Buck had taken my absolutely perfect moment away with Emry that I could swear I felt my blood boiling within my veins. I felt hot tears rush into my eyes as the other fact entered my mind. I'd been caught. What would become of me now, and what were they going to do to Emry?

Buck slammed his fists into the desk in front of me. I flinched at the noise. And here, I hadn't given him enough credit. I didn't think he could find it within himself to have enough intimidation to be a good cop.

"How could you do something like this?" he screamed at me.

I pushed my shoulders back and smoothed out the skirt of the dress. There was a slight tear up the side of it. Carlin was going to kill me, though she was the least of my worries now. I straightened and sniffled slightly, trying to get my emotions under control. I would not allow Buck Brady to break me down and make me weak.

"What were you thinking?" he yelled out again, his eyes dark and full of an intense hatred. Was it me? Emry? Seeing the two of us together?

I looked him straight in the eyes. "I won't answer to you, *Buck Brady*." I put as much demeanor into saying his name as Carlin did when she called me Annie. I knew he would feel degraded and hurt, especially by someone like me saying it, someone he had once took out on a date and cooked dinner for, perhaps even had feelings for.

It worked. His fists pounded down onto the table again, a growl escaping his throat in a sudden fierceness that even shocked me.

"Then you can sit here!" he shouted.

I watched as he turned and exited the room. I lowered my head as all of the emotions I was struggling to keep out of Buck's sight came rushing to me just now, all at once, and my shoulders heaved as my entire body shook with violent sobs. I let them come on, knowing that I was probably being watched and yet, just as long as I wasn't face-to-face with Buck, I allowed the sobs to take over. I buried my face in my hands, looking down to see the black from the mascara and gray eye shadow covering my palms. I must look a disheveled mess. I could only hope that I didn't look as horrific as I felt.

I lifted my head as the sobs started to dissipate, and my eyes scanned the dreary, dull green walls of the room I was in. So this is where they put suspects to drill them with questions. I'd barely been questioned and already felt like a criminal myself sitting here like this. It was as if the room itself toyed with your mind before the questioning even began; a prelude to what was to come.

So what was to become of me now? Would they transfer Emry to

189

be away from me? Would they throw me in jail, too? My parents would think the James name was forever ruined. I would surely be scorned and never again be seen as the same Anna James. Then again, the Anna James they knew had already been long gone. It seemed ages ago instead of months that the only thing I looked forward to when I woke up in the morning was going to the antique store. What a sad, pathetic girl I'd been. At least now I felt like I had a purpose. Love filled every empty void I had ever felt, thanks to Emry Logan, an inmate I was almost certain that I had instantly fallen in love with from the moment our eyes met. We were drawn to each other in a way that most people only dreamt about. And now, we were connected, too; bound together by his secret, by his magical strength and the intimate lovely world he had accidentally revealed to me, his Evadere. I already longed to be back there and in his arms, his lips against mine as a glowing sun with red hue behind it shined overhead. I felt as if his kiss still lingered on my lips. It had only been moments ago.

My heart was aching with the sudden realization that if they were treating me like this, how worse it would be for him. They actually *liked* me. I closed my eyes tight, saying a prayer under my breath, praying with all my might that they wouldn't hurt my beautiful Emry Logan. Surely they couldn't touch him. *Yeah, right*, I thought to myself. Prisons get away with more than they should every day, and something fueled their strong hatred of Emry. It was a bone-chilling kind of hatred that came on strong at the mere mention of his name. I had seen that hatred in Buck's eyes, and every ounce of me longed to save Emry. But I couldn't. He had been right. We were both trapped, caged in like animals, and the only hope we had

190

was knowing that we belonged to each other, and that someday that would be powerful enough to break through all of this unjust agony. Our connection was magical. There was no turning back now. I had to face whatever was in front of me and get past whoever dared to try to stop my being with Emry. I thought about the realization of loving him just then, a pleasant thought, but also one of cruel torment. An unjust kind of love.

I heard voices speaking and the heavy door made an eerie, creaking sound as it came open just a crack at first.

"What's going on? They called and said there was an emergency, but told me nothing."

I recognized the voice immediately. It was my father. I wiped my cheeks with the back of my hand and tried to smooth out my hair a little. I knew I looked a wreck, but I could do no more. I had run out of time. My time to mope had come to an end. It was now time to face whatever doom was lurking in the future as I could feel it headed straight toward me.

"Just take a look, sir," another officer said.

I looked at the door to see my father enter, and then his eyes widen in disbelief as he saw that I was the one sitting in the dark room. I could only imagine what was going through his mind just then. I tried not to think about it, but pushed my shoulders back and sat straight up as I had in the presence of Buck.

"What are *you* doing here?" he asked, still surprised and confused.

Remember how you despise this man, I reminded myself. Picture him with Mrs. Anderson, dig up the memory of those emotions, and don't let him intimidate you.

Another officer, who I didn't recognize, entered the room behind him. "We found her in the courtyard kissing one of the inmates, sir."

"What?" My father's eyes never left mine. I didn't dare look down or reveal any signs of weakness.

"Who?"

The officer hesitated a moment.

Then my father turned to look at him. "Which one?" he asked again, his voice rising.

"Emry Logan."

That had done it. Just the mention of his name made my father's anger spring to life. His eyes were fierce and almost had a fire about them. They were very similar to how Buck's had appeared.

He walked over to me and wrapped his hand around my forearm. His grip dug into my skin. He pulled me to my feet.

"Is this true?" he screamed in my face.

I wanted to shrivel up and melt into the floor, but I held firm to my ground and stared back, never giving him the satisfaction of hesitating. "Yes." I was surprised at how calm my voice sounded when the word finally came out.

My father released his grasp on my arm and glared at the other officer. "How did this happen?" He turned back to me. "Why are you dressed like that?"

"She was wearing this wig." The other policeman tossed it down onto the table. "Nobody recognized her. She claimed to be Emry Logan's attorney."

"What? This is ridiculous. Where's Buck?" he demanded.

"I don't know."

"Well, go find him!"

I had never heard my father speak to anyone that way. It was like he had some sort of control over these policemen, like they answered to him. It was strange to see him like this as if he were some sort of war lord. He turned to stare at me again. He didn't recognize me, and I didn't recognize him. We were on equal footing with one another.

"Anna, why would you do such a thing? How do you even know Emry Logan?"

Buck must have not been too far away as he entered the room with the officer who had gone to retrieve him. He hiked his pants up in an arrogant manner as he approached me.

"She first met him when she came down here to the jail," Buck explained for me.

My father gave him a confused look as if he had no clue what he was talking about.

"The day she passed out *your* pamphlets to all of the prisoners."

My father covered his gaping mouth with his hand as if it had all come back to him now.

"Don't forget to tell him about the part where you accidentally slipped and told Emry who I was," I belted out boldly.

Buck cringed. "You may as well take a seat, Anna." He gestured toward the chair.

"I'm fine standing, thanks."

He shrugged as if not really caring. "You could be here a while."

"This is so stupid!" I cried out. "Let me out of here!"

My father and Buck met glances. What kinds of thoughts were they exchanging?

"Do you have any idea of what laws you've broken here?" my father yelled out at me. "Do you understand what kind of mess you're in?"

"Maybe she does know what laws she's broken. She's an attorney, after all." Buck grinned at me.

"You're in trouble here as well," my father snapped at him.

"Me?" Buck smirked. "I have no blame here. You're the one who can't control your family."

"How did she get in here and fool everyone? Anna, you've always been so … honest. What has gotten into you? I just don't understand how any of this has happened. Emry Logan? Of all people," he mumbled.

I wasn't sure if I was supposed to explain or what. He seemed to be talking at me and yet about me to Buck all at the same time. I decided I wouldn't give him any information, anyway. He was the enemy.

"Sit down, Anna," my father commanded. I ignored him. "Sit down!" he roared angrily.

I decided not to push it and sat down in the chair as everyone else hovered above me.

My father knew he had lost his temper and tried to take deep breaths in order to compose himself.

"Just … sit," he said, although I already was, but repeating it as if

194

he hadn't meant to be so out of control the first time. "Let's just talk this thing through, shall we?" He looked toward Buck. "A few more chairs, please?"

Within minutes, Buck was dragging in two more chairs. I eyed them cautiously as they sat directly across from me. My father put his elbows on the table and crossed his hands in front of him. "I need to know everything, Anna. This is very important."

"Why is it so important?" I asked, maybe a little too quickly.

"You have no right to question *us*," Buck snapped at me. "Just sit there and answer the questions as they come to you."

I glared at him, but pressed my lips together. They weren't going to give away any information. It would be a waste of breath to continue to try to press them.

"What do you want to know?" I asked, my voice a little less harsh and a little more on the quieter side, a little more like the old Anna.

A sigh escaped from my father's mouth. He tapped his finger lightly on the table now and closed his eyes for a moment to gather his thoughts. "What contact did you have with Emry Logan after that first day when you handed him the brochure?"

My mind was spinning. Should I tell them about the letters? Of course not. What kind of traitor would I be then? The next question would be where the letters are, and then they would go take them away from me. What if they were all I had left for now to physically hold onto? I couldn't bear the thought of them ripping up those cherished pieces of paper. No, I wouldn't tell them anything. But they weren't going to stand for me saying

195

nothing. *Think. Think!* I screamed at myself. Send them on a wild goose chase. But how? What could I say without getting him into even more trouble?

"I've made it a habit to come down and visit inmates like this," I told them. "This is just the first time you've caught me."

My father pushed the table away from him as he jumped to his feet in rage. His chair tipped over on the floor with a loud slam behind him as he did so, and the edge of the table hit my ribs. I gasped as the sudden pain took the breath away from me for a few seconds.

"I'm not going to sit here and try to figure this out if you're going to act like this!" my father yelled, his arms flailing about as he did so. "You're an ungrateful, spoiled child! You've been handed everything! Everything! This is how you treat *me*? You disrespect me and our entire family in this way!"

"I won't tell you anything!" I screamed back, feeling that familiar hate for him suddenly from deep within as all of the powerful emotions I had felt toward him from that day seeing him on Mrs. Anderson's porch exploded within me as they surfaced. "You've given me nothing but lies, so that's all you deserve in return!"

"What are you talking about? She's out of her mind!"

"No!" I shouted. "For the first time in my life I can see clearly, and I see you clearly for the blasphemous hypocrite that you really are!"

His eyes shifted to Buck, who lowered his head, knowing it was coming.

"Don't look away, you coward!" I shouted at Buck. "You were

there. You saw what I saw!"

"What did you see?" my father asked. "Buck?"

Buck stood too, and began pacing back and forth in the room. "Anna, I told you you're wrong about this."

"Now secrets are being withheld from *me*?" My father had a wild look about his eyes. I didn't trust it because I didn't recognize it. Who was this man? The same one I thought I had known my whole life?

"And the fact that you can stand there and blame me for disgracing the family? Take a look in the mirror. How can you do this to my mother, to all of us?"

"Are you in love with him?" Buck yelled at me, attempting to start another conversation. Was it a diversion or because it was really on his mind? I couldn't tell.

My father looked uneasy, yet still fierce with anger at both of us. "What is she talking about? What have I done to our family? I've done nothing but try to protect this family along with its reputation, which you are squashing by coming in here and looking like ... a whore!"

I gasped at what he had just called me. "I'm a whore?"

"Anna, tell me if you're in love with him!" Buck stepped in between us.

"I'd rather be a whore than an adulterer!" I screamed at Father.

My father's face twisted. He was shocked, that much was obvious. And now he would know that Buck was in on it, too. We knew his secret, and I was willing to expose it now for all that it was worth to get him out of my life, our lives.

"Anna! Stop it!" Buck grabbed my shoulders and began to shake me violently, my limbs tossed carelessly like a rag doll. "Do you love him? Do you? Tell me if you do!" I watched his hand draw back then as he got ready to hit me, but before he was able to my father grabbed his arm and jerked him around.

"What's the matter with you?" my father scolded him. "This is turning you into a monster."

Buck's chest was heaving up and down with his fury. "Take a look in the mirror, old man," he hissed back and turned to give me one final glare.

"You need to leave," my father told him.

"I'm already on my way out." And with those words, Buck was gone.

I ran my fingers down through my hair, certain I was now more disheveled than before. I couldn't believe that Buck had just been about to hit me. What was the reasoning behind it? It just didn't make any sense. It's not like he had been in love with me? Right? No, he hadn't tried to call me for weeks. There was no way this could be out of jealousy. There had to be more.

I sat down in the chair and folded my hands in front of me on my lap. I noticed a run in my panty hose scurrying all the way up my thigh, a small line of whiter skin exposed. I blinked at it for a few moments, my mind going completely blank. Emry was right. This whole situation was becoming dangerous. I had never been around any type of violence in my life, and I had almost just gotten backhanded by a man. I rubbed my face where I assumed the blow would have taken place, grateful that it hadn't, but even though my father had saved me from Buck's wrath, it still didn't change the way I felt about him. He sat oddly positioned in the same fashion across from me, his face blank, his eyes lowered to the table. He looked exhausted.

After a few minutes of silence, my father finally spoke. "This is going to rip us apart."

"We were already there."

"Anna, you think you know everything about everything, but you really have no idea."

I looked up at him. He seemed slightly calmer but still not willing to render any sort of explanation for what was going on or what he meant.

"You think I'm still a child, blinded and naïve, but you're wrong. I think I deserve a little more credit. I know more than you think I do," I replied.

"Do you?" My father sighed and ran his thumb and pointer finger over his grayish-white beard. I was frustrating him. He had taken a blow to his self-esteem and knew he couldn't make up for it.

"This is not going any further. I want you to know this so you can handle it in a mature fashion and not overact or try anything irrational."

I frowned and narrowed my eyes at him. "What's not going any further?"

"Whatever is going on between you and Emry Logan. He's a murderer, and I can only imagine the string of lies he's told you to get near to you."

"He hasn't done anything wrong," I snapped.

My father pressed his lips together at my reaction. He should have known better than to think I would just give up because he simply told me I had to. "He's a terrible man, Anna, and I am telling you the truth because I love you, and I don't want to see you go down this path of destruction with him, only to get hurt along the way, or killed."

"You honestly think I'm going to sit here and believe that Emry Logan is capable of killing me? Do you think I'm that stupid, Father? You're the one here who is a liar."

He closed his eyes for a moment, the anger building back up as he slammed his palms down on the table and gripped the edge of it with all his might. "That's enough!" he shrieked. "I can get you out of here without charges, but you will never *ever* see Emry Logan again! Do you understand?"

My heart thumped in outrage and also throbbed in pain at his words. This was just his scheme to get me to break down, to become weak enough so that I would believe what he said and not pursue my heart, which now belonged to the beautiful Emry Logan. "I won't give up," I told him honestly. "You can't stop me."

"You just watch me," my father warned. "What's your plan? Are you going to live happily ever after with him in the state penitentiary? He's never getting out."

I closed my eyes as I felt a hot flush and the tears instantly returned. I didn't care now that they were gushing down my cheeks. I was tired of his games. "We belong together, Father, and no matter how hard you try, you won't be able to keep us apart."

Another officer stepped into the room and whispered something into my father's ear. He nodded and then the officer left again.

"Is there anything else you want to tell me?" my father asked, his tone borderline between smugness and assurance that he was getting his way.

"Is there anything else you want to tell *me*?" I asked him right back, narrowing my eyes as I watched him become angry again.

"Very well," he snapped. "I'll go see what I can do about getting you out of here."

I felt very sad and alone after he had gone. I sat slumped over in the chair, feeling the sorrow pulsing through me, but not having any more tears left to cry. I was worried that my father was now interrogating Emry, asking him all sorts of things. I thought about Buck hitting him and how my father probably wouldn't stop that. It made me wince, and I tried to shake the thought from my head.

I felt defeated, for now. This felt as if it had been the longest day of my life composed of the most astonishing and also devastating memories I had ever experienced. My plan had worked. I had got to see Emry. I had gone to his world and seen firsthand what he was talking about. My feet had walked over a foreign land that was filled with such breathtaking magnificence that I longed for another taste of Evadere. But even more wonderful than all of that was the kiss that kept running through my mind and the feel of Emry's soft lips moving simultaneously with my own, full of passion and love. It felt as if all of my senses were still connected to that very moment, and then as quickly as it had happened, it had gotten ripped away by Buck.

Defeated, definitely for now, but I was proud that I had stood up to Buck and my father as much as I did, and I had let nothing slip. I was sure that I had enough strength to overcome the both of them and whatever was behind their hatred for the man I had come to love. He was my reason for living now. I would get him back and be with him if I died trying.

My head jerked up as I heard the door opening again.

"Anna James?"

The police officer that had first accompanied my father appeared.

"You're free to go now."

I didn't know how free I was exactly, but I forced myself to stand as I unsteadily walked out of the room in my heels, the blonde wig in my hand. I thought about plopping it back on my head, but then decided against it. I walked down a long corridor alone, my footsteps pounding nosily along the cement as I did so until I reached the lobby where I knew desks of the policemen that had stared at me going in would surely be staring at me in a different way going out, the wig no longer on my head.

Once in the lobby, I made sure to keep my head down, not daring to make eye contact with anyone.

The room was completely silent. And then I felt a little relieved as the gush of cold wind greeted me at the main door, and I was outside, away from all of the commotion. But the relief quickly vanished as I reached my car and got in. A single tear escaped and ran down my cheek as I turned the key in the ignition and pressed my foot on the accelerator. I had to leave, but Emry had to stay.

Chapter 10

I drove way over the speed limit. I didn't care. I was furious that I had gotten caught. I could have gone back tomorrow as Amelia Roberts and been in his arms again. The more I thought about it, the crazier I drove. The houses and buildings zipped by, and before I knew it, I was on the other side of Seneca, heading out of town.

I took a deep breath and slowed the car down, pulling off on the shoulder. I wasn't going home right now. I couldn't. There was no way I was walking in like this, and who knew what my father had told all of them by now. I didn't care if I ever walked back into that house. I looked at myself in the rearview mirror and gasped. Wow. I *did* look awful, straight out of a zombie movie. My skin was covered in black makeup smudges and streaks from the tears that had washed portions of the foundation away. Then there was my hair. Had everyone really seen me like that? *Oh well*, I thought, immediately casting the care away. It was their fault I looked like this, anyway.

I did a U-turn and headed into the depths of Seneca again, toward the antique store to get cleaned up and out of these clothes. I thought momentarily about what I was going to do with this dress. It was beyond repair at this point. I would probably just end up hanging it in Carlin's closet in this condition.

She would be furious when she found out. It amused me to think of what her facial expression would be like when she first discovered it there.

I drove a little slower now, a little safer, my eyes scanning over the properties as I passed them.

Neon lights came into view as I recognized and read the letters on a sign: JD'S. All the bulbs were out on the letter D, though. It was a well-known yet deadbeat bar at the edge of town that seemed to have its own sort of crowd. I had only been in there once. It had been on my twenty-first birthday, and I could remember Mandi Liswich's car pulling in here as we met a few more of our friends from high school. I had remembered feeling so uncomfortable sitting at the bar, so out of my element, as Mandi and the other girls chatted away as if they had done this a million times. They probably had now that I thought about it. I only had one drink that night, a cranberry and vodka, as I sipped on it nervously wondering what was happening to my body while I did so. Would I be drunk after just one drink? I was so worried about how my body was going to react and worried that someone would tell my parents that I had been there. What a joke that had been. None of the people that had come in there that night were recognizable to me. I doubted many of them went to church, let alone my father's. I had felt a little strange after just that one drink, so I didn't dare have anymore. Mandi took me home afterward, smiling as if she didn't care that I was being a party pooper. Then she took off back down the road again after dropping me at the house. *She had probably had gone back to the bar,* I thought to myself now. A bar might just be enough of a loud, distracting environment to get my mind off the day's events if only for a few hours. I needed to do *something*. I had nowhere else to go.

My foot pressed harder on the accelerator, and the car took off toward the direction of the store.

***

Pulling back into JD's parking lot, I felt that same familiar kind of anxiety I had felt on my twenty- first birthday. At least then I had Mandi, but now I would be going in alone. I thought about turning around and going home, but that disturbance outweighed the one of going in here by myself.

I took a peek in the rearview mirror again. My face was now clean and didn't have a trace of makeup on. I had tried to brush my hair out as best I could, and I was now wearing a pair of jeans and a faded red sweatshirt.

Here goes nothing, I thought, opening up the car door.

The smell inside JD's bar was of cigarettes, hot wings, and spilled beer. It wasn't a huge crowd being it was a weekday, and I avoided the looks of the few people that were there and plopped down on a red-cushioned stool. I set my purse down on the counter and watched as a partially balding bartender with sunken in cheeks and creases permanently formed into his forehead approached me. He wiped his hands with a white cloth and tossed it on the counter.

"What can I get you?"

I looked at the shiny-topped counter and tried to think of something to say. What should I order?

What drink did I even know of to order? A beer? Did I even like beer? I had never tasted it before.

But then again, there were different kinds of beer. You couldn't just say you wanted *a* beer. This was ridiculous. I must look like an idiot. Why was I even here? I had no idea what I was doing.

"I'll have a rum and Coke," I said. I had heard that once on a movie. I was relieved it had popped into my memory so quickly.

He nodded and then turned to make the drink.

I shifted my attention to the others that were in the bar. There was an older man sitting by himself directly across from me on the other side of the counter. He looked up at me once and then quickly away when he realized that I had been staring at him. There were two girls sitting a few seats down to my left that were busy chatting away to each other, and there was a small crew sitting at one of the tables near a window, eating pizza with a pitcher of beer in the middle of them. They were being fairly loud, their laughter carrying above the hum of the music playing in the background.

"Here you are." The bartender put a napkin down and then my drink on top of it. I dug through my purse for some money. "Keep the change," I told him.

He eyed me curiously for a moment, but then said nothing and walked away.

I sat there for a few moments, trying to blend into the atmosphere around me, taking a few sips of the drink. It wasn't too bad, actually. I was glad I had chosen this over beer. I tried to keep my mind occupied with the music, an old classic rock tune lightly thumping in the background from an old jukebox lit up in the corner. It sounded like something I may have heard before. I tried to focus on the smell of the cigarettes, something I strongly disliked, by trying to come up with a list of reasons why exactly I disliked them so much. Anything to keep my mind from wandering back to my father and Buck, the prison, Emry, the kiss. Oh, the kiss. It was etched into my memory and made me almost tingle with the excitement of remembering, but everything else that took place directly afterward would return to my mind as well. I wasn't doing a good job of blocking it out. I frowned and began playing with the tiny black straw in my drink and watched as the ice melted, watering down the mixture.

The door of the bar opened, and I could feel the cold air against the back of my calves. I shivered and heard the loud voices of what sounded like a boisterous group of men entering. They were laughing and talking so loudly as to draw attention to themselves that I immediately knew that they were already drunk. They stayed behind me for a few moments chatting on, but the one man's speech was so slurred that I couldn't really understand what he was talking about. I tried to block out their conversation and return my attention back to stirring my drink. I took another sip.

One of them that I supposed belonged to the group came around to the corner of the bar to my right where I could catch a glimpse of him. He was a middle-aged man with a heavy navy-blue coat on.

"How about a round of shots for my friends, Richie?" he asked the bartender clear and loud enough that I was sure every other person in the bar knew what he was ordering.

The bartender reached underneath the table and pulled out six shot glasses and lined them in a row on top of the counter. He began filling each of them with a brown-colored liquor.

"Come on over here, boys!" he shouted, motioning for the rest of his crew.

I felt a little withdrawn again as I saw that the rest of the group of men were all just about as tall and husky as the first guy. They all had similar colored coats, some with ball caps on, others with varying degrees of winter hats, but there were six of them that gathered in the corner, all holding up a shot glass in the air. One of them mumbled something. A toast perhaps? And then they all mumbled in agreement after him and downed the liquor in a grizzly fashion.

Then every inch of me suddenly wanted to make a sprint for the door as I caught a glimpse of one of the men. Just a few feet away from me, standing alongside the man who had ordered shots, was none other than Buck Brady. I immediately looked away so as to not draw attention to myself by making any sort of eye contact. My hand snapped away from my drink as I pulled both hands up into the sleeve of my sweatshirt and lowered my head so that my hair would fall over that side of my face. I had to get out of here. Now.

My head began spinning again as I felt as if I wanted to melt like the ice in my drink and slither away under the door to get out of here. Of all places to run into him. I didn't know Buck was a drinker. If he was like the rest of his jolly crew, he probably had had one too many also.

I wondered how I was going to be able to get out of here without being noticed. What could I do? If I stood up and walked away, surely he would notice. He was right *there*. I could practically reach out and touch him. Maybe I should run. That's what I wanted to do, make a mad dash for my car. I still thought it was too risky. He would recognize me for sure. But what other choice did that leave me with? I had to continue sitting here and pray with all my might that he just would be too drunk to care or take notice. He hadn't paid any attention to me yet. Maybe tonight would be my lucky night. Then again, the rest of the day hadn't exactly been what I would label as lucky. *Far from it, in fact*, I thought. The last thing I needed right now was another confrontation with Buck Brady. He'd probably try to hit me again, only this time my father wouldn't be around to stop him. I remembered the piercing hatred I had seen burning in his eyes earlier. I shivered.

"You need another one?"

I looked up. The bartender stood directly in front of me, motioning toward the glass sitting in front of me. I looked at my drink. It was almost gone. I had drunk it already. Panic seized me. This would surely draw attention to me. I didn't want to speak, to move, to breathe.

"No, thanks, I'm good," I whispered.

"You sure?"

I wanted to scream. Just go away already. "Yeah."

The group of men were suddenly quiet, a little too quiet. I could feel their stares burning a hole into the side of my face. *Stupid bartender,* I thought. I turned my head to look at them. They were all turned facing me, Buck Brady in the front. We made eye contact.

210

He grinned and walked over to me. He slammed a mason jar full of beer onto the counter beside me. "Well, well, look who it is!" he bellowed out.

He was drunk for sure. I supposed he had figured he had had a long, difficult day as well. I turned my head around and tried to look away. Everyone else seemed to be staring at us too.

"I can't believe perfect, little, Christian girl is sitting here having a drink!" Buck yelled, laughing hysterically at himself. The rest of the men were still in place where they had been before, staring at us. "Gentlemen, I'd like to introduce you to someone. This is none other than Anna James." He patted me on the back and a snarled laugh escaped from his throat.

I remained silent and perfectly still. If I made a run for it now, would they follow me? I didn't want to face them outside in the cold. I'd rather be in here in front of witnesses. Buck seemed a little too unstable. I bet he would follow me just to harass me further. I cursed myself for having made the choice to come here. I would have rather faced my family. Something told me this wasn't going to be pretty. I made eye contact briefly with the bartender who then quickly looked away and made a little more distance between us.

"Need a little pick me up after the day?" Buck asked, still thinking his own words were hilarious for some reason.

"Leave me alone, Buck."

"Aw, what's the matter, Anna? Have you come to drink your woes away? Thinking about never seeing your precious Emry Logan again?"

I could feel his prodding in my temples as they began to ache. I

211

caught a glimpse of the silent group of men standing behind him just watching. They seemed concerned that I was here. Perhaps they were policemen, too. They probably knew everything. Maybe it had been me they had been discussing when they first came in the door. Maybe they hated Emry like Buck did, and hated me, too. I decided not to give Buck the pleasure of any sort of answer. Allowing him to have the knowledge that he was getting to me would only make things worse. Give him the satisfaction of having been able to stir up my emotions again, and he'd probably harass me all night then. If I didn't give him that satisfaction, maybe he and his group of hoodlums would leave.

"I can't believe it's been Emry Logan this whole time." Buck snorted and then threw his hand down on the counter, the beer in his glass shaking as he did so. "He's sick," he said, his eyes burning with fury and hatred. "A sick freak."

It was obvious that Emry's slamming Buck into a tree had not been overlooked. Buck had been afraid of Emry that night and ran away. He had been a coward, and he knew it.

"He deserves to rot in jail for the rest of his life, whatever his life even means," he mumbled, picking up his drink and chugging down the remainder of its contents.

One of the other men from the group came over and filled up Buck's cup with more beer from a pitcher. He lingered there to listen to what was going on. Buck didn't even seem to notice that he was there. He continued to point his finger in my face as he talked.

"You have no idea how he's using you," Buck went on. "It

212

seriously makes me sick to my stomach to have seen you … kissing him." He gave a disgusted face like he was about to vomit before picking up his now full glass and taking a few more gulps. "What the hell is the matter with you? I don't even recognize you."

"You don't even know me, Buck," I told him.

"I grew up with you. I know you. I know your family." He shook his head. "I try to kiss you and you give me a black eye, but you'll kiss Emry Logan?" He turned around in a circle as if he were in pain.

So there was a little jealousy combined in there with everything else. I had ruined his self-esteem that night with the whole he cooked me dinner thing.

"Freak of nature. Right?" He looked to the other guy standing there for reassurance who only nodded, his eyes fixated on me. "And your daddy gets you off the hook, as always."

"What's that supposed to mean?" I snapped. "When has he *ever* gotten me off the hook before?" I glared at him then. I didn't care if he was drunk, his assumptions were ludicrous.

He snorted out a chuckle as if I were a hypocrite. "You're a spoiled brat. It's almost like you're an only child in that house with Matthew. I bet you're glad he is the way he is."

I stood up just then, fury now pulsating through me as I looked him straight in the eye. "You would sink so low as to bring Matthew into this, you cold-hearted bastard."

His smirk disappeared as if he had realized what he said. He saw the other men looking at him and instantly shook off whatever guilt I had placed on his conscience. "You disgust me." He spit on the floor. "It's pathetic how stupid you are. You choose someone like Emry Logan to be with, a monster. You're clueless."

"Enlighten me. Please."

"I wasn't sure at first," he began. "I thought he had broken my shoulder from that tree, but then, I hadn't seen him hit me or anything. It was weird. Something that's never happened before."

I tried to keep eye contact, afraid he'd lose his train of thought and stop feeding me information if I looked away.

"It's a good thing I found that witchy woman," he continued. "She knew what he was, what to do."

"What witchy woman?" I asked.

He ignored me, speaking even louder. "We couldn't let his kind continue about in Seneca. No, we had to rid our society of him. He needed to be locked up, and for good."

"You think he's dangerous?"

He snorted. "Of course he's dangerous! That's how you like them, though, don't you, Anna? You like the thrill of chance, the ones with all the magical powers. Don't you worry; we got him rounded up good. We only hunt to capture and never release."

"You have a big mouth, Mr. Brady."

We both turned toward the sound of the voice. Mrs. Anderson strolled through the door as she carelessly came our way. She wasn't the least intimidated by the group of intoxicated men beside me. I narrowed my eyes at her. Then I suddenly put the pieces together. Mrs. Anderson was Buck's "witchy woman."

"Gather up your things now and be on your way," she instructed him in a very calm fashion, placing one palm on Buck's back and guiding him toward the others.

Buck looked as though he had instantly sobered up. His eyes looked full of shame now as he said nothing more, just did as he was told and strolled over to the corner of the counter where the others were putting on their winter hats and gloves. I watched in awe at the power she seemed to have over each and every one of them. Was that the same kind of control she had over my father as well? Then one by one they turned and almost formed a line as they walked toward the door without glancing my way again. Mrs. Anderson was the last one in line. She gave me a quick look as she strolled by. Our eyes met for a second. I couldn't get any kind of read on her. There was no facial expression at all. There was something peculiar about the way she moved and the way she spoke. She was a witchy kind of strange, as Buck had described her. I sat there for a moment, contemplating the words he had used. *We only hunt to capture and never release.* A modern day witch hunt. Only Mrs. Anderson was the witch and Emry was the one she had made everyone believe was the threat, not her. They listened to her. Did she have some sort of spell over them? I wasn't so quick to rule it out as I would have been yesterday. Today was a big eye opener for me, a revelation. Things weren't what they seemed. There was magic and mystery in the world, even if it wasn't given birth in this world, it still lingered here and walked among us. Seneca, the new Salem. And they weren't done with my Emry yet.

Chapter 11

I woke up the next morning, realizing I had slept in. It was nearly 10:00. I couldn't remember the last time I had slept that late. The sun illuminated my room as I opened my eyes and winced. I had left the curtains open last night, something I couldn't ever remember doing before.

I sat up in bed and took a moment to gather my thoughts. What time had I finally had the courage to leave the bar and find my way home last night? I had sat there and thought about Buck and Mrs. Anderson for hours, drinking a few more rum and Cokes in the meantime. I remember pulling in front of the house and not seeing a single light on. I remember trying to be careful as to not make any noise when entering the house, and I also recalled how I had tripped over a stray shoe right inside the doorway and making a loud thump as I tumbled to the hardwood floor, but no one came to see what had happened. Everyone had been asleep. I had wondered what my father had told my family of our eventful day in Seneca County Prison. I didn't know how I should act, or what kinds of things Carlin would say to me if she did know.

I sat still and listened. Silence. Had everyone just let me sleep and gone about their day without the slightest curiosity of my well-being, or where I had been late last night without even a phone call to tell them I was all right? I jumped out of bed and made my way to the hallway. My hair stunk of cigarette smoke and my mouth stuck together miserably from the aftertaste of the rum.

I took a peek inside my mother's bedroom. The bed was neatly made and everything tidied up. I tiptoed downstairs. The TV was off, and there was no one in either the dining room or kitchen. The dishes were stacked up on a thick white towel, some still dripping. Everyone was gone for the day, even Matthew. I felt relieved, yet slightly uneasy about the situation. I rubbed my eyes, as if to persuade myself that I wasn't still asleep. This house was rarely empty. I couldn't help but feel slightly abandoned at the moment.

I took the opportunity to go back upstairs and take a long, hot shower. I needed to get ready for today's to-do list. I pushed the thoughts of my family to the furthest corners of my mind and brought back the details of what I had decided to do. I had to find out exactly what was going on. Today I would go give Lainey Tritt a little visit.

***

As I was pulling my car into the driveway that belonged to the little run-down home, my stomach fluttered with a sensation of anxiety. I wasn't sure exactly why. Perhaps it was because this was the place that Emry had grown up, where he had spent his time as a child and a teenager, or perhaps it was because it had an eerie appearance to it that made me want to turn around. Was I at the wrong place? No, this was the right house for certain. The mailbox said TRITT in large, handwritten white

217

letters. I pulled my car up to the top of the driveway and turned off the motor. I stepped out into the cold air and let my lungs take a refreshing deep breath as my eyes studied the exterior of the home.

It was small and looked almost unbalanced as the top where the foundation stuck out of the ground on one side didn't match the opposite side. It was as if the one end was sinking into the ground little by little. It had jagged grayish siding that was peeling off in sections and a roof that also had missing shingles in spots. There was one single window facing this part of the house, and it was closed by pale yellow curtains from the inside. A stray chicken brushed past my foot just then, making me jump. I looked down at it for a moment, curiously. I watched as a few other hens came around the corner of the yard to follow that one. There was an old shed to the far right of the yard. It was falling down and obviously hadn't been maintained in years. I imagined that there had been animals in there at one time or another. Perhaps cows? Horses? My eyes shifted to large rocks sticking out of the snow and forming a line around the house. I stepped on each one as they led me to the front porch, which was just as broken as the rest of the place. I cautiously stepped up onto the floor of the porch, hoping I wouldn't fall through. The screen door groaned painfully as I pried it open. I searched for a doorbell. There wasn't one, so I lifted my fist and tapped lightly on the door.

No answer. An old run-down red Ford truck was parked on the other side of the house. It must have been from the 1950s I guessed. I pounded on the door a little louder this time.

I backed away as I heard the door being unlocked and opened. A frail, elderly woman with frazzled, long gray hair sticking up every which way possible gave me a blank stare as I stood before her.

"Yes?" she asked, annoyed or angry that I had disturbed her, I wasn't sure.

"Um, hi," I said. "Are you Lainey Tritt?"

Her thick eyebrows raised above the large glasses that sat on her nose. "Do I know you?"

I shook my head. "No. I'm, uh … a friend of Emry's, and I wanted to know if you could answer a few questions for me."

"You'll have to speak up," she said, pointing to her left ear. "Hard of hearing."

I sighed, frustrated already. "I know Emry," I said more clearly and with more volume this time.

"Oh." She smiled, revealing a row of half-rotted, half-missing front teeth. "Well, come on in." She stepped back from the door so I could go inside.

It was cold and damp in the house, and I realized that Lainey was wearing a heavy coat. *She is probably unable to keep a good fire going herself*, I thought. The house was a mess and very dirty.

A few cats glared at me as I strolled by them, their only movement the flicker of their tails as they eyed me.

There were a few pictures up on the walls. I glanced at them as I went by. None of them were of Emry as a child as I had hoped to see. They were older pictures, mostly groups of people, and they were in black and white, some of them faded from the sunlight draining them over the years.

"How is he doing?" Lainey asked, taking a seat on an old green recliner at the back of the L-shaped living room.

I took a seat on the edge of a matching green couch directly across from her, a cat on either arm rest. "He's good," I replied. She had no clue he was in jail I guessed. Emry had said she had dementia.

My eyes shifted to the mess of papers on the floor. That's when I really took notice of how bad this place smelled. It was a combination of garbage and cat feces. I looked around to see if I could find the exact source of the smell, but there were so many things on the floor that it made it too difficult to pinpoint.

"And how is Candy doing?" she questioned me. "I was glad to see those two marry."

I cringed at the name and also the memory that Lainey was rekindling. She had no idea they were divorced. I decided I might as well just play along. It was amazing that this woman was able to stay here on her own. I only imagined how inefficient she was at cooking and bathing herself as I could tell by her housekeeping that she was mentally not equipped to be living here on her own anymore. Then again, she was probably the type that wanted to stay in her home until she died. A nursing home was probably out of the question for her. I doubted she even went to the doctor's.

"Candace is good, too." I realized I had said her full name. I just couldn't bring myself to call her Candy. It seemed like the kind of name that belonged to a stripper.

Lainey nodded her head approvingly at my brief answers and then looked up at me. "How did you say you knew Emry again?"

"We work together," I blurted out.

"I don't remember what you said your name was."

"Anna. Anna James."

"Anna James," she repeated, biting her lower lip and squinting up toward the ceiling as if in deep concentration. "I believe I recall that name. You're that preacher man's kid, ain't ya?"

Wow, I thought. I couldn't believe she would know something like that, let alone remember it.

"That's right. I am."

Lainey nodded and stared at me in silence.

I looked at the orange and black cat to my right. Its eyes were closed as it slept carelessly on the arm of the hair covered piece of furniture. "You know, Emry has told me so much about you. He said how you adopted him."

"I did," she said proudly. "My late husband and I never had any kids. I decided I didn't want to be alone no more. I went and found myself Emry. A perfect match." She pressed her lips together and smiled.

I flashed an uneasy smile back at her. "So was it hard to be a single parent?"

"What was that?"

I swallowed and took a deep breath so I could yell it out at her once more. "I said, was it hard being a single parent?"

"Nah," she replied. "Emry was a good boy. He never got into much

221

trouble. He never said much. Boys will be boys."

We sat there in silence for a moment. I wasn't sure what to say to her next.

"You do know what happened to my late husband, don't you?" she said suddenly.

I raised my eyebrows. "No."

Lainey changed her position in the chair as an odd smirk crossed her lips. "That nasty Earl Connor was sneaking around here again."

I tried very hard to make myself concentrate on what she was saying. I felt so distracted with the way she looked, by knowing this was where Emry lived, by her strange smile directly after mentioning her husband's death, by the cats. It was exhausting to have to sit here and really focus.

"Who is...?"

"He was a looker, that boy," she quickly interrupted me. "Handsome devil. Black, slicked back hair in beautiful waves and dark eyes. All the girls went crazy for him. But me, no, I knew better. That Earl Connor wasn't getting to me, no, sir. He always comes around, but I told him no, to get on out of here. I would have nothing to do with him. But he wouldn't have it. No one had told him no before."

Lainey was speaking so fast now. I was glad she paused so my brain could try to catch up. "So what happened?"

She smirked again. "Well, he knew I was a married woman. He knew Larry. They had graduated together and all. But he still didn't care. He came around, and I straightened him out and put him in his place good.

222

Well, that must have done it. Earl Connor, he snapped. I came home one day and found Larry hanging from one of those slaughtering hooks out there in that shed." She lifted her arm to point toward the door. I had already guessed she was referring to the one with the roof caving in that I had noticed on my way in. "The tip of the hook right through his neck. It was awful."

I cringed at the picture she was creating in my mind. "You think Earl Connor did this because you … rejected him?"

She nodded. "Oh, I know he did it. He stabbed Larry first before hanging him up there. Awful, just awful."

"How do you know it was him?"

"Such a waste of life. Poor Larry," she mumbled, ignoring my question.

I wondered then if what she had said was even a true statement. How could I take anything she said as the truth? She had severe dementia, and her memory couldn't be that good at the moment. Then again, she knew who I was and remembered my father.

"A murderer in Seneca?" I had never heard of a so-called Earl Connor before, one who killed the husbands of the women he wanted for himself. It sounded too made up to be true.

She nodded, her disheveled hair springing back and forth with the sudden movement. "He was a sly one. Sometimes he still comes around here, but I always say the same thing. He'll never get to me."

I lowered my eyebrows. There was no way she knew what she was saying now, right?

"Earl Connor. You remember that name, and you remember to stay away from him and his good looks, too."

"I'll do that," I whispered.

"How is Candy doing, by the way?"

I sighed. The noise stirred up one of the cats on the armrests. It turned to stare at me and flicked its tail in annoyance. "She's fine." The words came out just as annoyed as I had imagined the cat was sitting next to me.

"Everyone thinks of a kid in a different way, you know?" Lainey continued. I realized it probably had been some time since her last human interaction or conversation. "I didn't give birth to him, but he's my son. You can put your nose up to me all you want. You think adopting a little boy who has no one is still not right. It's just not right to you people, but I don't care what you say."

"Lainey, I didn't say anything…"

"You come in here with your snobby attitude and your good clothes."

I looked down at myself. Good clothes? Anything would be considered good compared to living in your own filth.

Lainey stood up just then. She shook her finger toward me. "At least I didn't pretend like all of you!"

I started to panic. She was getting upset. What could she be capable of? I wasn't sure. Her mood and affect were so unstable. I stood up too, not sure if I should make a run toward the front door or not. My eyes shifted toward it, to the door knob, on how to maneuver it in a hurry if the need may suddenly arise.

"No, all of you are fake!" she cried out. "When they adopted you, it was the same thing, but they made *me* feel bad about it and they just pretended that you were theirs, but you ain't never belonged to them and you know it, don't you?"

I gasped in horror. Now she was trying to accuse me of being *adopted*? She was truly crazy.

"I can see it in your eyes!" she went on shouting and still shaking and pointing her index finger at me, taking a few steps closer. "You've always known! They're convincing, I know. They tried to convince me, too!" She stepped even closer still, too close for comfort.

Suddenly, I ducked underneath her arm and sprinted toward the front door. My hand quickly twisted the door knob and I swung it open and looked back at Lainey, who had a wild look in her eyes. She remained positioned as before, still pointing to where I had just been standing. She turned her head then and our eyes met once again.

"You'd better be careful. Earl Connor might be lurking in the shadows out there." She grinned. I stepped out onto the porch and slammed the front door behind me. I hesitantly looked around.

Nothing but the falling down shed and a ground full of snow. I carefully walked on the rotten floorboards of the porch and was so glad when I was finally back in the safety of my own car again. I started it up and sped away from Lainey Tritt as fast as I could.

She had genuinely freaked me out. I never wanted to step foot in that place again. It made me feel stranger still to know that Emry had grown up there in that creepy place. Perhaps it wasn't always so creepy? Who knows? I kept getting flashes of images of Lainey's husband hanging from a hook dead in that shed. No wonder no one ever kept it up. *Stupid*, I told myself. *That story isn't even true.* She's just a woman without a properly functioning mind. I should be feeling sorrier for her than I was. She was living there in that filthy house in her own delirious world. The thought of another world sparked up the memory of Evadere. How I longed to be there right now where I had felt safe and perfectly at ease for once.

The houses blurred past me as I sped down the road, barely even conscious of my driving. Why would such a thing come from Lainey's mouth about my being adopted? It couldn't be true. I felt the tears come on quickly, and I angrily wiped them away with the back of my hand. I couldn't sit here and allow myself to get upset over something I knew wasn't true. My baby pictures were plastered all over the house. There hadn't ever been even the slightest mention of it to me before by anyone. Surely *someone* would've slipped it to me if it were true. *That's because it's not true*, I convinced myself and slowed down my driving speed as I began to calm down a little. But a sick feeling in the pit of my stomach lingered. It was that small portion of doubt that I knew nothing about everything, that I had been blinded for most of my life and that nothing I knew was of any sort of truth that everything around me was only as my parents wanted me to see it. I had to find out for myself. I had to look my mother straight in the eyes and find out what exactly the truth was. There was no way around it. If it wasn't true, she could tell me I was being ridiculous and that would be that. If it was true, then … I shuddered at the mere thought of it. Everything around me would change even more drastically than it already had.

The anxiety I had had before about being around my house and my family didn't even occur to me now. That ache that Lainey Tritt had put there was still in my stomach, eating away at me piece by piece.

I pulled in front of the house and got out of my car. I didn't even bother to put on a pair of gloves or hat as the wind whipped around me. I didn't even seem to notice it as I took long, steady strides up the walk, then up the steps, opening the front door without any sort of hesitation. I shut the door behind me and listened. The TV was on, and Matthew sat in front of it. He grinned and waved to me. I waved back and stomped through the house, my boots still on and leaving wet shoe prints behind me.

"Anna, is that you?" I heard my mother ask from the kitchen.

I took a few more long steps into the room and leaned against the kitchen table. My mother stood over the counter as she peeled potatoes and tossed them into a pot beside her. "You slept in late this morning, Honey. Are you feeling okay?" Then she turned to look at me, and her eyebrows lowered in hesitation. "Anna?" She put down the peeler and potato to spin the entire way around to face me.

"What's the matter?"

"You tell me," I spit out.

She gave me a questioning look. "What do you mean?"

So my father hadn't told her about our wonderful adventures at the prison yesterday. Or, maybe he had told her, and she decided to act

227

clueless about it. Sometimes she did things like that, ignored circumstances as if they never existed and went about her merry way. No, I decided. He hadn't told her.

I swallowed down the lump forming in my throat.

"You look pale. Honey, please sit down," she insisted in a soft voice, reaching out to touch my arm.

I jerked away. "I'm fine standing," I snapped at her.

She gave me a look of uncertainty as if she didn't recognize the person standing before her. Perhaps she was unrecognizable to me, too. Perhaps this whole family thing was merely a charade. Maybe Lainey Tritt was right. Maybe I didn't have a *real* family.

"Am I yours?"

"What?"

I shut my eyes tightly and shook my head as the words escaped out. "Am I adopted?"

The look on her face just then was one of pure horror as it twisted up in a moment of grief as well as deceit. I gasped, my hand extending over my gaping mouth. So Lainey Tritt had been right all along. No wonder she remembered my family. They stuck out as the other ones who had adopted a child.

"I can't believe it," I whispered. It felt as if my legs were going to give out from under me. I caught myself on the edge of the table. The tears were there but barely. It was as if the shock of this moment was even more powerful than the overwhelming urge to cry.

"Anna, please!" My mother grabbed my arm and pulled me away

from where Matthew could hear us speak. She peeked in at him as he was still happily watching his show as she led me into my father's study just off the dining room and shut the door behind us. "Please look at me," she begged.

My eyes fell to the floor. I couldn't look at her. I just couldn't.

"Say something," she pleaded again.

I shook my head and leaned against the front of my father's huge cherry desk. My head was still lowered. "You're unbelievable," I snapped. "You want *me* to say something? It seems to me that I'm the one owed an explanation here."

My mother sighed. You could tell she was trying to gather her thoughts. She always did this. She thought too much before she spoke. It always drove me crazy and even more so now. I had always thought of her as being so honest, one of the best people I had ever met in the way of values and the goodness of the heart, but now all I could think about was that her pausing to say anything meant that she was only stalling to allow herself more time to come up with an even better cover-up lie. She played the part well. Her and my father deserved an academy award.

"No more lies!" I shouted, weary of her lingering silence.

She began to cry. "It's true," she cried out. "It's true." She covered her face with her hands as she began to sob.

I looked up. Seeing her like that almost made me feel sorry for her again, but no, I would stand my ground and demand nothing but the truth.

"I'm so sorry, Anna." She continued to wail as she bent downward toward the carpet. "It wasn't supposed to happen like this."

"No, you hoped it would never happen at all; that I'd never find out!"

She looked up at me, her face soaked in tears. "I never meant to hurt you. I have always felt as if you were truly mine, Anna."

"The *truth*," I insisted again, crossing my arms. I went over and pulled her to a standing position. I looked her straight in the eye so that she would know I meant it. I was so tired of these games.

She gave me an apologetic look again. "I could never have children. Something's wrong with me."

She shook her head. "I didn't know if I could feel complete without having children in the house."

"So Matthew, too?"

She nodded. "Yes."

I tried to think back to the time when I was little and Matthew had come into the house. I would have been around four. I couldn't remember what it was like before he came or when he came. I had been too little to understand at the time, I supposed. "Why didn't you tell me? How could you have kept this from me?"

"I thought it was best this way. I'm sorry. I was wrong."

"You're just sorry you got caught."

"I know you're angry. You have every right to be, but please know that I love you, Anna, more than anything, and I have never wanted anything but the best for you and your brother."

She was probably right. I shouldn't be so furious at her, but I was. This was just too much to bear right now on top of everything else.

"It's hard to find out, but it changes nothing," my mother continued.

"It changes *everything*," I corrected her.

"Please," she began to beg again. "I love you."

"It's like I'm living a nightmare. Maybe I'm not really even here. Is somebody going to pop out and tell me I'm dead next, that I'm really just some spirit wandering around?"

"What are you talking about?"

I took a deep breath. I had been rambling. I had to calm myself down and think clearly.

"I know it's a huge shock, but you are still my daughter and I'm your mother."

"Who are they?"

"What?"

"My real parents?"

"Oh." She sat down in a large chair stuffed into the corner of the room. She ran her palms over the smooth leather exterior. "I don't know."

I raised my eyebrows at her.

"I really don't know, Anna. You had been abandoned as an infant. Someone had found you and took you to the adoption agency where I then got you shortly after you were born."

Abandoned. The word rolled around in my head like a heavy log. "So my birthday?"

"Well, the doctors were certain that you had only been a few days old when you were found. I guess it may not be completely accurate, but

…"she whispered.

Unbelievable. I had no real name, no real birthday. I might as well not exist at all.

"Anna, you can't tell Matthew. He'd never understand."

I glared at her. "I'm not going to tell Matthew," I said with irritation in my voice.

"Hardly anyone knew," she said. "Please tell me how you found out."

I hesitated. Should I tell her? It didn't seem to me that she deserved to know. "Lainey Tritt," I suddenly blurted out.

She removed a tissue from her pocket and began dabbing her nose with it. "Who's that?"

"She's the woman who adopted Emry Logan."

My mother's face twisted up again at the announcement of the name. What did it mean to her if my father hadn't told her about our little rendezvous yesterday in the prison courtyard?

"What do you know of him?"

"I should ask the same of you." I stared at her, wondering what my father told her and what he didn't. It was obvious she knew *something*.

"Well," she began hesitantly again. "I probably shouldn't be telling you this, but I guess I will anyway."

I tapped my foot impatiently.

"A group of townspeople in Seneca have gathered together against him. He's dangerous, a man to stay away from," she said.

"Dangerous how?"

232

She eyed me as if still trying to figure out how I knew of him. "A threat to society. A killer. He …"she hesitated, but then looked at my face and knew she had to spill everything she knew now. It was the only way to regain what little trust I had of her. "There's something different about him. He has this special gift. Well, I shouldn't even call it a gift. He's into black magic, Anna. He worships Satan."

I almost laughed aloud, but I quickly removed the smirk from my face. "How do you know this? Does he go around wearing all black and have horns growing out of his head?"

She frowned at my sarcasm. "Anna, you have to believe me." A sound similar to a snort escaped from my throat.

"Of course you have every right not to, but about this, I am telling you the truth. Your father has told me things about him. He isn't someone to take lightly. Please tell me that you're having nothing to do with him and his kind. Mrs. Anderson knows things."

His kind. How very ironic. Emry didn't even know who his kind was. My father thought he was a devil worshipper. Now it was starting to make sense. He would feel it his duty to rid the town of such an evil, and so they had formed a group of people to seek him out and take him down, to lock him up so he wouldn't be able to get anyone else involved with his witchery. I was assuming that the only thing that Mrs. Anderson knew was what Buck had told her about his ability to move things, things such as Buck.

I took a deep breath and looked at the woman I had always assumed was my birth mother. She had always seemed fragile, yet had this strength about her, a way with people that could calm them down and get them to trust what she said, but now that image was completely destroyed. She only looked fragile, sad, and pathetic. I almost wanted to shake her and ask how she got this way, but then I really should be shaking myself and asking the question of why hadn't I ever figured this out before? Why had nothing seemed out of place as far as my belonging until today?

"So Mrs. Anderson knows things, you said. What do you mean? If she knows things, doesn't that make her a witch, which technically would put her into the category of *her* practicing black magic also?" I crossed my arms and raised my eyebrows at her.

She began chewing on her nails nervously. "Mrs. Anderson is … different herself, but not in that way. She can be trusted. She knows what she's talking about. She's helped gather a group of strong men in the community, who can also be trusted and who will help rid Seneca of any black magic and send out the message to anyone who might be like Emry Logan, that we don't tolerate such practices here. We're a God-fearing community. They're actually meeting again tonight. All of them."

"The witch hunting the devil. Interesting." I couldn't hide the smirk this time. What she was saying was all too ridiculous. Of course, they probably weren't to blame for their lack of understanding of what was really going on with Emry. Worshipping Satan was the only kind of logic they would pin on him for what had happened that night with Buck.

"I really shouldn't be telling you this," my mother blurted out, pacing back and forth in front of the chair.

"I just don't get how you can trust anything he says."

"Who?"

"Father."

"What do you mean?"

"Oh, come on, as if you haven't recognized it."

She gave me another puzzling glance. "I really don't know what you mean."

"Oh, come on!" I shouted out. "The affair. Why do you even make me have to say it? You have to already know."

She became very still and very quiet, more tears streaming down her face as she stood there and stared at me. "He's not having an affair," she whispered.

"Of course he is! I *saw* him with *her*. He tells you he's going over there to talk about what? Satanic people in Seneca? Don't you think they've spent a little too much time together *alone*?"

Her eyes moved to the floor and she crossed her hands in front of her and clasped them together.

"You don't know what you're saying."

"No, of course not," I snapped. "I never do. I don't know anything. Everyone treats me like a child, a child that's not even theirs to begin with."

She ignored my remark about the adoption. "John's a good man. A great man. He loves me. He loves all of us. You're mistaken," she said in a voice so soft I had to strain to hear every word.

"Well, I've said my peace about the subject. I won't bring it up again." *Pathetic*, I thought to myself. I was almost glad she wasn't my real mother now. I didn't want to be anything like her. I headed toward the door and then looked back. She was still standing there, staring at the floor. "Just tell me one thing."

She refused to make eye contact with me.

"Why won't you stand up to him?"

She remained very still for a few moments before making any kind of response. "I trust him."

Chapter 12

I shivered as I opened my eyes. The chill of the night felt as if it had crept into my bones as I huddled my arms around my stiff body. Piles of snow were heaping all around me. I squinted as my burning eyes seemed to refuse to open, revealing how tired I still was. I could see that most of my car was now covered with snow also. My hand fumbled around blindly in the air until it felt the dangling keys sticking out of the ignition. The car whined from the cold as it finally gave in and started, and I waited for it to warm up before I could blast the heater.

I had fallen asleep in my car. I was sitting in an abandoned parking lot of a boarded up building that had once been a local grocery store before the main stream of commercial food places pushed their way into town and bullied the local companies out of business. I pulled my coat around me tightly.

Somehow while I slept, it must have fallen off of my shoulders, and it, too, was cold from lying on the seat beside me.

The air shooting out of the heater felt warmer. I sighed in relief as it hit my skin. I turned the knob to high and just sat there, trying to stretch out my rigid limbs. I tried to clear my mind, too. Hadn't I had a strange dream? Oh yes, I remembered, it had been about Emry. I smiled. It wasn't strange at all. It had been wonderful. We had been lounging on the sparkling beaches of Evadere, his arms wrapped around me. I laughed at the irony of it all. I had first thought that he had only imagined such a place, and here I was recreating it in my mind. I felt my heart ache suddenly as I realized how much I longed to be near him again, to touch his perfectly smooth tan skin again and feel the warmth of his breath on my neck. I closed my eyes and tried to hold still, waiting for a numbness to come on to block out my misery of being forcefully separated from him. Then I remembered my mother, crying on her knees in my father's office and telling me that I was not their child. And the numbness came then, another sort of pain but less severe and different from the one I felt when thinking of Emry. This I could tolerate, and so I allowed myself to continue feeling it.

The heater began to thaw me out as I thought about how I had gotten to the point of falling asleep in my car in the middle of nowhere in the first place. My eyes shifted across the street. Just almost out of sight behind a line of barren trees I could see the edge of Buck's driveway. I hoped he hadn't come home while I was asleep. I looked at the green glowing numbers on my dashboard: 10:21p.m. I had been asleep for almost an hour, and the snow had fallen heavily between now and then, too.

Great, just great, I thought to myself as I made sure my boots were on tightly. I reached in the backseat for the ice scraper. I exited the vehicle and began to clean off the front windshield. The night had suddenly become very peaceful and calm. There wasn't a single snowflake in the sky, and there were no clouds. It was clear and brisk, the moon shining down bright against the blinding snow. Even the abandoned parking lot looked serene and beautiful, renewed by the fresh coat of white it had just received.

Out of the edge of my vision, I saw taillights heading up the driveway leading to Buck's house. My heart skipped a beat as I felt a sense of urgency rush over me. My hand brushed off the snow in long, rapid motions as I headed to the back of the car and cleaned off the rear windshield as well. I looked down at my boots as they sunk into the snow. A couple of inches, at least, had to have fallen, I guessed. I finished up the car and hurried back inside to the warmth. I shuddered, my eyes glued to edge of the driveway. I wasn't sure how this was all going to go down tonight. I wasn't even sure if I had a plan.

My mother had told me that the whole group was going to be meeting tonight, which had led me here to his creepy lot where I could be hidden, as well as be able to see Buck at the same time. I had hoped that he would come home first to change out of his police uniform before going to meet up with Mrs. Anderson and the rest of the group, and I was glad I had been right. I was also glad that I hadn't slept any longer, or else I would have missed his coming home at all. Now I had to wait until he had changed and somehow follow him to this meeting. That was all I knew for now. When I got there, I had no idea what I was going to do then. Being a stalker didn't come easily to me. Too much anxiety was attached to it.

My mind shifted to Emry again. The whole thing angered me. They thought he was pure evil, and I thought he was pure heaven. I wondered when I'd be able to see him again. It was too painful to even consider that it would be never. It was something I just wouldn't allow myself to accept. Things couldn't end where they had between us. Life wasn't that cruel. Was it? Everything else was falling apart around me. Surely Emry was the only solid thing I had left to grasp onto. He was the only thing I had going for me now, my only sense of belonging, my escape from the bitter reality of realizing that nothing else in this world had been real up until now. The aching returned in my heart. It hurt so badly I was struggling to breathe. Whatever it took, I had to find something out tonight or the chance might be lost forever; the chance for Emry to be freed from those bars that locked him inside, away from the rest of the world, and also from me.

I saw the first traces of headlights coming back down the driveway. Buck had changed quickly.

Perhaps he was running late. Without stopping, his vehicle pulled out onto the road and drove away in the opposite direction from where I was. I began to panic slightly as my mind raced with what I should do. I started to count slowly in my mind. How many seconds should I let pass before pulling out behind him? I had to keep some sort of distance or he would know something was up. No one would be on the roads tonight with all the snow that had just accumulated on the ground. But then I thought I should probably just go for it right now. I couldn't risk the chance of him getting too far ahead where I couldn't see him turning off and not be able to know where he went.

My foot pressed down on the accelerator. I felt the snow underneath my tires as I pushed harder on it and began to slide slightly. I made it out to the road, relieved I hadn't gotten stuck, and attempted to be alert and cautious, although the aching along with the exhaustion that I was feeling was a weary combination.

Where was Buck? I couldn't see him at all, but then I realized that I could just follow his car tracks.

This wasn't going to be as difficult as I thought, and it was more discrete this way as Buck couldn't see a car behind him at all. I'd raise no suspicion.

I followed the tracks for what seemed like endless miles as the roads were very slippery, and I tried to be cautious so I wouldn't end up in the ditch. I hadn't seen any other cars on the road at all. It was almost 11:00 p.m. before Buck's tire tracks darted off to a section toward the outskirts of Seneca.

I began driving down a familiar back road. It led directly toward Mrs. Anderson's house. It was the same road that Buck had gotten the flat tire on the day we caught my father with Mrs. Anderson on her front porch. I felt my heart speed up. *Of course this is where they would meet*, I thought. It shouldn't be that much of a surprise. Her house was the perfect location, out of the way and private. She lived alone. Perhaps even her sons had been let in on what was happening. It was just so nerve racking to be here again. I didn't like the feeling this place gave me.

I remembered there was another lane just before Mrs. Anderson's main driveway. I assumed it had been created for another access for farm equipment to get up to the fields. I pulled my car into that lane. It had a little hill to it as I reached the top, and then I felt my tires sliding as I began to go backward down the hill. I pressed the brake, and the back end of the car fishtailed to the side of the lane. I pulled the emergency brake. The car lurched to a sideways stop. I took a deep breath and decided against trying to start over again at the bottom of the lane, afraid I'd get myself stuck for sure. At least this way I was fairly certain I could get back out of here.

I began piling on layers of clothes and winter garments, finishing off with a heavy pair of gloves, a thick wool hat and a fuzzy warm scarf. I twisted it around the back of my head and tied it in a gigantic knot, securing it into place. I was wearing almost all dark-colored clothes. I felt around under my seat for the flashlight that my father had insisted I keep in my car, grateful that it was still there. I turned it on. It worked. I shoved it in the front of my coat pocket and my keys on the other side.

Well, are you ready to do whatever it is you're going to do tonight? I asked myself. I pictured Emry's face in my mind again, his arms around me as he had been in my dream. I let the painful emotion that followed come on for a moment before jumping out of the car and quietly shutting the door behind me.

The night was so serene without any wind that it was eerie. There was always wind in Seneca. I could even hear my footsteps crunching into the old snow underneath the new, the old frozen solid. I cut through the little patch of woods toward Mrs. Anderson's house. I didn't even need to use my flashlight. The moon provided enough light to see what was in front of me.

I rounded the corner of the driveway and crossed over onto the

242

piece of land in front of her house, instead of walking any farther down the actual driveway. I found an old, broken down tractor that had been rusting away for years sitting a few yards away and ducked down beside one of its massive tires, knowing that the house was directly in front of me now. I got down on all fours and stretched my neck out far enough to get a good look at what was going on inside the house. Not a single light was on. It sat in front of me, still and dark. No one was there? My thoughts began to swirl. Had I missed where Buck's tracks had gone? No, I was certain he pulled in here. And there had been fresh tire tracks going to the lane that I had walked across.

I stood. There were no cars parked in front of the house either. I clenched my fists inside the gloves. I tried to think of my next move. My eyes searched all around the house as I walked up to it now, only feet away from the front porch. I headed to the side of the house to where the tracks were. I began to walk along them, my feet leaving prints where the lines were. It led to the back of the house and then up another small hill toward the woods. Buck had driven back here and then into the woods.

My thighs burned from the vigorous exercise of climbing the hill in the deep snow along with the layers of clothing weighing me down. I hoped I wasn't going to have to run away from anyone tonight. I would surely lose the battle if that were the case at the speed I was going now.

I was huffing and puffing, my lungs burning from the cold inhalations when I finally reached the top of the hill and walked forward through the woods to a clearing. I could now hear plenty of noise, people yelling and others clapping their hands together. A haze of smoke lifted up into the clear, starry sky of the winter night as a large bonfire blazed in the middle of the field. A large group of people were gathered around it, their backs to me as they all faced something, someone. I stared in astonishment at the scene before me. What were they doing out here in the middle of the night shouting—more like almost chanting—at each other? And then my eyes caught sight of something else, something shiny above my head. Hanging from the barren, icy tree branches were large pieces of metal that twinkled as they turned and mirrored the reflection of the fire. They were round and had two diagonal lines going through them. They were everywhere. I had no idea what kind of symbol it was, but they made a circle around the field, around the group of people standing in the opening of the field.

I realized suddenly then that I was exposed. The trees I was positioned behind were thin, and the moon was too bright along with the fire that I couldn't stand here forever and not expect to be seen. I quickly searched for a place to hide. I scanned through the trees in fear, praying that there was somewhere I could hide after making it this far.

Through the trees to my left, I caught sight of a rock large enough that I thought I could stoop behind.

I looked back to the group of people in the clearing. They seemed to be focused on whatever was going on in front of them. I made a mad dash for it, not giving it a second thought. It was now or never.

My boots made loud noises with every step as I crunched snow and broke icy branches and twigs beneath my feet. I didn't bother looking over to see if anyone was watching. I couldn't. My lungs felt like they were going to explode when I finally reached the rock and pressed my back against it, trying to catch my breath and calm down as I allowed myself to slide down it and just sit there for a moment. I could hear the voices chanting in unison now, but I couldn't make out what they were saying. When I decided to peek out from behind the rock, I expected someone to be standing there looking back at me. There was no one there. I had made it safely, unnoticed.

The group of people were now circling the bonfire, their arms held high in the air as it seemed they were trying to make their voices carry into the sky. What were they doing? *Singing?* I thought. Was that a hymn I recognized? I strained my ears to try to catch the words, but they were so loud it was as if their voices mumbled together.

"Silence, everyone!" I heard someone yell out clearly above the rest of them. They all stopped moving at once and edged away from the fire, their backs still facing me as someone came down the middle of the group, coming closer to the fire. It was a woman. She was bundled up in just as many layers of winter clothing as I had, but sticking out from the hood overtop of her head was a white lace shawl. Mrs. Anderson.

"I would like to thank everyone for coming on this cold winter's night!" she yelled out, her arms held toward the sky as she did so. "I would like to thank Mr. Barnabas for starting out the ritual so powerfully!"

Mr. Barnabas. I recognized the name right away. It was an older gentleman that went to our church.

I felt my stomach getting sicker by the minute as I listened to her words. Ritual, power. It *was* a modern day witch hunt, only it was as if

245

they were the ones using black magic here. My eyes scanned the men as I searched for my father, but they were all so close in height and all wearing heavy coats and hats. It was impossible to single him out from the rest of the group.

"All of you have been handpicked to save our beloved Seneca, and you were called here tonight to replenish the sanctity of the ritual!" Mrs. Anderson then shouted something out that I couldn't understand. Everyone else seemed to understand what she had said, and they all raised their arms up high along with her.

Another man came forward, standing next to Mrs. Anderson. He was carrying a large wooden pole in each hand, both with circles on the very top.

"These represent the two that have already been found!" she screamed out. "These represent the Satan worshippers! We can't have these men in Seneca, teaching our children the works of the devil!"

"No!" some of the people shouted back in agreement.

"We have to rid ourselves of these dark enemies!" Mrs. Anderson said. "This one!" She pointed to the one in the man's right hand. "Lucas Banesberry, he was powerful in his works. But this one," she yelled out while pointing to the other circle on the wooden pole, "Emry Logan, he is even more dangerous than Lucas Banesberry. He possesses an even greater power and even more intelligence. It's something I've never seen before. We must make sure, my friends, that he never escapes or a great evil will come over all of us, and we shall all be doomed." All of the people shouted in agreement.

"You see, I believe he knows not the extent of the dark power within him. We mustn't give him opportunity to explore it. We must make sure he is locked up behind bars forever, never to be free!"

More people yelled out.

"You are the strong ones of this town. You are the leaders. You have to take control of your town. You have to rid the world of people such as Lucas Banesberry and Emry Logan. No matter what it takes, my friends, Emry Logan cannot be set free!"

"Cannot be set free! Cannot be set free!" they shouted in unison and agreement.

Another metal ornament turned slightly above my head, and I looked up at it curiously as it revolved. I was unnerved and frightened. Mrs. Anderson was crazy. It was as if she had all of these people under some sort of spell of her own. These were respectable, probably most of them Christian, men who were out here in the middle of the woods shouting back at some crazy, old woman who lifted her arms to the sky and hung weird metal objects from the trees. These were her *followers*. My stomach began to churn. I knew I shouldn't be here. I was putting myself in grave danger. If I were to be seen, what would she have them do to me? Kill me? I wouldn't put it past her at this point. My mother said she knew things. Did she have some sort of strength as well? She was making these people hate Emry, but for what reason exactly? There had to be a motive.

I felt a chill go up my spine. I figured that even if this had been the middle of summer, I probably still would be getting chills just by being here. Mrs. Anderson had a strong influence over this group.

Even my father was under her spell. They should be throwing her behind bars for her practice of witchcraft.

"Throw them in the fire!" she commanded the man still holding up the poles. "Throw them in! This is how you destroy evil! You burn it up and watch it wither to nothing!"

The man tossed the wood into the fire. I watched the two round circles, representing heads, I supposed, curl up first and burn in the flames and then the two poles stood there burning as well.

"Only you can seek out the evil and destroy it! Be courageous, my friends! You can't let Emry Logan out! Never let him out of the cage he so rightly deserves to rot in for the rest of his life!" Mrs. Anderson held her arms upward to the sky again. Everyone repeated the action in the same fashion as her. "Drink up, my friends!" She pulled something out from within her coat and outstretched her arm to the fire. "Drink, be filled with peace, and go!"

I watched the first person take a swig of the container Mrs. Anderson had handed them. They passed it onto the next person, and after each one would drink, they would turn and walk away from the bonfire. They formed a single line as they headed to their vehicles parked across the field in a plowed area. They got into their vehicles and drove down another path on the opposite side of the field that must have led to another way out of Mrs. Anderson's farm.

After each man had left and gone, only Mrs. Anderson remained. She still stood in front of the fire, her eyes seemed to be focused on the burning poles that were now blackened and burned through. She stood all alone and very still for a long time. She was also facing in my direction, so I leaned back against the rock, let the coldness settle in until I felt completely numb, even with all of the layers of clothing on, and hoped that she wasn't going to be there for a long time. There was no way I could get out of here while she was facing me like that. She would see me for sure if I made any sudden movements.

I listened to my heart beat within my chest like a drum for a while as I waited. I realized I was scared to death. Never had I expected their meeting to have gone in this direction. Never in a million years could I have ever pictured my father or Buck Brady joining in some sort of ritual like this. Did they believe that they were truly doing good? Was that it? I tried to find some way of reasoning with the logic behind it. I couldn't. It was too creepy for Seneca, way out of the range of normal. I could only decide two things: Mrs. Anderson was not right in the head, and everyone that believed what she said was under the influence of her insanity.

I memorized the other name she had called out as I repeated it again and again. *Lucas Banesberry.* She had said that he had been powerful, too. What significance or relation did this man have to Emry?

It would have to be my next step in finding out anything I could about this Lucas. I doubted I would forget the name. I doubted I would ever be able to forget this night and all its sinister charm.

Halloween had been a few months ago. Maybe someone should have told them. Oh, that's right. They think Emry is the one worshipping the devil.

I wanted to bend my neck over again and see if Mrs. Anderson was still standing there. I was too terrified yet. I couldn't let her see me. I was all alone in these spooky woods, the shiny things dangling above my head, taunting me with their strangeness. I guess this was the kind of thing that Emry had warned me to be careful about. He had had a bad feeling, and he had been so right. Mrs. Anderson had just had a pep rally for her miniature army she had created in Seneca, Ohio, the most normal place in the entire world where nothing out of the ordinary happened. Wow. Even I surprised myself at how blind I had been my entire life to believe any of that. Seneca was turning out to be the epitome of weird. Maybe every place was like this. Or, maybe I had just been so out of it my entire life that I genuinely had no clue about what was going on in the world around me.

I realized that I was beginning to not be able to feel my feet. I sat still for a few more moments, listening to the silence of the night, trying to get enough courage to look around the rock again. *You have to do this*, I told myself. You can't sit here all night and freeze to death.

I turned around slowly and placed one gloved hand on the rock to brace myself as I cautiously moved my head far enough away from the barrier of the rock to get a good look at the bonfire.

No one was there. Mrs. Anderson had gone, but she hadn't walked down the same path as I had come up to get to her house. I was grateful for that anyway. She would have seen my footsteps on the way down. But where had she gone? I scanned the area one final time before deciding it was probably safe enough to stand. I took a few steps away from the rock. Nothing. Still silence. No one was in sight. All the cars had gone, and Mrs.

Anderson had seemed to vanish into thin air. I was trying to debate what I should do. Should I go down the same path as I had come up where I would have to cross in front of Mrs. Anderson's house in order to get back to my car, or should I cross this field and go down the lane that the cars had driven down and see where it led me? But then I thought that Mrs. Anderson had probably left down that path herself. I wanted the way with the less chance of me crossing paths with her. I finally took a deep breath and headed the way I had come up. Hopefully, I wouldn't fall down the slippery hillside.

My feet tingled and burned with every step. I was freezing. I made my protesting body work as I trudged my way down the hill, my eyes wide and alert for any signs of danger as I repeatedly scanned the area in front, around, and behind me every few minutes. This had been such a bad idea. What if I had been caught? I probably would be the one burning in that fire right now. Buck would have gladly thrown me in.

When I had reached the bottom of the hill and also the edge of the woods, I hesitated at the back of the house. There was a dim light coming from one of the windows. Mrs. Anderson must be inside. I tried to listen to see if I heard any voices coming from within. I heard nothing and continued to walk very slowly around the side, and stopped again before I headed into the open area in the front of the house. I put one hand on the siding and peered around. I looked at the front porch. No one was there, and no car was parked out front either. Taking a deep breath, I tried to compose myself. I knew I had to force myself to keep going. I trudged on, starting out slow as I walked directly in front of her home, and then I saw movement from inside one of the windows. I started to sprint as fast as I could with what I was working with, deep snow and layers of clothes, and before I knew it, I was already halfway up the road and my car was in sight, still sideways, up the other farm lane.

I wanted to kiss my steering wheel once I got inside. Had I really made it out of there without being seen? That seemed impossible in itself. I still had to get my car out of here and far away from this place. I think I would have rather been sleeping in Lainey Tritt's house of horror right now than spend another moment in the presence of Mrs. Anderson.

The car roared to life, and I was grateful the battery hadn't given out on me in this bitter cold. I released the emergency brake and turned the steering wheel hard as I attempted to maneuver the car into a straight line. It didn't work, but I was still somehow sliding down the lane, my front end suddenly coming forward, and I slid right out onto the road. I put the car into gear and away I went. The thought of my house was now a welcoming one at the moment. I had never missed my bed so much in my entire life.

Chapter 13

I got to the library early the next morning. I waved to Jeannie, the librarian, as I went in. She waved back. She was used to me being here. I hadn't even bothered going to the antique store yet. It had been a few days since I had gone to the store, since the night that I had changed there from coming from the prison and then going to the bar. It surprised me at how little I even cared if it ever opened again. My mother was up and around once more. She could go tidy it up if she wanted to. I was probably through with that place. I felt as if this attitude was partly her fault. So much had happened in the recent months. I didn't want to be in Seneca anymore. I didn't want to be in Ohio. But the one thing keeping me here was Emry Logan. Then again, if it hadn't been for running into him and falling madly in love, none of these other things would have probably occurred either. It had been a gradual cycle, an awakening that had only been brought on by a matter of chance and events. I could only imagine how dull my life would have continued to be if I had stayed in that slump for the rest of my life. The sad thing was that I could picture it happening that way, too.

I began my morning by plopping down in a chair and going on the computer, searching for anything that would give me a clue into who exactly Lucas Banesberry was. Periodically I would take a sip of the piping hot coffee that sat beside me. I had never been much of a coffee drinker before, but today I decided I liked it.

After a couple of hours of searching, I felt frustrated. I could find nothing on any Lucas Banesberry.

Then looking through some old newspapers that had been scanned onto the Internet, I came across an obituary.

Lucas W. Banesberry, birth March 14, 1947, death September 28, 1965. Son of Lawrence and Juanita Banesberry of Elverson, Pennsylvania. Brother of Adam Banesberry. Faithful son, loving friend. He'll be deeply missed by all who knew him.

This couldn't be the same Lucas Banesberry I was searching for. I set the obituary down and tried to find out more information on anyone else with the same name, but came up empty handed. I looked down at the printed out piece of paper beside me. I took another gulp of coffee while holding it up and taking another look at the dates again. If this was him, it had happened a long time ago. For Mrs. Anderson to have known him, she would have been fairly young herself. I guess I had been expecting to find someone still alive, perhaps in another prison, some article telling what crime that had committed and so forth. I sighed. This had to be the one. There was no other information on anyone else by that name. Elverson, Pennsylvania. Where was that? I went online to find a map. It was near the border of Ohio. I glanced down at my watch. Then I stood and headed for the door, tossing the half empty coffee cup into the trash on my way out.

***

I wasn't sure exactly what I was expecting from this sudden trip to Pennsylvania. Then again, most mornings I woke up unsure of how the day was going to unfold anymore. Surely someone in Elverson knew something about Lucas Banesberry. Maybe they'd remember what had happened to him or lead me in the direction of someone that did. As always, my nerves were getting the best of me, but today wasn't nearly as bad as what I had experienced last night at Mrs. Anderson's little field ritual. The memory of the night's events was still haunting me in the bright sunlight of the day. Seneca was repulsive.

I picked up a GPS on my way out of town. I had never been very good at reading a map, and it just seemed simpler this way. I was grateful that I hadn't ever been much of a money spender. I had gone to the bank and gotten out plenty of cash for the trip for gas and food, even a hotel room if need be.

As the highway winded on before me, Emry crept back into my mind again. His face was always there, his beautiful eyes staring into mine. I thought about him every second of the day. All of my actions revolved around him. He had freed me, helped me gain a sense of independence I had never known before, and now I must help free him. I could only imagine what he was going through. What had they done to him for kissing me? Were they still punishing him? Such a beautiful creature. It was pure torment to think of them injuring his face or for him to be in any kind of physical pain, pain that had been caused by my sneaking in to see him.

I wondered if he thought about me as much as I did him. Would he question when he'd see me again or what had happened to me? I was convinced we were on equal ground when it came to our love for one another. Our connection was too strong to ever doubt that it could fall short in any way. My chest ached for him to be near me again. I wanted so desperately to go back to the prison and see him again, but I knew for sure that they would be on the lookout for my being there. I knew it would be an impossible task and a waste of effort to even try. My car lurched forward as I pressed on the gas a little harder. It was as if I thought by getting to Elverson at a faster rate, I could somehow speed up the time we were suffering apart so that it might end quicker. I missed him so much that it was as though I could literally feel my heart breaking. It was the worst kind of pain I had ever experienced before, the not knowing, the inevitable future already mapped out for us yet snatched away for the moment, possibly to never be.

Stop thinking like that, I commanded myself. There was such negativity pouring out from me. I had to remain optimistic about my future, *our* future, or else I knew I'd be hopeless and make careless decisions.

There was no room for errors in this game. This was a battle between good and evil, although I wasn't exactly sure yet who was on either side, and I would bet that those battling didn't have a concrete grasp on the side taking part yet either. I decided to turn on the radio and settled on the first station that had an upbeat, happy song on it. I tried to block out all the pain and all the anger that had been building up lately. I had to put it all behind me and move forward.

After what had seemed like a long time of driving, I sighed a breath of relief when I saw a sign that said welcome to Pennsylvania. According to the GPS, I was almost at my goal. I drove a little further and then began to see businesses that had Elverson in their title. So I had made it. Great. Now what?

I pulled into a little diner that was made up of a small rectangle building that had been painted a dull pink color called Tillie's. There were only a few other cars in the parking lot. I thought maybe I'd go in and check the place out, see if anyone in there knew anything about the Banesberry family and maybe even grab a bite to eat. My stomach growled viciously just then at the thought of food, and I realized that I hadn't eaten a thing yet today.

The inside of the diner was very much like its exterior, rundown but still tidy and clean. I sat at a little booth with black and white checkered seat cushions and looked around. The soft sound of a country music station on the radio was playing, and other than a couple people talking to a waitress up at the counter, the room was very quiet.

"Here's our menu," a waitress said, plopping a copy down in front of me. "Can I start you out with a drink?"

I looked up at the lady. She looked very tired. "Yeah, I'll take an iced tea, please."

She nodded. "I'll be right back with that."

My eyes scanned the menu for a few moments, but it was as if I couldn't truly concentrate. Should I say something to the waitress about

257

the Banesberry name? She didn't look that friendly to me. I reread the same words that I had just looked over in the menu, trying to focus once again. I just wanted a sandwich. Where was the sandwich section?

"Here you go." The waitress set down my drink. *That was fast*, I thought.

"Have you decided?"

I frowned, my eyes finally finding the right section I was looking for. "I'll take the turkey club."

"With fries?" I nodded. "Coming right up."

"Oh, hey," I said, wondering how the words were going to sound coming out of my mouth. The waitress turned her head to look at me again, a curious expression on her face. "I was wondering if you knew anything about anybody named Banesberry in town?"

"Waynesberry?"

"Banesberry," I corrected her, saying it more slowly and more pronounced this time.

She put her finger to her lips as if thinking for a moment. "No, sorry. I have actually only lived here for a few months, though."

"Oh, okay. Thanks," I mumbled through my obvious disappointment.

"I'll go ask my boss. I bet he'd know."

Before I could say anything more, she had turned and disappeared around the corner. After a few minutes, the waitress had returned with both my food and an answer for me.

"My boss said that the Banesberrys have a place at the end of Birch

Street. Just keep going straight on this road," she instructed me, pointing out of the window. "Pass the courthouse in the middle of town, and then you should run right into Birch. Turn right, and he says it's the last place."

"Thanks," I said to her, a little more cheerfully. I stared down at my plate of food and quickly reached for the ketchup bottle to dump all over my fries. I sat there and thought while I ate. What was I going to say exactly when I knocked on the front door of their house? *Hi, nice to meet you. I'm looking for someone to tell me how Lucas Banesberry died.* It sounded rude, even though he had been gone for a long time now. I decided maybe it wasn't such a good idea to overanalyze and think about what I was going to say exactly. I should just see what happens and wing it. Dwelling on it only made the nerves in my stomach increase, making it difficult to eat, even though I felt almost sick from hunger. I tried to pay attention to the words coming out of the speakers on the wall of the diner. I was getting better at distracting myself when need be.

I ate quickly and was surprised when I put my hand down to get another fry that everything on my plate was gone. I had been hungry. *I should take note to take better care of myself*, I thought.

I threw money on the table to cover my bill and the tip and put my coat on. I felt better on a full stomach, a little less agitated. I got back in my car and headed back down the road, destination Birch Street.

I had to turn around once as I missed the road. It had crept up on me too quickly, and I hadn't turned on my GPS for it. When I got on Birch, it was a short road with only a few houses. The fourth house was the final one, right where the road turned into a dead end. It sat right next

259

to the road, a faded green color that looked abandoned. I parked the car and stood in front of the house. Brown dead weeds that had grown above my head were waving fiercely in the winter breeze as they carried themselves halfway up the beams that held up the porch roof. I climbed a few steps up to the porch.

The wood underneath me creaked in agony as if it had been a long time since someone had put weight onto the beam. I stepped back and looked up at the second story windows. Nobody had lived here in years, maybe even decades.

I felt that freaked out feeling, very much like the one I had had inside Lainey Tritt's, starting to overwhelm me again. This place felt like a gigantic tomb just waiting for me to go inside before crashing down and burying me underneath its heavy, rotted roof. I ran my hand along the peeling paint of the banister attached to the steps. A few flakes of paint flew into the air as I released them. I sighed.

I had to go in. I knew it felt wrong and everything within me screamed not to, but I couldn't just stand here hesitating all day. Maybe there would be clues inside, who knew, but I had driven all this way and would find *something* out even if it meant going in alone.

I ran back to my car and grabbed the flashlight. The house looked dark and gloomy. Dust filled my lungs as I stirred it just by opening the front door and taking one step in. I fought back the sudden urge to sneeze. I turned on the flashlight as thick drapes covered all the windows. Cobwebs hovered all over the ceiling like nets bending down toward my head, the spiders waiting for their prey. There was a set of steps directly off the front door and beside those steps; an old piano, the white keys now dirty and covered in dust. There were a few pictures sitting on top of the piano. I walked over and shined the light on the picture frames. The first picture had a young couple in it, a woman dressed all in white, holding up a daisy and the man in a Navy uniform, his arm around her waist. It looked like it might be a wedding photo. Another one just as large sat beside that one. It had the same young couple in it, along with a little girl who sported blonde curls and a little boy about the same height with dark brown hair and a large grin. A smaller photo was on the other end of the piano. It was a headshot of the little blonde girl smiling, one of her front teeth missing as it looked like she might be in second or third grade. I picked up this one and attempted to blow the dust off. I studied the little girl's face. She was beautiful. I put it back and rounded the corner to a living area. There were two red velvet couches in there and an overstuffed green chair. There was a small coffee table with some magazines sitting on top of it. Someone had moved out of here in a hurry and hadn't bothered to take much of anything with them. There was a large mirror on one of the walls in this room, and it made my heart flutter as I kept staring up at it, half expecting someone to be there in the mirror, staring back at me.

A small book sat under the coffee table on a shelf. I sat down on the edge of the dusty sofa and picked up the book. I blew the dust off of it, and this time I did sneeze. I opened the front cover. It was a photo album. There were tons of pictures of the little girl and boy together, the same ones that belonged to the photo on the piano. They were smiling, swimming, and some pictures showed them riding in the back of an old truck down the road, the kids smiling from ear to ear at whoever was taking the picture as they drove off. I picked up one of the pictures out of the book and turned it over. There was writing on the back. It said: *Lucas and Cassie, 1955.* They looked like partners in crime, brother and sister perhaps, very happy being with one another.

"You shouldn't be here."

I screamed, startled, the photo album sliding off my lap and crashing onto the floor. I looked up at the face of a young girl who was a little on the heavy side, her light brown hair pulled back into a messy ponytail, her hands on her hips as if she were pleasantly irritated to find me here like this.

I jumped to my feet and stared at her, my heart pounding in my chest. "You scared me." She didn't say anything, just continued to stand there with an annoyed look on her face. "Are you a ghost?"

"Yes," she said quickly.

I frowned. "Well, I don't believe in ghosts." I thought about my last comment. No, not ghosts, just other worlds and beautiful men with supernatural powers and witches who can convince respectful townspeople that they need to chant around a bonfire in the middle of the night. I almost laughed, but instead I walked over to the child and I poked her shoulder with my finger. "It looks like you're just as human as I am."

She glared at me, upset I had revealed her secret so quickly. "Who are you?" she asked in a demanding tone.

"I'm Anna. And you are?"

She remained silent again, pressing her lips together as if forcing herself not to speak. "Oh, come on," I said. "Don't ghosts have names, too?" I raised my eyebrows.

She was not amused with my games. She let out a huffy sigh. "Lucy."

I held out my hand to shake hers. "It's nice to meet you, Lucy."

She cautiously reached out and shook my hand, her eyes never leaving my face.

"So what are you doing in a creepy, old house like this?" I questioned her, reaching for my flashlight that was lying on the coffee table behind me.

She smiled. "I'm the groundskeeper."

"Huh," I mumbled. "Of this house?" She nodded her head proudly. "Surely you don't live here. I bet it gets awfully cold at night."

She ran her fingers along an old wooden rocking horse that sat in the corner of the room. It rocked a little as she touched it. "No, I don't."

"Can I ask you another question, Lucy?"

She turned around to face me and nodded.

"Does the name Lucas Banesberry mean anything to you?"

She put her finger to her chin as if in deep concentration for a moment. Then she looked up. "No."

"So your last name isn't Banesberry?" She shook her head this time.

I watched her go around the room, running her hand down the furniture, a small book shelf, an old toy truck behind the chair. The disturbed dust flew up in clouds behind her as she did so.

"But my great-aunty's is."

Hope flickered inside me. "Can you take me to your great-aunty? I'd like to speak with her for a moment, if that's okay with you, Lucy."

She grinned at my asking her permission. "Sure. Follow me."

I walked behind her as she went outside and darted down off the porch in a hurry. She started running when we had reached the backyard and headed toward a wooded area behind that.

"Lucy, wait!"

She stopped dead in her tracks and turned around to look at me.

"My car is over there. Let's just take that."

"But it's right through this path," she argued.

I shut my mouth and followed her again. There was a narrow path in the woods behind the abandoned Banesberry house. It wasn't long before we came to another clearing where another house was. It was more kept up, a stream of smoke lifting into the sky from a thin chimney sitting on top of the roof.

"This house?" I asked.

Lucy nodded and sprinted toward the front door. I hesitated for a minute before starting to jog myself. Lucy had already gone inside once I reached the front door. She reappeared with a middle-aged woman who was also heavyset, her hair pulled back into a bun piled loosely on the top of her head. She looked exactly like an older version of Lucy.

"This is who you wanted to show me?" the lady asked. Lucy nodded her head in excitement.

"Hi. I'm Anna James."

"We're not interested in buying anything today," the lady snapped.

I smiled awkwardly. "I'm not a solicitor."

"Then what do you want?"

I bit my lip for a moment. "I came to find out about Lucas Banesberry."

"Lucas?"

"Did you know him?"

She looked me over again. "He was my cousin." She looked around behind me for a moment and then opened the door wide. "Come on in. It's too cold to be standing at this door."

Warm air greeted me once I was inside. I could smell some sort of pie baking, the aroma spreading throughout the house.

"Don't be impolite, Lucy. Take the lady's coat." Lucy held out her arms as I handed it over to her.

"Thanks," I mumbled.

The woman turned and went into another room. I followed her. It was a small living room but neatly kept. There was another lady in there who seemed pretty old, who looked like she was sleeping as her head bent backward leaning against the back of her wheelchair.

"Take a seat," she instructed me.

I sat down on the couch, my eyes fixated on the elderly woman's face.

"That's just my aunt. She won't bother you. She took a stroke a few years back, and she just mostly sleeps all day. She can't talk no more."

I nodded as if I understood. Lucy came over and sat right beside me, her curious eyes burning into my face. I tried to force a smile at her. At least I wasn't freaked out by this house or these people. It was a nice change.

"I don't know what you want to know about Lucas. It's been a long time since I've talked about him."

"You said he was your cousin?" I was grateful that she wasn't asking why I wanted to know about him. If she did, I wasn't sure what I'd say. I hadn't had enough time to come up with something.

She nodded. "That's Pearl Banesberry." She motioned toward the lady sleeping in the wheelchair, soft snores escaping her throat. "Her and her husband used to live in a big house just through those woods outside. They owned this house, too, and used to rent this place out, but they decided to move back in here after the incident happened."

"Incident?"

"Yeah." She cleared her throat before continuing. "Her husband's been dead now for almost ten years, and now just Lucy and I take care of her. Poor thing. She belongs in a nursing home. I just don't have the heart to leave her."

Lucy jumped up from her position on the couch and walked over to be beside her great-aunt. She stroked her wrinkled cheek lovingly.

"Anyway, the incident was the day their little girl went missing." I lowered my eyebrows focusing on following the story. "Cassie," she said. That had been the name on the back of the photo. It must've been the little blonde-haired girl with the curls. "She was their only child. One day she came home with another child, Lucas. He had been hanging around the old store the Banesberrys used to own in town. They had caught him sleeping there. He was a runaway orphan. Anyway, Cassie took to the boy right away. My uncle had shooed him away from the store a couple times, but Cassie just kept bringing him right back. Finally, she brought him to their house and said that she always wanted a brother. Lucas stayed with them then, ate dinner, had his own room, and everything. They even went to the courthouse and got the adoption of him in writing so he'd be a true Banesberry. They were happy for a long time. Then one day, Lucas and Cassie decided to follow the train tracks to the lake."

"I've already heard this story," Lucy whined.

"Hush now," her mother scolded her. "Go into the other room and play with your dollies for a while."

Lucy began to interject, but then saw her mother's commanding eyes and stood up and left without a word.

"I'd like some tea. Would you like some tea?"

"Oh." I looked down at my intertwined hands. "No, thank you."

I watched the woman stand and go into the kitchen. I glanced back at the person beside me, still sleeping away in her wheelchair. She made me feel slightly uncomfortable alone in the room with her, so I decided to go into the kitchen and hear out the rest of the story.

"Lucas wasn't a normal boy. Anyone could tell that just by being around him for a little while."

"What was different about him?" I asked, watching her fill up a pot full of water from the spigot.

She shrugged. "He was always polite and nice and all, but he just seemed like he was in his own little world half the time. He was spacey. He didn't click with other kids, but he sure loved being around Cassie."

"You said they were headed to the lake?"

She put the pot on top of the stove and turned the burner on. She turned around to face me, her arms crossed in front of her chest. "Well, I guess they never made it that far. They took a break on the tracks. It wasn't just Cassie and Lucas, though. Another boy went along with them. What was his name?" She closed her eyes as she sifted through her memory. "I can't remember. Anyway, that boy and Lucas got into an argument. Lucas got really upset and supposedly he started shaking all over."

"Shaking?"

"Yeah, like he was having a seizure or something … only different. Cassie tried to help him. And then the next thing they knew, Cassie was gone," she said.

I frowned. "What do you mean by gone?"

"Just like poof, vanished into thin air." She looked at me, studying her face, and laughed. "I know, sounds crazy, right?"

Not entirely, but definitely out of the ordinary, I thought. "So they never found Cassie?"

She shook her head. "Not even a body, not a trace. Poof!" she repeated, throwing her hands in the air to demonstrate. She turned around to check on whether or not her water was coming close to boiling. "It tore up my aunt and uncle. They couldn't have any more kids. Cassie was all they had, and now she was gone. They blamed Lucas right away and

268

themselves, too, of course, for letting him into their home."

"So what happened to Lucas?" I asked. "He was a little boy, right?"

"Yeah, he was still in elementary school when this happened. Lucas swore he didn't know what happened to her, and even the other kid that was with them told everyone how Lucas just started shaking right before Cassie's disappearance." She slapped her hand against her thigh and grinned. "Gary!"

"Gary?"

She nodded. "Yes, that was the other kid's name. It just came to me. Funny how a mind works." She laughed. "They didn't believe Lucas or Gary. They were out to point the finger, and they had every right to. Cassie couldn't have just vanished like they said. And Lucas was a strange boy. So they locked him up."

"Like in prison?"

"Yeah. There was this young woman who convinced everyone he was a danger, a murderer who would only kill again if he was set free."

"Who was she?"

"Now wait a minute," she said. "Just give me a moment to think." The pot started whistling, startling us.

"What are you making?" Lucy asked, popping her head inside the kitchen.

Her mother frowned at her, knowing she had been eavesdropping on a story she didn't want her to hear. "Tea. Now get on back to your room," she commanded her.

I watched Lucy turn around and obey against her will. The woman poured the water into her cream- colored coffee mug sitting on the counter. I remained silent, hoping she would go on.

She dipped her tea bag in the water. "She was kind of pretty. She had brown curly hair that was always pulled up. Hanley was her last name."

Hanley. I thought about the name for a moment. It didn't ring a bell.

"She was bossy, the know-it-all type," she explained. "I forget what her first name was, but oh, she always wore this white lacy shawl around her head."

White lacy shawl? Could it be? Mrs. Anderson. It *had* to be. She was always wearing that shawl.

And she was the bossy, know-it-all type, too. That explained why she knew so much about Lucas Banesberry. She had helped in keeping him locked up even as a young girl at the time.

"This family hasn't been the same since Cassie's disappearance. It's one of those things that wasn't ever solved and just wore on my poor aunt and uncle. You had to pity them, for not knowing and all. It ate away at them all these years, and then after my uncle died, my aunt just deteriorated further. I don't think she'll hang on much longer."

"But I thought Lucas died, too?" I asked, puzzled by how exactly that fit into the story.

She took a sip of her tea as a little puff of steam lifted from the top of the cup and disappeared into the air. "He was in jail the rest of his life then. When he was a teenager, they had another trial. Someone had paid some top of the notch lawyer to come in and defend him."

"Who?"

She shrugged. "Who knows? But he got him out of it. And then on the day he was released—I remember it clearly because I was actually there protesting his release like everyone else—he took a few steps out of that courthouse, and someone shot him dead right then and there."

"What?" I asked in astonishment.

She smiled, proud of the fact that her story had affected me that much. "Never did find out who, either."

"Did it have anything to do with that Hanley woman?"

"Huh," she replied. "I never thought of that, but no, I doubt it."

You have no idea what she's capable of, I thought. She has violence written all over her face, and I wouldn't ever put murder past her agenda if she thought it were the only way to get her way. "It's kind of an odd, little story, I know, but there it is. You now know how Lucas Banesberry died." She smiled again and took another sip from her cup. "Why is it you wanted to know again?"

I stared down at the floor for a moment. "Thank you for your hospitality," I blurted out. "Please tell Lucy goodbye for me, and I'll pray for your aunt." I practically sprinted out of the kitchen, through the living room with the sleeping woman, and straight to the front door.

I was horrified. I was trying to get Emry free, but it didn't matter. Mrs. Anderson would have him assassinated the moment he was free. They were out to get him. They were out for blood, if that's what it came down to. What on earth was I going to do?

Tears streamed down my face as I traversed the little patch of woods that Lucy had taken me through. The old Banesberry house was just ahead. Poor Emry. I had to warn him. I had to get to him again. But how? It seemed so impossible. *Nothing's impossible, though*, I told myself. I had gotten in there before in disguise. They'd be watching for me now, probably checking everyone's IDs, too. I had to come up with a plan. I couldn't let them try to kill him. He had to have the chance to be properly set free again, and happy with me.

I thought about Lucas' story as I started up my car and pulled out of the Banesberry driveway. I'm sure it was a legend in a small town such as Elverson, which was very similar to Seneca. Strange things didn't happen in small towns, and when they did, everyone panicked. It seemed like the more I was listening to people these days, everyone had a story to tell. Well, the story of us, the story of Anna and Emry, wouldn't end so abruptly, so brutally, if I had anything to do with it. Nothing else mattered. No one was going to shatter the only smidgen of happiness that I had in this awful world.

Chapter 14

I woke up in my car again the next morning, freezing to death. My mouth was dry and stuck together as I attempted to sit up. All my muscles were aching. Why did I keep doing this to myself? I couldn't live in my car. I had even brought enough money for a hotel.

I realized I wasn't in Elverson anymore. I was back in Ohio. I was in Seneca, parked in front of the antique store. The sun looked as if it were still trying to come up for the day. It must be very early. I turned the key in the ignition so that I could see what time it was. It flashed on. 6:02a.m.

My eyes felt matted together. I remember I had had a bawling fit last night. I had just let all of the balled up tension and emotions pour out of me. It seemed like it had lasted for hours as it felt good just to release it. My life was such a mess. It was utterly phony. Somewhere out there I had two parents who had given me up, who were leading probably totally different lives than the one I had grown accustomed to here in Seneca. Somehow in the midst of it all, I had gotten in the middle of people from another world. Other worlds did exist, at least one I knew of so far. There was life outside of our planet. It was an amazing revelation but an overwhelming one at that. The bigger picture was much more complex. We thought we were so intelligent, but really, humans were idiots, blinded by their own selfishness and narrow mindedness, terrified of the unknown, striving to rid the world of anything out of the ordinary because of fear of the unknown. It was a ridiculous and vicious cycle, and now I saw it plain as day. How many others knew these secrets? It seemed like more people *should* know and seemed impossible to have kept it a secret so well. I assumed that most, like I had been, were completely clueless. Even those chasing evil, such as my father, truly didn't know the extent of what their actions meant. Again, they were just scared of any kind of change.

I glanced at the door of the antique store one more time before driving away from it and toward my house. I wasn't sure who'd be home, who I'd have to face, but right now, I didn't really care. I didn't have to answer to anyone there. I just needed a shower, and then I'd be on my way again.

The house looked still in the early morning as I parked and didn't bother being discrete about slamming my car door. I even opened the front door of the house as loudly as possible, my keys jingling as they dangled in the keyhole. I might as well make my entrance known this time.

I hung up my coat and saw that the kitchen light was on. It was quiet in there. I peeked my head in.

My mother was sitting at the small kitchen counter with a cup of coffee and a muffin in front of her.

She looked up at me. Dark circles were underneath her eyes. She looked more drained than I felt, but the pity that I used to get when seeing her look frail didn't come to me then. I just felt like she used it against me to lure me in and suck the life out of me to regain some of hers. She had a worried look on her face.

"You want one?" she asked quietly, meaning a muffin.

My stomach growled. I ignored it. "No. I'm going to take a shower." I turned around to leave.

"Anna?"

I clenched my fists together and turned back to face her. I raised my eyebrows in question.

"Are you alright?"

What did she expect me to say? I wasn't going to open up to her right here right now at 6:00 in the morning after crying my eyes out all night; partially because she had turned out to be such a hypocrite and a liar, and partially because my father was in cahoots with Mrs. Anderson in trying to keep Emry locked away forever. I had every right to be a little grumpy and not quite in the mood for a heart-to-heart.

"Yeah," is all I managed to say before heading up the stairs.

On the way up, my father was coming down carrying a newspaper under his arm. His hair was wet as he had just gotten out of the shower. We stared at each other but said nothing as we walked away in opposite directions.

I locked myself in the bathroom upstairs and turned the hot water on full blast. The mirror was already all steamed up from my father just having been in here. I wiped it away to catch a glimpse of myself. My hair was sticking up everywhere and my eyes were red. Wow. *Gorgeous*, I thought sarcastically. I pulled my sweater up over my head and tossed it onto the floor. *Well*, I thought, *time to get beautified. Today's the day I make another venture down to the jail.*

After the shower, I shut the door to my bedroom and sat down on my bed. I looked around at the room that had once been my place of comfort, of rest. It seemed so childish now with the girly paint and dolls that I had had since I was a toddler sitting on my bookshelf. It seemed small and uncomfortable.

I stood and walked in front of my mirror in my towel. I studied my face. I looked the same, but different. More tired and probably even more aged, but I looked better, more alive and my skin had more color than before. I tore the towel off my head, letting my wet brown hair fall over my shoulders.

How was I going to get to Emry today? I had asked myself this a million times already over the course of the morning. For some reason, I couldn't answer myself this time. I had no clue. I was starting to feel hopeless about the idea, but I knew I had to try. Emry was now more in the dark than I was for once. I couldn't bear the idea of not seeing him again or of something terrible happening to him. I forbid myself to think like that again. It was too crushing. It was something I couldn't handle to even think of, let alone to live it out. No. I didn't have a plan, but I knew I was going to get myself dressed and head straight down there.

A sliver of sunlight filtered in through my slightly parted curtains. I looked back at my face. What should I wear? I knew the contents of my closet without searching through it this time. I had nothing that I'd want to wear, so I decided on a pair of jeans and a long-sleeved T-shirt with a sports logo on the front. Well, at least I could put some makeup on. I didn't want Emry to think I looked like a disaster *if* I even made it that far for him to get a chance to see me. It probably wouldn't make much of a difference, though. I'd probably just end up crying for some reason, and the makeup would streak my face.

I dried my hair and ran a straightener through it quickly. I was feeling anxious already, the adrenaline making me jittery and unable to stand still. One final look in the mirror. I sighed, dissatisfied but knowing it was probably as good as it was going to get today. Without allowing myself to stay in this room for a minute longer in case I'd try to talk myself out of going, I reached for my purse and headed for the stairs.

"Anna?" I heard my father say when I had reached the final step.

I stood still, not knowing if I should turn around. He'd notice I was wearing makeup. He'd force me to go upstairs, sabotaging me before I even got a chance to leave the house. My heart beat faster. I started to turn around and look at him. He was sitting in a recliner in the living room with the lamp on, reading his paper.

"Are you on your way out?" he asked.

"Yeah," I mumbled.

He didn't bother to ask where. "May I just speak with you for one moment, please?"

His tone of voice was a lot nicer from the last time I had been face-to-face with him. I wasn't quite sure how to react. I took a few steps forward, careful not to get too close to the lamp thinking that the more I was in the shadows, the more difficult it would be for him to see my glistening lips and black eyeliner.

"Helene told me that you two had a conversation the other day about ... well, you know, you having been adopted," he said.

I sighed again. "I'd prefer not to talk about it."

"I'm sure you don't," he went on. He took his reading glasses off and looked up at me. "I just don't want you to get the wrong idea. We thought it was better not to tell you, because we didn't want to hurt you. You're still our daughter is what I'm trying to say. You always will be and nothing will ever change that. I hope your heart still feels the same way."

"It doesn't," I snapped.

He actually looked hurt by my comment. "Anna…"

"No." I put up my hand for him to be quiet. "Under different circumstances, I might be actually listening to you right now, but you and I both know that things are different." Life was too complicated to go back and make any sort of attempts to rekindle anything with my father. "I have to go." I turned to leave, expecting him to interject, to block the doorway with his body until I told him that we were still all a family or something, but he didn't. He didn't say anything at all.

***

There weren't many cars in the parking lot when I had reached the prison. It was still fairly early yet. My stomach growled, reminding me that I hadn't bothered to eat any breakfast. Probably not the wisest choice, but too late now; I was already here.

I parked the car as the panic settled in once again. Had my father followed me? I was being paranoid, but for good reason. The realization that I had no plan terrified me once again, and I tried to push the emotion out of my body, pushing it down into the depths of my stomach so that it couldn't totally control me. I lifted up my hand. It was already shaking.

I got out of the car. The sun felt good on my back. It actually wasn't too cold today. Maybe I was just sweating from being so nervous and wasn't a very good judge of the temperature. I started pacing around the parking lot, trying to think. Again, I came up empty handed. So I started to just walk around the prison. My boots shuffled against the sidewalk that had been freshly salted. I walked past windows of the prison, fully aware that someone may recognize me.

I got off the sidewalk and began going through the snow. It wasn't very deep on the one side of the prison where the wind had made it drift. I stared down at the cold ground as I went, down at my feet.

Then I glanced up at the huge building towering above me and the frustration settled in. What was I doing? I can't just waltz on in there. They'd probably arrest me this time. This was just plain crazy and a really bad idea. I started picking up the pace a little. I decided I would walk completely around the prison and then head back to my car. I was already halfway around, anyway. I looked up just then. I froze dead in my tracks.

Straight up ahead of me was a fenced-in recreational outdoor area for the inmates. There were basketball courts and picnic tables. And more importantly, to my surprise, there were actually people out there this morning. I squinted my eyes in the sunlight to try to get a better look. There were a lot of prisoners out there. A flicker of hope swelled in my heart, bursting through the frustration. I walked a few yards closer to get a better look.

"No!" I gasped, a smile instantly appearing on my face. It couldn't be. It was. There, sitting on the edge of a picnic table with his back almost against the fence sat Emry. He was slouched over like the first time I had seen him, his hair in his face as he sat there perfectly still. It was definitely him. Joy shot through every inch of me. Fate. This was truly fate today.

It took all I had not to run over to him. I had to move casually so as not to draw too much attention to myself. I knew I would only have a few minutes at most until someone did realize I was standing there, but I'd take it.

I was almost there and couldn't contain myself any longer. "Emry!" I said in a loud whisper.

"Emry!" I walked over to the fence and wrapped my fingers around the tiny holes in it. "Emry, turn around. It's me!"

As if in slow motion, Emry's body rose to a more upright position as he turned his head and his beautiful blue eyes locked on mine. His lips turned upward in a closed smile, and that's when I noticed it. His face. He had a huge black bruise covering his right eye and his bottom lip was slightly swollen and scabbed as it had been busted open.

I gasped and put my hand over my mouth. "Oh, Emry, what have they done to you?"

He walked over to me with his head down, ashamed that I had seen him like this. He wrapped his fingers around mine in the fence. The warmth of his touch overwhelmed me. My heart ached to see him like this.

"It's nothing," he mumbled. "I'm so glad to see that you're alright. I wasn't sure what they had done to you. It was killing me."

"Who did this?" I demanded. "Was it my father? Buck?"

He shrugged. "Doesn't matter. It's fine."

He was being too quiet. Maybe he wasn't as excited to see me as I was him. This cloud of sadness drifted around him. I wanted to hug him so badly, to touch his wounded face and ease his pain.

"I had to come see you. I've missed you so much," I blurted out right away. I knew I should be on the lookout to see if anyone had caught onto my being there, but my eyes couldn't leave his face. It felt like it had been so long, like I needed to memorize it all over again or else I'd forget what he looked like when I was away from him.

"Anna, you have to be careful. Tell me you are," he whispered, his fingers still gripping onto mine. "Emry, they're after you," I told him. I had to get it all out. He had to know before I wasn't able to tell him. "A woman named Mrs. Anderson is leading a group of men who are against you. They think you worship the devil after what happened with Buck. But she's like a witch. I saw them perform some sort of ritual."

"You saw?"

"Well," I said, knowing he was probably going to be upset with me that I had put myself in such a vulnerable situation, "yes, but they didn't see me."

"Anna," he said in a worried tone.

"Emry, please," I begged. "Just listen to me. There was another, Lucas Banesberry. He had some sort of strength, too. Mrs. Anderson had him killed, Emry. She's a murderer, I just know it. You're the one who has to be careful. She's dangerous. She'll stop at nothing to get what she wants."

Suddenly I heard whistles being blown and shouting I was certain was directed at me.

"Hey, you there!" someone yelled out. "Get away from there!"

Emry didn't bother to turn around. "Run, Anna. Get out of here. Now!"

I looked at my fingers intertwined around his. The tears started to flow. I couldn't bear being separated from him again. He stared at me with those blue eyes, which were full of fear as he tried to urge me to leave.

"Go!" he hissed.

I nodded as the tears dripped from my cheeks. He took his hands away from mine. I turned to go. "Anna," he said.

I turned back around.

"I love you."

The words tore through me and made my lungs feel as if they were suffocating me instead of helping me to breathe. How could I leave such a beautiful creature as Emry Logan behind, not knowing when I'd ever be able to get an opportunity again such as this one? I had fallen in love, and he had felt the same, and now we couldn't even see one another. It was unbearable.

I started to run as fast as I could through the snowy patch of grass that I had just come through. I heard footsteps behind me, policemen shouting. I had almost made it back to the sidewalk when I got tackled from behind. I fell to the hard ground, my face digging in the snowy mud beneath me.

"Don't move!" he told me.

I recognized the voice immediately. It was Buck. I didn't bother to put up a fight. It was no use at this point. He forced both of my arms behind my back, my shoulders hurting from the sudden force. Then I felt him slap cold handcuffs on my wrists as they cut into my skin. He pulled me to my feet.

"I figured you'd be back," Buck said.

I stared him straight in the eye and didn't bother to say a word. My heart was aching, but a sense of joy was somewhere in there, too. Emry Logan was in love with me.

***

Later that night, I was curled up in a ball on my side of the couch, a blanket wrapped around me. Matthew sat beside me, watching TV and giggling away. I stared at the wall in front of me. I hadn't stayed at the prison too long after Buck had handcuffed me. He took me into a little room in the prison and left me there. It wasn't long before my father had come down to retrieve me. He told me to stand up and come on, but we barely exchanged any words, nor made much eye contact with one another. I followed him outside to my car where he told me he'd have someone drop it off at the house later. I was to go with him in his car. Again, the entire way home he said nothing, nor I to him. And here I was, lying on this couch, wallowing in my agony.

This house was just as much a prison to me as the actual prison itself was to Emry. At least when I was down there, I knew he was there also. Here, there was no one I could turn to. Besides Matthew, everyone inside these walls was as good as enemies to me now. I pulled the blanket up to my chin, and after a while, I started to drift off to sleep.

"Anna?"

I opened my eyes.

"Here, Anna, I made you some chicken noodle soup."

My mother set down a little bowl on the end table beside my head. I closed my eyes again.

"I'm not hungry."

She sat down on the edge of the couch and put her hand on my knee. "Now don't be silly," she said. "You have to eat something."

I sat up and faced her. "If there's something you need to tell me, just tell me."

Matthew let out another laugh and pointed excitedly toward the cartoon he was watching.

A very serious expression came over my mother's face. She looked down at her hands as she crossed them in front of her.

"I'm very worried about you," she confessed.

"Don't bother," I lashed out.

She didn't move a muscle. "I want you to be careful, Anna. Mrs. Anderson, well, she's dangerous. Don't mess with her."

She knew about me and Emry now. My father must have finally told her.

"Listen," she whispered, turning to face me. "I know you don't want to talk to me like you did before. I know I've screwed things up, but I want you to know I'm still here for you. I know that you have to be suffering all alone and need somebody to talk to."

I studied her eyes. I still didn't trust her. If Mrs. Anderson could have some sort of hold on my father, how did I know that she didn't have one on her? No. I couldn't risk leaking any information out to her. I started to feel slightly guilty, though, about snapping at her. Maybe she was being genuinely nice without any other motive besides worry.

"I appreciate that," I said.

She smiled and patted my leg, satisfied with some sort of answer. "I always thought you'd end up with Buck Brady."

I cringed at the mention of his name.

"Buck always seemed like such a kind man. It's not that way at all, is it?"

It surprised me that she would know that, let alone bring it up to me. I took a deep breath. "It's like he's bipolar. He does have this nice side to him, but then on the other hand, he can be pretty mean, too."

She nodded as if she understood. Perhaps my father had a similar way about him. "So now you love someone else?"

I stared at her, clenching my jaw together. She was trying so hard to get me to open up to her about Emry. She had always been curious about any type of social life I had, because it hadn't been much growing up. But now, I couldn't decide if she was prying out of that same curiosity or because my father was banking on her ability to be able to get me to talk. I said nothing.

She laughed and touched my cheek with the palm of her hand. "Of course you do. It's written all over your face."

"Funny you would think that," I said. "I feel so sad."

She swallowed hard. "Well, not so much your face, but in your eyes. They have a sparkle about them that wasn't there before. It's okay. You don't have to tell me about him. I understand."

Reverse psychology now? Did she take me as a fool?

"Sometimes love is a hard thing to manage. It interrupts the thought process to the brain." She looked over at Matthew, who didn't seem to be paying one bit of attention to our conversation. "There had been a time when I couldn't bear the thought of leaving Russell, but look at me now, where I am. There are other people out there in the world."

Which world? I wanted to ask. Emry belonged to Evadere, and I belonged to him. This was something she wasn't going to be able to grasp even if I could explain it to her. What had happened between me and Emry couldn't be described. It was something that had to be seen. Even I had doubted him before he had shown me. Our love ran deeper than most. I knew things that no one else knew. I had seen a place so extraordinary and beautiful that it was impossible to duplicate with words. We now had a history, though barely knowing each other. I was drudging up demons from the past and virtually putting my life on the line for this love, and what did she know of that? She compared her and Russell's flimsy relationship that had happened ages ago to mine and Emry's?

"I'm just trying to tell you that sometimes we don't think we're doing the right thing at the time. Our hearts blind us by love even when we know we should move on. The hardest thing I ever had to do was leave Russell. But I did. And it was the right choice. I can honestly look back now and say that. And you will too."

So she thought I was being forced to give up. Well, she didn't know me that well then. I would never give up. Never.

"Thanks for the pep talk," I said, a little on the sarcastic side. "But you have no idea what you're talking about." I stood and tossed the blanket back down on the couch. "I doubt you've ever been in love if you think you have to manage it."

My mother looked horrified. She probably thought I was the bipolar one now. But I didn't care. I couldn't believe I had actually felt sorry for her a moment ago. What was wrong with me? This woman was as crafty as Mrs. Anderson. She worked the angles she knew were my weaknesses. I was proud I hadn't gone past any boundary. She still knew nothing.

Carlin stepped into the living room just then. She had on a gold sweater and a tight black skirt. She looked annoyed as usual.

"Did I overhear you two talking about love?" she asked, raising her eyebrows pettily at us. She threw back her head and chuckled. "True love doesn't exist. You're a stupid woman, Annie, for putting all of your trust in something that isn't really out there."

I wanted her gone so badly. She was such a nuisance around here. Why was she still hanging around since mother was getting so much better now? I couldn't stand to look at her for another moment. Carlin turned around and left the room.

"So," I said calmly to my mother. "You keep bringing Russell back up. Do you still think about him?"

"Every day," she confessed.

"Huh," I said. "Maybe you really did love him. Maybe you shouldn't have given him up for *that*." I looked toward the entranceway of the living room, indicating Carlin. "Seems like a waste of life to me." And without bothering to look and see what kind of face my mother was making at that moment, I turned around and stormed out of the room.

Chapter 15

I had become so utterly disgusted with my life that I couldn't even get out of bed anymore. I locked myself away in my bedroom, each day passing and blurring into the next. I had nowhere to go, no one to see, and no one to turn to. I had no responsibility to anyone else. I felt completely hopeless, the very life sucked out of me. I didn't care if I laid there and rotted to death. What was the use of trying to even put on a show anymore? I was too worn down for that.

Sometimes I wouldn't think at all. I'd just stare at the ceiling and trace the way the plaster circled around the ceiling fan. Then when I thought I had almost reached the brink of insanity from the repetitive eye motions, I would return to my misery and overanalyze everything that it brought along with it.

Why had Emry even bothered to say he loved me? Why would he have chosen *that* exact moment in time? Was it because he truly did love me and had to confess it that second or he'd explode from keeping it in? Or, was it for a different reason altogether? I started to think that maybe Emry knew that was the last time we'd see each other. It was his way of telling me that it was the end. It was more like a *thank you* instead of an '*I love you*.'

Life was unjust. It had teased me into believing that I could find some sort of happiness here, and I had been just naïve enough to believe it.

What an idiot I was. How could I allow myself to get mixed up with someone that was impossible to be with? Why had there been such a connection? Why did I still miss him so much that my heart felt as if it were being ripped apart little by little, the torment slowly killing me from the inside out? I wanted to scream. I even tried once, but no sound came out. I was becoming a hollow shell now. The emptiness consumed me.

I hated this house. I hated this town. But where else was there to go? Everywhere else would be the exact same, and I didn't even feel I was independent enough to try to make it on my own. My misery would follow me wherever I went. I was sure of that. But I didn't belong here, with *them*. I wasn't even really a part of the family. I didn't have a family. I had no one. How did it come down to this?

Wasn't I happy just a year ago at this time? I shouldn't have found any of this out. I should have continued being who I had been. But then, I wasn't happy then either. I was merely fooling myself into believing that I was. Meeting Emry opened up a part of me I never knew existed. What a terrible waste I had been.

I missed those blue eyes. How unfair it was to have met such a man and feel like I was so in love with him and yet, on the other hand, feel as if I barely knew him. We should have had a life together. We could've lived in Evadere, our perfect escape, where no one would be able to find us. I missed the way he pushed back his hair out of his eyes with his hand, only for it to fall right back down again. Now I knew what it felt like to have a broken heart. Such relentless agony.

The desolation poured into me, clawing its way into my soul so that I could almost feel its grasp on me. Slowly, it would suffocate me, wouldn't it? I could only pray for some sort of death here. I welcomed it. There was nowhere left to turn to.

Day turned into night and night into day. I barely noticed. My curtains were drawn closed so that not a single speck of light could come in. I needed a shower. I needed to eat. But I just didn't care.

Sometimes I would hear whispering outside my door. Sometimes I'd hear knocking on the door, but it was too faint, too drowned out by the pain. I wouldn't move a muscle, knowing they wanted to come in. I really just wished they'd all disappear. The mere thought of them totally vanishing actually made me feel slightly better. Knowing they were here just plummeted me further into the depths of despair.

"Anna? Anna?"

My eyes flickered open momentarily. Had someone been calling for me?

"If you don't open this door, it will forcefully be opened." A threat. I didn't budge.

Soon I heard the noise of some sort of power tool as my door was being taken apart at the hinges. It swung open from the wrong way. A pool of light filtered in through the hallway. It was bright. I shielded my eyes with a blanket.

"Leave me alone," I grumbled.

I heard a sigh and a few more whispers. It was my mother and father. I didn't know why I still referred to them as that. I really should start referring to them by their first names now.

"You have to get up and eat something. Please," she pleaded with me. I closed my eyes again and pretended they weren't there.

"If you don't get up and eat something, we're taking you to the hospital. They'll put an IV in your arm and give you nutrients that way," my father threatened.

I knew he wasn't bluffing by the tone of his voice. Very slowly, I rose up on my elbows and made a good attempt to sit upright. My muscles were so stiff, they burned in agony at my trying to disturb them for use now.

"Fine," I mumbled. I watched my mother reach for the switch on the lamp beside my bed. "No, don't turn it on."

She hesitated and then her arm retreated. She set down a bowl beside me on my nightstand and a glass of water. My stomach growled and actually hurt when I saw the food. Nausea overcame me, and I almost threw up. *So this was what starvation was like*, I thought. How long had it been since I'd eaten anything that had even a little bit of substance to it?

I realized that they weren't going to go anywhere until they actually saw me eat with their own eyes.

I huffed for a moment before picking up the bowl and shoving a few bites in my mouth.

"Anna, you have to talk to us," my mother pleaded, her voice full of desperation. "You have to tell us what's going on with you. I've never seen you this way before."

"A lot has changed," I told her, my voice still soft but grim. The bites of soup went down hard as I swallowed. I reached for the water to wash it all down. "I don't want to talk to you. I want you to go away and leave me alone."

"I've had enough of this!" my father yelled out. "You are a grown woman acting like a child! You will eat all of that, and when you're done, you'll take a shower and come downstairs and at least spend a little bit of time with your brother!"

"He's been asking about you," my mother added.

Ah, Matthew. A soft spot. I suddenly felt guilty that I had left him down there to deal with them; although in his mind, he still thought they were wonderful. A wonderful, united, faithful, devoted family. I almost threw up all the bites of food and water I had just eaten. They really did make me sick.

A little while later, after a hot shower and clean clothes, I physically felt better as I sluggishly walked down the stairs, my hazy mind and heavy heart tagging along with me. I took one step into the living room, and immediately everyone stopped talking and just stared at me. They were all there; my parents, Matthew and Carlin. They had been waiting for me. It felt like a trap.

"What's going on?" I asked them.

My mother stood up and pointed to the couch. "We want to speak with you, Dear. Please, just take a seat."

I took two steps backward, the sight of all of them together and all wanting to try to intervene on my life suddenly pressing upon my chest. I could feel a slow panic taking over me.

"Sit down, Anna," my father said in a stern voice.

I stared at them for a few more seconds before pressing my lips together, and against my better judgment, taking a place on the couch.

"Matthew, why don't you go into the office and draw for a little while?" my mother suggested.

Carlin reached for his wheelchair. "I'll take him."

My eyes trailed the back of Matthew's wheelchair, and then returned to the other sets of eyes in the room staring at me. Carlin returned quickly.

"What do you want from me?" I snapped, wanting nothing more than to return to my tomb upstairs. The three of them exchanged glances amongst themselves.

"Well, we realize a lot has happened over the past couple of months for you," my mother began.

"And now you're not able to handle it anymore."

"I'm handling it!"

"By locking yourself up in your room?" Carlin said.

"Why are you even here?" I asked her in an angry tone.

She glared at me and then pressed her back up against the wall.

"We have all talked about this," my mother went on. She looked up at my father hesitantly.

"About what?" I asked.

My father sighed. He too was standing. "We've all agreed it would be in your best interest to take a little trip, get away from what's bothering you."

Now they wanted rid of me. How convenient. Was their spotless reputation in this town blotted black by their once seemingly perfectionist of a daughter?

"I'm not going anywhere."

"Anna, just listen to us for one moment…" my mother pleaded.

"No!" I shouted. "You don't get to decide my life for me. I mean, where do you think I should go? I don't have money to go somewhere. This is ridiculous."

My mother bent down on her knees in front of me as if making herself a human barricade so I wouldn't run out of the house. "I know you're upset."

"You have *no* idea what I'm going through," I snapped, giving her the dirtiest look I possibly could. She let out a frustrated sigh.

"You can go anywhere you want," my father told me. "Anywhere in the world. I mean it. We have money saved up. Just get away. You won't be going alone."

"Oh, yeah? And who exactly do you have in mind to go with me?"

They all looked at each other. They had obviously planned this all out way in advance, and it irritated me that they had been talking, scheming about me in such a way.

"Me." Carlin took a step toward me.

"What?" The thought horrified me. "I can't stand to be in the same room with you. What makes you think I'd want to take a trip with you?"

She smiled, a smug look on her face.

I felt the fury rising in my throat. It took hold of every aspect of me. I wanted to lash out and hit her. I loathed this person. Only she could make me so infuriated that I couldn't even think anymore.

"Anna, be reasonable," my father said, his tone still relatively calm as he tried to convince me.

"Reasonable? You want me to go with *her*?" I couldn't even say her name. The very idea of her, let alone her name, made me want to vomit.

"Take a few weeks' … months, whatever you need."

"You think time is what I need?"

"It is what you need," my mother blurted out. "Time heals all."

"You're so stupid," I told her. "You all are. You have no idea. It kills me that you have no idea."

"You think you're the first girl to have your heart ripped out by some jerk?" Carlin asked. "No, you're the stupid one. You really need to grow up, Annie."

"Ugh!" I cried out, jumping to my feet, my hands balled into fists at my sides. "I will *never ever* go anywhere with *you*!" I screamed out at the top of my lungs, my voice sounding like a raspy growl as the words came out. "I hate you!"

"Anna, don't, please," my mother begged.

"Don't what? Say what you can't? You hate her, too. You say you love me, but yet you want me to go away with someone that you can't even stand yourself?"

"Carlin's the one with a lot of travel experience here," my father tried to explain.

"No, it's alright." Carlin crossed her arms, but she wasn't raising

296

her voice at all. She narrowed her eyes at me and then lit a cigarette in the middle of the living room. "It's totally fine that she doesn't want to go with me. It's not really about me, anyway." She exhaled, the smoke fleeing from her nostrils. "None of this is about anything that's been going on with us. All of this has to do with *him*, the one she's supposedly in love with. What was his name again?" She took one more hit of the cigarette, and then a smile crossed her lips. "Oh, that's right. *Emry Logan.*" The way she pronounced his name so slowly and with such arrogance made me almost lose what little self-control I had remaining.

"Thanks for the little chat," I snapped, hurrying out of the living room.

"Not so fast."

Someone from the shadows near the front door took a few steps my way, making me back slowly into the living room again. As he came into the light, I glared at the face in front of me.

"You need to know everything about your precious Emry," Buck said, his boots clanking on the wooden floor as he entered the room and came into full sight in the glow of the lamps.

"I can't believe this!" I exclaimed. "What are you doing here?" I looked at my father. He stared right back at me.

"Emry Logan isn't who you think he is," Buck continued, "and you're not the first one he's fooled."

He pulled an envelope out from underneath his arm. "I'm not allowed to be showing this to you." He pulled out a stack of papers from within the envelope and handed them to me. "But I will, because despite what you think of me, I actually care what happens to you, Anna."

"Right," I said sarcastically, realizing immediately that this was Emry's file from the prison as I recognized his mug shot on the first page, so beautiful even in such a grim photo. My heart throbbed in an instant ache as I saw him staring back at me on the page.

"I don't know what he's told you," Buck continued, ignoring my remark, "but I doubt he's told you about his past. This is proof. He's been arrested several times for theft. Has he told you that?"

My eyes skimmed the pages fast as the words entered my mind. Emry, robbery, pleading guilty, combined with other words that didn't make much sense to me. I lowered my eyebrows. Emry could never be a thief.

"That's not even the half of it. Did you know he's been married before?"

"Yeah, I did," I whispered, my eyes still scanning page after page of information.

"Well, don't think he didn't lie to her, too. He abandoned that poor girl after barely being married to her. He drained her bank account and left her in loads of debt with a little girl of her own to take care of," Buck said.

"And he's a murderer. Wes Campbell isn't the only one he's killed," my father stated.

I lowered the papers and stared up at all of them. All of their eyes were on my face, assessing my reaction to the facts that they were trying to explain to me now, facts backed up by a police record with Emry's name and face plastered all over it from various ages, beginning as a young teen.

"Who else?" I whispered, afraid of what they were about to tell me, afraid that Emry was going to slip away from me suddenly. It was as if I could almost feel myself releasing my grasp on him.

Carlin finished her cigarette and then exited the room to dispose of the butt.

"When he was a teenager, he was accused of another's boy's death, another so-called friend of his," Buck said.

"But what happened with that?" I felt a few of the papers fall from my fingertips as they spread out on the floor, but I barely noticed. I was too focused on the information Buck was feeding me now, things I didn't know, that Emry had never bothered to tell me.

"He got out of it," Buck continued. "It helped that he was under eighteen, too. He gets these top of the line lawyers. It baffles us how he does it. He has the same one defending him now that defended him against that."

"He got out of it," my father added. "Only to be able to do it a second time. But this time, he won't get away with it."

"He's not a good person," my mother said softly. "He's a monster."

"Do you really want to end up like anyone else that's been close to him? Dead, or just end up used and alone again like his ex-wife? I thought you were smarter than that." Buck clenched his jaw together as he examined my reaction again.

What was my reaction? Horror? Complete shock? All of the above? I felt devastated, unlike the pain I had felt before. I was confused now in a different way. My mind was spinning and buzzing with all kinds of thoughts and voices. My mother was hurrying to gather up the papers that were still falling from my released grasp on the floor. My eyes darted from my father to Buck and then over to Carlin, who just leaned against the wall staring everywhere else other than toward me.

Could this be true? Was Emry Logan not who I thought he was? Was there the possibility that I was so infatuated by his sudden interest in a person like me that I was blinded from seeing him for who he really was, the monster they were all telling me he was? *No*, I scolded myself. He had taken me to Evadere. He had shown me his secret and this remarkable new world that no one else knew existed.

None of the other stuff mattered. Or did it?

"He's just using you," Buck continued. "You're just someone to make him feel better about himself, to get under our skin even more because you're the daughter of Pastor John James, because you're my friend."

"I hardly consider us friends, Buck," I snapped. "Seems like that blew up a while ago." He narrowed his eyes at me, obviously disturbed and angry by my remark.

"Show some respect," my father yelled out. "The man is here as a favor to you."

"Really? Or is it a favor to *you*?" I yelled back. "Or perhaps it's a favor to Mrs. Anderson?"

His face twisted as I'd hit a nerve. I couldn't deal with this any longer with all of them in front of me, staring at me, watching my every move. I had to get away from them to think. My mind was spinning as I felt a gush of dizziness come over me.

"I'm sure his ex-wife thought he was some sort of a saint, too," Buck blurted out. "Maybe you should go have a little chat with her and let her tell you about who Emry Logan really is."

Emry couldn't have committed such crimes. He was an honest man, a beautiful being, and this world wasn't good enough for him. Surely they had planted all of this against me, one thing after another. Maybe they had been onto him for years now, trying to get him locked up. He wasn't a bad person. He wasn't. These were the bad people, standing in front of me and trying to get me away from Seneca, away from Emry, to go with Carlin, of all people. They were making good attempts at trapping me emotionally now by playing these little mind games on me. This is how they worked. I should know this by now. They had never been on my side, always against me. They had been scheming, and they wanted me out of Seneca no matter what it took. Mrs. Anderson wanted me out of her way so she could get rid of Emry once and for all. I was a problem. I had to be dealt with. Carlin should take me away. She was well-educated on culture. The entire thing made me sick as my stomach now churned with the heavy weight I felt pressing down upon my shoulders, trying to force me to my knees.

I knew what my heart felt. It ached for Emry. He loved me, and I loved him. We belonged together. I shouldn't listen to any of this. My eyes moved to the police record that my mother now handed Buck, and I watched as he stuffed it back into the envelope. It had said he had pleaded guilty to all of the accusations of theft. Why would he do something like that if he was innocent?

I closed my eyes. My head spun, and I felt the vomit starting to rise in my throat. My eyes looked at all their faces. They were staring back. Or were they? Their eyes became a blur as I suddenly felt very lightheaded and hot all over. Tiny white specks flashed before me, intruding on my line of vision.

"Anna?" I thought I heard my mother cry out. "Anna? Are you alright?"

Emry Logan wasn't a murderer. Emry Logan was a beautiful creature of the supernatural world.

Emry Logan was all mine. They couldn't have him. They couldn't make me abandon him now, not when he needed me the most, even if it meant staying in the same town with him, just so he knew I was with him.

I took a step forward, the sudden heat that radiated through my veins, through my entire body and the white dots flashing in front of my pupils getting the best of me as I collapsed onto the hard, wooden floor.

Chapter 16

I was back to my old self; the boring, routine-oriented, Anna James. Over the next few months, I had become accustomed to everything that had made up my life before Emry had stepped into the picture and confused me, made me someone I was never meant to be. I had come to accept the fact that him and I would never be together again. Our relationship had been doomed from the very beginning.

I had no idea why I had been so adamant about pursuing it. I had been naive and foolish. I had allowed him to get into my head and mess me up. Perhaps the mystery surrounding who he was, the magic of it all mystified me. I would never forget Emry Logan or Evadere, but I had to think of it all as if it were merely a dream. It was the only way to move forward. Besides, it really did feel like a dream, anyway, so that made it slightly easier.

I slowly started spending time with my parents again. I scolded myself for having been so mean to them about the whole adoption ordeal. The holidays helped to remind me that no matter who had given birth to me, whoever they were weren't able to take care of me or didn't want a child, and so why should I even waste an ounce of time thinking about where they were, who they were, what their reasons had been? I had made it this long without knowing any different. John and Helene James were the ones who had given me a home and plenty of love to grow up with.

They never told me to get my own place or pay rent. They simply loved me for me, and had totally forgiven me, despite my having treated them so badly. All had been forgotten.

Carlin had spent only a few more days with us after our last little family meeting we had had the day I blacked out in the living room. Buck had caught me before I could fall and injure myself. They had taken me to the local emergency room, and the doctors there, after a thorough evaluation of my heart and brain, determined dehydration and fatigue combined with emotional disturbance had caused my little spell. The entire time I was there, I felt it utterly ironic how they had to rule out my heart and brain first. They would have been the first things I would have thought to be disastrous, but no. I was healthy and had regained my strength in a few days after allowing my mother to nurse me back to health again. There hadn't been any sort of effort made to make amends with my aunt. She had just packed up her things suddenly one day and headed down the stairs, her suitcase in hand, her stilettos on her feet.

"Do you know anything about this?" she asked me, holding up a torn and dirty, little dress.

I was sure my flushing red cheeks had given my guilt instantly away. Oh, how I remembered that dress and how I looked in it, everyone staring in the prison. It was a shame I had ruined it beyond repair.

"Anna, do you?" my mother demanded after I had kept silent.

Carlin still held it up in the air almost as if rubbing it in my face. I couldn't blame her for being angry about it. It had to have been expensive.

"Sorry," I mumbled.

"Sorry?" She raised her eyebrows and gave me that annoyed look she seemed to always get when talking to me. "That's all you have to say?"

"You did that?" my mother asked, as if horrified that I could be capable of such a thing.

I shrugged. "Yeah. I used it to get into the prison."

"This was part of your little disguise?"

I pressed my lips together. I did feel somewhat genuinely apologetic now. That had been the best day of my life. Emry had kissed me in that dress. I immediately shook the memory from my mind.

"Yeah."

"You took this out of my closet and then put it back looking like this?" Carlin was now shaking the dress clumped up tightly in her hand at me.

"I said sorry." I hated having to repeat myself, especially to her.

She eyeballed me for a few more moments before tossing the dress my way. It landed on the floor in front of my feet.

"Do me a favor and throw that in the garbage for me," she said in a calmer voice as if her despair over her dress had just been a show.

"Anna, you should pay your aunt for that. What are you doing, Carlin?" my mother asked her, turning her attention to the zipped suitcase she had been carrying.

She stopped at the closet behind the front door and pulled out a thick, fur coat and tossed it around her shoulders. "I think my time here is done."

As if she had done her duty and was off, like some sort of soldier.

She was such a phony. Her intentions of making amends with my mother didn't seem to have brought them any closer. Perhaps the two of them were incapable of being anywhere near close like sisters should be. It made me a little sad. Though I couldn't stand the mere sight of my aunt, they were biologically true sisters, and here they were, almost strangers, yet they had been under the same roof all this time. It just didn't make sense to me that Carlin couldn't forgive my mother or whatever it was that was preventing her from being truly nice for more than an hour at a time. Maybe she was just a moody, selfish person who couldn't get over herself. I was sure that no one would be able to guess they were related if the fact hadn't been stated aloud. Carlin was nothing like her sister, and so here she was, running away again. Maybe my words of telling her I hated her had struck a nerve and gotten to her somehow. The more I thought about that, the more I doubted it. I was sure Carlin had felt the same exact way about me. She had always hated me, and so we had that mutual feeling in common at least.

"Please stay," my mother begged her. She could kill people with her kindness.

Carlin smirked as if she didn't believe her sister really wanted her there anyway. "You're all better. It's been fun and all, but I don't think I can take Seneca for one second longer."

My mother sighed and opened her arms to hug her sister, realizing that nothing she said could keep her here. Maybe deep down she wanted her gone as much as I did. The thought of her leaving overjoyed me.

"Thank you so much for all your help during these difficult times."

She hugged her tight as I saw Carlin glare at me over her sister's shoulder during the embrace.

"*She* sure didn't make things easier on you," Carlin hissed.

I clenched my jaw together and felt my fists tighten into little balls again. It was as if she could always start a fire of fury within me and then continuously dowse it in gasoline as more words spilled out of her polluted mouth.

"The past isn't worth thinking about," my mother said, almost as a reminder to her sister. "It's a dark evil that can creep up on you if you let it. What's ahead in one's future, that's what we should always be looking to."

Carlin pulled away from her sister and gave her a look as if she thought she was crazy. "Whatever you say, Sis. Tell John I said thanks for the hospitality and stuff. I already told Matthew goodbye upstairs."

"Anna, tell your aunt goodbye, too," my mother instructed, turning around to look at me. I uncurled my fists and let my arms drop to my sides.

"See ya," I quickly blurted out. My mother gave me a disapproving look.

Carlin smirked. "Bye, *Annie*."

Ugh! Good riddance, I wanted to scream, and don't show up for another decade or two. I watched as my mother and aunt exchanged a few quiet words and then Carlin picked up her suitcase and headed outside and down to her car parked along the road. I quit watching after that. I didn't want to give her the satisfaction of actually seeing her off. It seemed like a waste of time. I could be doing something else of more value, like lying down on the couch and listening to the peace and silence of her no longer being in our home. And so that had been the last I had seen of Carlin. And life went on as it had before she had ever shown up.

The weather was turning a little warmer now, the wind dying down slightly as winter was now thawing out into spring. The ground was still soggy from all of the freshly melted snow, but you could sense everyone anticipating the warmer season as cabin fever had gotten the best of the people of Seneca.

During the weekdays, I spent my time helping to manage the antique store with my mother. I really had dove into things there. I believed I had a good handle on knowing all aspects of the business.

Antiques still weren't a passion of mine, but I knew a lot about them; what was valuable, what was junk. Sammie still helped out. She had recently gotten engaged and had asked me to be one of her bridesmaids. I happily accepted. The girl still annoyed me to death, but we did talk often, nothing of too much significance, but I had never been in a wedding before, and so I was a little excited about it.

It wasn't for a few more months, but that's all Sammie talked about. Her engagement wasn't even to the two guys she had dated at the same time before. It was to a new guy, someone she had barely dated a month before jumping the gun and getting herself a fiancé. She had met him while in a bowling league downtown. He was at least ten years older than her, or more, but she seemed thrilled; more about the wedding than the man was my suspicion.

I never told Sammie about Emry. No one ever asked me about him. Maybe no one knew, or if they did, they had been keeping it to themselves. I no longer knew anything about him. I had received no more letters from him. I had no idea if he was even still at Seneca County Prison or not. Emry Logan was an unmentionable name. It was as if he vanished into thin air, a ghost. He was dead to all of us now. Sometimes the thought of him fluttered into my mind, but not as often, and I was usually able to get rid of it more quickly and not allow it to control me as it had in the past.

Buck wasn't really around all that much anymore either. I guess we had had our little falling out. That was just fine with me. His personality and mine clashed. I would rather we not interfere with each other's lives. We brought out the worst in each other. No one needed that type of negative energy around to bring them down. And so it was as it was. John and Helene James had their family back together, miraculously so, and it seemed that those few months of darkness in our lives had just been a mere bump in the road. Now it was back to smooth sailing for all of us.

On the weekends, I would indulge in Bible study groups and church organizations. I was always helping with something, becoming involved and keeping myself occupied. I needed to be around people, put myself out there a little more and help those who needed it. I hadn't really done that before as much as I should have. I couldn't say I was really making any new friends. I was mostly dealing with people I had known since I was a little girl and some missionaries would come in for a few days and leave again. Seneca had sucked me in once more, but this time, I was making myself be content with what was to be of my life. I belonged here with my family in Ohio. Only dreamers believed they would ever end up in such a place as Evadere. It had been a once-in-a-lifetime opportunity, and I embraced that fact. I would be thankful for having gotten out of Seneca just that once. I had actually been in a completely different world and no one would ever know. It made me chuckle just thinking about the irony of that fact. The one remarkable thing that had ever happened to me, I would never be able to tell. Who would believe me even if I tried?

On Sundays I tried to fill myself with as much hope as possible from my father's sermons. He hadn't been in as much contact with Mrs. Anderson anymore, and he seemed happier these days.

One Sunday in particular, I was feeling inspired at the end of one of his sermons on using our talents to go out into the world and teach others about Jesus, to embrace those talents and put them to use within the community and church. Mostly all of the people had filed out of the building. Only a few stragglers were left chatting to one another as my father stood in the open doorway of the front of the church, the sunlight pouring in. I was just debating in my mind what my true talents were when I caught sight of someone out of the corner of my eye. I immediately stood very still and strained my eyes as particles of sun burned brightly into them as I struggled to see who it was. They had approached my father rather quickly and had been dressed in ordinary every day clothes. Our church was big into dressing up on Sundays. It wasn't like it was mandatory, but it wouldn't surprise me if some of our members gave someone a dirty look who came strolling into the building in jeans and a T-shirt. That was considered disrespectful.

I darted around the pew I had been sitting in and to the far corner where I could shade my eyes a little and get a better look. I ducked down using another pew as a shield. It was a middle-aged man talking with my father. Who was it? I struggled to see again. Could it be? No. But it was. Lauren Anderson, Mrs. Anderson's son, was standing there chit-chatting with my father. I had only seen him a handful of times, but I was sure it was him. He was peculiar-looking and had the kind of creepy face that you couldn't forget. He had a large scar going diagonally across his face, little black beady eyes that looked too small for his head, and slicked back dark hair and a complexion so white, you'd think he was a vampire at first glance. I focused my attention on the two of them. It didn't look like chit-chatting at all. It looked odd and suspicious.

After watching them for several moments, it was clear that Lauren was upset about something, and he was quietly telling my father all the details of his sudden anxiety. I watched my father look around in the church hesitantly. There were still some people talking amongst themselves, not noticing my father or the man standing beside him as they were too engulfed in their own conversation. My father held up one finger to Lauren, motioning for him to wait. He walked over and took his coat from the coat hanger a few feet away and then quickly exited the church with Lauren Anderson.

I stood from the pew I had been ducking behind, staring at the open, empty doorway. Without even thinking about what I was doing, I was practically running out to the parking lot toward my car. I had driven myself and Matthew to church separately today from my parents, as they had had an early meeting to attend. I quickly scanned the almost deserted lot as I shielded my eyes from the brightness of the sun with my hand. There was no movement anywhere. Had my father and Lauren already gone?

I jerked open my car door and hurried to start the engine. I found myself driving down the road, headed toward Mrs. Anderson's house.

I felt the same familiar obsession I had once had for Emry Logan come roaring back full force within me as if it had never really gone away. The sick, stalker-like fixation engulfed me, making my foot press down harder on the accelerator. Adrenaline rushed through me, and I suddenly felt as if I had come alive once again.

I pressed the brake. My tires squealed as the vehicle lurched to a stop in the middle of the road.

What was I doing? This sudden impulse I had had was absurd. Why on earth was I trying to figure out where my father and Lauren Anderson had gone? Why should I even care? Emry Logan didn't love me, and I didn't love him. I had thought this whole foolish thing was over and done with. I had found my old, true self and had promised myself that I wasn't going to behave in that manner ever again. I felt my body sink down a little in my seat so that I could no longer see the road in front of me. After Buck had told me all of those terrible things contained in Emry's police record, I had felt very weak and frail. Even so, even on my worst days, deep down I knew that I was growing stronger little by little. Even in the depths of the pit I had dug myself into as I lay in my bedroom, sulking and refusing to eat, even through all the emotional turmoil, I had somehow convinced myself to believe that that experience had been formed purely to serve as a lesson and from that, I had grown as a person. Hours ago I had felt strong, strong enough to go on living my life as a normal human being, as the Anna James that everyone in Seneca had familiarized themselves with. But now what? Now I felt even stronger with this surge running through my veins, with a sense of adventure and passion that drove me to even get in my car and attempt to follow my father. What was happening to me here? I couldn't allow this to start all over again. But then, I felt the sudden epiphany become clearer still. I had convinced everyone, including myself that I was over him. I had convinced myself that the calm, kind-natured Anna James was the real me, but that person was merely an illusion. Being her had helped me to overcome the emotional grief that felt like it had been swallowing me whole. I had brought the numbness back to life by being *her*.

I became startled as a horn from a truck blasted my eardrums as I had been blocking the road. I sighed and sat straight up quickly to get the car off of the road. I let the truck behind me pass and then started driving again, only slower this time. I tried to clear my mind and push Emry out of my thoughts. I tried to think of anything except those luscious lips and the way they had briefly touched mine in that single kiss of passion, his gentle blue eyes, and the way I loved his dusty brown hair and the way it fell into them. My heart thumped in my chest, feeling heavy and sad at the same time. The sensation of loneliness lurked up from behind me, followed by the familiar longing, a desire to be near Emry Logan in any way I could, even if it meant not literally being with him but even by being consumed with something as small as following Lauren Anderson to try to unveil something to grasp onto. Just by doing that, I would be able to feel a little piece of Emry, and that would suffice the yearning. For now. I wasn't sure where I was headed, and when I did finally focus my attention to actually just driving again, I realized where I was. I was in front of Mrs. Anderson's driveway.

After deciding that it was probably safer to pull my car into the next lane down from her driveway where I had parked the same night as that infamous field ritual I had stumbled upon this past winter, I stepped out into the warmth of the early afternoon sunlight and reached back in my car for a pair of sunglasses before heading through the patch of woods that would run right into the side of the driveway. I was very careful with each step that I took. I was wearing a long dress and shoes that had a medium-sized heel on them which sunk into the soft clay beneath my feet. The grass was just beginning to turn green, which helped to make this area not seem as depressing or frightening as it once had to me before.

Mrs. Anderson's house came into full view in the clearing past the woods. I tromped down the slight curve of the driveway and squinted my eyes through the sunglasses to see if anyone was around.

The house looked still and peaceful. There were no cars parked out front. I walked freely in front of the house and went around the corner to see if anyone had parked out back. Empty. No one was here.

I took a few steps back and peered upward at the house before me. What was I going to do now without anyone to follow? I went around to the backside of the house and again just stared at it. It seemed like the house was calling to me, wanting me to go in and check things out. It had to be somewhat interesting with someone like the witchy Mrs. Anderson living there. I was curious, too curious perhaps. The motion of a swaying white curtain caught my eye as the warm breeze blew in through an open window. A smile crossed my lips as soon as I saw it. Before I even gave myself a chance to think things through, I was already standing right before the open window, peering in at the contents of the house. I had to do this. I had nothing of Emry to hold onto.

The window was slightly above my head. I had to use what upper strength I had to pull upward and then brace myself to hold steady for a moment while I looked in to see if there were any signs of movement or life inside the house. I listened for a moment. All was quiet and peaceful from within.

There was a little wooden chest sitting directly in front of the window with a few porcelain birds placed on top of it. I tried to slide my body in through the window very gracefully and carefully so as not to break anything. When I finally stood up in Mrs. Anderson's house, my feet on the worn circular rug in the middle of the floor, I put my hands on my hips in satisfaction that I had accomplished getting in here so easily and without breaking anything as well.

I looked around. I stood in the middle of a living area. There were old paintings and photos hanging from the walls, two long couches with beautiful handmade throws on the backs of them, and a bookshelf covered in thick hardbacks. It looked like a typical farmhouse would look. It wasn't sparkling clean, but it wasn't filthy either. It was a little cluttered for my taste. Furniture seemed to be shoved together, more or less. I listened again for any sounds. Hearing nothing, I decided to snoop around the rest of the place.

A large kitchen extended to the front of the house. There were dishes stacked up in the sink, and the smell of maple syrup lingered as if she had had a few guests over for breakfast this morning. I reached above my head and opened up one of the kitchen cupboards. There were just the normal every day bowls, plates, and cups stacked inside. Nothing out of the ordinary. Nothing that would render any hints of what was going on with Emry.

I walked into another room, which was obviously a dining area with a large table in the center. It seemed as if this room was barely used, though. The chairs were covered in dust and the table was covered in mail, opened envelopes, and newspapers. I sifted through them for a few moments and again came up empty handed. I wasn't sure exactly what it was that I was searching for, anyway, I reminded myself when the disappointment started to settle in.

I turned around another corner and ran my hand over the gray-speckled wallpaper in the hallway.

There was a large, gaping, dark hole at the end of the hallway, and

I quickly realized what it was, a staircase leading to the second floor. My stomach fluttered in both anticipation and anxiety.

Should I attempt it, or should I just go? *I should probably go*, I told myself. The darkness of the stairs themselves should've been enough to make me feel unwelcome up there. What if I found dead, rotting bodies or worse, became one of them myself as Mrs. Anderson could cast an evil spell, forbidding me from ever leaving? An image of remembering Mrs. Anderson in the middle of the snowy field, holding up what was supposed to represent Emry as a piece of wood as she tossed it into the bonfire, spread itself out across my mind. I took a deep breath. I would only go up for one minute, take a quick glance around, and then come back downstairs and out the window again. I glanced down at my watch.

Every minute more that I lingered in this house was putting me at even greater risk of getting caught. And then what? I didn't think I wanted to find out.

The stairs creaked one by one as I took slow strides toward the top. Why was it so dark in here?

Were there no windows, or did she just have them all drawn shut? The lack of sunlight after the conclusion of a gloomy winter annoyed me. My hand brushed over the banister at the top of the stairs as my eyes struggled to focus in the shadowy light. There weren't any windows up in the open area. I headed down another hallway. This house was larger than it appeared from the outside. I guess that's how these old farmhouses went, though. A bedroom on the left, another one on the right, a bathroom. It was a lot of space for just one person to be living here. Then again, her children did visit often, I assumed, and could stay here if they wanted. Maybe she even had grandchildren for all I knew.

There were two more rooms at the very end of the hallway. One of them was another bedroom, and the other was filled with junk from wall to wall. Maybe there wasn't an attic in this house, and this room served the purpose for storage. There was a window in the room, and I reached across a pile of papers stacked up from the floor to grab onto the string of the blind to pull it up so I could get an even better look at what was in here. Particles of dust spread out in the air as the sunlight touched them. There were a lot of older pieces of furniture in here, antiques for sure that could easily fit into my mother's collection at the store. One lamp caught my interest as I studied it momentarily. Farmhouse memorabilia corroborated with statues of strange animals and pictures of shapes in a multitude of colors all shoved into anywhere they would fit in this small square room. I blew the dust off another strange statue of an animal that resembled a monkey, its face twisted in a menacing expression. If these things belonged to me, not that they really represented my taste or anything, I would want to display them, not hide them away up here, letting them collect all this dust. It seemed like a waste. But what did I know about Mrs. Anderson? I thought she was odd, and if anything, this just went along with the strangeness that seemed to coincide with my opinion of her.

In the midst of all the clutter sat a desk that was in desperate need of restoration. It looked as if it had been left out to weather for years by the color of the wood. I ran my hand over the jagged surface on top of it.

There was a single drawer with an open area underneath it, piled full of papers. I opened the drawer. There was a navy blue metal box inside. It had a place to insert a key on the outside. But to my surprise when I attempted to open the box, it willingly flung open. There were stacks of envelopes inside, banded together by rubber bands. I picked up one of the stacks and took off the rubber band. I glanced through them. They appeared to all be old electric bills, farm supply receipts, etc. I went through the next few stacks of envelopes that were composed of the same things. I shoved them all back together as I had found them and put them back in the metal box, closing the drawer. My eyes moved downward to the papers in the open area below the drawer. They were thrown together wildly, making it difficult for me to hold onto them as some were sideways in the stack. The papers themselves were simply more paid bills. They were mixed with old newspaper clippings of obituaries and some weddings that had occurred decades ago. I recognized the town immediately on one of the headlines of the newspaper. The article was about Elverson, Pennsylvania. Still seeing nothing of any real value, I threw the papers back in the space just as recklessly as I found them.

I folded my arms across my chest. Now what? There was nothing here. Mrs. Anderson was a packrat of strange antique memorabilia unlike anything I had ever come across in my mother's store. That didn't prove anything other than the woman had an odd taste of collections, collections that she didn't like to share with anyone else. I quickly pinched my nose as I felt a sneeze coming on. I winced as my eyes burned while I forced myself to hold it in. I must have been kicking up too much dust.

I walked back over, stood in front of the desk and stared at it, the sunlight still dancing with the particles of dust. I frowned. There *had* to be something in here, but there was nowhere else to look.

I opened up the drawer again and peered down at the metal box. I lifted the whole thing up and set it down on top of the desk. The drawer was entirely empty now. I pushed my hand down on the bottom of the drawer and felt the bottom piece of wood move loosely within it. I squinted my eyes to try to get a better look inside the dark compartment. That wasn't the bottom of the drawer. Someone had put another piece of wood in here that didn't quite fit. I was able to dig my fingertips down along a tiny gap between the wall of the drawer and the edge of the piece of wood. I struggled to pull it up.

Finally it gave, and I was able to lift it upward and out of the drawer. I set it down on the floor beside me. There were more folded papers in the drawer. I quickly took them out and into the sunlight as I unfolded them. One was a small painting without a frame. My heart began to beat in the same combination of excitement and apprehension that I had felt moments ago when entering the house. My mouth dropped open as I examined the painting further. It was slightly faded, but I still easily recognized those rocky cliffs, red hazy sky with brilliant white speckles and high golden grasses in the background. This was a painting of none other than Emry's Evadere. It portrayed the real thing perfectly. What was this doing in Mrs. Anderson's house? Who could have painted such a thing or had any knowledge of the place? As questions began to surface inside my head, I unfolded another piece of paper. My mouth gaped open. It was a birth certificate for Emry Logan.

I felt a little dizzy all of a sudden. All the dust was getting to me, along with the way the sunlight poured in brightly into just one spot of the room, the rest of the place dark with black shadows. I braced myself against the wall for a few moments trying to take deep breaths. I would not allow myself to pass out here. My heart beat furiously. I tried to calm myself down, hoping the rhythm of my heart would cooperate as I did so. After a few more moments, I started to be able to see clearly again. I allowed myself to attempt to stand straight again without the assistance of the wall. I steadied myself, praying I wouldn't fall over. I waited, just standing there, the papers still in my hand. I felt okay, just a little sweaty.

I looked back down at the birth certificate. Emry Logan born on July 21, 1988, son of Henry Logan and Trisha (Fisher) Logan of Seneca, Ohio. These were the names that Emry had given me; the ones he thought were fake. Underneath the certificate was a small envelope. Inside were some Polaroid pictures of a small, beautiful child; a little boy with bright blue eyes. It was Emry as a child. He was a baby in the one, standing up in his crib and the others were taken of him as a toddler, maybe a little over a year old, outside playing in someone's yard. What was she doing with this? I wanted to scream it out as loud as I could as it roared within my mind. Had Mrs. Anderson stolen this from Lainey Tritt's house? But why? It didn't make any sense. Why would she care about any of this as long as he was behind bars? What kind of case was she building up against him?

There were a few other papers underneath the envelope, folded up as well. I went to unfold one, when suddenly I felt someone wrap their arms around me so tight that I could barely breathe. The papers fell from my reach and scattered on the floor. I struggled with what little strength I had to break their grasp, but it was no use. They were too strong. They squeezed even tighter, and I winced as the rest of the air fled from my lungs. They dragged me out of the little room and down the dreary hallway. I couldn't see who it was. My back was against their chest. I was certain it was man, though. My legs flailed about as I tried to put up whatever fight I had left within me.

They forcefully carried me down the stairs, my elbows and head bouncing violently off the narrow walls on the way down. I grunted as my lungs pleaded for me to expand them. A sharp pain radiated across the front of my chest. The force of the violent suffocation felt as if they were breaking my ribs one by one. A numbness made its way into my face and blackness crossed my field of vision as I wasn't sure exactly where I was anymore. My feet were now limply dragging on the ground behind me as they refused to put up a struggle.

I heard a door open and then the back of it slamming off the wall, echoing. Then with one giant heave, they tossed me like a rag doll, and I fell down a staircase, my body rolling, jolted by each turn and twist as different parts of my body smashed into the steps. Finally, everything stopped as I landed with a hard thud on the cold, hard dirt at the bottom of the stairs. My chest heaved in pain as my lungs lapped in the moldy air around me. I could feel something wet running down my forehead. *Probably blood,* I guessed. But the worst pain was my ankle. The pain was so deep, so intense that I curled over on my side into a ball, making a failed attempt to rid myself of it.

"You were warned!" a husky male voice hollered down at me from the top of the stairs.

I felt like I needed to cry, but the sting and burning, as if my ankle had been ripped wide open, outweighed the emotional upset. Panic overtook me. Was I dying? I felt as if I were. My fingernails dug into the dirt around me, trying to reach out to grasp something, anything to take away what was happening. But I found no relief from my anguish.

Chapter 17

The pain surging up my leg was almost unbearable. I realized instantly that I had been viciously thrown down stairs that led to a basement area. The floor was merely dirt, but compacted down so much that it felt like cold cement underneath me. There were no real walls as all the electrical wiring was exposed, and the ceiling was pretty much the same way. It stunk of mold and dampness. There were a few old crates sitting in a pile in the corner and a coal furnace adjacent to these. There was a single window at the top of the far wall that looked smaller than my head, allowing a sliver of sunlight through. There was also a wooden door with a huge metal lock shining in front of it as if it were brand new. I didn't know what my chances of escape were at the moment, my head frantically trying to process the amount of pain I was in, but I didn't think my chances were that great.

I pulled away the palm of my hand that had been covering up my wounded ankle. The shock from the sight hit me intensely as a puddle of blood surrounded my foot, and the jagged edges of a red- tinged bone protruded from my leg, surrounded by pink meaty flesh that had been split wide open from the sharp bone.

My stomach churned. I wasn't sure what was nauseating me more; the intensity of the pain or the revolting sight of the wound before me. I twisted over on my side and vomited in the dirt. I wiped my mouth with the back of my hand. Vomiting had given me little relief. I started to feel the panic settling in. What was I going to do? What *could* I do? I was crippled in Mrs. Anderson's basement, locked up, and no one knew I was here except for whoever threw me down the stairs. I was going to bleed to death. No one would find me, and this would be my tomb.

The realization was too much to handle. This was all my fault. They were after Emry, and I was the only one trying to save him. Me against them, and they were too powerful. I should've expected something like this. I had acted without thinking about the consequences of breaking into someone's home, especially someone like *her*. She was dangerous and I knew that, but somehow I thought I was unstoppable, probably because I had gotten away with so much before.

My father would come to save me. Or maybe not. Maybe this would push him over the edge, an unforgivable act of one too many, and he'd finally abandon me. I wasn't his real daughter. It would be easier to rid himself emotionally of me knowing that fact. He thought I had changed things around, that we had all been back to normal over the course of these last few months and that Emry Logan had been ripped from my mind and my heart forever. Knowing I'd been snooping around Mrs. Anderson's house would be too much disappointment for one man to bear, even that of Pastor John James himself.

The tears started to flow. The feeling of entrapment, combined with being so physically injured tore at my heart. I took a deep breath. My ribs throbbed and a headache was quickly forming as I felt around on my head and a large lump was growing on the top of my skull. The fire radiating up from my punctured skin burned intensely. I closed my eyes for fear that I might accidentally look down and see the bone again. Closing my eyes would make me unable to see the gruesome sight. I put both hands behind me and felt the bloody wetness on the cold dirt and brought up both hands horrified. Death would soon conquer me.

Emry wouldn't want things to have ended like this for me. He had warned me to be careful, and I had been such an idiot this time. I was messing with the wrong people who couldn't care less about what happened to me. They only wanted one thing, Emry Logan destroyed, and if it meant destroying me too, then so be it. I had proven loyal to the wrong side in their eyes. I was just as much a criminal and threat as he.

What was I thinking? I scolded myself for even thinking that Emry would still be caring about what happened to me. Whatever had happened between us had been hopeless. He was a smart man. He would have given up. Only I had become the foolish one, had put myself in this situation, and now I was in too deep. There was no way to get myself out of this one.

I was so pathetic. I deserved to die down here like a worthless thing. My life was meaningless. I had no purpose, no one to believe in me, nowhere to turn. I felt the same despairing emotions rush over me, similar to those that I had felt after the realization that me and Emry Logan would never be, only this depressed feeling was even worse.

The dizziness came over me then, integrating its way throughout my entire body. I couldn't think. I couldn't move. I felt my consciousness fade in and out, in and out. I felt my body fall over onto my side, my hair caked in vomit and blood, as the cold, damp earth beneath me engulfed me until all I could see was black.

The sound of voices awoke me partially. I had no sense of how long I had been down here. I couldn't move. I could barely breathe. My wounds still throbbed uncontrollably.

"This is what I needed to drive the whole way down here to see? What did you do to her?"

"I caught her upstairs in the room, nosing around."

"So just to get this straight, you snap, lose your temper, and need me to get you out of this mess, does that about sum it up, Lauren?"

"Who else was I going to call?"

"You could've killed her. Just look at her. I'm surprised you even called. Why not just let her die?"

"I couldn't."

"Really, Lauren? You mean you actually have a heart thumping around somewhere in there? Who is she?"

"Anna James."

"Why does that name sound familiar? Wait. The pastor's daughter?"

"Yeah."

"Just great, Lauren."

I felt my eyes flitter open slightly. They immediately snapped shut again as the bright light from a flashlight was being shined directly on me.

"What a mess. What's mom going to say about this? Does she know?"

"Not yet. It's her own fault. She was supposed to stay out of it."

"It?"

There was a long silent pause between them.

"Never mind. I can only guess what she's been up to. I told you all long ago I want no part in any of this. I mean it. Don't tell me one thing more."

The flashlight moved out of my face and off to the side. I tried to open my eyes again. There was just enough light in the room for me to see the faces of two men. One was Lauren Anderson, the one who had just confessed to finding me upstairs and who had caused me this cruel misery, and the other looked familiar. I tried to squeeze out the pain for a moment so I could concentrate and think. It was another one of Mrs. Anderson's sons. I believed he may have been the oldest, but it had been a long, long time since I had seen him. He had moved away.

"Can you fix her?" Lauren asked his brother.

The man let out an overly irritated sigh. "I don't know. I can't do anything down here. These conditions aren't exactly sanitary."

Oh, that's right. I remembered that Mrs. Anderson's oldest son had moved away, because he had gotten a job out of town in a nearby city as a physician. A little hope fluttered through me. I wasn't dead yet. Perhaps he'd be able to help me.

"Do whatever you can."

"She's lost a lot of blood. You didn't have to be so violent."

Another pause. Then I heard footsteps walk closer toward me and the flashlight shining again in my face.

"Anna? Anna James? Are you able to open your eyes? Are you able to speak?" the man asked me.

I felt my lips part slightly, but a wave of pain swept over me again. My eyes squinted from the light as I tried to open them as well. I felt the light touch of his fingers on my neck as he checked the rate of my pulse.

"She's bad, Lauren. Real bad. We have to move her, and quick. She has a fever. She's in shock. Here, take this. Anna? Anna, listen to me. You're going to feel a pinch in your arm."

I felt the needle go into my arm but barely. It was nothing compared to all the other things I was feeling right now.

"She's not stable enough to go back up those stairs. We'll have to take her out that door. Go open it."

I prayed for some sort of relief. Then all at once, the light of the flashlight began to dim, and I saw blackness once again.

***

When I opened my eyes, I was still in the damp basement. I no longer felt the cold dirt beneath me and realized that I was on some sort of a cot. I tried to sit up, but winced. My ribcage was bandaged, and there was an IV in my arm. I remembered how badly my ankle had hurt but couldn't feel the pain as much now. Looking down, I saw that my leg was casted. He must have helped me. Mrs. Anderson's son must have somehow repaired the injured ankle and given me pain medication. I was a little groggy but overall much improved. I reached up and touched my hair. It was damp. Someone had cleaned me up as well. But why had they brought me back to this place?

The door at the top of the basement stairs creaked open, and I could hear multiple footsteps stomping down the stairs toward where I was. I lay back down on the cot. I wondered if I should pretend to be sleeping, but before I could think it through properly, I looked up and saw them gawking at me.

"Finally she's awake. Ms. James, how do you feel?"

I recognized Mrs. Anderson's oldest son, the one who I presumed had saved my life, as he stood directly over me, his eyes intently staring at my face.

"Better," I managed to whisper, although my voice sounded a little muffled and raspy.

"Good, good." He put a cuff over my arm and took my blood pressure. "This is the last time I'm checking on her, and then I'm out of here." He shined a pen light in my pupils. "I suppose I can't talk you out of what I've already told you."

"No." Mrs. Anderson stood from a distance, looking harshly at me. She had her hands clasped together in front of her.

"She needs to be in a hospital," her son told her.

She quickly shook her head as her mind was already made up. "Why, so they can just release her? Absolutely not. Not until this whole thing is over and done with."

He frowned, his face illuminated by the glow of a small lantern at the bottom of the stairs. "If there are any signs of infection, another fever, yellow drainage from the wounds ..."

"Yes, we understand," Mrs. Anderson whispered.

I didn't like the way she spoke. She seemed overly calm all the time when there was this treacherous storm really going on underneath the surface. And the way she talked about me, as if I weren't in the room or a child or something, was so irritating.

"I don't want to be called if that happens," her son went on, being persistent in the way he spoke to them.

"Take her to Seneca General, but I am done here."

"You don't have to repeat yourself ten hundred times," Lauren grumbled.

A loud knock echoed all the way down to the basement from the front door upstairs. Within only a few moments, the knock repeated, even louder. Everyone stared at each other uncomfortably. I was hopeful for whoever it was, anyone but this grisly family in front of me.

"Don't just stand there. Go see who it is," Mrs. Anderson snapped, only allowing her tone of voice to rise slightly.

Lauren rushed up the basement stairs, taking two at a time. I could hear the front door open and another pair of feet anxiously shuffling inside the house.

"Where is she? What's going on?" It was my father. He was panicked.

"Down there."

"What? Why is she down there?"

And then he made his way down into the dully-lit basement, his eyes locked on mine and the condition I was in. He looked pale even in the shadows.

"Anna!" he said, horrified. "What happened?"

He rushed over to my side and took my hand in his, his eyes scanning frantically over the various bandages and my cast, the IV plugged into the vein in my arm.

I opened my mouth to speak, but no words would come out. Tears flowed freely down both cheeks, and I could do nothing more but sob and bury my face into his chest, trying to mumble how sorry I was for everything.

He turned around and glared at the Anderson clan, demanding an answer from them. "She fell," Lauren lied.

His mother gave him a stern look and took a step closer to my father. "There was an incident in which Ms. James was found meddling with my affairs upstairs."

"Was found?" he asked. "What exactly does that mean?" He glanced back down at me. "It means we weren't home and she broke in," Lauren said bluntly.

Mrs. Anderson held up her hand, motioning for her son to keep quiet.

"Is that true?" His eyebrows furrowed. It was the look of disappointment I was dreading, though inevitable, to see. "Anna? Please tell me there's a better explanation than that."

I closed my eyes and squeezed his hand. I opened my mouth and cleared my throat. "I'm sorry."

"But why? What were you doing? What were you thinking?" he demanded from me, his tone no longer holding even a twinge of sympathy.

"John, you know exactly why she was here," Mrs. Anderson told him, giving him just an extra nudge to confirm his suspicion.

He released his grasp from my hand and stood, backing up as he did so, so that he was a few steps away from me now. "No. It can't be that. You're done with him. I thought this whole thing was over."

"Love is such a difficult thing to turn on and off." Mrs. Anderson smirked at me. Anger burned within me at her mockery. I absolutely abhorred her.

My father was starting to fall apart. He stood there, rocking back and forth on his heels as if he could barely take it. His mind was going a million miles an hour, and I couldn't tell which direction he was taking as he processed all the information. I had betrayed him. He had trusted me to have been *me* again, the "me" he had always liked, always thought I was. He trusted that Emry Logan was out of the picture entirely and that it would never come down to this again, this vicious cycle of disillusionment that twisted all of our lives uncomfortably upside down, forcing us to have to reevaluate who we were, what we've become. I could feel the instant strangeness between my father and me, as I had once felt in Seneca County Prison after Buck had caught me and Emry in a moment of brief passion. It was as if my father didn't recognize the child he had watched grow up before him, nor did I recognize my father, my pastor standing there whose eyes had grown as black as the shadows surrounding him.

"So you found her, Lauren?" he asked, his voice just as jittery as his body language. Lauren nodded.

"And then what?" he questioned him. "You beat her up? You taught her a lesson?"

"Not exactly," Mrs. Anderson answered for him.

My father was on the verge of losing all control. You could hear the edge to his voice. It was still undetermined, though, if he'd lose it on them or me. "Then please, enlighten me."

"I already told you, she fell." The gruffness in Lauren's voice grew as if he were ready to defend any accusations thrown his way.

"That's not true," I quickly said. "He threw me down the stairs."

My father bit his fingernail anxiously. Then he closed his eyes. I could tell he was trying to fight the emotions writhing within him. He was fighting to remain as calm as possible.

"Don't strain yourself, child. You'd better just rest and be silent," Mrs. Anderson told me.

I glared at her, trying to project the hatred from within my eyes. "I won't be silent. He tried to kill me. You want rid of me, like you want rid of Emry."

She scowled back at me. I had said his name. I had struck a nerve. It was written all over her face, but she didn't reply. She simply took my father by both hands and turned him around to make him give her his total attention. "John, listen to me. She's fine."

"She doesn't look fine to me."

"Of course not, but it's all been taken care of. My Richard has performed surgery on the girl."

"Surgery?" He tore his hands away from hers and then backed away, moving closer to me. His eyes searched the shadows, searched to see Richard Anderson's face in the darkness. "Is he here?"

"He's here."

The oldest son stepped out of the darkness and near the lantern, a worried expression on his face.

"She's stable. She had a good bump on the head, a few fractured bones, and her ankle needed the most work, but it's been pinned and casted, and I've given her IV fluids and some pain medication."

My father turned around to look at me again, realizing what I had just gone through, his face pained with the thought of it all.

"Now, if there's nothing else needed, I must be on my way." Richard gave his mother and brother a stern look. "Remember what I said." Then he faced my father for a brief moment and gave him an apologetic look. "I'm sorry, Pastor."

I watched him walk slowly but steadily up the basement stairs. He probably hadn't wished to be as involved as he was, nor had he wanted to see my father face to face. He was in a big hurry to get out of here and far away from Seneca and the drama his family was deriving here.

"Why are you keeping her here? I'm taking her to the hospital," my father shouted out in a demanding tone.

Lauren stepped in between him and me in a bullying manner. "She's not going anywhere."

"Are you going to throw me down the stairs, too?" The two men eyed each other warily.

"If I have to," Lauren threatened.

A soft chuckle escaped from Mrs. Anderson's throat. She smiled as she now stood beside the two of them. "Now, now, let's not do anything drastic here. This can be discussed rationally. Shall we go upstairs and talk over tea?" she suggested.

"No," my father snapped. "We can't just leave her here all alone."

Lauren sighed as if my father were being totally unreasonable. His mother gave him a look of disapproval.

"That's fine, John. You just have to understand the situation she's put us in."

"There's no excuse for what she's done by breaking into your house and all," my father stated. "But if Lauren tried to kill her…"

"If I'd wanted her dead, she'd be dead." Lauren put his hands on his hips.

"That's enough, Lauren. Maybe you should go upstairs and take some time to cool down."

"Fat chance of that happening," Lauren said, his eyes still focused on my father.

She shook her head. "Fine. The girl can't leave, John, and I know that you know why."

He backed away from them and leaned against the bottom railing of the stairs. His eyes darted about at everyone around him, including me, as if trying to think of some form of persuasion, some sort of offer, yet coming up empty handed.

"And certain things should not be discussed in her presence either," Mrs. Anderson added, giving him a gentle reminder.

"Yes, I'm aware," he replied, sounding as if he had already surrendered to her intentions.

I wondered what they were talking about. What was happening to Emry? What had they done to him? My mind swarmed with all kinds of terrible thoughts, and now, suddenly, I was the one panicking. I had to get out of here. My father had to get me out of here.

"What's going on?" I asked before thinking. "What have you done to him?"

No one turned in my direction, though. They all ignored me as if I hadn't said anything at all, as if I didn't matter, because in their eyes, I didn't.

"Okay." My father stood straighter for a moment. "I don't understand, though, why you can't take her upstairs and put her in one of the bedrooms."

"No way," Lauren said without taking the suggestion into consideration.

"That's out of the question, John. She has a greater chance of escaping up there. Only down here will we have peace of mind that..."

"These conditions are ridiculous!" he shouted. "Would you want to be down here like this; a cot in the dirt with an IV? This is insane."

"Is it?" She walked around in a small circle, hands now clasped together behind her back. "She broke into my home, John. She was

337

digging around for information on him. If she gets out, she'll ruin everything. She'll stop at nothing."

"You have to get me out of here!" I shrieked. They were scheming against Emry. They were going to try to kill him, I was certain of it.

"Do you see, John? See how she's acting." Mrs. Anderson stopped moving and stood directly in front of him, blocking his view of me. "It's proof that he's got her under his spell."

"His spell?" I could feel the tug of pain in my ribs as I attempted to sit up. I fought through the pain so I could get a better look at her. "You're the one who has everyone under a spell, you witch."

Mrs. Anderson ignored my remarks. She simply sighed and continued to watch my father's reaction to the scene before him.

He clamped his fists together at his sides and looked down at the floor. "Are you going to check on her?"

"Of course."

"I mean, really check on her, make sure she's fed and given plenty of water along with the pain medication?"

Mrs. Anderson flashed him a warm smile as if he were being silly by asking such things. "Of course, John. Please don't worry. Everything will be okay. Everything will work out, and all of our hard work will not have been for nothing. You'll see. Just trust me, John. You do trust me, don't you?"

He frowned.

"John?"

She was so annoyingly persistent in the way she acted with him.

338

"I trust you to do the right thing."

She nodded and placed her hand on his arm as a gesture of extra reassurance.

"I don't know about Lauren. Seems like a loose cannon to me." My father met Lauren's eyes as they exchanged nasty glances again.

Mrs. Anderson raised her hand, motioning for Lauren to calm down. "I will handle him." Lauren snorted as if her words were a big joke to him.

My father looked at me then, and I knew he was going to leave me here with them, all alone. I already felt so lonely and abandoned, though he was still in the room with me. He had barely defended me, barely put up any sort of struggle with them. I knew I didn't deserve his defense, but I needed it. He had been my only hope. I know he felt that I had failed him. I had failed Emry as well. I had failed everyone.

"She'll be free to go after it's all over," she told him.

He remained very still and silent for a few moments, taking everything in and running it through his mind. "Your mother is worried sick," he told me harshly. "You've broken her heart." And with those words, I watched him turn away from me and walk up the basement stairs. I heard his footsteps for a brief period of time on the floor overhead and then the front door open and slam shut. He was gone. He had actually done it. He had left me here in this forsaken place with these murderous people.

Mrs. Anderson and Lauren then headed up the stairs also, without saying anything further to me. I wondered if they would take care of me as

339

they had promised my father. I wished Richard wouldn't have intervened. I wished he would have left me to die. I didn't know what was going on with Emry, but I could only imagine their intentions for him. I got a sick feeling in the pit of my stomach every time I thought about what their plans could possibly be. My poor, sweet Emry Logan. How long had it been since I'd seen him? How I longed to be in his arms again. I had repeatedly pushed his memory far from my thoughts for months now. Had he done the same? I was tired of trying to figure out his thoughts when I knew so very little about him. There was no way of knowing, and there was no way I'd ever get the chance to find out either. I couldn't believe it had come down to this.

My eyes scanned the dark walls around me. They settled on the locked door at the other end of the basement. I couldn't even walk, but it was so tempting to try to escape. I knew if I tried, and if I got caught, which I probably would, they'd surely kill me without hesitation. They'd tell my father I hadn't made it through the night, that they'd done everything they could but to no avail.

I laughed out loud. At least I was thinking things through, trying to get an angle on what *could* happen and that there were consequences to my actions. Perhaps Lauren had really taught me a lesson.

I wasn't used to my mind working like this. I barely thought through my actions ahead of time completely. Exhaustion started to settle in as I looked out the small window and saw that it was already dark. I wondered what time it was, what day it was, how long it had been since the actual surgery on my leg. I gave up and didn't try to fight my heavy eyelids any longer. I felt them shut and then stay closed. I just didn't have the strength left to keep them open for another minute longer. And then I fell fast asleep.

Chapter 18

The next few days were blurred together, partially by the pain medication that made me groggy and partially by the fact that I no longer had a sense of day or night. Sometimes loud footsteps coming down the stairs would stir me awake. It was always Lauren, never Mrs. Anderson, who brought me trays of food and glasses of water. He never spoke to me and always gave me mean glances when he'd come. It was against my better judgment to ingest anything they'd brought to me. I was fearful it'd be poisoned, but then I'd end up eating it anyway. I had to get my strength back. I wouldn't give them the satisfaction of dying down here. Not now. Sometimes he'd change my dressings and check my temperature for a fever, but that was all. He'd give me no more information or even question how I was doing. He didn't care. He was only doing what he was told to do by Mrs. Anderson, who was only nursing me back to health because of her relationship with my father, which still confused me. She seemed to be more affectionate with him than he was with her the last time they were together down here. I knew they had to have had a strong friendship as I strongly believed she had him brainwashed in some fashion, but on the other hand, I was starting to doubt the affair I was once convinced they were having. Perhaps it had been all in my mind, twisted by the images I had seen of the two of them together. Perhaps it was merely a friendship of some sort, probably connecting on a level that suited both of them, but maybe no boundaries had been crossed. Maybe they had only been spending so much time together to really be scheming against the so-called evil in Seneca, aka Emry Logan and his black magic and satanic ways that Mrs. Anderson had convinced him if left alone, would begin to corrupt and pollute their beloved community like some sort of virus.

If it were true that they were just friends, nothing more, only something more created by my warped mind, how much pain and suffering I had caused by the misinterpreted communication I had seen them share. I felt a twinge of guilt inside me as I wondered if I had been wrong about the entire thing. I felt remorseful and embarrassed at the same time. What a horrid accusation if it hadn't been true, and to even put that kind of bug in my mother's ear about her husband. What a monster I had been.

As I became less sleepy throughout the days and more aware of my surroundings, my injuries less intense in their pain, I found myself utterly bored out of my mind and so helpless. There was nothing left to do but wait, and even then, I wasn't sure what it was I was waiting for. Something was happening out there, something involving Emry. It was killing me not to know. It just surged my obsession with him into an intense, uncontrollable fire that burned within me. The more I was kept away from him, the greater my desire was to be with him. I wasn't sure what was worse, the pain I had felt initially after being tossed down those stairs, or the desperation of needing to know what was going on with the only man I had ever and would ever truly love.

I occupied myself with replaying every memory I had of the two of us together in my head, trying to remember every detail of his facial features and his body, the way he moved, the way he spoke ever so softly, his words luring me in. I found it disheartening that his face was slipping from my memory.

He became a distorted figure in my mind, and I became angry with myself for forgetting such a beautiful creature as Emry Logan.

When the emotions became too unbearable, I would travel to Evadere in my imagination and try to retrace my steps of the brief period of time I had been able to spend there with him. I would remember the beauty of that world and the mystical atmosphere of the seductive caves and glorious golden grasses. I tried to imagine what life would be like if everything had worked out differently, if Emry and I had met under different circumstances, under more normal circumstances. I pictured us actually dating and getting married. We could've lived on Evadere forever with no one being able to come between us. It would have been beautiful, our life together, our love and the world we lived in.

And perfect. No Mrs. Anderson to intervene. No violence or scheming against him or me, just us together, forever. It was such a shame that all was lost. Happiness just wasn't in the cards for us. The rest of my life certainly would be one of constant misery and of living in a past that seemed to have gone by so quickly like a whirlwind, leaving me overwhelmed with a love too strong to break and a life too desperate to forget. I hated to think about what the future held for me now without any possibility of Emry in it. It seemed so desolate. What a cruel play of fate. I would have to be content with a life of loneliness.

It felt as if I were in this hole of hell for weeks, though I was sure it had been just days, left alone with all my thoughts as if I were slowly losing all remains of sanity within me. My ribs weren't hurting quite as badly, and my healing ankle was beginning to itch. I began to wonder if pins had been placed in the ankle and if so, when exactly those should be removed. I was tempted to ask Lauren about it one day when he was down here, but his grim expression made me decide against it. It felt like it'd be more a waste of breath than anything else, so I didn't say anything to him. I ran a hand through my greasy hair and wrinkled up my nose in disgust. I needed a shower badly. I was sure they could probably smell my stink upstairs by now. And I was sure they didn't care either.

The basement door opened, and I heard footsteps coming down. I sighed as I wondered what Lauren wanted now. He had just given me food not too long ago. The steps were a little lighter than usual. I looked up, knowing it had to be Mrs. Anderson and wondering what she was going to tell me. I was completely shocked by the face that turned to look at me from out of the shadows.

"Holy crap."

"Carlin?" I had never thought I'd be so happy to see her as I was at this very moment. I sat straight up in the cot.

"What have they done to you?" She rushed to my side and quickly assessed my injuries.

"Lauren threw me down the stairs."

She looked horrified to know such information. "I didn't know all this."

"What are you doing here? How'd you get in?"

She shrugged. "I figured if you could do it, so could I." She grinned.

I laughed. I must really have lost my mind if I was happy to be having a normal conversation with my aunt.

"I had to pry the information out of Helene to find out where you were, but she didn't tell me they had done this to you," she quickly explained. "Maybe she didn't know. Maybe John didn't tell her."

"I thought you left Seneca. When'd you get back?"

She shook her head, motioning for me not to ask so many questions all at once. "I did leave. We can talk about all of this later. I have to get you out of here." She examined the cast on my leg and then looked around the room. Her eyes rested on the door across the room with the humungous lock hanging from it.

"Yeah, I don't think it's possible to get out that way," I said, reading her mind.

She rolled her eyes. "Yeah, I must've left my bolt cutters at home this time." She laughed, and I couldn't help but laugh along with her at her sarcasm. "I guess you would've already thought about that anyway. I can't believe you've been down here."

"How long have I been down here?"

"I'm not sure exactly. I came back and you were gone. It took me a couple days to sweet talk Helene just enough to get her to slip. I was thinking about getting her drunk and getting her to talk that way."

"But she doesn't drink." I winced as she put an arm underneath my shoulder and helped me stand.

My muscles ached from lack of use.

"That's what made getting her drunk so impossible."

She helped me to both feet and gave me a moment to steady myself and regain some sort of balance.

I lifted the injured left ankle in the air behind me and depended upon balance on the right leg.

"Sorry if I stink," I said, sounding like a joke but really serious as I could only imagine how horrible I really did look and smell.

"You do, kind of." She smiled at me and then helped me move over to the bottom of the basement stairs.

"We're going out *that* way?" I raised my eyebrows, questioning her decision.

"Can you think of a better way?" she asked, irritated by my lack of trust. "Besides, they're not here."

"How can you be sure?"

"Because I came in through the front door, and because I know they wouldn't be missing it."

"Missing what?"

She helped me get up a couple of the stairs as I still hobbled on one leg. She looked hesitantly at me. "The end of the trial."

"What?" I hissed as the realization of what they had been talking about swarmed my brain.

"Emry's?"

She pressed her lips together as if she might be sorry that she had

347

told me and then nodded her head. "They're giving him the jury's verdict this afternoon. I've come to break you out of here. We don't have much time to waste."

I paused a moment to look her over. "Wait. You mean you're going to help get me there; to the courthouse, I mean?"

She raised her eyebrows. "That's right. Do you want to stay down here and talk about it some more or get the hell out of here?"

I shut my mouth and concentrated on hopping up the stairs. We made it to the top, and I didn't even bother to glance behind me at what had been my cage over the past few days. I nervously glanced around the open rooms upstairs as we passed by them. Carlin was right. No one was home. And then we walked outside, the warm, fresh air, heaven to my lungs from the dampness I had been inhaling all that time. I felt even stronger and knew that a shower would make me feel even better.

Carlin's car was parked right in front of the porch. She helped me hobble down the steps, and within a few minutes, I was safely inside her getaway vehicle. Relief washed over me.

"Let's get out of here," she suggested.

"No argument here." I focused on her getting out of the driveway and smiled as I thought of how Mrs. Anderson would feel when she knew I'd escaped. It was a brief moment of satisfaction. I couldn't go back to my house. My parents would forbid me to go to the trial. Once I saw we were securely on the road and speeding quickly away from Mrs. Anderson's house, I decided I should probably voice my concerns to her. "I don't think we should go back to my house."

"We're not," she replied, her eyes glued to the road, every once in a while glancing in her rearview mirror as if to make sure no one was following us.

"I have to get a shower and get cleaned up before…"

"You need to just relax," she said, interrupting my little rant. "I'm not an idiot, you know."

"I didn't mean that you were."

She looked over at me and gave me a little smile. "Don't worry. I wouldn't dream of taking you back to that place. We're going to my place."

"Your place?"

She nodded. "I'm not staying with John and Helene. I have my own motel room a few miles away. You can get showered, and I'll let you borrow some of my clothes, since you're so fond of borrowing them anyway," she added.

I blushed then, the dress of hers I had ruined popping up into my mind. "Thanks, Carlin. I really mean it. Thanks."

"I couldn't let John get away with just leaving you there with those crazies. I never did like the Andersons. They're a little off, don't you think?"

I laughed at the word she had used to describe them. "No, they're as normal as they come."

She chuckled. "See, I always knew you and I had more in common than met the eye."

Within minutes, we were pulling in front of a small motel that had doors on the outside leading into the rooms. She pointed to which one was hers.

"I'll help you get settled in there, and then I have to go see what I can do about finding you a pair of crutches."

The room was neatly kept as I wondered how long Carlin had been back in town. I figured not long.

I wondered why she had come back here and why she wasn't staying with her sister. Maybe they had had a fight. All sorts of questions popped into my head, but mostly I was wondering what the rest of the day had in store for me.

Mrs. Anderson and Lauren, even my father, were all hiding the trial from me. I felt as if I had a thousand questions squirming around in my head about that as well. And what was everyone going to say when they saw me there? Would they throw me out? Could they throw me out? I had so many emotions rushing through me all at once. I had this new sense of adrenaline from Carlin helping me to escape, that I had lived through that situation, and now I was going to see Emry today. But then I had to realize that it might be a sad day. Mrs. Anderson's scheme may have worked as she had tried desperately to turn everyone against him, to get enough false evidence to make the jury believe he was a murderer and call out the guilty verdict. He might be going to spend his entire life in jail. The sudden sadness didn't go well with the adrenaline. I felt a little woozy from it all. I hopped over and quickly sat down on the queen-sized bed.

"Are you okay?" Carlin asked me, walking into the bathroom and grabbing towels and shampoo for me to use and tossing them onto the sink.

"I will be."

"A little overwhelming for one day?" She peeked her head back out and smirked.

"You could say that." I rubbed my temples with my fingers and tried to focus solely on just breathing.

"Listen, I need to get you some crutches. Are you going to be alright showering on your own? I have this plastic bag that you can use to cover up your cast so it stays dry." She held up the bag for me to see.

I nodded. "Just give me a moment. I'm trying to absorb this thing called my life at the moment." Carlin laughed aloud. "It's not really that funny." She had this odd habit of inappropriately laughing when she shouldn't. I didn't know if it bothered anyone else, but it always struck a nerve with me.

"Sorry." She flashed me another quick smile. "It's just, you sound like a whiny teenager."

"Do I?" I narrowed my eyes at her. "I will be forever grateful for you rescuing me, but please don't pretend to have a clue about what I've been through or compare it to a drama-filled teenage girl. There's no comparison."

"No? Alright, I'll shut up." She threw a few more things in the bathroom and then arranged them so I could have easy access to them with my gimp leg. When she appeared again, she paused to look at me. "It's just, it kind of is the same."

Why did she always have to be like this? Couldn't she just ever let things be without giving me the full analysis of her opinion? I didn't ever want to hear it, but especially not right now.

"You know," she continued, "first loves and all. The obsession, the desperation. I mean, it's totally normal, but it's worse with first loves."

"You make it sound as if there will be others."

She shrugged. "Perhaps. Who knows? But the first one, that's the one that seems to always stick with you. The memories linger throughout the years. They're vivid, clear, haunting."

"I know what you're comparing this to, Carlin." I ran my hand over the smooth burgundy-colored comforter underneath me. "I know all about Russell."

The mention of the name alone seemed to pain her. "Helene told you." I nodded. "Well, you'd better get showered and all prettied up. You look like you just got ran over by a truck."

"Thanks."

"I'll be back. You sure you're alright on your own?"

"Yeah."

I watched Carlin leave. If I had known that all it took was talking about Russell to let me alone, I would have used it as ammo in the past. I immediately felt remorse as I thought that. She had been in love with him, and it obviously still bothered her. I actually felt sorry for my aunt. Then I glanced at the clock on the nightstand beside the bed. It was almost noon. She hadn't told me what time the verdict was being read, but I assumed I'd better hurry nevertheless.

It had taken a little getting used to at first from the awkwardness of not being able to use my left leg to stand on, plus hoping that I had the plastic bag on tight enough so that no water leaked in to make the shower a little tougher than I had anticipated. The warm water rushed over my dirty skin and felt wonderful, despite a few balance issues. I had never enjoyed taking a shower this much before. Then again, I had never been this filthy before either. I wrapped a towel around myself and opened the bathroom door to peek out. Carlin still wasn't back yet. I wondered where she was going to find crutches. Then I used the palm of my hand to wipe the steam off the mirror so I could get a look at myself. I had some bruising on the side of my face that had turned dark purple. I took a closer look. I hadn't even remembered feeling any sort of pain or discomfort there. My body was probably full of bruises and scrapes that I had been unaware of, masked by the stronger pain of the ankle and ribs.

Richard had initially wrapped a large bandage tightly around my ribcage, so I decided to try to wrap it back around myself, but it was too hard to manage alone. I would have to wait for Carlin to get back and ask for her help.

I looked down at the sink full of all kinds of things in front of me; powders, lotions and soaps. I doubted any amount of makeup was going to fully cover up that bruise. I would just have to do what I could to make myself look decent. I laughed out loud, thinking that that could even be a remote possibility.

I started with drying my hair first as I ran one of Carlin's thick brushes through it. I felt a million times better scrubbing Mrs. Anderson's basement off my body. My ankle suddenly began throbbing as I realized I had no more pain medication. Lauren had been in charge of that. Oh well, I would have to do without. Maybe Carlin had some ibuprofen or something lying around.

"Choose anything to wear?"

I heard the hotel door click shut as Carlin had returned. She walked over to me in the bathroom.

"Wow."

"What?" I asked.

"Nothing. You clean up well."

"Ha, ha." I glared at her.

She smiled. "No, I mean it, Annie. You look so much better. Let me help you with your makeup."

"First, I need help with this bandage around my ribs."

She looked surprised. She hadn't known that my ribs were injured. "He did a number on you, didn't he?"

"Yeah."

"Lauren Anderson always was a scary beast."

She helped wrap it tight enough so as to ease the pain.

"You don't have any pain pills by chance, do you?"

"One sec." She disappeared around the corner and grabbed her purse. She opened it and dug around for a moment. "Here," she said, pulling a bottle out. "Better double the dosage by the look of you."

"Thanks."

"Sure."

Carlin helped me with my makeup and then continued to straighten and smooth out my long brown hair. She stood back admiringly. "Take a look."

I peered at myself in the large mirror. She had done a good job. The bruise was barely noticeable, and I actually looked pretty fantastic. Satisfied, we both walked out into the larger room. There were two crutches leaning against the side of the bed.

"You found some?"

She nodded as if extremely proud of herself.

"Where on earth did you find them?"

"Oh, I have connections in this town." She grinned. "Come on, try them out. Ever had to use them before?"

"No."

"No? Of course not." She rolled her eyes and walked over to retrieve them for me. "You put them under your arms like this and then walk like this."

I watched her demonstrate for me. "Yeah, I've seen people use them before," I said in almost a borderline nasty tone. But Carlin never cared when I was like that. She always looked amused when she pushed my buttons and I retaliated.

"Okay. Let's find something for you to wear." She sorted through her open suitcase, pulling out outfit after outfit. She held up a purple dress.

"I'm not wearing a dress," I warned her.

She quickly tossed it aside. "No, of course not." She pulled up a pair of white slacks, followed by a light green V-neck. "How about this?"

I stared at it. It wasn't bad. A little fancy for my taste, but everything about Carlin screamed fancy or rather, wannabe fancy, I should say. "Not bad."

"Try it on. We're about the same size."

I stood in front of the mirror, the crutches securely under my arms for balance. I still looked pretty damaged, but overall much improved. "So, you were pretty mad that father left me there?"

She tossed up her head as if mad were an understatement. "I couldn't believe it. Well, he wouldn't tell me where you were. I knew he knew. I knew it had to be bad. Good thing Helene breaks a little easier than him. I don't think he'd ever tell me. I don't know if I would have thought to look at the Anderson place either."

"Where else would you have thought?"

She shrugged. "I don't know. I just knew I had to get Helene to talk."

I sat down on the bed and waited for Carlin as she seemed to be sorting through her purse of what she did and didn't need. I watched her toss a few items into the trash can that was sitting along the wall. "I was pretty upset when he left me. He just turned around and walked up the stairs. Horrified was more like it, but I can't say I blame him. I mean, it's not like I'm even his *real* daughter anyway."

She turned around to look at me, surprise written all over her face.

"Oh, come on. Like you didn't know."

She returned to what she had been doing. "No, of course I knew. I just didn't know you knew."

"Yeah. I found out in kind of a strange way. Emry's adopted

mother actually was the one to tell me."

She stopped again and turned to look at me again. "Really? What else did she tell you?" "Not much else. I went home and questioned Helene. She started crying and everything."

Carlin rolled her eyes. "Of course she did. So did you ask her who your real mother was?"

"Yeah."

"What'd she say?"

"Well, basically that my mother abandoned me and someone found me and took me to some adoption agency."

"What?"

I gave her a hard look. "That's not how it happened?"

"Absolutely not."

"Helene lied to me?"

"Unbelievable. I can't believe she told you that."

I took a deep breath. The force of the hard expansion against the bandage caused me to wince slightly and bend over in pain. The pain pills hadn't kicked in yet. I was probably in need of something stronger. "Tell me what you know, Carlin. Please," I begged her.

She sighed and then zipped up her purse and tossed it on the nightstand. She came over and sat down beside me on the bed. "Annie," she began.

"I hate it when you call me that."

"I know." She pressed her lips together. "I have something to tell you."

"What is it?"

"You already said your day was overwhelming enough."

"Just tell me. You can't just say something like that and leave me hanging."

"Alright."

She swallowed hard as my mind raced with what she was about to tell me. Maybe she knew who my real parents were.

"I'm your mother."

I felt my throat grow instantly dry. "What did you say?"

"I'm your real mother."

I tried to stand up and get away from her. Now she was lying to me, too? How could she say such a thing? We were nothing alike.

"Just sit back down before you hurt yourself," she instructed me. "I came back here for you. It's time you knew the truth. You're miserable here with *them*. I just know you are. It's written all over your face. Then, when I found out you were missing, I went absolutely crazy."

"Wait." I held up my hand to stop her. "You're my real mother?"

She nodded, giving me a moment to absorb it. It seemed utterly impossible to wrap my mind around. "*You* gave birth to *me*?"

"Yes."

"Why would Mother lie about that?"

"Because she's a coward."

I sat down as my head began to spin again. I needed to eat something.

"I know it's pretty hard for you to believe, given that you can't even stand the sight of me and all, but we're more alike than you think. This little rebellious thing you have going on here right now, that's all me."

"Now isn't the best time for jokes."

"Okay, okay, sorry. I've never been so good with the serious stuff."

"Well, try."

She took a deep breath. "Alright. Here's the cold hard truth. Helene told you about Russell, right?"

"Yeah."

"We were in love. I mean, I can't even begin to tell you how inseparable we were, but he was a little older, and when you're a teenager, a few years makes a big difference."

"But she said that he was in love with her, too," I interrupted, wanting to get all of the details exactly right this time.

"Well, not exactly. I always suspected he had a thing for her, too. I know she liked him and was jealous that he was with me. I always thought they hung out together because he felt sorry for her because he knew she liked him. The whole triangle thing was kind of complicated, but anyway, a long story short, I got pregnant."

"So this Russell is my real father?"

"Right. Russell Flaherty."

"So what happened?"

"Well, if you let me get to it."

"Sorry." I tried to remain quiet so I could listen, but I couldn't guarantee that I wasn't going to interrupt again.

"So I was only fourteen, a freshman in high school. I wasn't ready for you yet. I had no means of taking care of you. But I couldn't just get rid of you. I never abandoned you like she claimed. You meant too much to me. You were mine and Russell's love child." She paused a moment so as to let that all sink in. "Helene was furious, but we came to an understanding. She and Russell were supposed to get married and take care of you. It was perfect. She was my sister and so we figured you'd look similar to her, that it'd all work out, all fall into place. That way, at least you would have your real father with you."

"So they were really engaged?"

"Right, but not for long. He only stuck around for a short period of time after you were born. He got cold feet. He didn't want to marry Helene. He wasn't sure he could handle a child at that age either, so he left her there all alone with you. I helped her as much as I could, but I was so very young and incapable of such things. I hit the road the first chance I got when I turned eighteen to get out of Seneca. But it broke my heart, especially the older I got. I never stopped loving Russell, wondering where he went. I couldn't stand that Helene was raising you, but what could I do? I couldn't tear you away from the only home you'd ever known. It just didn't seem fair to do that to you, so I stayed away as much as possible. It was easier that way."

"So what happened to Russell?"

She folded her hands in front of her and clasped them together. "I don't know. Never heard from him again."

"So, Matthew?" I asked.

"They really did adopt Matthew a few years after you from an

360

adoption agency, but not you. You were mine."

I stared at her for a moment. Maybe I was more like her than I thought. Maybe that's why we never got along because of our similarities. "This day is insane."

"Enough drama to fill up the life of a teenage girl." She winked at me. I rolled my eyes. "I didn't really expect this from you. I thought you'd be mad."

"Huh," I said, thinking about that for a moment. "I would've thought so, too, but for some odd reason I'm not. A strange twist of fate for sure, though. I wasn't expecting that one coming."

"You see, Helene loves you so much. You were the child she always wished she could've had with Russell. She lives in a fantasy world, Helene does. I'm so sorry that you found out that way and thought that you'd been abandoned like that. I'm just plain old sorry."

"That story makes more sense, though," I admitted. "Being fourteen and Russell's leaving."

"So you see, we are all family. You have a real family. You were loved by everyone in different ways. You don't have to call me mom or anything. I mean, I'm not expecting anything to change. You can still hate me if you want to."

I stared into her eyes, the reality and shock of it all hitting me. Carlin was my real mother. Wow. "I don't hate you."

"Anyway," she said, motioning toward the clock, "we'd better get going. Don't want to be late."

"Can we go through a drive through or something on the way? I'm

361

starving."

"Sure. Whatever you want."

I put the crutches under my arms as I stood and practiced on them by heading toward the door. They were a little awkward as I struggled to get a steady pace going with them.

Carlin grabbed the keys to the room and shoved them in her pocket. "By the way, the reason I call you Annie in that way?"

"Yeah?" I looked back at her as we left the motel room.

"It's because the deal I had made with Helene was that she could name you. I didn't want you to be named Anna. That's why I just say Annie. It was always hard for me to swallow that I didn't get to name my own kid."

"So what would you have named me?"

She thought for a moment as she opened up the passenger side door of her car and helped me in.

"Juliet."

"Really?"

"I always liked that name."

For the first time in a long time I had a sense of belonging, even if it meant Carlin was my mother. It was as if one of the many voids from within me had been filled. I did have a family, and I was loved.

"I came back to help you find your love. I don't know how it's all going to pan out, but I don't want you to lose him like I lost Russell. If you love someone, you have to fight for them. I admired your courage of standing up to Helene and John when I was staying there," she told me as we started to drive down the road.

"You said love didn't exist."

"It doesn't matter what I said. That was just part of the act. I do believe in love. I do. I don't know who this Emry Logan is, but if you like him, there has to be something good in him. Plus, he's hot." She flashed me a big smile.

"You've seen him?"

She nodded. "I've been attending the trial."

"You have to catch me up on that. I need to know everything."

Chapter 19

I stuffed a huge bite of hamburger in my mouth and leaned my head back against the leather headrest in Carlin's car. The window was down halfway as a warm breeze tumbled in, tossing my hair about playfully. I tried not to think for a moment. I just sat there, letting the sunlight burn into my skin and enjoyed the warmth of it, enjoyed the feeling of the taste of a greasy hamburger in my mouth. I tried to relax myself entirely, knowing that my fate would soon be determined with what the jury decided, that Emry's verdict was also my own.

"So, you ready to know what's been going on in there?" Carlin asked, gulping down a sip of her sweet tea and then putting it back in the cup holder beside her.

I sighed and then looked over at the courthouse in front of us. The sight of it worried me. I guess quiet meditation time was over. "Yeah, let's hear it."

"They had this witness come forward. I think Helig was her name?"

"Stacy Helig."

"Right. Do you know about her?"

I nodded. "I know what Emry told me about her; that she wasn't even there and that somehow they had probably paid her off to get her to say that she was there, knowing it was her word against his."

"Oh." Carlin picked up her sweet tea again and held it in her hand. "Well, she did a good job at pretending she was there then."

"Thanks, Carlin. I mean it."

She gave me a look of uncertainty. "For what now?"

"For being on my side."

"I've always been on your side, kid." She gave me a quick wink. I laughed and finished off the rest of the hamburger.

"She gave all these details about Wes and how he had been pushed by Emry and even knew the details of where he had fallen on the ground."

I sighed, irritated. "Of course she did, because *they* knew that and coached her."

She shrugged. "Right. So this Helig woman was pretty convincing. I was sure it was all downhill from there for poor Emry."

"Great."

"No, but listen. Emry has this top notch lawyer."

"Really? How'd he afford that?"

Carlin made a loud slurping sound as she sucked down the rest of her tea with a straw. "No idea. But he's really good. I mean, *really* good. He made that Helig woman look like a fool, even made her stumble a few times. You should've seen the look on Mrs. Anderson's face when he did that. It took all I had not to laugh out loud."

I saw a few people walk up the steps of the courthouse and go inside. I still didn't feel ready to see Mrs. Anderson, Lauren, my father, Buck, nor did I feel ready to see him, Emry. It had been so long.

What if he didn't even notice me there?

"So then they questioned Emry," Carlin continued. "He was very straight forward and kind of quiet in his manner. He never got upset or lost his temper."

"Not violent enough to be a criminal, huh?" I smiled.

"If his only crime is breaking hearts." I glared at her.

"Sorry."

"So how did he do against their lawyer? Did they trip him up?"

"Not at all, actually. He said that Stacy Helig wasn't even there, that he thought there was some sort of underlying conspiracy going on behind his back, that he wasn't sure why, and then his lawyer jumped in and connected all the dots with the conspiracy, that no one had any real proof on him, that Wes and him were best friends. Wes's mother was even called as a witness to say how wonderful of a person Emry is, how Wes and him would've never fought, that it had to have been a huge misunderstanding. I mean, if Wes's own mother can assume it an accident, how can the jury not? The victim's own mother doesn't believe Emry could've killed her son."

I thought about it all for a moment. "So was anything brought up about black magic, anything said along those lines?"

"Actually, yes. What do you know about that?" Carlin asked me.

Another gust of wind came in through the open window and I inhaled deeply, my lungs welcoming it. "Well, that's what they're accusing him of. There was some sort of incident between Emry and Buck, and Buck ran off and told Mrs. Anderson and they deemed him a worshipper of the devil."

Carlin let out a loud chuckle. "Too funny. That's exactly what Emry's lawyer made it out to be, too; a huge joke. He made Buck look like a total fool."

"Buck was questioned?"

"Yeah. Buck isn't very smart, is he?"

"Not at all."

Carlin smiled as she must've been remembering Buck's face as Emry's lawyer interrogated him.

"The lawyer was like, look at Emry Logan looking all satanic with his piercings and gothic mannerisms. Everything about him just screams the dark side."

Now I burst out laughing. It sounded more nervous than happy, but I was so thrilled to be hearing how well the trial had gone for him. It was giving me more hope by the minute.

"They tried to bring in his past offenses. I don't know. His lawyer seemed to prove all of them as moot, that they had never been proven either, and that this whole thing was based upon a group of people that just didn't like Emry and had built up a case around him that didn't have any solid foundation to it whatsoever."

More cars pulled up and a few more people entered the building. We both sat there in the silence for a few moments. Then Carlin turned toward me.

"Listen, I want you to be careful in there. I mean, I don't know what could possibly happen. I doubt much, but still. Everyone will be in there, but I'll be by your side, like I should've been all along."

I stared at her, dumbfounded by her sudden motherly nature about her, surprised that she had it in her, but I supposed it had been there all along. She had been bitter all these years, not just about Russell, but about me, too. She had tried to make the right decision for both of us at the time, and I agreed; fourteen was very young. How could I be angry with her? How could I not sympathize with her? We were two lost souls drifting around this world without a seemingly knowing cause, the men we loved out of reach. She was trying to help me make mine somehow within my reach.

"They're going to be furious with you, too," I said, reminding her of her role in my escape and how easily they would guess her involvement.

"Those people don't scare me." She chuckled lightly. I wasn't sure if it was just a cover-up. Maybe they really did frighten her on some level. "So, you ready for this?"

I inhaled deeply and then let it all out, trying to rid myself of the butterflies starting to accumulate rapidly in my stomach. I was dying to see Emry's face again, but I was terrified of his reaction. I was terrified that he was going to hear the word guilty. I was terrified that he was going to reject me.

"As ready as I'll ever be."

Carlin got out of the car and hurried over to my side. She opened my door and pulled out the crutches, then helped me up and onto them.

"You good?"

I nodded, the anxiety overwhelming me as I felt like I was about to enter the dragon's lair.

"We're a little late going in for the verdict, you know."

"Are we?" I raised my eyebrows up at her, unsure of what she'd meant.

"Well, yeah. I'm sure they haven't started yet. There's probably a bunch of preliminary stuff they have to get out of the way beforehand. I just kind of figured it'd be best if we were the last ones in.

That way everyone would already be seated inside, and no one could try to stop us before even getting through the doors."

Carlin was being pretty smart about this whole thing. I don't know that I would've ever thought of that. I gave her an immediate look of both surprise and approval. "Okay then. Let's do this."

We walked side by side, estranged mother and daughter, up the courtroom stairs as I hobbled along and she helped to steady me. She opened the heavy front door and I stepped inside. All was quiet. No one else was in sight.

"Down there." Carlin pointed to an already closed door just ahead of me on my left.

I hesitated but continued, my hands feeling already clammy with sweat as I gripped onto the crutches. We met eyes one last time as she lurched open the door to the courtroom and held it open for me to go inside first. I tried to compose myself as I forced myself in.

Everyone had their backs turned toward me. A group of jurors sat just ahead. They were the only ones facing me. There were rows of benches, and they were mostly already filled up. I didn't know what to do.

Where should I sit? Where was Emry? And then I saw him, just the back of his head, his hair slightly longer than I had remembered, his figure positioned upright as if eager to know what would become of his future as well. My heart instantly leaped into the air, and I actually gasped at the sight of the back of his head. I had to get his attention, but how? No one had noticed I'd come in, or even looked my way. And then Carlin stepped in. Her stilettos immediately echoed off the hardwood floor as she took just a few steps forward. Everyone turned their heads to see whose shoes had made that sound.

Great. Good job, Carlin, I thought to myself.

I now recognized everyone as I felt the heat of redness gush into my cheeks at the sudden attention.

Mrs. Anderson and Lauren were toward the front, closer to Emry. They were gawking at me in astonishment. I wondered if they had been home yet and learned of my sudden disappearance from their comfy little nest of a basement, or if just now the realization had hit them. Lauren looked so furious I thought he was about to leap out of his seat and lunge for me. I quickly looked away from them. And then I saw, just a few rows back, my father sitting with some of his police buddies, Buck among them. He, too, looked completely dumbfounded that I was standing there at the entrance of the courtroom with Carlin.

"Come on," Carlin urged me, pulling on my arm toward an empty spot to sit in the back.

I started to follow her, but then stopped dead in my tracks. I felt the pair of eyes on me and instantly knew they belonged to him. They could have burned a hole straight through me and if they did, I wouldn't have cared. I turned toward him and met his stare, his beautiful blue eyes locked on me. His face twisted up in a look of pain as he saw me, and I quickly realized why. I had come in with bruises on my face and on crutches. He was probably imaging the worst, and I knew he was right for thinking so. I had stuck my nose in too far, and this was my consequence, and I knew he could read it all from my face. I pressed my lips together and gave him a little smile. I was glad that he knew I was here, knew that I supported him still, and hoped that deep down he knew that I was madly in love with him still.

I tore myself away from his stare and took a seat beside Carlin. I recognized the woman sitting in front of me. The smell of her cheap perfume invaded my nostrils the moment I got too close to her. It was Candy, Emry's ex-wife. She gave me an unwelcome look also, but then hurried to turn back around so all I could see was the back of her bleached hair in its sprayed to death up-do position.

As I set the crutches up beside me and leaned them against the side of the bench, I looked over toward Emry once again. He put up his hand and waved to me in front of everyone there and added a gentle smile as he did so. My mouth dropped open. Everyone immediately stared at me once again. I felt tears well up in my eyes at the gesture, and I, too, raised my hand to give him a little wave. And then I watched as he turned back around and faced forward.

I felt Carlin put her hand on mine and realized that my hand was shaking in a nervous tremor. I had gotten through the worst of it. I was here. I had made it. No one had stopped us. No one had tried to kill me...yet.

After several minutes, a short man with a bald head came to the front of the room. I immediately realized he was the judge, and my heart began to speed up once again. The anticipation in the room was thick and heavy.

"Good afternoon," the man bellowed out.

"Good afternoon," everyone mumbled back.

He put on a pair of glasses and looked out at Emry sitting before him. "We are at a conclusion to the trial of Mr. Emry Logan and the charge of the murder of Weslie Campbell. Mr. Logan has pled not guilty. Jurors, have you made a decision?"

A thin, tall man stood. He was at the end of the group of jurors. "We have, your Honor."

"Good. Please come forward."

The juror walked up to the judge and handed him a piece of paper. The judge inspected it for a few moments and then took the glasses back off his face, folded them, and set them down on the desk in front of him.

"On the charge of first degree murder of Weslie Campbell, how have you found Emry Logan?" the judge asked.

The tall man smoothed his hand down over the jacket of his suit. I thought it seemed like an eternity before he opened his mouth.

"We find the defendant, not guilty."

"Oh my," I hissed, relief rushing over me. Had he really just said those words, or had I misheard them? I looked over at Carlin, who had a huge smile on her face. She shrugged. The whole room began buzzing in awe and surprise. It was obvious that the majority of them totally disagreed with the decision the jurors had made. I, on the other hand, was so happy I was almost tempted to start crying right there. "Does that mean he's free?"

"Free," Carlin repeated, nodding.

Mrs. Anderson immediately stood and made a big production about stomping out of the courtroom.

She scowled at me before exiting the room. I watched Lauren follow. He, however, did not bother to look down at me.

"Well, congratulations, Mr. Logan," the judge said. "It appears you have your answer."

I wanted to go over to Emry right away before my father or Buck could get to me first. I didn't want to talk to them. I reached out for my crutches as I saw Emry stand and shake the hand of the man next to him. I realized that that must be his top notch attorney as Carlin had described him. He was older but very neat and well-kept. He smiled at Emry and shook his hand furiously as I was sure they were both exchanging excited words about their victory.

"Carlin?"

"Huh?"

"Who is Emry's lawyer?"

She took a moment to try to recall the name. "I think it was something like Ben. Ben Hanley, I believe."

"Hanley?" The word sliced through me just then like a knife. I immediately became stricken with panic. I knew *exactly* where I had heard that name before. When I had visited the town of Elverson and ran into the little girl named Lucy and she had brought me into her mother's house, who had told me about a woman named Hanley, the same woman presumed to have been Mrs. Anderson, perhaps her maiden name, but the same person.

Carlin instantly read my face. "Why do you look like that? What's wrong?"

I closed my eyes for a moment as I felt Emry's tiny moment of freedom, of happiness vanishing quickly, moment by moment. Mrs. Anderson had planned this whole thing out. She didn't want him to be sentenced as guilty. She wanted him free to walk out of here so she could have him killed. I felt the tremor return in my hand and I felt wobbly even with the crutches.

"Annie?" Carlin reached her arms out as if she were about to catch me if I passed out. "Are you okay?"

"No. It's bad, very bad," I mumbled.

A crowd of people still lingered in the courtroom. I caught another glimpse of Emry speaking with his attorney still and another man who had approached him.

"I have no idea what you're talking about."

"I know." I had to think fast, but my mind was spinning. How could I stop this from happening?

"You said his name's Ben Hanley."

"So?"

"There was another case similar to this one. I don't have time to tell you the whole story, but another guy was found innocent just like this and was murdered as he left the courtroom. The woman believed to be involved in helping to get that man behind bars originally was named Hanley also."

She gave me a stumped expression. "I'm really not following."

I sighed, irritated that she couldn't understand, but really, how could she? She had no idea what was going on. I was the only one in this entire room besides those who had evil intentions for Emry who even had a clue. "It was Mrs. Anderson. Mrs. Anderson's name used to be Hanley. That man's name is Hanley. Don't you see? They're related. They have to be."

Carlin looked past me to see where Ben Hanley stood. "Like siblings?" I shrugged. "You think Mrs. Anderson is going to try to kill Emry when he leaves the building?" She was finally catching on. I nodded. "Are you sure?"

My stomach felt like there was a brick in it. I felt as if I could throw up at any moment, but I had other things to worry about than my emotions. I tried to focus on how I could get Emry out of here, alive. "If that guy is her relative somehow, maybe he was in on it," I whispered. "This was all a scheme of hers. Don't you see? Ben Hanley was in on it. He's working *with* her so Emry will get out of the building and that'll give her, or someone she's hired, the chance to get a shot at him."

"I don't know how you know all this," Carlin said, "but you have to go to him and tell him everything you've just told me."

My eyes skimmed over the thinning crowd of people. I saw Emry, now turned in my direction. It looked like he was searching for me as well. Our eyes met. Sadness flooded over me at the thought of someone trying to kill him, of someone wanting him dead. He was too beautiful to be lifeless. He was too beautiful to be mine, but I wanted him, selfishly so. Then he smiled.

I started to make my way over to him, struggling with the crutches on the way. And then I stood before him, finally. There were no barriers between us. There was just us, face to face. I felt the tears rush into my eyes as I buried my face into his chest. He wrapped his arms around me and held me tight, just letting me cry on him for a moment. Then I bent my head backward and peered up at him. He grinned again.

"What happened to you?" he asked.

I wiped away the wetness from my face with my arm. "You don't want to know."

"No, probably not." He gave me a wary look as if trying to figure it out but regretting doing so. "I can't believe you're here."

"I would've been for the whole thing had I even known, or had I …" He raised his eyebrows. "Like I said, never mind."

A sudden anger burned within him as I could tell he got the general concept. He hugged me tight again, pressing his head down against mine. I wasn't sure who was watching us. I'm sure people were staring, but this was one time I absolutely had no cares about anyone else but the most important person holding me in his arms. I had craved for this moment for months. I had tried to even forget about him, but Emry Logan wasn't someone to just cast out of the mind so easily.

"We can let it all go now," he whispered, putting his hand underneath my chin and pulling my face upward next to his. "We have our beginning now. Nobody can stop us."

"No, Emry, wait …" But my words were interrupted by his lips pressing down on my own in a kiss that made all the bad dissipate from within my mind at that moment. All I could focus on was this beautiful moment and the way his lips felt against my own, the way his breath felt hot on my tear- stained cheek.

"I almost thought you'd given up on me," he whispered.

I blushed just then, feeling the shame of what he didn't know; that I had, well, at least tried to. I had been so convincing that I had almost tricked myself into believing it as well. What an idiot I had been.

"I love you, Anna James." He smiled at me again.

"I love you, too," I whispered and pushed up to kiss him again.

"And who is this?"

Emry released his hold on me at the sound of the voice. He put his hand on my back being cautious of my crutches holding me up. He turned me around to face his attorney, Ben Hanley.

"This is Anna," he said proudly.

Ben extended his hand out to me. I slowly balanced my crutch against my hip so I could have a free hand to shake his. I gritted my teeth together but tried to force a smile and be polite.

"It's nice to meet you, Anna. I'm Ben Hanley, Emry's attorney. He's told me so much about you. You're pretty much the only thing that got him through all the time he spent in prison," Ben said.

He had a warm smile and a gentle face. He looked very professional. It was hard to hate him as much as I did at that moment when he was such a likable guy. Looks were so deceiving sometimes, I reminded myself. I couldn't let his pleasant personality sidestep my attention to the task at hand. I had to tell Emry about his untrustworthy lawyer and his evil intentions. I hoped he was going to leave, at least give us a moment to ourselves.

"I don't know if that's entirely true," I managed to get out, the words feeling like they were sticking to my tongue.

Emry laughed. "Yeah, right. You're so modest."

Ben clasped his hands together. "Well, alright, let's get you out of here. I'm sure you're anxious to go."

"That's an understatement," Emry replied.

The panic overtook me again. Ben Hanley wasn't going to leave. He was actually going to be the one to guide us out the doors. I had to do something, but before I knew it, Emry had his hand firmly on my back again as he led me toward the doors out of the room.

"If I didn't think you'd be embarrassed, I'd carry you out of here so you didn't have to use those things," he joked.

I didn't smile. I couldn't think of anything else but that something terrible was about to happen if Emry got near the front entrance of the courthouse.

"Emry, I need to…"

"Hey, congratulations, Man," a guy said, quickly shaking Emry's hand and making him incapable of paying attention to what I was trying to tell him.

"Yeah, thanks," Emry said.

Before I knew it, we were already outside of the room and in the hallway. There were a lot more people out here, most of them not happy about the verdict and glaring at Emry, especially now that they saw that I was by his side. My father and Buck were leaning up against the wall. When Buck saw us together, his face turned pale. I looked away from them. I refused to worry about what they were thinking right now as I continued to get dragged along by Emry.

Ben, who had only been a few steps ahead of us, turned quickly on his heels and faced us. "Listen," he said in a low tone so nobody else could hear what he was saying, "I think we should go out through the other doors; the back way out."

Emry raised his eyebrows suspiciously at him.

Ben frowned. "I just think there's going to be too much publicity, even more when the press sees her." He nodded toward me.

Emry wrapped his arm around my waist and pulled me closer. "You're right, Ben. Where's the other exit?"

"Let's just try to do this discretely," Ben suggested.

"Emry," I tried to say.

"You do want to come with me, don't you?" he asked as we moved slowly but steadily toward the back of the courthouse.

"Yes," I answered. "But shouldn't we…"

"They're following us," he said.

"Who?"

He glanced over his shoulder. "Pastor James and Buck Brady."

I didn't bother to look myself. I took his word for it. I found myself distracted. Emry wasn't listening to me. I wasn't being forceful enough. But what should I do? I couldn't make a scene in front of Ben. I was afraid he'd kill him right then and there if I confronted him. I could be making it worse.

But why had he suggested the back way? My heart thumped wildly in my chest. He probably had someone out there waiting for Emry, maybe even waiting for the both of us. The back door was now in sight. Adrenaline raged within me as I didn't know what to do. I didn't know how to stop it. I was sure that we were both about to die.

My eyes darted around madly for something, anything that would be able to help me in my moment of pure desperation. There wasn't even anybody down at this end of the hall. I could hear footsteps behind us, though, and I knew that it was my father and Buck hot on our heels to come retrieve me, to convince me of what a horrendous mistake I was making.

We were almost to the door now. It was just up ahead. A door opened at the corner of the hallway. A woman stepped out just ahead of us. She had long, sleek brown hair and appeared to be in a hurry.

She looked up at me just then, her green eyes with a hard stare toward Emry. A feeling that I had seen her face somewhere before at one time or another filled me. I *had* seen that face before. A pretty girl with a hard face and grim expression. Then it hit me. I had seen her at the hospital when my mother had been admitted for her heart. That same woman had been sitting outside in the hallway of the hospital and had given me the same cold stare that I now saw she wore. And then I looked down and saw the shimmer of a silver knife blade gripped tightly in her hand. She was coming directly at Emry. Without even having time to panic or even think about what I was doing, about what was happening, I released my crutches and swirled around. Buck and my father had caught up to us. I reached toward Buck and ripped the gun viciously from his holster, and in another split second, turned back around. Ben and Emry had stopped dead in their tracks, distracted by what I was doing. They weren't even facing the woman. They had no knowledge that it was about to happen. The woman lunged directly for Emry, the knife held out in front of her, and I felt my finger instantly find the trigger as I aimed and fired Buck's gun at her. The noise of the gunshot echoed off the walls of the hallway and pierced through my ears. I watched the look of surprise on the woman's face as the bullet had sliced through her body and she fell backward onto the floor, her blood gushing from the wound that had ended up very close to her heart. I heard people screaming down the hall.

I knew I had got to her before she had got to Emry. I knew she was dead, that I had been the one to have killed her, and that I had saved Emry. My mind was now overwhelmed with emotion as I realized that I was still standing there with the gun aimed upward, my finger still locked securely on the trigger. I felt someone wrap their arms around me, forcing my extended arms down as their hands quickly wrapped around the gun and squeezed, forcing me to release my grasp on it. I felt my legs buckle underneath me and the sudden pain in my bad ankle as I had accidentally put weight on it. I fell down to the ground, hunched over and sobbing.

"I have the gun," I heard Buck shout.

"Anna!" Emry rushed over to me as other people rushed over to the woman. He picked me up in his arms and cradled me to his chest. "Anna, please talk to me. Are you alright?"

I looked up at his marvelous face, and I shook my head and started laughing at the same time as I was crying. "Oh, Emry," I sobbed. "I'm just so glad you're still alive."

"That girl tried to kill him," Ben Hanley said.

Emry turned around and I could see the small group of people that now surrounded her, most of them police officers.

"There's the knife," Buck said. "She was definitely almost up to Logan. She almost got him and would've if …"He turned around and looked at me.

"You saved my life?" Emry asked me.

A state of confusion settled as everyone tried to figure out what had just happened. "Is she alright?" my father asked, coming over to us. I nodded.

"I think she's just shaken up," Emry told him.

"I thought *he* was going to kill you," I managed to say.

"He?" my father asked.

I pointed to Ben, who, shocked by the accusation, gave me a horrified look.

"Ben?"

"Yes. I thought he was Mrs. Anderson's brother."

Ben now narrowed his eyes at me. I guessed by his reaction that I might have been right about the relation to her.

"What?" Emry asked, stumped by what I'd said. "Ben's a good man, Anna. He's very trustworthy, believe me."

I still had my eyes locked on Ben, who stared back at me, and then I looked down at the woman lying motionless on the floor in front of us.

"Put me down, please."

Emry gave me a worried look.

"It's okay," I reassured him. "I'm fine."

He set me down, and Ben bent over and retrieved my crutches and handed them to me.

"I'm sorry," I said to Ben, realizing that he may have not wanted to harm Emry. "I just assumed … and then I saw that woman with the knife. I'd seen her before at the hospital. She must've been following me then." I know I wasn't making sense to them. It was just a bunch of garbled-up words as they tried to listen and understand.

"Wow," Emry mumbled. He put his arm around my waist and held me tight. "You saved my life, Anna."

"Indeed she did," my father said, as if not completely happy about it.

Emry turned my face away from the dead woman and the pool of blood that was pouring out and coming close to where we stood. "You must really love me or something."

I sighed and closed my eyes as I felt the warmth of his hands cupping my face. I felt the stresses of the day melting away now. The joy of being together with him again filled me and I let myself just be happy, savoring the moment for what it was.

"Yes," I whispered. "That must be it."

***

The rush of the wind danced along my skin as we walked barefoot on the pearly beach of Evadere.

Crystal clear waters rushed up underneath my feet. I made my grip tighter on Emry as we continued on hand-in-hand and marveled together at the beauty of this wondrous world before us.

I looked at him. He flashed me a grin and I gave him one in return. He glowed here in this light as the red sky hovered above us, and a million white stars that never seemed to go away danced in between the clouds. I couldn't imagine him looking happier than he did at this very moment. We were here, away from everything, and it was just the two of us. We could linger as long as we desired and had no one to answer to when we got back. We could just be us.

"You look overly happy today," I teased him.

He tugged at my arm and pulled me into his chest in one swift motion. I felt the hardness of his muscular body against mine as I gazed up into his shimmering blue eyes and touched the dimple in his cheek as he just couldn't seem to wipe the smile from his face.

"I am. Aren't you?"

"Hmmm…" I put my finger up to my lips, as if I had to think about it. "Extremely."

"The happiest you've ever been in your whole life?"

"Without a doubt."

"I don't know what I'd do without you," he admitted, his fingers tracing the outline of my face.

"You're stuck with me now, you know."

"I don't know how I'll ever manage being stuck here with you."

He grinned and then leaned in and wrapped his strong arms around me. He lifted me off the ground so I was face to face with him, and then we kissed again and again, the breeze swirling around us, drops of sunlight falling on our skin.

"Hey there!"

He instantly dropped me to my feet in shock at the sound of someone else's voice. We both looked over and saw a figure standing in the distance. It was a man wearing white clothes that matched his white hair as he waved his arm wildly in the air to make sure he had gotten our attention.

Emry took hold of my hand. We were both surprised and feeling a little guarded at the sight of someone else on Evadere. Never in his entire time here had Emry ever seen a single soul, even a single animal or an insect. This had always been just his own private secluded beach. The man walked closer to us.

"Hi. Please don't be afraid," he said cheerfully.

Emry eyed him and had put me slightly behind him, making himself a barrier in between the man and me.

"Are you lost?" he asked.

We both just gawked at him for a moment.

"Are you hurt?" he asked, when not getting a response from either one of us.

"No," Emry finally managed to say. "You just surprised us is all."

"Oh." The man smiled warmly at us. "I'm sorry. Didn't mean to startle you. The name's William."

He extended his hand out toward Emry.

Emry shook his hand. "Emry, and this is Anna."

"Nice to meet you folks. Where are you from?"

Emry and I just turned and looked at each other, reading each other's minds. So we weren't all alone on this beautifully strange world. There was life on Evadere.

Acknowledgements

This journey would not have been possible if not for the two biggest supporters of my dreams, my mother, Harriet Muir Payne, and my husband, Bradley Zook. Thank you for being there for me and for the encouragement to keep writing.

Also, I would like to thank my two closest friends, Jill Lichtenfels and Melissa McFeaters, for being my guinea pigs and giving me their honest opinions.

"With God all things are possible." Matthew 19:26

Dear reader,

I hope that you enjoyed Strange in Skin and will continue on the journey with Anna and Emry in Evadere and Solace, the final book in the trilogy.

Good reviews are important to a novel's success. If you enjoyed Strange in Skin I would appreciate it if you would leave a review on Amazon.

Sincerely,
Sara

Contact Sara V. Zook

Website: http://www.saravzook.com
Email: saravzook@gmail.com
Facebook: https://www.facebook.com/SaraVZook

www.ingramcontent.com/pod-product-compliance
Lightning Source LLC
Chambersburg PA
CBHW071159250626
47159CB00001B/134